The daycare center was supposed to be safe, so how could her son just vanish?

Kingsley glared at the staff, several of whom were in tears.

"We checked the sign-in-and-out book, thinking one of you might have taken him. Nobody had. We looked everywhere, even called those authorized to pick him up, hoping they'd forgotten the rules. When that yielded nothing, we called Mr. Henning and Security."

Pandemonium erupted as the security chief burst through the door and everyone started talking at once. Kingsley broke from the group and ran to Billy's crib, which someone had returned to its normal position. It was empty except for a doll and a small, wadded-up blanket. She sprinted from room to room and corner to corner. She checked bathrooms and under the tables, hoping one of the four-year-olds had adopted him to play house. She demanded an answer from two little girls who immediately broke into tears and clung to a daycare worker's legs. Startled by the confrontation, other children started to wail.

Billy was nowhere. Kingsley circled the rooms a second, then a third time, reopening every door and cupboard, irrespective of logic. She even opened the children's play cook stove. Wild-eyed and panicked, she confronted Miss Alicia. "Billy! Where is my baby?"

"Ms. Henning," she said in a trembling voice. "We can't find him. It's like he vanished."

Todd jumped in the security chief's face, fists clenched and red-faced with fury. He bellowed orders. "Shut down the building. Nobody leaves until every person and every inch is exhaustively searched. Get the police and whatever other bodies you need. And go over every scrap of security footage. Our son couldn't just vanish. Find him!"

It was supposed to be the kidnappers' last job, snatching the infant of a poor single mother for an unsuspecting wealthy client. But the kidnappers grab the wrong baby—Billy, the son of high-profile bankers, Kingsley and Todd Henning—from their employer's secure daycare. Realizing their mistake, the kidnappers plant evidence to implicate the parents then dismantle their operation. No ransom call comes. Detectives, convinced the parents are guilty, interrogate relentlessly as they uncover planted evidence.

The parents can't face the mosaic of guilt, blame, and despair or help each other. On day ten, they are called to the morgue. The deceased is not Billy—this time. Shaken, they recommit to each other and vow to find him themselves. They scrutinize the bank's security footage for incongruities only insiders might spot and follow the flimsiest clues into the murderous underworld of illegal adoptions. As novice detectives, they are exposed to extreme danger, skirting the law while keeping one step ahead of the villains and the police.

But is it too late? Will the kidnappers eliminate all trace of the baby? Or are they no match for two angry, determined parents?

KUDOS for *Vanished*

In *Vanished ~ A Trust Mystery ~ Book 3* by Nancy A. Hughes, Kingsley and Todd Henning have just had a baby boy, which they entrust to the new daycare center at the bank where they work—a daycare center that is supposed to be as secure and safe as any place can be. But when their baby is kidnapped, the local police blame Kingsley and Todd, who are outraged and determined to find the baby themselves, without the help of the police if need be. But as they dig for and get closer to the truth, they discover that the kidnappers will do just about anything to make sure they don't get caught, and Todd and Kingsley might be endangering not only themselves, but their baby. Well written in Hughes unique and intriguing voice, this one will keep you glued to your seat all the way through. A really great read. ~ *Taylor Jones, The Review Team of Taylor Jones & Regan Murphy*

Vanished by Nancy A. Hughes is the third book in her Trust Mystery series. In this episode, Kingsley and her husband Todd Henning leave their new baby at the daycare center at the bank where the two of them work. However, kidnappers intent on stealing a single, struggling young mother's baby, end up kidnapping the Henning's baby by mistake. Since Todd and Kingsley are well to do and have powerful friends, the kidnappers fear they will be discovered, and they plant evidence to make the local police think the parents are responsible for their son's disappearance. When the police fail to find their son, and don't even seem to be trying, Todd and Kingsley start their own investigation, determined to find their son at any cost. But they are not dealing with everyday kidnappers, a fact they soon discover as the case becomes more and more bizarre. With Hughes marvelous character development, a solid plot, and an intriguing mystery, Vanished is sure to be one that mystery fans will love. I thoroughly enjoyed it. ~ *Regan Murphy, The Review Team of Taylor Jones & Regan Murphy*

OTHER BOOKS BY
NANCY A. HUGHES

The Dying Hour

The Trust Mystery Series

A Matter of Trust

Redeeming Trust

Vanished

A Trust Mystery
Book 3

Nancy A. Hughes

A Black Opal Books Publication

DEDICATION

In Loving Memory of Esther Jane Filer

Prologue

March

The attorney and his subordinate scrutinized the details that delineated their final operation. Volumes of research, patiently culled from weighty documents, lay in orderly stacks on the massive oak table, summary sheets topping each pile. "The prospective parents—have we a winner?" he asked.

She said, "There was a problem with the couple in Erie. Turns out he does business in France, which gives him European connections. I recommend we drop them. He could investigate our European operation, or lack thereof."

He nodded agreement and pushed that folder aside. "Next."

"Also a bust. The husband checked out negative for military connections, but we overlooked his wife. Turns out she served overseas in the army."

"Nice save. She could have numerous contacts. Zero risk is our tolerance level. How about the third couple?"

She thumped a finger on that file. "They're perfect! Both only children with no living relatives. He's a self-educated CEO who made a fortune in doc.com technology and got out before the shit hit the fan. They tried to get pregnant for years, failed three times at *in vitro*, then adopted a baby who was reclaimed two years later by the teenage birth mother. They mounted a huge legal battle, but the judge ruled for the birth parents. Seems the father never signed off. Now in their mid-forties, they're out of options."

Pulse quickening, he motioned for her to pick up the pace. "The husband's a match with our model," she continued. "Adores his socialite wife and would pay anything to make her happy, but couldn't give her what she wants most. Here's a bonus—he's an egotistical social climber who lives for the country club life. He insists the baby must be a perfect white male and didn't bat an eyelash at four hundred fifty thousand dollars for the right kid. And we can milk him for additional expenses."

"Did they agree that, due to the risk of embarrassing foreign governments, they could never know the baby's nationality? And that the birth certificate says he's American, which protects everyone's interests?"

"They were especially excited about that. They'll do whatever it takes to never lose a baby again."

"Did you get any sense that either is idealistic, deeply religious, or apt to raise ethical questions somewhere down the road?"

She grinned. "He's a narcissist who won't tolerate losing or not getting his way, in spite of his finely-honed public persona. He may come from poor white trash, but you'd never know it now. There are claws in his golf gloves."

The attorney smiled with lazy contentment. "Tell them we'll approach our European connections immediately on their behalf then make the deal. Now—about the birth mother."

Rifling through her impeccable Coach briefcase, she extracted the summary sheet and slid it across the table to him. "She's a perfect match. Bright, pretty, and spunky. Ran away at sixteen from a dysfunctional family in Chicago. There's been no contact since. She found work in LA, juggled several minimum wage jobs while getting her GED, then started community college. Met some jerk who abused her. As soon as she realized she was pregnant, she fled the state, ending up in southeast Pennsylvania."

"And now?"

"She has a back-office job at Keynote National Bank and goes to community college part time. Baby stays in the bank's ground-floor daycare, which abuts a large parking lot. Bank's right on a highway with no traffic lights to impede a smooth getaway. Better yet, there's an abandoned gravel road behind the daycare's parking lot that leads to a small subdivision. The asphalt's decaying, but passable. Locals have forgotten it's there."

"How about the girl's resources?"

"She has no money to hire a PI and no family to help her. She lives week to week."

The attorney turned to the building's blueprints. "Have any trouble getting these without arousing suspicion? And how much did they cost?"

"Not one cent. The owner of that defunct high tech company was adamant that he had been cheated—foreclosed upon prematurely by the same bank that now owns his building. I let him pick my brain for free legal advice then told him I'd consider his suit."

"Does he have a case?"

"Of course not. The lender had been exceptionally lenient. The owner spent like the faucets gushed money. Went with whatever the architect loved. Talk about excess! Furnishings belong in a sheikhdom. And they paid way too much for obsolete technology."

"And he just gave you these drawings?"

"He had a bunch of them strewn all around. After a pint of Glen Fiddich he was in no shape to count them. If he complains, well hell, I did say I'd consider his case."

He smoothed each sheet, delighted with the areas that interested him most. He traced the various routes the kidnappers would take while she followed his drift. "These floor plans look pretty straightforward," he said. "Enlarge the lobby, the connecting corridors that lead to the daycare, and the stairwells, along with the security, plumbing, and wiring diagrams. Have copies ready for our people at our planning session."

The man rocked back in his swivel chair, his manicured fingers laced behind his head. He grinned at his lovely associate. "As usual, you've done excellent research. I'm comfortable giving the order. Who knows—maybe we're doing this gal a favor, eliminating an obstacle in her career path. While that's in the works, I'll wrap up the practice."

"Do we have other business pending?"

"Nope. My temp secretary knows to turn down all prospective clients. In just three more weeks, with this completed, I will retire."

Chapter 1

A Few Weeks Later

*I*f anyone ever harms one hair on your sweet little head—

Kingsley Ward Henning smothered her incongruous oath as her baby's baptism continued. The priest placed his hand on the infant's forehead and, with his thumb, drew a cross with oil of Chrism. "William Todd, you are sealed by the Holy Spirit in baptism and marked as Christ's own forever. Amen."

Seven-week-old Billy blinked at the priest, yawned, then refocused on the pendulum light suspended from the ornate gothic ceiling. Sunlight streamed through the stained-glass windows splashing rainbows of gold, ruby, emerald, and sapphire onto the baby's white heirloom gown. His silky dark hair shined with the water of baptism.

Kingsley forced back tears as she stole a glance at her husband Todd's dignified face. *Our precious child. The one who was never to be. Ours, and now God's.* The aura of Easter, wafting its scent of lilies, hyacinths, tulips, and daffodils that mingled with beeswax, filled Kingsley with awe. Kingsley's mother, Sarah Alderson, flanked the opposite side of the hundred-year-old marble font. Blinking rapidly, Sarah caught her daughter's eye, prompting both sentimentalists to grin.

"Let us welcome the newly baptized," the priest intoned. And everyone prayed on Billy's behalf.

Golden child, Kingsley thought, momentarily overwhelmed by the emotion of new motherhood and an inexplicable feeling of impending doom. It wasn't responsibility—that she could handle with ease. But what was it? She snapped back to the moment, as the voices of 200 congregants welcomed Billy into the household of God.

"The peace of the Lord be always with you," the priest announced as the congregation broke into greeting each other. "Meet your new family," he said to Billy, as he strolled down the aisle, turning left and then right for the adoring congregation to peek at the baby who had fallen asleep in his arms. In what seemed to Kingsley like the blink of an eye, the milestone was over.

Two hours later, the caravan crunched down Todd and Kingsley's private country lane, flanked by vibrant crocuses and snowdrops that glowed purple and yellow through a late *onion snow*. Three generations of Hennings and Aldersons had already spilled into their restored 1803 stone farmhouse. "We're late," Kingsley lamented to Todd, as they brought up the rear.

"We couldn't be rude to the people at church who surprised us with a reception. Besides, you know our mothers and aunts will handle the kitchen. And your dad, the consummate barkeep, will keep mimosas and bloody Marys flowing." Then he added with a chuckle, "We aren't the stars of this show. We've been demoted."

Billy's godparents, Randall Shannon and Barrie Brown, flanked the baby's carrier in the back seat. "Randall, will you please take Billy in by the living room fireplace for pictures?" Kingsley asked. "I want to get family portraits before his gown gets any more rumpled."

Stocky and craggy, Randall's kisses and coos contradicted his redheaded temper and wisecracking nature. He disengaged the carrier's clasps and scooped up the baby.

"C'mon, Ace. Let's dispense with the pics so they can get you out of that dress."

Kingsley lagged behind to give Barrie a hug. "Before things get hectic, I want to tell you again how much it means having you as his godmother. You're my best friend—the sister I never had."

"If you make me cry and ruin my makeup…"

Kingsley laughed. Barrie would be gorgeous with a scrubbed face. One hundred pounds of fire and determination, brains and endurance belied her delicate, child-like features. At five feet eight, Kingsley towered over Barrie, yet she knew her friend was the mightier.

"Come on," Barrie urged. "Bloody Mary is calling my name."

Inside the grand foyer, the scene took Kingsley aback. To her left, in the living room, the men exchanged hearty banter before a blazing fireplace while her dad, Henry Alderson, butlered their drinks. Behind the living room archway, the dining room table groaned with a feast arrayed on Grammy's best lace cloth. Grammy, now gone almost fifteen years. If only she'd lived to see this.

Kingsley followed the sound of women's voices to the right of the foyer, beyond the library's open glass doors, to the kitchen in the rear quadrant. The women fussed and ferried specialties, reserved for auspicious occasions, across the back hallway behind the staircase and into the dining room. The kitchen's walk-in fireplace hissed and popped with aromatic apple wood.

She caught Todd's arm. "Do you realize *everyone's* here? Our entire families? Except for funerals and weddings, when does this happen?"

"It's times like this that make up for the bad stuff. One perfect child overshadows all of life's disappointments."

"We are so lucky. If there were a way for life to be any more perfect, I can't imagine what that could be."

Hours later, as dusk settled over the quiet Pennsylvania countryside, Todd escaped from his duties and slipped up the staircase. He paused at the landing's window to survey the rolling countryside to the north, brittle with frost. The neighboring Amish farmland beyond their own acres lay fallow, awaiting the bite of hooves, plows, and seed.

He rounded the landing and, mounting the last six steps, stood unobserved at Billy's door on his left. He gazed at Kingsley, nursing the baby. Billy's mouth quivered then dropped away from his mother. After hours of being passed around, his son was dead to the world.

Kingsley, Todd thought, looked even lovelier than on their wedding day. Long, sleek body curled in her bentwood rocker, the cream chenille throw on her lap as soft as her spirit. Shiny dark hair against flawless skin, her sweet mouth, and green eyes recapitulated in his son.

She looked up, smiling, and motioned him toward his grandfather's oversized oak rocker. "This time last year we were planning our wedding, knowing we couldn't have children. And on our honeymoon we decided we could travel the world every May after you dispatched the share-holders meeting. Never, in my wildest dreams, did I think we'd have Billy and a day like today."

"He's out cold. Why don't you put him down?"

She shook her head, eyes misting over. "Today was so special. Yet, at the same time, I'm sad, knowing he's only on loan for the next eighteen years. I want to hold him a little while longer. I feel, in a moment, that he will be grown. And next week he starts daycare. Are you sure I'm doing the right thing? Returning to work? Putting him in daycare with strangers?"

"I suppose if it's right for you, it'll be fine for Billy."

She ran her internal pep talk again. *He'll be in our building. We can drop in whenever we wish. And from what we learned during orientation, the program is excellent, and the staff, capable and caring. Besides, it's not like we've signed a contract. If it doesn't work out, I'll come up with plan B.*

"You don't have to be gainfully employed unless that's

what you want. There will be years to practice your profession."

She shook her head. "I love commercial lending. To be offered the departmental head at twenty-six was such an opportunity. At my level, there are no part-time positions. Besides, I've always thrived on a hectic lifestyle. Even though I've only been home seven weeks, I've run out of projects. I'd lose my mind baking cookies."

"You accomplished a lot in two years. And you've been missed. 'When's Kingsley coming back? *Is* Kingsley coming back?' You should hear them."

Kingsley glanced at a table on which was folded a growing pile of wee summer clothes. He followed her gaze. "Just think—instead of cruising like last year, we'll be vacationing on Kiawah Island with Randall and Barrie."

"Except on May fifth. They'll baby-sit while we do something special for our first anniversary."

"Not as special as last year," she said, nodding toward Billy.

"Oh, it will be special. Count on it!"

Kingsley rose and snuggled Billy into the cherry spindle cradle her father had crafted for his first grandchild. Looking around, she smiled at Noah's Ark animals, armadillos to zebras, with which her artist-mother had encircled the room. Their adorable faces complete with eyelashes never failed to amuse her. "I've loved every minute of our life together, and Billy makes us complete."

"Come here, K," he said, drawing her onto his lap. "Do you have any idea how much I love you?"

Chapter 2

Kingsley pulled into Keynote National Bank's parking lot with its towering fountain and rock garden where weeping cherry trees overhung rioting tête-à-tête narcissus and grape hyacinths. Approaching the boomerang-shaped building's main entrance, she steered left around the architectural wonder. Its copper-pink windows set between bands of rose granite and stone reflected a crystalline sky and cumulus clouds.

She circled the building, stopping near Keynote's daycare entrance. As she cut the engine, she peered into the rearview mirror at Billy, asleep in his car seat. The baby stirred and yawned, but resettled without opening his eyes.

Turning, Kingsley watched him, conflicted. *You can do this*, she told herself. *It's already ten, a short day, and just two hours until lunch. He'll sleep until then.* She looped Billy's bag over her shoulder, then retrieved him from the back seat. Later she'd move the Lexus to her assigned parking spot and rescue her leather tote and purse.

As she emerged, her eyes swept the vast parking lot, overbuilt as was much of the opulent structure. Designed by a high-tech firm that had gorged, then disemboweled itself on excess, it was a prize pluck for Keynote, which had needed a new corporate office, main branch, and back-office facilities.

As she started across the lined asphalt, motion caught her peripheral vision. Turning toward the grass and hemlock hedge that bordered the lot, she caught sight of a vanishing figure and the gleam of red metal. Odd—the momentary flash of color reminded her of someone in Mennonite dress. Straw hat, deep blue shirt, black pants. She blinked. No one was there. It must have been her imagination, triggered by her sudden exposure to sunlight. She turned her attention back to her mission, repositioning her precious bundle. She strode toward the daycare entrance, pretending this was her normal routine.

"Bell," Kingsley said to Billy as she rang it, which brought a slight Mennonite girl to the heavy exterior door. Dressed in a homemade calico dress, knee socks, and sneakers, she wore her blonde hair center-parted and skinned into a bun beneath a stiff white gauze "*capp*." She glanced at Kingsley's employee ID badge and smiled shyly.

"Ms. Henning? We've been expecting you." She led Kingsley down a long corridor. At its end, an overhead security camera blinked a red light. Turning, Kingsley spotted its twin mounted over the exterior door through which they had just passed. Halfway, to the right, the daycare's interior door stood ajar.

Alicia Wright, the head of daycare, swept forward to meet them. Short and round, Miss Alicia's wide-set brown eyes were wrinkle-fringed from decades of smiling. Her crisp, well-chosen words, however, underscored her devotion to her responsibility.

"Do you remember our routine from orientation?" Miss Alicia asked. She began ticking off rules in a voice more suitable for little children.

"Show my ID, coming and going, until everyone knows me by sight, then sign Billy in. When collecting him, don't cross the yellow line without signing him out." She pointed to the three-inch stripe painted on the entryway floor.

"Do you have your pictures?"

Kingsley pulled an envelope from her suit pocket. "My

parents, Sarah and Henry Alderson. I've also listed Barrie Brown, who's the assistant controller here at the bank. She wears an employee ID badge. The last photo is Billy's godfather, Randall Shannon, though I doubt that he'll ever pick Billy up."

"Remind them," Miss Alicia intoned. "Not one toe over that yellow line with Billy without signing him out *in our presence*." Even though spoken in her little-girl voice, there was no doubt in Kingsley's mind that the woman meant business. Kingsley nodded dutifully.

"Miss Alicia, I'm just wondering—what's behind the parking lot, beyond the dumpster, the grass, and the hemlock hedge?"

"Why, nothing. I'm not sure who owns it…perhaps the county…but that's where the undeveloped countryside begins. No, wait. I remember now. Something about a new housing development. A decade ago an access road was started, but it dead-ends and has fallen into decay. No buildings sprang up as a result. Why do you ask?"

"I thought I saw somebody. I guess security was on my mind."

Miss Alicia dismissed that with a flip of her hand. "Hikers or cyclists, perhaps. If you're worried about our little ones, trust me. It would be easier to break into the vault. Our exterior door is locked at all times. The security cameras are monitored by real people, and nobody can pass unobserved into our daycare."

"But what about fire? That corridor looks rather narrow, and hundreds of people occupy this building."

She smiled indulgently. "In the first place, most employees wouldn't be near this corridor and would exit elsewhere. Not only would we be the first ones out, but look at our double-hung windows." She pointed across the daycare's main room. "They're wired and security's armed, but if the electricity's out, we can override the system, opening them, and step over the sills."

"It sounds redundant even to me."

"Nonsense. You're a diligent mother. Now—if there's nothing else, let's get our little guy settled." She led Kingsley through the main room with its glowing waxed floors and cream-colored walls on which was painted a secret garden with woodland creatures, flowers, ferns, and foaming ponds. To the right, low dividers that picked up the motif separated areas for arts and crafts, stories, and games. Play centers lined the exterior wall, where light streamed from the parking-lot windows. Two little girls were pretending to cook while little boys pushed matchbox cars and fire engines, imitating truck sounds.

"We separate and then subdivide our little ones by age." Miss Alicia reiterated her orientation speech as she led Kingsley into the infants' area. To the left stood all manner of baby contraptions—rockers, bouncers, and walkers on a colorful flat-napped rug. "Meet one of our grannies. She's a retired teacher who comes in a few hours a week to help with the toddlers and play with the babies." A white-haired woman in black polyester pants, a mannish white shirt, and black Reeboks stopped soothing a fussy toddler long enough to exchange a quick greeting. She then resumed placating the child.

Miss Alicia motioned Kingsley toward the far-left interior, softly lit for napping infants. "This crib will be Billy's," she said in hushed tones. "Every day, he gets fresh linens, and while he's sleeping, one of our staff checks him every ten minutes. Each day you'll get a report card telling when he slept, ate, was changed, what songs and games we played, and so on. Don't forget to take home your forms— we need to know what he did while he wasn't with us."

Another infant slept in a second crib. "That's Sammy." Miss Alicia looked back and forth between the two babies. "Why, Billy's as big as Sammy, and Sammy is five months old!"

"We joke that Billy was *overbaked*. He weighed ten pounds, eleven ounces." Kingsley felt her anxiety melt. The facility was even nicer than she'd remembered—bright, new, and squeaky clean. And safe. Safer, in fact, than the money stored in the vault with its timer and multi-ton door. "Billy still sleeps most of the day. He's a real night owl like his dad."

"We'll watch him closely. And when he's awake, loving hands will give him lots of attention. If he's hungry early, we'll give you a call. Come—tuck him in. He'll be just fine." When Kingsley hesitated, she gave Kingsley's arm a reassuring pat. "And you will be too. Now, over here—I'll show you where to leave his bag and spare clothes."

⌘

"Welcome back!"

Marle Jenkins, Kingsley's administrative assistant, jumped from her seat and hurried to greet Kingsley as she stepped from the fourth floor elevator and into the Commercial Lending Department.

Kingsley felt a flush of appreciation as her coworkers called and waved greetings. She eased through the knot of lenders who demanded to know why she hadn't brought Billy in for a peek. Finally, she escaped into her private office, trailed by Marle, who chattered nonstop from notes about myriad accomplishments and problems. The latter she refused to call *challenges* and never used the word *issues*.

"Love that new bag." Marle stopped for a breath and pointed to the leather satchel hanging from Kingsley's shoulder.

"It's lightweight," Kingsley said, passing it to Marle by the strap. "It's on loan from my friends in the Controller's Department. They insisted a banker wouldn't be caught dead on the job with a diaper bag."

She set it on one of her guest chairs and opened the latches for Marle's inspection, tipping it to reveal the expandable configuration. Her laptop, several file folders, and a variety of baby accessories fit inside with room to spare.

Marle grinned. "Why, it's roomy enough to smuggle Billy into your office. I can picture him now, peeking out of the top like an Anne Geddes picture." With a quick check of her watch, Marle reverted to business. "Did you hear they finished upgrading our fire alarm system? Had you come later, you could have ducked our first scheduled practice. It's due to go off any—"

Shrieking blasts buried Marle's explanation, as Lending jumped to its collective feet. Billy! What if it scared him? What if they dropped him? She was less prepared than she'd convinced herself about leaving Billy with strangers. She thought of what Miss Alicia had said. "In case of an emergency, our staff will take our little children to our designated spot in the rear parking lot. In case of a real emergency, wait for instructions to come get your child." She had pointed in the direction of the hemlock hedge that was flanked by a commercial dumpster.

Kingsley double-timed with the others into the stairwell, emerging into the rear parking lot. Joining other departments, they circled en masse to their assigned spot on the right side of the building. She edged from the group, trying to glimpse the opposite parking lot where Billy would be, but Marle, clipboard in hand, was starting roll call. Just like a cruise ship's lifeboat drill, Kingsley thought, as her dear friend Margaret Stiles, head of Residential Real Estate Lending, motioned her into position. Sandwiched among them were several customers, outsource professionals, and visitors, trapped and instructed into the drill. "Why the roll call?" Kingsley whispered.

"Every department must account for each individual. That way, rescue workers don't take unnecessary risks." Marle finished the task, then joined the footrace of other departmental appointees who were dropping their sheets with the designated captain.

Kingsley envisioned someone putting a check mark beside Billy's name. William Todd Henning IV. She smiled. Such a long handle for a twelve-pounder. When the all clear sounded, Margaret tucked her arm through Kingsley's. Together they trudged back upstairs. "Welcome back, Kiddo," Margaret said in her deep mellow voice. "Can't wait to catch you up on the latest politics." Kingsley grinned at her friend whose sapphire eyes, accentuated with bifocals, matched her crisp linen suit. Yes, this felt good. She had missed stimulating work, her professional friends, and the challenges. This *was* going to work.

☙❧❧

Kingsley drank in the April eighth sunshine that streamed through the daycare's windows. Billy's birth, in the midst of the Valentine Day blizzard, seemed light years ago. No longer a newborn, he was sprouting like the asparagus in her late Grammy's garden.

Callie Smith, Sammy's mother, had already fed her baby his bottle. He lay on her thighs, watching her coaxingly. When Callie tickled his tummy, the five-month-old belly laughed, crunching his eyes shut, then looking at her expectantly.

Kingsley bent over Billy's crib and found bright eyes looking back. As she scooped him up, he gave his mom a gummy grin. "Hey, buddy, you hungry?" Billy stuffed the back of his fist in his mouth and smacked on it loudly. "First the pants."

"I wish I could have nursed longer," Callie said sadly, watching Kingsley settle into her rocker. "But Sammy was so allergic to cow's milk that I couldn't eat one little cookie that contained dairy. By the time I figured it out, it was too late. At least he stopped throwing up."

Kingsley studied Callie's anxious face. Her ash-brown hair escaped in ringlets from a banana clip. Below fringed bangs, pointed eyebrows gave her hazel eyes a quizzical look. Freckles splashed her straight, short nose, and her pretty mouth was tinged a faint pink. She wore a short khaki bib jumper over a white turtleneck, and she'd kicked off her clogs. Callie could have passed for sixteen had worry not etched its toll.

"He seems to be thriving," Kingsley said of his double chin and dimpled arms. Callie buried her face in his belly and blew, which made the baby squeal. Kingsley noticed her wince then touch her jaw, eyes watering, as she lifted her head.

"Are you okay?"

Callie darkened and shook her head. Before Kingsley could frame an apology for prying, Callie explained. "My ex wasn't what you'd think of as an alcoholic. He didn't stagger, slur his words, reek of booze, or hang all day at a bar. He'd get off by himself and brood about things—the last job he'd lost, his mother not loving him, his ex-wife— then he'd come in and have a few beers.

"By the time I'd get home, even small things displeased him, and he'd pick a fight. He'd never apologize—just excuse himself by saying *we'd* hit a bump. One day he backhanded me. Hard. Loosened a tooth." Callie touched her cheek gingerly. "That time he apologized profusely, begged my forgiveness, but I knew things would only get worse. I'd seen enough of that as a kid. I was relieved when the tooth seemed to tighten, but now it's hurting like hell."

"You'd better have that looked at."

"Can't. Not now anyway. I don't have the money to go to a dentist."

"Is it possible that Sammy's father could help you? Legally, he's responsible for child support."

She looked down, blinking rapidly. "Not an option. Never was. He wasn't interested in marriage or kids. Detested the notion of responsibility. I paid the bills while we were together."

Kingsley nodded and tried to keep still, even though she was dying to offer advice. "Do you have any family?"

"I ran away at sixteen when we were passing through the Midwest. There's been no contact since then. Ultimately, I ended up in California. I wanted *big*—thought it was the best place for a sixteen-year-old to find work. And warm. Chicago was awful in winter. Then I met my ex. At first, it seemed wonderful. Someone who wanted my undivided attention. Said I was beautiful, loved how I cooked, how I made love, how I listened. But after the novelty wore off, he changed. Or probably reverted. It's true what they say. I replicated my father, who abused my mother.

"One of the things we fought about most was my having friends. He wanted me all to himself. Boy, did I get an earful from my girlfriends about possessiveness, control freaks, abuse. I spent hours at the bookstore, speed-reading self-help books in the restroom. As soon as I realized I was pregnant, I split. Worked my way cross country and ended up here. Sammy's father doesn't know he exists. Not that he'd care…"

"And now?"

She swept a hand, as if to encompass the entire Bank's campus. "I may have a back-office job, but as long as I get A's, Keynote reimburses me one hundred percent for related college courses. B's are worth eighty percent, but I won't settle for that. I'm sorry," she whispered. "I sound so pathetic."

"Hardly. It took guts to do what you did. And a willingness to assume responsibility alone. Many girls would have punted."

Callie smiled at Sammy, who had been watching her face intently. He smiled back immediately. "This little guy is the best thing that ever happened to me. The first person who is totally mine. There isn't anything I wouldn't do to protect him; help him grow up strong and responsible." She flinched again, touching her jaw.

"You should see a dentist. You could have an infection. Didn't you take the Bank's dental plan? It costs so little."

She shook her head. "It seemed too expensive at the time, and every cent counts. What is it they say—penny wise and pound foolish?"

"Callie, if you'll let me, I'll get information from Shirley Granger. She's our head of HR among other things. We just started a new benefit program, and as I recall, we're still within the sign-up window. May I inquire for you?"

Callie looked up, almost pleadingly. "Could you do that for me? I'm not comfortable approaching an executive VP like Ms. Granger."

"Sure—it's no biggie. People did so much for me during my maternity leave."

Her smile faded. "Another problem—I don't dare burn even a half day's vacation. I've got to save them for Sammy's appointments and sick days. I have absolutely no one to help me, and I can't afford to pay a sitter."

"Have you considered asking your supervisor to let you work a split shift from time to time? Seven to eleven, then three to seven? Some of our fulltime employees work split shifts routinely. That would give you four hours midday. Sammy could go to the dentist with you. Bet their staff would be overjoyed—he's such a good baby."

"I suppose I could ask…"

"Worst case scenario would be they'd say no, and you wouldn't be fired for asking."

Alarm overspread her face. "Please! Don't ever repeat to anyone what I said about my ex. I must protect Sammy. My ex can't find out where I am. He was dreadfully possessive, and I can't risk his using Sammy for leverage. And I don't want him spending one minute alone with my boy. I've experienced, firsthand, the devastation an abusive father can cause."

"Of course not." An awkward silence hung in the room. "So—what department are you with?" Kingsley filled in.

"Item processing. When checks are cashed at the branch, our department routes them back to their originating bank for payment. I key them into a proof machine. Next, they're sorted electronically. I can key hundreds in minutes."

"You must be good."

"It's a start. When I get my degree in banking and finance, I'll already have my foot in the door. Then I can give this little guy a wonderful life. The thought of us living hand to mouth forever—" She bit her lip. "Really, I'm doing okay. It's just that, well, I don't have anyone to talk to whom I can trust. Sometimes I feel overwhelmed."

"Are there friends in California you can call?"

"I severed all ties—just took off. I did confide in one special friend, in case the police thought I'd been kidnapped or murdered, but told her I wouldn't be in touch. I left whatever stuff wouldn't fit in one bag. No doubt he threw the rest out, snapped his fingers, and installed the next girl within days."

"Callie, you can trust me, I promise. I won't say a word. Besides, it sounds like you have a great plan and a future full of promise."

"That's generous, especially for someone in your position. I mean, you and your husband both being senior officers."

"You'd be surprised how hard that can make things sometimes. Just think of me as somebody's mom. My biggest fan does." They rocked and chatted awhile, then Kingsley put Billy back in his crib.

Callie said. "You are so lucky."

Kingsley straightened, remembering her first husband Andy and her hellish existence after his murder. A flickering memory of Andy's face the last time she saw him. His soft flick of a kiss. Ducking into the storm as he flipped his rain jacket's hood over his head. The police at her door with bad news. The crash. The fire. Her life shattered—unprepared as she was for anything beyond her charmed, mainline Philadelphia existence. "We all have dragons in our lives. They just aren't obvious to others. If you give me your phone number, I'll call you about that dental plan. And don't worry—this *will* work out."

Chapter 3

"The cook needs a hug." Todd flipped the eggs then plunged the knobs on the four-slice toaster. Kingsley wiggled between the counter and his kiss-the-cook apron, locking him into a bear hug. Kisses bestowed, she rubbed her cheek against his smooth face and savored his scent. Six foot two, her gentle giant, his laughing gray eyes that changed with his mood, his short dark hair that kept trying to curl in spite of his efforts. She willed it for Billy—and maybe a daughter. Someday.

"Are you ready for week number two?" Todd asked her.

"Well…" She strung out the word. "I need to get back to rest up from the weekend. I love Billy's long naps—time to pamper his daddy. You better look out, mister. I don't plan to neglect you."

"I'll hold you to that—"

The toaster interrupted. Seizing the slices, Todd reached for the butter.

"I'm so much happier than one week ago, though it'll be a bit lonely today. Callie's working a split shift to go to the dentist. Billy and I will do lunch alone."

"I have meetings in Plymouth Meeting and Conshohocken. If you need me before three, call on my cell phone. What's your day going to be like?"

"Piles of paper to push. A dairy farmer is meeting me at a restaurant midday. A large loan presentation to finish for

Committee. I'm getting caught up. Staff did a yeoman's job during my absence, although they're relieved that the crunch is ending."

"Why would a dairy farmer meet you at a restaurant? Why not at his farm? Or at the bank?"

Before she could answer, she heard Billy cry. She set down her untouched piece of toast. "If I were to design an emblem for motherhood," she tossed over her shoulder as she left the kitchen, "it would be a cold cup of coffee."

❧❧❧

At eleven thirty that morning Kingsley hustled into the daycare to feed Billy. The disorganized scene that greeted her stopped her mid-stride. Both Billy and Sammy's cribs stood in the outer area along with the other accessories that belonged in their quiet room. Inside, a woman wearing a facilities' uniform was mopping errant puddles. Noticing Kingsley, she stammered a contrite explanation. "I'm sorry—I was told that both of you mothers would be out over lunch, so I cleaned other areas first."

"That's okay. Don't worry about it," Kingsley said, locating her baby while the woman wrung out the string mop and attacked the floor with renewed vigor.

"See, the night shift woman didn't show up, so I have double duty."

Kingsley dropped her leather bag onto a nearby table, pulled a *spitty-up* cloth from its depths, and draped it over her shoulder. She smiled at her newfound efficiency. Baby spit on her sleek black suit would not be corporate-chic. Selecting a rocker away from the traffic, she settled Billy into her arms. He attacked greedily.

"The floor will be dry in a jiffy," the woman called. "I could turn on a fan."

"No, this is fine. Really." As she fed and rocked Billy, she allowed her mind to drift from her hectic routine. Their vacation in May was a few weeks away. She closed her eyes and pictured the ocean, the house on the beach at Kiawah, the fun they would have with Randall and Barrie. And she needn't worry about Billy when they returned, knowing that Keynote's daycare was the perfect solution. "You better take some really long naps. And no midnight wailing," she cooed to Billy.

"I'll ask someone to push the cribs back into position as soon as the floor's dry. And again, I am so sorry. Please don't complain to my supervisor. I had no choice."

"I wouldn't dream of it. And thank you." Kingsley sighed. This conscientious woman was not responsible for the employee who had skipped without giving notice.

Kingsley rocked Billy until the cleaning woman was gone. His crib, she noticed, was now blocking traffic. With her hip, she edged it to a better location near Sammy's.

As she turned to stroll with Billy, she collided with an unfamiliar employee. The woman quickly regained her balance. "I'm so sorry!" Kingsley sputtered, appalled that her elbow had almost decked the pregnant young woman.

"No harm done." She held out her hand. "I'm Ethelda Blake, Miss Alicia's new assistant." She smoothed her form-fitting maternity outfit. "Kind of handy, my working here, wouldn't you say?" She gave Kingsley a sorority smile. "May I?" She reached for Billy.

Kingsley hesitated for a split second and then nodded agreement. Billy eyed the new woman with wonder as Ethelda swayed, smiling sweetly at the mesmerized baby. Without breaking her gaze, she whispered to the baby, "If Mommy needs to leave, I'll take care of you, you dear little thing. I need lots of practice."

Kingsley hated to leave Billy with yet one more stranger, but she had promised to meet that dairy farmer. And she had left herself scant traveling time. Ethelda patted Kingsley's arm reassuringly. "Really, we'll be just fine. I promise. Oh, he feels so good. I can't wait for my own little one to be born."

Ethelda whispered, as if her words were intended for Billy alone. "My husband and I lost our first one. He was premature and stillborn. I'd been horribly sick. In fact, I had told everyone that nothing good could come of it. He had pitiful deformities. But this time everything's different." Bringing Billy's face close to her own, she whispered into his ear, "We feel wonderful, don't we?"

Billy yawned and, closing his eyes, rested his head on her shoulder.

Feeling slightly resentful, Kingsley wanted to snatch back her baby but had to admit that this young woman did have a way with babies. Kingsley relaxed. "When is your baby due?"

"I have eight weeks to go. Even if he were born now, he'd just be small."

"Speaking of going, I'm running late, and my car's on the other side of the building."

"Go. We'll be fine. I promise we'll call if you're needed." Kingsley smoothed and kissed Billy's silky head, then rescued her bag. She stuffed the cloth into its depth, then checked his cubby for clothes to take home. The tiny blue sleeper with its embroidered red beaver barely fit him—ten weeks old and already outgrowing his clothes.

Smiling, she added his laundry to her bag. He'd be packing for college before she knew it. After a quick stop in the ladies' room, she retrieved her bag, leaving Ethelda settled in the rocker with Billy. Satisfied that all would be well, Kingsley rushed toward the exit.

ℛ

Kingsley snapped a disgruntled glance at her watch and conceded the obvious. The farmer whom she was scheduled to meet was a no-show. What a waste of time. She struggled to re-channel her anger and stalked toward her car.

Back at her office, she forced her most professional voice and participated in a conference call. Then she immersed herself in another customer's request for an extension on an overdue payment. She paged through the file. How unusual—this customer was always rock solid. What had made his situation go south? She probed deeper, losing herself in the minutia.

The piercing alarm jolted her to her feet as she momentarily forgot what the racket meant. A fire drill—damn! What else could go wrong? She followed the others into the stairwell, down and out to their assigned location. Marle, clipboard in hand, stood tall, ready for roll call.

"What's the deal?" Kingsley asked Margaret, who had a Real Estate client in tow.

"We were supposed to have a second unannounced drill, but I didn't think it would happen this soon. It's just been a week. This shouldn't be—"

A fire engine, pumper truck, ambulance, and police cruisers tore from the highway into the complex, their sirens blasting competitively. "My, god! It's the real thing!"

Kingsley's gaze followed where Margaret was pointing. She strained toward the commotion while scanning the building for smoke. Everyone started to pace and chatter. Minutes passed without explanation. Time dragged, her coworkers panicked about records and personal items at risk from water and smoke, but Kingsley's thoughts were for Billy alone. She knew that everything else was just stuff. Being captive on the back side of the building, she lost sight of the emergency vehicles, growing impatient as an hour crawled by. Descending clouds obliterated the sun, encircling them in raw mist and chilly wind. She shivered, hugging her body, and prayed that Billy was warm and dry.

Just when she had decided to break from the group, the all clear rippled throughout the complex. As the trucks pulled away and bankers re-entered the building, the corridors buzzed with the particulars. Some kid had tripped the lobby's fire alarm, which was located behind the atrium garden. Apparently, the lush trees and tropical plants, which thrived beneath the five-story glass dome, hid the perpetrator's actions from the employees who worked inside the branch. Rumor suggested that the child had escaped via the stairwell located to the right of the alarm.

ೞೞೞ

Back in her fourth floor office, Kingsley dropped into her chair and tried to refocus. She picked up the threads of her customer's dilemma, disjointed as they were by the interruption.

She formed a plan and made a few calls before moving to the next challenge that screamed for attention. Realizing the day was flying unchecked, she glanced at her watch. Three-twenty already, and still that big loan presentation was not ready for Committee.

As she swiveled her chair to root for its file that was buried on her credenza, she paused, captivated. The beauty of rural south central Pennsylvania was emerging from winter at last.

Beyond her expansive window-walls rose gorgeous wet greens, dripping with moisture. She imagined the smell of damp earth, pine, and hemlock that mingled with wild rhododendron. Todd slipped into her office so quietly that her trance was unbroken until he snapped her door shut.

"K..."

She loved the soft way he said it, spelled it, with no period, meaning no end. "Hey!" She rose to greet him. Her smile faded as she digested the alarm on his face. She circled the desk. "Todd, what's wrong? Are you all right?"

"K, come with me."

"Where?" Instinctively, she reached out to hug him, but he grasped her shoulders instead.

"It's Billy."

Adrenaline shot her into fight-or-flight mode. "Billy?

What's wrong? Is he sick? Wet from the rain? Did somebody drop him?"

Todd squeezed her arms as if she might fall. "K. He's missing."

She flashed to the earlier mix-up in the daycare and sighed in relief. "Todd," she said calmly. "It's okay. The cleaning woman left his crib out of position. There was a scheduling mix-up, furniture out of place—"

But Todd was shaking his head with increased determination and gripped her arms tighter. He took a deep breath and started again. "K, he's not in his crib. Or any crib, or a playpen, or with anyone. They can't find him."

Kingsley stared in disbelief and, then registering what he had said, wrenched her arms free. She bolted through the Lending Department, Todd in pursuit. She battered the elevator button with her palm, and when it didn't appear instantaneously, sprinted for the stairwell. Taking the steps two at a time, she raced, trailed by Todd, down four flights to the ground level. Gasping, she muscled the fire door open and dashed across the corridor into the daycare.

"Where is he? Where's Billy? Where's my baby?" she demanded of the daycare workers who were frozen in place, mouths open, unable to speak.

Miss Alicia came forward, voice quavering. "When the shift changed at three o'clock, one of our grannies went to his room to check on him. He was asleep on his side, so she didn't disturb him." Alicia paused when her voice wouldn't stop shaking. She cleared her throat and began again. "The granny went back a little while later and touched his head. It was stone cold. She panicked momentarily before realizing it wasn't Billy. It was a doll. 'Very funny,' she said that she'd thought then went looking for him."

Kingsley glared at the staff, several of whom were in tears.

"We checked the sign-in-and-out book, thinking one of you might have taken him. Nobody had. We looked everywhere, even called those authorized to pick him up, hoping they'd forgotten the rules. When that yielded nothing, we called Mr. Henning and Security."

Pandemonium erupted as the security chief burst through the door and everyone started talking at once. Kingsley broke from the group and ran to Billy's crib, which someone had returned to its normal position. It was empty except for a doll and a small, wadded-up blanket. She sprinted from room to room and corner to corner. She checked bathrooms and under the tables, hoping one of the four-year-olds had adopted him to play house. She demanded an answer from two little girls who immediately broke into tears and clung to a daycare worker's legs. Startled by the confrontation, other children started to wail.

Billy was nowhere. Kingsley circled the rooms a second, then a third time, reopening every door and cupboard, irrespective of logic. She even opened the children's play cook stove. Wild-eyed and panicked, she confronted Miss Alicia. "Billy! Where is my baby?"

"Ms. Henning," she said in a trembling voice. "We can't find him. It's like he vanished."

Todd jumped in the security chief's face, fists clenched and red-faced with fury. He bellowed orders. "Shut down the building. Nobody leaves until every person and every inch is exhaustively searched. Get the police and whatever other bodies you need. And go over every scrap of security footage. Our son couldn't just vanish. Find him!"

Chapter 4

Activity swarmed around Kingsley as security personnel posted checkpoints at all exterior doors. Employees and visitors showed police the contents of parcels voluntarily, all of which yielded nothing. Inside the branch, tellers and customer service representatives gazed, transfixed, at the activity swirling beyond the glass wall that separated the branch from the atrium lobby and garden.

"It looks like they're having everyone stop and look at the security camera before leaving the bank. Why are they doing that?" a teller asked the branch manager.

"I was told they want to know who was here, when they left, and what they were wearing."

"Their clothes? Why would that matter?"

The manager shrugged. "I have no idea. Back to work, please. Unless I miss my guess, they'll shut us down, and we have to be ready."

"Did you notice anything unusual?" one asked another.

"Only that little boy who was hanging around the stairway next to the fire alarm. That was strange. I thought at the time that he should be in school."

Inside the daycare, Kingsley watched with surreal detachment as the nightmare continued. Uniformed officers protected the scene and began to interview potential witnesses. Detectives from the special investigations squad arrived and assumed command. Ethelda Blake, red-eyed and shaking, mopped her tear-rivered face as she stammered answers to their clipped questions.

"When the fire alarm sounded, I picked up Billy and headed outside. He's such a good baby—slept right through the racket. I sat with him on the grass at the edge of the parking lot. The weather went south on us, and I was afraid he'd catch cold. So I kept him bundled against me for warmth. We huddled there for what seemed like forever. I thought they should have let us go in. When the all clear sounded, I carried him back into the daycare."

"Did you see anyone who shouldn't be there? Any strangers? Innocent-looking people taking a walk?"

"No one. But I wasn't watching that closely. My responsibility was for the children. And it was starting to rain."

"Did you notice if anyone entered the building while you were waiting?" She shook her head.

The detective watched her with hooded eyes. "Continue. What happened once you were back inside?"

"I settled Billy in his crib then read a story to the toddlers in the gathering area. We played Duck-Duck-Goose with the three-year-olds for maybe ten minutes. Then I left."

"What time was that?"

"It was around two thirty, my quitting time. See, I start at six and get a half hour for lunch. Some of our officers travel to early off-campus meetings, and some back-office staffers report at seven. The daycare opens early to accommodate them."

"You said you left after two. Why did you come back?"

"Miss Alicia called me at home. Told me that Billy was missing. To get over here fast, so I did."

The detective made a few notes dispassionately in a small spiral-topped notebook. "Did you check on Billy before you left?"

"No. Well, I mean yes. Sort of. I peeked in the door, and he was asleep. You see, by then I was assigned to game time with the three-year-olds who no longer take naps. Billy's such a sweet baby. I couldn't resist taking one last peek."

"Are you sure it was Billy?"

Tears welled in Ethelda's swollen eyes. "I had no reason to think that it wasn't. Maybe if I'd come closer. If only I'd touched him…" She paused, covering her mouth with a tissue. "I feel sick." She bolted in the direction of the bathroom.

The detective took a deep breath and approached the security chief who had motioned him into the corridor. "Well?"

"It's all on the video. You can see for yourself. During the fire drill Ms. Blake carried him out and back in again."

"Are you sure?"

"Right down to the monkeys on his blanket. And that's still in his crib. So we know he was still in the building at two."

"When did the Blake woman leave? And was she carrying anything?"

"She left the building at two thirty-four, keys in one hand and a little purse in the other. It was way too small to conceal a baby."

"What about the surveillance footage inside the daycare?"

"They don't allow cameras in the baby's quiet room where there's privacy issues with nursing mothers. But there are panoramic shots of the interior. That shows nothing useful."

"Are there any blind spots?"

"Just that one area, but we still can see anyone coming or going, and nobody used the main door, emergency exit, or the windows on the far side of the room."

The detective eyeballed the ceiling's two-by-two tiles. "Get property management. I want to know what's above those tiles and whether someone could access the crib from above."

Time crawled, and darkness settled as the police processed the scene. The building emptied, except for second shift personnel who slipped around, speaking in hushed tones. Employees who arrived to claim their infants and toddlers grabbed them and fled. Kingsley stood shivering beside Billy's empty crib. Gingerly, she picked up the blanket, which had been a gift from a college roommate. She stroked its soft fabric. Burying her face in it, she smelled the essence of Billy.

"Ms. Henning! Don't touch anything!" Startled, she dropped the blanket back into the crib as if it might burn her fingers. She glanced at her palm and noticed what appeared to be a few strands of Billy's hair. She rolled the hairs between her thumb and index finger into a ringlet and held it close to her face. It had an odd smell. Glancing around, she surreptitiously tucked it into her pocket, not wanting to surrender the tiniest remnant of Billy.

Todd paced, questioning officers who repeatedly reminded him to leave the scene undisturbed. An evidence technician dusted for fingerprints, and a handler arrived with a bloodhound.

"Ms. Henning, have you an article of clothing that your baby wore recently? Other than the blanket? We need that for evidence."

"He wore this hooded sweater this morning," Kingsley said, taking it from Billy's cubby and offering it to the handler. The bloodhound, she thought, looked as sad as she felt.

"Find," she commanded, following the dog from the daycare. The animal halted in the corridor, looked right, but turned left, and trotted, nose down, ears dragging, toward the exterior door.

"Are they crazy? Do they think Billy could walk out of here?" Kingsley asked Todd.

"That isn't it," an officer interjected. "His scent could linger. He could be out there."

"What?" Her eyes widened, chin trembling. "Oh dear God. Do they think somebody left him out back in the woods in this rain?" She couldn't stop her voice from quavering. "Or in the dumpster? We've got to get out there!"

Todd caught her arm as she started to bolt, struggling to keep his voice calm. "K, wait. We cannot go out there! We might contaminate the trail. If he's out there, they'll find him faster than we can. Perhaps they can pick up a trail or find footprints or tire tracks or something they dropped."

"They?" Again, Kingsley tried to lurch toward the door, but Todd hung fast to her arm. After what seemed like an eternity, the handler returned with the bloodhound. The animal was sneezing and panting. "The scent ends at the edge of the parking lot," the handler said. "There's a scent pool a few yards from the dumpster, but no closer. I understand that's where daycare personnel waited during the fire drill." She bent to scratch the dog's ears and murmur appreciation. The bloodhound turned baleful eyes toward his master, tongue lolling lopsidedly.

The detective approached them. With a soft, empathetic voice he said, "We're treating this as a kidnapping. We'd better go to your home—in case there's a ransom call. You'll need to be there, and we need to set up equipment." He nodded his head in agreement with himself.

"Come on, K. There's nothing we can do here."

The detective scanned his notes and said, "We'll need those documents we discussed—your son's footprints, photos, identifying marks, addresses and phone numbers of people we should contact. And please give more thought to possible enemies."

His voice blurred away as Kingsley covered her ears and closed her eyes tightly to blot it all out. Opening them, she swept the room, as if awakening from a bad dream. The woodland creatures that encircled the room now seemed to mock her. How strange. Their eyes were following her. Speak! What did you see? Numb, she let Todd lead her out of the daycare.

∞∞

The cold front that swept in that afternoon blanketed the area with drizzle, fog, and bone-chilling dampness. Todd unlocked the back door, cleared the security code, and strode their center hall toward the front foyer, turning on lights as he went. Pandora, their longhaired tuxedo cat, took one look at the invasion and bolted upstairs.

Kingsley tore into the dark library to check the phone for messages. The red number blinked twelve.

"Wait," the detective said, lighting a lamp. "We need to hear too." Without shedding their coats, they played the messages. Three were from Kingsley's parents, two each from Barrie and Randall, a couple from friends, and two from the press. The mailbox exhausted itself before number twelve finished.

Kingsley shivered and clutched her thin raincoat as activity swirled around her. The police installed trap and trace devices while Todd went through the motions of lighting a fire. Flames from the stone fireplace, centered on the side wall, soon cast a softening glow on the ten-foot-high cherry bookshelves that covered the side and back walls.

"Hon, why don't you make us some coffee?" She nodded numbly and went to the kitchen. She glugged spring water into the Krups reservoir and dumped coffee beans into the filter. She turned it on. Only this morning, she thought. Or was it yesterday now?

She looked for the mugs, and not finding them in their right spot, started to cry. *Billy! Where are you? Everyone, everything, should be where they belong. Why aren't you here? Please, please, please, let me wake up.*

She noticed the carafe, filling at last with what looked like dirty water. What had she done? The beans—they should have been ground. She dumped the mess into the garbage, scalding her hand. She yanked at the faucet, drenching her fingers with cold water, and then started the process again.

The tall-case clock in the foyer chimed each quarter hour, but time had no meaning. Whenever the phone jangled, everyone jumped. On cue, Todd took the call. Everyone watched intently, the only noise being the crackling fire. Finally, he spoke, giving a brief update to family. An audible sigh escaped the assemblage. The vigil continued, their time divided between pacing and sitting, then pacing again.

Todd finally took up a station at one of the library's double-hung windows, half-sitting on the deep windowsill. He stared at the dreary landscape outside. Two hundred-foot oaks sent huge raindrops great distances, frothing puddles beside their suspended white cedar swing.

"It's getting light," he finally said to Kingsley without turning around. "You must be exhausted. Why don't you try to grab a nap?"

She looped her hand through his arm and rested her cheek on his chest. "No way I could sleep. And I can't go upstairs. The thought of passing his room, and Billy not in it." Just thinking of Billy made her milk let down from her engorged breasts. She squeezed her forearm against them to stem it. "I need to pump. My equipment's upstairs."

"I'll find it. Then maybe you can lie down on the couch."

She nodded, remembering that the officers had been on duty all night. "I'd better make them some breakfast. I couldn't sleep anyway."

Chapter 5

Kingsley lay fetal-like, her back wedged against the living room couch cushion, a butter-soft leather remnant of Todd's bachelor condo. Head on scrunched pillows she huddled, clutching the edge of a throw in one hand, the cordless phone in the other.

Her head throbbed, eyes raw, neck muscles threatening to give up support. As shadows lengthened outside the west window, calls had become less frequent. Well-wishers and the curious had been asked politely to keep the line free. Time edged past twenty-four hours without a ransom demand or someone knocking, miraculously, returning with Billy. Kingsley agonized over the anguishing details of needing to find missing children within the first twenty-four hours. She refused to go down that dark tunnel.

As the tall clock struck four, the quiet rumble of approaching male voices startled her. Rubbing her eyes, she realized that she'd been asleep. She sat up, tossing the throw from her rumpled clothes and smoothing her skirt. Todd directed a man and a woman into the living room, whom he introduced as detectives. If they had names, Kingsley didn't catch them. Both angled chairs beyond the steamer trunk that served as their coffee table. Todd sat down beside her and drew her close, his hand anchoring her shoulder.

"What have you learned?" Todd asked.

"As you know, several procedures were implemented immediately. Every square foot and possible place of concealment was searched uneventfully. We photographed and dusted the daycare for prints and gathered trace evidence."

His speech was measured, professional, objective as he ticked points from a small spiral notepad. "Every individual exiting the building passed through security. All were asked to voluntarily show the contents of purses, brief cases, or totes, which everyone did without exception. And nobody objected to personal cars being searched. Same lack of results."

"What about the bloodhound and his handler?"

"That produced nothing beyond the area where Ms. Blake was known to have sat during the fire drill. Her coworkers have verified her and your son's whereabouts."

Todd scowled. "Somebody had to access that daycare."

"We found no other way into or out of the facility above two feet that wasn't visible to the cameras. We even took the entire ceiling apart and checked all the vents."

"What's under the room?" she asked.

"Concrete. Dirt. Rock. Not even a crawlspace. As you know, that wing is an add-on. All mechanicals are in the walls or above the ceiling."

"Then how do you explain it?" Kingsley asked. "My baby couldn't just vanish. Somebody had to carry him out, and somebody had to have seen that. You can't just sneak into a secure daycare, pick up a baby, and stroll out. Could the security recording have been altered? A previous day's version run in its place?"

"No."

"How do you know?"

"We tested them for tampering then checked the clothing of employees as they arrived in the morning, came and went for the fire drill, and again as they exited. Everything matched. Besides—it's a live feed, with real people watching."

"Surely, they take breaks."

The detective shook his head. "Not at the same time."

Kingsley, feeling the bile rising in her core, cast agonized eyes at her husband.

"Detective," Todd said, "you've told us succinctly what you did *not* find. What *do* you know?"

"We believe this was no random abduction. That it was expertly planned. Do either of you have any enemies? Has anyone threatened you? If you've kept anything from us—if you know anything at all and are not telling us—you're not helping your son's situation."

Kingsley wrenched herself free from Todd's arm. "No! Of course not. We would have told you. We haven't heard anything. When would we?" She turned desperate eyes to Todd. "We don't know anyone who would hurt us, do we, Todd? Surely not to this extent."

The detective raised his eyebrows. "This extent?"

"Of course, I routinely turn down unqualified loan applicants. And there's a former Keynote executive whom I helped convict in a loan scam. But he's still in prison," she said. The detective jotted a note. "And my husband's killers are also in prison."

Todd said, "My ex-wife hates my guts, but she lives in Europe. Besides, she's all mouth, no brain, and physically harmless. And she wouldn't know what to do with a baby."

The other detective, who had been quiet, weighed in. "I have to ask. Both of you are committed professionals. As the bank's president, Mr. Henning, just thirty-seven, you could be chairman in less than three years. And Ms. Henning, I understand as Vice President for Commercial Lending, you're on the fast track to head all of Lending." She paused, then proceeded in casual tones that missed their mark as compassionate. "Might you have given someone, even inadvertently, the idea that your lives would be less encumbered without the demands of a child?"

"Of course not! Everyone knows we were thrilled about Billy."

"Not according to the human resources director at your

former bank. Ms. Henning, he said that during your initial interview you were asked where you pictured yourself in five years. You said you wanted to head a lending department. He asked about children. And you said you had no intention of having any. Ever. He said his reaction was two-fold—that he was shocked by your answer and that he remembered, too late, that it was an improper question. He was relieved that he wasn't reprimanded. That's why he remembered."

"That's ridiculous! Responses to interview questions like that are canned. You can read them in any how-to-get-that-job book."

"But we do have information from multiple sources that you weren't happy about having a baby."

She jolted. "Who said that?"

"We aren't at liberty to give out that information."

Kingsley bolted to her feet and tripped over the throw, sending the cordless phone clattering across the trunk onto the Persian rug at the detectives' feet. "Are you trying to say we're somehow responsible for Billy's disappearance?"

"Ms. Henning. Please. Sit down. We have to ask to eliminate any possible involvement—"

"Involvement! That's obscene! And cruel! And malicious! Do you have any idea how much Billy means to us? Well, I'll tell you." Fists clenched at her sides, she half leaned over the trunk, words spitting like daggers. "Our child is a miracle. I miscarried badly when my first husband was killed, and Todd's ex-wife altered documents to say he was sterile. But we loved each other so much that we married anyway. Billy—he was our honeymoon baby. If he needed my heart, I'd cut it out for him. And you have the audacity to compare our precious child to our jobs? Go do your homework. We don't need money. We need our son back."

"There are certain documents that we'll like to access. Just to rule you out. It's routine. Your bank records—"

Todd jumped from his seat. "You have absolutely no

reason, no probable cause to pry into our finances. No judge will allow it."

"It's our job to investigate. And, yes, a judge would."

"Get out! Get out of our house!" she screamed. Ragged sobs accompanied her high-pitched screech as she shook her fist. Todd caught her flailing arms and locked her close to his body. Solemnly, he jerked his head toward the door.

"Okay. For now." They let themselves out the front door.

☙❧

Day blurred into night and into the morning of the third day. Todd came downstairs and entered the library where Kingsley huddled in a wingback chair, hugging her knees to her chest. She looked up from the quiet phone and technical paraphernalia. Todd, who had showered, shaved, and dressed in khakis and a long-sleeved polo shirt, looked rather normal to her. "I'll stay with the phone if you'd like to shower and change," he said. She shook her head. "Well then, why don't I bring you fresh clothes? There's the powder room—"

She smiled in spite of herself. He was trying so hard. "My jeans, the old faded ones, and my Penn sweatshirt. Thanks." He disappeared and was back in five minutes, also carrying some funky peacock blue underwear, her cosmetics basket, and fuzzy purple socks.

"What are you going to do?" she asked.

"Got to take a brief run to the bank. I shouldn't be gone for more than two hours. Even in an emergency, responsibility can't be ignored, especially during the countdown to the shareholders meeting. I'll ask my reports to brief me on their areas. They'll run with the ball. And I need to give Marketing my speech for the meeting and review their press release. That can't be emailed since it contains inside financial information. It's times like this that I'm glad we have good key people. I'll ask them to communicate on my cell phone—keep this line free." He started toward the back door, then called back over his shoulder. "You'll be okay?" She nodded. "Then I'll be back as soon as I can."

She made her way to the Harry Potter door tucked under the staircase and shut herself into the powder room. The face in the mirror couldn't be hers. She pulled a thick hand towel and washcloth from their rod and soaked the cloth in cool water. She held it against her eyes. Her hot face quickly warmed the cloth. She soaked it again and finally looked up. Her eyes were swollen to slits. Billy! It came rushing back, and she smothered her sobs in the washcloth, drawing water into her nose.

She tried to pray but couldn't find words beyond *please, please, please* and rash promises to govern the rest of her life. Like the crack of a bat, it suddenly hit her conscious mind. The phone had not rung. Not once! If nobody wanted to deal, Billy might never be found. For the first time, she could not block the inconceivable word from her mind. Her baby could be dead.

She sank to the toilet lid and, closing her eyes, grasped her knees. She rocked back and forth. *Think. Billy couldn't just vanish.* She had to know, whatever the outcome. What had she seen? What was she missing? Step by step she walked herself mentally through that last hour—the new cleaning woman! Could she be involved? She'd left before Kingsley and according to security hadn't returned.

Kingsley had fed Billy. Rock, rock, rock. Billy had been fussy—couldn't seem to burp. His crib. Where had she pushed it? Beside Sammy's? Did that make a difference? She had stroked his warm little back. In her mind, she could see him. Feel him. Smell him. She'd been preoccupied, hoping to settle him into his crib before time forced her to leave.

Enter Ethelda Blake, the new daycare worker, who had calmed her anxiety and was holding Billy when she left the daycare. Ethelda, who had cared for Billy during the fire drill and brought him back safely. Security had confirmed Ethelda's movements. Kingsley had left by the stairwell opposite the daycare to meet a prospect. Leaving the building, she had passed no one. She got into her car. No. First, she had opened the trunk and tossed in her leather bag. Kingsley backed up her mental tape. The last thing she did before leaving the daycare was go to the ladies and pick up her bag. *Then* she had left the building.

In a flash of irrelevant horror, Kingsley bolted from the powder room through the back hall. Not finding the bag in its usual spot by the door, she raced through the rooms, searching for it. There! Under her desk in the library. Todd must have dropped it in there. Overwhelmed with dread, she tore it from the kneehole and, crouching on the rug, flung open the closures.

Nothing—except her laptop, a few client files and Billy's laundry, just as she'd packed it. Instantly, she felt ridiculous, even though there was no one to observe her bizarre behavior.

Trancelike, she lifted each object. The thermal receiving blanket edged in blue that she had thrown over her shoulder. Some newborn outfits, already outgrown, no longer suitable as daycare spares. Baby accessories—gifts from her friends, adorable in themselves, but never used. She sighed. How ridiculous to think. How grotesque. Unthinkable. They would have noticed his body long before now.

Mechanically, she folded the newborn clothes. Then something clicked. Frowning, she looked through the pile. The beaver suit—the blue terry sleeper with the charming little creature embroidered in red—it wasn't there. And she was positive she'd seen it in his cubby before she left the daycare. Kingsley shook off the creepy feeling she couldn't explain.

ᘒᘖᘒ

"Kingsley?" Sarah Alderson called to her daughter from

the back door. Henry trailed his wife into the kitchen where he planted a large cooler on the yellow pine floor. Kingsley wandered into the kitchen, stocking-footed and hitching her threadbare jeans. They three-way hugged, no one wanting to move.

"Food," Sarah said finally in a brisk motherly tone, disentangling herself. "I didn't know what else to do, so I cooked and baked." She lifted the lid of the Coleman. "Comfort food—soup, stew, a roast sliced in gravy, a casserole. You've got to eat."

"Mom, you're the best." Kingsley felt enormously better just knowing her mom was on duty. A subtle blend of urban chic and country elegance, Sarah exuded a softness that went beyond the sweep of her auburn hair and her casual knits. Her creativity captivated people as did her paintings. Once she started a *well-now-dear* speech, Kingsley knew she could make sense of the inexplicable.

Henry cleared his throat. "And I've got the chocolate group covered. Everyone kept asking what they could do, so I divulged all of your weaknesses. It got out of hand."

"Daddy!" She hugged him again. He disappeared and re-appeared juggling myriad Tupperware containers.

"Where's Todd?" Henry asked.

"Outside somewhere. He can't seem to settle."

"I'll check on him."

Kingsley smiled appreciation to her dad. From the time she was little, she'd been his shadow, tromping their acres in St. Davids, or playing banker at the small table he kept for his only child in his Philadelphia office. Tall and straight, his hair touched with silver, he commanded respect while being well liked. Just being around him made her feel protected.

Sarah eyed her narrow daughter's five-foot-eight frame on which her size two jeans already gaped. "You won't be any good to yourself or anyone else if you don't keep up your strength. How about a nice soak in the tub? I brought you a fantastic new bath gel. Then you must eat."

Kingsley looked helplessly at her dad who merely shrugged. "Mom, I can't go upstairs."

"Grammy would say, '*Put can't behind the door and try.*' Come on, sweetie. One step at a time."

"But—"

Sarah tucked her arm through Kingsley's and propelled her toward the staircase, up and past Billy's door, parking her in the bathroom.

⊱⊰

Kingsley forced herself to take the first mouthful of soup and willed herself not to gag. She didn't. She waited a moment then took another taste. Vegetable beef, from Grammy's recipe, made with beef shin. The three lingered at the old kitchen table that Todd had bought at an antique auction before they met. Finding and renovating an old stone farmhouse had been his dream but having a family was for somebody else. Yet he had bought and stored antique treasures nevertheless for this *someday house.*

Henry pampered the fire that crackled in the walk-in fireplace, smiling with satisfaction and a bit too much cheer. "I wasn't sure it would draw, but it's so chilly and raw in these woods." He and Sarah exchanged surreptitious glances at Kingsley's empty bowl.

"Guess I really was hungry," Kingsley said, separating and buttering a second homemade clover-shaped roll. "I just wish I were stronger, like Grammy. What a survivor she was."

"You helped make her strong when she needed it most," Sarah said of her own mother. "It never crossed your mind that she couldn't do anything, and you were vocal about that, even as a small child. Do you remember your grandfather?"

"In snatches. I remember her stories about him better, and the two melt together."

"Even though your grandfather was fifteen years older, she thought he was indestructible. So when he died unexpectedly…"

"Did they really meet the way that she said, or was that just a story?"

Sarah smiled, an only child remembering her mother, also an only. "He was a CPA and guest lecturer at her sophomore accounting class. He said it was love at first sight. They eloped, you know, but he won her family over, insisting that she stay in college. In her day, a female accountant was unusual. He loved all of her, especially her mind. He sought her counsel, brought her into his firm, and insisted she have a maid and a nanny when I came along."

"How old was I when Grandpa died?"

"You were four."

"I remember she could do anything—have a career, a family, a garden, bake, be active in the community. She was way ahead of her time. I remember wanting to be just like her."

"Actually," Sarah said, "she fell into a deep depression when he passed away. Grief counseling, mediation, the church, family, and friends couldn't reach her. Then one day, she said she overheard you tell a little friend, 'When a grandpa dies, the grandma has to stop doing everything.' She said that was a terrible lesson to teach her only grandchild. So she returned to their accounting firm and resurrected the gardens that you remember."

"She was so wise. Always saying what helped. If she were here, what would that be?"

"She'd say, 'Pray, then step back. Let God lead and then follow. '"

"If only it were that easy."

"You must try. We all will, honey. Now—your dad and I have to get back, but we're only two hours away. Less if he drives and the officer writes quickly. Try to rest. You can't anticipate what further demands will be made on your time and energy. You need to be ready." She slipped into her sweater. "It's awfully hard to be the responsible grownup sometimes. You have what it takes, but you must take care of yourself."

No sooner had the Aldersons' taillights disappeared up the lane and onto the secondary road than Kingsley felt overcome by exhaustion. Warmed by the food and her parents' devotion, she calmed. A few minutes, she thought, as she located the cordless phone. She curled into the living room couch and adjusted the throw. Pandora, her beloved cat, appeared from nowhere and pounced beside Kingsley's stomach. The feline snuggled into the bend of her mistress's knees and began licking her forepaw rhythmically. The last thing Kingsley remembered was the white noise of Pandora's purr.

∽∾∽

A vehicle crunching slowly down Hennings' lane finally broke into her dream. Unlike friends and family, who circled around back, this car halted by the brick walkway that stretched from the lane to the front porch. Instinctively knowing it wasn't her parents returning for whatever reason, Kingsley crept to the living room window. A nondescript sedan was stopping out front from which two people emerged simultaneously. Immediately she recognized the male detective who had questioned her and Todd the previous afternoon. His companion was a rather plain woman in a poorly cut brown pantsuit and dusty shoes. The detective sharply rapped the pineapple knocker. One. Two. Three. Kingsley opened the door.

"Have you heard anything?" she demanded, not waiting for introductions.

"This is Detective Flynn, Ms. Henning. May we come in?"

She eyed them suspiciously. They looked neither friendly nor helpful, and she still stung from their recent encounter. Stepping back, she allowed the massive walnut door to swing open and motioned them into the foyer. "Lovely old home," the woman said in a soft, appreciative voice. "Has it been in the family for generations?"

Taken somewhat aback by her pleasant tone and the mention of a favorite topic, Kingsley heard herself answer politely. "My husband and I bought it just before we were married then tore into a massive restoration. Insanity runs in the family." She instantly regretted the latter comment when that didn't bring smiles. "It's a joke."

"Ms. Henning, I must apologize for my partner's rudeness the other day. Diplomacy is not his long suit. He spends too much time with hardened criminals. We thought you could help us."

Kingsley studied her face a split second longer, unable to read an ulterior motive. Although her better judgment was screaming like hell, she went along with the ruse. "I'll try." She led them into the living room where the two sat in the same seats the men had occupied previously.

"Wonderful old windows," she said. "That's the original hand-made glass, isn't it? Twelve over twelve? And those windowsills must be two feet deep."

"I'm sorry." Kingsley cut her off when she began to expand her appraisal to other architectural details. "I'm in no mood for small talk. What have you learned? Do you have any suspects? Any clues?" She wanted to ask, *are you clueless*?

"We thought, if you'd walk us through your recollections, perhaps that would jog your memory. Even the tiniest detail, the slightest thing that was amiss, an object out of place—"

"I've been over this a thousand times in my mind. The only thing out of place was his crib. The cleaning woman had moved it out of the babies' room to mop the floor."

"And that was unusual?"

"Very. I'm told that's done earlier in the day, but the regular woman had pulled a no-show, and the double-shifting substitute couldn't follow the normal routine. I don't pay attention to HR logistics—didn't need to know anything about staffing issues."

"Do you know this woman?" Without taking her eyes off Kingsley's face, Detective Flynn slid a color photo onto the trunk for Kingsley's inspection. Obviously, the woman in the photo was dead.

Kingsley's breath caught. "Who is she? What happened to her? She looks…"

"Do you know who she is?" she asked.

Vacantly Kingsley shook her head no. Detective Flynn started to collect the photo.

Kingsley pointed at the vanishing picture. "What's this about?"

"She is—was—the regular cleaning woman whose area included the daycare. When she didn't show up at her daughter's for dinner and couldn't be raised, the daughter went to check on her. Found the grisly scene and called nine-one-one."

"How awful!" Kingsley looked from face to face. "If this happened at the bank, I heard nothing about it."

"They found her at home, and, according to the ME, she died the previous evening."

"The day Billy was kidnapped?"

"No. The evening before."

"Let me see that again." She studied the photo and winced. The image was grotesque, the obvious result of a massive head wound. "Is that blood?" She looked again, trying to interpolate how the woman had once looked. "No, I'm positive. I've never seen her before."

She handed back the photo as if it could somehow contaminate her. "I normally visit the daycare at noon and return to my office before one. Even if her workday were rearranged, well, I've only been taking Billy to daycare for two weeks. And I only know the cleaning crew who work in Lending, and she's not one of them."

"I'd like to show you some photo enlargements printed

from surveillance equipment." He handed Kingsley a black and white eight-by-ten-inch glossy of herself, exiting the daycare.

She nodded. "That's me. It looks like it was taken the day—the day he—I had fed and rocked Billy, left him with the new daycare provider, and was on my way to my parking spot on the opposite side of the building. This shot was taken in the corridor between the daycare's entrance off the hall and the stairwell on the opposite wall that leads outside. A prospect had insisted on a midday meeting. I had fed Billy a little bit early to accommodate the prospect's schedule."

"Where did the meeting take place?"

"I was supposed to meet him at a diner a few miles from the bank, but he never showed up. After an hour, I called the number he'd given me, but it was a disconnect. He had sounded so harried, so disorganized when he made the appointment that I didn't find his behavior unusual."

"Did you see other coworkers or friends at the diner?"

"No. Most of us take a half hour in our break room or eat at our desks, unless we have a lunch meeting. If a meeting is a really big deal, we reserve a private room at a nearby inn or have lunch catered in our conference room."

"So nobody saw you."

"Well, sure. Other people whom I don't know were having lunch. And the waitress who refilled my coffee. And refilled it. And refilled it." She grimaced. "Total waste of time. And I jangled for hours."

Detective Flynn pointed to Kingsley's image in the glossy again. "Nice bag. Would make a great airplane carryon." She tapped the indentation on Kingsley's shoulder. "By the looks of that strap, it must weigh a ton. What you got in there, rocks?"

"My laptop, bank folders, baby stuff."

"What kind of baby stuff?"

Kingsley took a closer look at the woman and processed her attitude. Hard face. No-nonsense expression. Kingsley felt her heart rate pick up, her body go hot. She couldn't quite get her mind around where this woman was going, and she prickled. "I don't understand what you're asking. What does the contents of my bag have to do with anything?"

Flynn placed another eight-by-ten of Kingsley on the coffee table trunk. "What's happening here?"

"Oh!" she said. It came out as a sigh from somewhere deep in her soul, and she felt the scratch of threatening tears. In the photo, Todd was propelling her by her shoulder toward the exit, a police officer beside her. She could make out the keys to her Lexus dangling from the officer's hand. "After the K-nine officer finished, they asked us to go home and wait for a ransom call. One of the officers offered to drive my car home. That's him. On my left."

"And you're carrying the bag."

"Yes."

The man jumped in a little too quickly. "We need the bag." It was a statement, not a question.

"Why?"

"Ms. Henning, we find it curious that you were the only one leaving the daycare that day—twice—with anything large enough to conceal a baby. How do you explain that?"

She jumped to her feet. "That's crazy!"

"What's crazy?" Todd had entered the house unnoticed via the rear hallway, approaching the living room from the foyer.

She rushed to him, wild-eyed, her skewered emotions never far from the edge. "They're accusing me of taking Billy from the bank in my bag. They're crazy! Why would I do that? When? How could he fit?" She felt herself frothing questions that didn't make sense, even to her, but she couldn't stop the torrent.

Todd strode toward the pair, fury in his eyes. "Let me see that." Without waiting, he grabbed the photos of Kingsley. He pulled his reading glasses out of his breast pocket and jammed them onto his face. Eyes scrunched toward the corners, he flapped the first photo in the air. "What the hell kind of idiocy is this?" Jabbing the lower right corner with his index finger, he showed her the tiny four-point time stamp. "K, when must this photo have been taken?"

"Just after noon. I was on my way to the parking lot to drive to a meeting. I told them about that—the dairy farmer who never showed up at the diner."

"This time stamp says one fifty-five. The photo's been altered. K, where were you at one fifty-five?"

"In the parking lot behind our building, freezing, along with the entire department. The fire drill was in progress—remember? We were stuck there for nearly an hour."

"That timestamp's been altered." Todd looked at the other photo. "The bag—"

"Someone handed it to me. I don't remember who, but some kind soul retrieved my raincoat, purse, and bag from my office before we went home. Yes. I remember now. I wouldn't have left without my coat. Margaret, from Real Estate Lending, that's who it was. She also checked my office, turned off my computer, and filed sensitive documents. You can ask her."

"We need to see that bag."

"Not without a search warrant, you don't," Todd said without blinking.

"I can get one. Easier for you if I don't have to post an officer while we get it. That could take hours."

"You do that! But while you're at it, make sure that warrant specifies Keynote National Bank records contained in that bag by specific customer, as well as all records on the bank's laptop. Oh! And the bag itself is bank property." The pair paused. Todd smirked sardonically. "Thought so. You're fishing. And clueless. Get out. Now!"

Reluctantly they headed outside.

He hugged Kingsley to him. "What did I miss?"

She gulped back tears. "Seems I'm a suspect. How could anyone ever think that? Or hate me enough to tell the police that I didn't want Billy? Several of them! What have I done?"

"I've had about enough of this. We're talking to our lawyer."

"Won't that make us look guilty?"

"Guilty of what? Kingsley, why would you think that?"

"Isn't that what the police always do when they can't figure it out? Blame the parents? How can they not? I blame myself. I never should have left him alone."

"K, he wasn't alone. That should have been the safest place in the world."

Outside, the detectives piled into their car. "That went well," he said dryly to Detective Flynn. "Where did that photo come from anyway? And how could the date stamp be wrong?"

"Someone went to a lot of trouble. We should have checked the timeline ourselves. Not taken a shortcut. Too much pressure to act quickly. I feel like an idiot."

"Well, don't. We have more information implicating the parents than any case I can remember. If they did it, we'll nail them. We'll just have to check out our sources more carefully. Start thinking about who could have helped them. And why."

Chapter 6

enry Alderson swept through the Pennsylvania Turnpike's E-Z pass lane and wedged into the Philadelphia East lane. Sluicing around speeding motorists and market-bound semis, he soon led the pack. Only then did he glance at his wife who was uncharacteristically quiet. He patted her thigh to get her attention. "You all right?"

Without raising her eyes, Sarah's sigh underscored her exhaustion. "It's a nightmare. If they don't find Billy immediately—you've read the statistics."

"Sarah, we've got to think positively. They'll find him."

"I can't help it. I feel so helpless. When Kingsley was little, there wasn't much I couldn't fix with a hug and a Snoopy Band-Aid. But this!"

"You helped a great deal. How you managed to keep yourself under control is amazing, given the circumstances. I could see her relax."

"Kingsley's *my* baby. I had to keep my focus on her."

They rode in silence for thirty more minutes then exited onto the Schuylkill Expressway at King of Prussia.

"Should we have stayed overnight?" Sarah asked, glancing at their bags stashed in the back of the SUV.

"She knows we'll come back, no matter what time or what reason. Hell, for no reason at all if she needs us."

Sarah frowned. "I know our daughter. If we stayed,

she'd feel obligated to buoy up our spirits, and that would drain what little reserve she has left. Besides, I sensed they need time alone."

"Was it my imagination or were they avoiding each other?"

"For a man that's pretty intuitive." Henry faked an insulted look. She continued. "You know how they are—the looks, the little touches, their private terms of endearment. The way he does things without being asked and the appreciation she showers on him. Their love is palpable. But now, when they need each other the most, they're like polite strangers. I thought if we got out of their hair, perhaps they would talk. Henry, she has always listened to you. Perhaps you could give her some hints on drawing him out."

"I'll call her when we get home." As he exited the Schuylkill onto the Blue Route and east toward the St. Davids exit, he drummed the steering wheel to the energized beat of a CD, pretending not to notice that Sarah had finally succumbed to tears.

∽∾∽

Executive Vice President Shirley Granger—head of Human Resources, Marketing, and Branch Administration at Keynote National Bank—rose to shake Detective Flynn's hand. She offered a facing visitor's chair to the intruder. Both sat and dispensed with small talk.

"As I said on the phone—" Shirley said, kicking off the interview. "—all I can tell you about an employee is when he or she was employed here and what the job description entailed. I cannot elaborate on personal details, why they were hired, quit, or were fired, unless you have a warrant. And I certainly can't discuss the quality of their work."

"I understand. Did you know Kingsley Henning personally? Outside of work?"

"We're professional acquaintances. Our lives beyond the

bank do not intersect." Detective Flynn remained silent long enough for Shirley to begin feeling uncomfortable. Without wanting to do so, she heard herself filling the void. "On a day-to-day basis, we cross paths at meetings and bank functions in the building—the usual places."

Now on high alert, Shirley would not let herself fall for that ploy again. She had conducted enough interviews herself to understand the reason for the long silences—get the subject to babble, divulging details.

"So you've had opportunities for informal conversation about non-banking topics?"

"Yes, I guess so."

"While you were chatting, outside of conducting bank business, do you recall her attitude about her pregnancy? Was she happy? Excited? Depressed? Overwhelmed?"

Shirley snapped back to control the interview. "Detective," she said in as polite a tone as she could muster, "I'm sorry if I failed to make myself clear. It would be wholly unprofessional, possibly actionable, for me to discuss personnel issues with you. What you just asked falls into the category of health issues. I've been a human resources professional for twenty years, which makes me a hard person to play. So why don't you just ask me directly what you want to know."

The detective uncrossed her arms, draped them on the upholstered chair's arms, and crossed her legs. She settled back and modulated her voice. "All right. The Henning kidnapping has taken some challenging twists. We've had several anonymous tips, presumably from Keynote personnel, saying that Ms. Henning did not want the baby. That she and her husband are somehow involved in his disappearance."

"That's crazy!"

"Why do you say that?"

"In the first place, any employee who talks to an outside entity about what transpires on the job, without permission, will be fired. No exceptions. None. And no one may talk to the media, either. All press calls are routed directly to our public relations officer, who researches the inquiry and routes it to Executive. No one can speak about our employees without clearance from the top. New hires sign off on that requirement before taking their seats."

Detective Flynn shrugged. "That wasn't really what I was asking, but okay. So it's a potentially threatening infringement to speak out of school. Yet several people have risked it."

"What I'm questioning is whether your sources are truly our employees. Maybe one person could be upset about an incident at work, but several? Most people can't afford to blow off their jobs. And I didn't use the word 'potentially.' They would be gone."

"But you said our information 'is crazy.' If you don't know her that well…"

Shirley pulled in a deep breath. "Detective. I'm speaking globally. About employees in general. Let me explain, hypothetically, the reality of corporate culture as it might relate to your so-called sources. I am not talking about anyone in particular, any job, or my knowledge of the Henning situation. Suppose you're a nineteen-year-old from the poor part of town. Bright, drug and alcohol free, with a modicum of ambition. You get an entry-level job at a bank, such as a phone center operator or even a janitor. You understand from day one that you're going nowhere without more education. You scrounge enough money to attend community college, one course at a time. You watch postings for higher positions at work and apply, even if the requirements are a stretch. You're turned down as *unqualified* most of the time but manage some modest progress.

"Twelve years later, you complete a bachelor's degree and apply for the first assistant officer position that comes along. That, however, goes to a twenty-three-year-old new college graduate, who joined the bank via its management-training program. Finally, at age thirty-six, you are promoted to bank officer and, in four more years, to assistant vice president. You're buried in debt and don't have time for a personal life, but you finally see success within reach. Then the position of vice president in Commercial Lending opens unexpectedly. Or Real Estate. Or Small Business Lending. You apply and make it through the first hurtles at a bank that prides itself on hiring from within. You want it so badly that you can taste it. The private office, prestige, huge bump in salary. But a handsome twenty-six-year-old steps off the elevator and is introduced to everyone as the new VP."

"And you think that's what happened—"

"No! I'm totally making up the specifics, but it happens routinely in the corporate world. Here's the point, Detective. We're a nation of idol topplers. Psychologists call the process *leveling*. By tearing someone else down, one can build oneself up. It's an illusion, of course. Look at another hypothetical situation. Imagine a young man who comes from a wealthy family with connections to excellent business prospects. In high school, rather than flipping burgers or changing oil, he has the luxury of time to excel academically and in athletics. Perhaps his family sends him to a prestigious prep school and an Ivy League college. He's a prize candidate for the best graduate schools. After two years' experience at a big New York bank, he applies to a little country bank. You get the idea?"

"He gets the job."

"And all the jealousy, resentment, false rumors, innuendoes, and subliminal desire to knock him off his pedestal."

"So, in our purely hypothetical scenario, you're saying that mean-spirited, ambitious, jealous people saw an opportunity to dispose of competition, such as, hypothetically again, the Hennings."

"More so. These people could be anyone from the ground up. A person who, no matter the level, perceives another as having been dealt an unfair, lucky hand. A hand that could never be his or hers. And helping to topple that person might right a wrong—that nobody should have it all without paying the price."

"Anyone? Not just your hypothetical loan officer? Say, a teller, administrative assistant or—" She paused, for what Shirley sensed was effect. "—property management?" And she added, with subtle emphasis that would have escaped the untrained ear, "—an item processor?"

Shirley's mind shot straight to Callie Smith. Keeping her expression cool, she opened her lower left file drawer and extracted a sheet. "Here. I'll give you a breakdown of all our positions. And here. A flow chart of all our departments so that you can see how everything meshes." She slid a third sheet across the desk. "And a list of our holding company's subsidiaries, the bank itself being the largest. There's our mortgage company, investment company—just for reference, since you asked." She smiled at the detective whom she now perceived as being at a disadvantage.

"Ms. Granger, in your vast experience with human nature in the corporate world, would you say it's unlikely that several people would come forward with similar *idol-toppling* stories about a crime unless it was true?"

Shirley could feel herself sliding back into the quicksand. Not wishing to be drawn into further speculation, she said, "I'm afraid I can't help you with that." She stood and extended her hand. "I have no relevant or firsthand information about the kidnapping." She glanced at her watch. "I'm keeping my ten o'clock waiting. I must get back to work."

Her guest rose and placed her business card in Shirley's extended hand. "If you think of anything, please give me a call. Thanks for your time—and the education about corporate culture." She left.

Shirley sank into her chair. Head tilted back, she closed her eyes briefly and reviewed what had transpired. On a new Word document, she reconstructed the interview to the best of her recollection.

Then she email attached it with a memo, flagged *personal and confidential*, to Todd Henning. She then deleted the document.

❧❧

Kingsley stirred from disjointed dreams, her dragons still dormant deep in her brain. For a split second, her mind was as uncluttered and pristine as the shore at low tide. As Todd descended the staircase, she became aware of the couch's cool leather, and reality crashed on her mind's beach. Friday. A fifth day had dawned. She jumped to her feet, which triggered a dizzying head rush. She sank back and tugged the chenille throw over her ice-cold legs as Todd entered the living room.

Dressed in charcoal suit pants, a white shirt, and silk burgundy tie, he carried the jacket over his arm. "Where are you going? And why?" she demanded.

"To the bank. I have meetings all day."

"But you need to be here." Todd averted his eyes, glancing beyond the foyer to the silent library beyond. "Are you giving up too?"

"Of course not. If anyone calls…"

"What? What should I say without the technicians or you to field their demands? Or to defend me from the detectives' attacks?"

"Kingsley, *if* the kidnappers call, which now seems unlikely, the call will be monitored, recorded, and traced. All you have to do is pick up and speak as instructed. Keep the caller on the line as long as possible."

"But if they're using an untraceable phone, the police won't have time to find them."

"They couldn't respond that quickly anyway."

"Whose side are you on? The police are abandoning us! They think it's our fault. They—"

Todd focused on the Persian rug under his feet as if memorizing its convoluted pattern. "Would you like breakfast? You need to eat something. I'll cook whatever you want," he said.

"You didn't answer my question."

"I *must* go to work. The shareholders' meeting is Tuesday, just four days away. Staff has done a yeoman's job preparing for me, but Warren, as chairman, can only report on the holding company. The bulk of the message must come from me since I'm the bank's president. Most of the corporation *is* the bank. Five hundred shareholders, analysts, and the press will be in attendance. What I say could affect stock prices, sales, customer and community relations. I shouldn't have to explain that to you, of all people. I can't let everyone down."

"But it's okay to let down your family."

"K, that's not fair. I need to do something, and there's nothing here I can fix." He switched his jacket to the other arm. "How about some orange juice? I could fire up the juicer. Coffee at least?"

"No thanks."

"All right then." He started to leave the room, hesitated, and then turned back. Stilted as an unpracticed actor, he spoke without making eye contact. "Maybe it would be better if you went back to work too. Filled up your mind with challenging distractions. Blotted some of this out."

"How can you say that? You sound like it's over. That he's not coming back. That he's—that, that he's—dead!"

"No, that's not what I meant. I'm sorry. Kingsley, I don't know what to say that you won't take the wrong way. I know you're angry as hell—we both are—but I won't be goaded into another fight. That won't solve anything. You've got to cut me some slack." He put on his jacket and, without further comment, retrieved his briefcase from the library. His retreating footsteps and the snap of the door latch echoed in the tomb-quiet house.

⌘

Barrie, smartly suited in gray sharkskin, let herself in the back door, rays of morning sunshine spilling around her petite silhouette. She found Kingsley at the kitchen table wearing yesterday's clothes. "How can he leave me alone when I need him? Switch into work mode and go off to his job as if nothing happened?" Kingsley asked without a preamble.

Barrie considered that while dumping the coffee dregs, assembling spring water and coffee, then flipping the Krups switch from 0 to 1. "Kingsley, that's two different questions. He's not leaving you—he's overwhelmed and needs to retreat to his metaphorical cave. Think about it. He's a man—a plan-of-action, take-charge kind of guy who's faced with the biggest challenge of his life. And he can't come up with a single solution. Todd championed the day-care, authorized its building with state-of-the-art security and, when the unthinkable happened, turned the place upside down without results. Now he can't even hire private detectives because they won't interfere with an ongoing police investigation."

"So he goes to the bank—"

Barrie shook her head. "He goes to his *cave*. He can close his door, think, and regain his equilibrium. And by making routine banking decisions, he can at least control *something*." At Kingsley's skeptical look, she added, "It's a male thing. They simply aren't like us. When Randall's stressed out, he quits talking. Disappears."

"That motor mouth?"

"Sure. When he's ready, he reappears with a plan. That brings me to your other question. What is it you need him to do that he isn't?"

Kingsley startled. "Well, to be here for me, of course."

"He can't do that until he understands what that is. You need to ask him to listen and understand what you *mean*, not just what you say. And, most important, that you don't expect him to provide solutions."

"He pulls away when I try. I don't understand what's happened to us. From day one we've been experts at dealing with crises."

"Sure, when it involved banking issues, home renovations, and solving a loan scam. But this! None of us is equipped to handle this kind of disaster."

"He blames me. How he must hate me."

"How could you even think such a thing?"

"It's my fault. We could afford a nanny. Or I could have stayed home. But I love my job—the challenge, using my brain, the professional contact, putting six years of college to work. I feel so guilty for being me. How many other women would love the luxury of staying home with their babies? Callie Smith sure would. I wouldn't feel so overwhelmed if Todd would let me off the hook."

Barrie grabbed Kingsley's shoulders. "Stop that! It isn't your fault. Billy is missing because some evil person did the unthinkable. Todd's not to blame either, and you've got to convince him of that. Then maybe together you can muster every shred of your energy to face this together." Kingsley nodded mechanically, but Barrie looked skeptical that her message had penetrated. "Just ask him if he thinks it's your fault. He'll say what I did—'don't be ridiculous.'" Barrie eased herself toward the door but paused and reversed direction. "I've got a meeting first thing, but I'll check on you later. If you need me, just call. My cell phone is on."

Kingsley nodded at Barrie's exiting back.

She started upstairs but paused, unable to go any farther, and sank onto the fourth step, gripping her head in her hands. Bent in submission, she raked her nails through her hair, incapable of forming a coherent thought. She rocked, head in hands, her eyes squinted shut, and pressed the lids with her palms. When it came to what really mattered, she was a failure. For the first time in her life, she hadn't a clue how to fix it. First Billy, then Todd.

Where had she missed that lesson? Surely not with her parents who doted on her to the point where she hardly listened. They never demanded A-plus accomplishment. She did that to herself. Don't be so hard on yourself, they would say. The tears of humiliation when her second-grade teacher made fun of her penmanship in front of the class and the subsequent hours she had spent practicing. Her mother had brought that to a halt, chastising the teacher that her gifted daughter would not address envelopes for a living. But the pattern was set—do whatever it took for 100 percent. Make that 110 or perhaps 120.

By seventh grade, it was the fast track, which accelerated through the last days of high school. The teachers intoned to each AP class, "You are the brightest and best. The future lies in your hands. If you fail, it won't be for lack of ability. You have a gift. Use it!" That, she had accepted as gospel, the reality being Life, Liberty, and the Pursuit of *Excellence*.

The brightest and best. Those destined to fix the ills of the world. Leaders in business and industry, as spouses and parents. Since failure was never an option, techniques for dealing with it were never taught. So far she had produced, never anticipating the inevitable head-on collision. She had no primer, no strategy, and no guidelines for coping with failure.

Kingsley leaned on the banister, hugging her knees to her chest, staring at nothing. She thought—*My mind is as blank as the air.*

ⒸⓈⒸⓈ

Randall Shannon backed his Dodge Ram pickup into Barrie's double garage, jumped out, and trotted to open her door. She had already slammed it. "Must you always be so damned independent? The least you could do is let me pretend I'm a gentleman."

Barrie flashed him a smile and mouthed a kiss. "That's so 1950s. Doesn't letting you give me flying lessons count for anything? All those times I had to play dumb?" She hit the remote button, and the garage door descended, enveloping them in forty-watt light.

"On your worst day, you couldn't fake *dumb*. You didn't tell me that when you were a kid you washed planes in exchange for flying lessons. I had to learn that from the mechanics." Before Randall could grab her paraphernalia, she shouldered her bags and climbed to her condo's first floor. He shagged what remained and followed.

"Any messages?" he asked as he trailed her toward the phone.

Barrie sighed. "Nothing of interest. There's got to be something that we can do. I feel so helpless. And the police, thinking Kingsley and Todd could be involved. Why do they always suspect the family? Or is it a smoke screen to hide their incompetence? Kingsley says they've come up with nothing. Nothing!"

Randall shook his head. "I'm betting they're withholding evidence to prevent the Hennings from going public and involving the press."

"With her history? Remember how the media hounded her when Andy was killed? They weren't sympathetic. Just wanted to sell papers. 'Daughter of Prominent Philadelphia Main Line Family Loses Husband in Fiery Crash.' Then the loan scam at the bank that she cracked. She'll never go near a reporter."

"The police don't know that. If they have a lead, they'll keep it close to the vest."

"Bet they're still pissed at her for showing them up by solving her husband's murder."

"Barrie! Wake up. *They* are suspects. That's why the police aren't sharing."

Barrie dropped her leather jacket onto a chair, straightened her sweater over her stretch jeans, then finger-combed and tossed her layered curls into some semblance of order. "This is just awful. And it should be one of the most exciting times of their lives. New baby. That perfect old house. Todd's incredible re-energizing of the bank, about which he should have the pleasure of reporting at the shareholders meeting. Last year's earnings were amazing! Then their anniversary at the shore—"

"They've got to find Billy by then.

"I feel so selfish."

"Why on earth would you?"

"In spite of it all, I'm excited about stuff that doesn't matter by comparison. I have a little surprise for you. I was saving it for a more opportune time, but, well—I passed my dual qualification to fly both the Cessna and the Gulfstream IV. That opens a world of opportunities for us."

"That's fantastic!" He swept her into a bear hug and kissed her. "You have every right to be happy and proud, logging thousands of hours while working full time. I've never known anyone with your focus and determination. Speaking of which—"

"Not now. Please. I can't handle another left-brained, plan-of-action, time-lined sales pitch about our relationship."

"I was thinking about lunch," he said. "Some of us can't live on celery and birdseed."

୧୦୧୦

Randall washed down the last of his microwaved pizza with Coke. "I have an idea," he said to Barrie who was prying the last maraschino cherry from a tall skinny bottle with overgrown tweezers. "Let's go pump the police. See what they know. While we're at it, stir the pot. Force them to think outside the box."

"I love it. How do we get them to see us?"

"I'll say we have information about the kidnapping— that we want to talk to the detective in charge."

"And that information would be…"

"We'll decide that on our way over. Once we're in, *we'll* question *them*. See what makes them twitch. Probe their buttons. Maybe they'll tell us more than they should. What say, I start asking questions while you watch their eyes? Then we'll switch. That should keep them off balance. But wear something drab. Nothing sexy or cute. Distraction is not what we want."

"Banker suit. And glasses! I'll take out my contacts and put on those black-rimmed Groucho's you hate. But Randall, what's our goal?"

"Honestly? I'd feel better just doing something. Anything. Maybe they'll say something that will trigger *our* thinking. At least we can learn if they're giving it two hundred percent."

Twenty minutes later, Barrie emerged from the bedroom, Ms. Assistant Controller down to her tie shoes. Randall hung up the phone and grinned at her getup approvingly. "He'll see us. We're in."

"Let's take my Acura. The pickup's not quite the right image."

"I wasn't planning on driving it into their lobby."

∽∾∽

Barrie circled the police lot, parked, and approached the public information desk, where they signed in at a safety-glassed counter. An officer greeted and escorted them through security doors to a small private office. Randall scanned it for surveillance equipment and mirrors but didn't spot any.

When no one joined them immediately, he eyeballed the organized chaos that covered the desk. Nothing looked re-motely germane. In fact, the office appeared to belong to someone who worked in community relations.

Minutes ticked. Finally, a man in a nondescript tan suit entered the room carrying a thick folder with fuzzy worn edges. He fit Kingsley's description of the detective who had made two trips to their home. Void of any outstanding features, he was just *bland*. Middle everything—height, weight, age, expression, brown eyes and hair that nearly matched his clothing.

Closing the door and setting the file on the desk, he offered apologies for the delay. "It's not like TV. We have dozens of cases going simultaneously. We try to distribute the workload evenly, but sometimes it gets overwhelming. Can I get you some coffee? A soda? Water?"

Barrie said no thanks, but Randall, seeing opportunity, accepted his offer. The detective disappeared, leaving the door ajar and the file on top of the clutter. Randall jumped to his feet. "Stand guard. I want a peek at that file." Barrie angled her chair toward the door and, craning her neck, watched and listened intently. He pulled a pen from his pocket and with it lifted the file's cover. He read upside down, oblivious to the outer office, even when footsteps approached.

"Randall! Close it up!" He dropped into his chair, concealing the pen with his hand. A female officer passed by the door and kept walking without breaking her rhythm. He hopped up again and squinted to decipher the unfamiliar jargon and messy handwriting. "He's coming!"

The detective reappeared, and taking no notice of them or the desk, kept his eyes on the brimming Styrofoam cups. "We've had numerous tips, all of which we must investigate. What a nightmare. It's human nature, I guess, wanting to be the bride at the wedding or the corpse at the funeral." Barrie and Randall sneaked peeks at each other as the detective tasted his coffee and winced. "Ouch! That's too hot." He set it down. "Now—you said on the phone you had information. What's on your mind?"

"It's high time somebody told you you're barking up the wrong tree," Randall said. "If you're thinking the Hennings are involved in their son's kidnapping, you are dead wrong. I've known Todd since we were little kids. That man doesn't have a mean bone in his body. And he loves kids. I watched him grow up, mentoring three younger sibs, the youngest of whom drowned in Lake Erie. He was the one who pulled his family through it. And Kingsley—that baby means everything to her. How you could possibly think—"

"I'm sorry if you're offended. I appreciate your loyalty, but we have procedures to follow and a different agenda from yours."

Randall raised his palms in supplication. "So? Where *have* you proceeded? What about that girl who last handled Billy? Ethelda what's-her-name? Surely you've tossed her place."

"Let me explain *probable cause*. Our Constitution protects us from unreasonable search and seizure. We must have a warrant. In order to get one, there must be circumstances to make a judge believe that evidence of a crime exists in that place. In plain words, less than a smoking gun, but more than a hunch. Ms. Blake is clearly visible on the security recording, carrying the Henning baby back from the fire drill. She is seen leaving the building alone and doesn't return until she is summoned after the kidnapping took place."

"So that eliminates her as a suspect? How about a co-conspirator?"

"We can't make public who we've eliminated."

The room grew silent as the three stared at each other. Randall knew the interview would end abruptly if he didn't pick up the pace. The detective unknowingly helped, his voice tired but polite. "We're focusing every available resource on finding the child. And we're following up on every call, no matter how far-fetched or mean-spirited."

"Mean-spirited? Who? I hope you're aware that people like the Hennings attract plenty of jealousy. Just look at their families' long history of leadership in business and industry, as well as their charitable activities and contributions. Are you aware that Todd and Kingsley headed the capital campaign to build our new youth center just last year? Do you know how few people would undertake a challenge of that magnitude?"

The detective rocked slightly in his chair. "Yes. I am."

"That can motivate mean-spirited individuals to say or do things to tear them down as if, by doing so, they can build themselves up. The shrinks have a name for that, which escapes me. We're a nation that loves tabloid intrigue, as I'm sure you know. Just look at the magazine racks in the grocery."

"I am aware of that too. We do have some experience here."

"So—who are these people and just what do they claim to know? Do they say that they work at the bank? That they overheard chitchat in the can? Did it cross your mind that these so-called sources could be the kidnappers?"

"I'm sorry. I can't share that kind of information."

"What about the press? Has anyone leaked information that only the guilty would know?"

"If they had, we would have them in custody. Since the crime took place on bank property, I'm told that any employee who speaks to the media, other than their official spokesperson, will be fired immediately. That tends to discourage even innocent speculation. We always withhold details that only a perpetrator would know."

Barrie spoke up. "What about the security recordings? Surely something's been missed."

"We have sophisticated technology and excellent professionals. As I said previously, all appropriate resources are being employed."

"I understand that camera recordings can be flawlessly altered," Randall said. "A segment showing no activity in the daycare corridor could have been copied and substituted for that brief segment when somebody left with the baby."

"Not in this case. During the fire drill, the bank's security officers watched the monitors like hawks for procedural problems. They saw nothing amiss. And, had the scene deviated from the live feed, they would have noticed, especially given the critical situation that unfolded."

"Thought you couldn't divulge details."

"Ms. Brown, you work for Keynote. Is what I just said common knowledge?"

Barrie frowned. "I suppose so. At least, among officers." When he smiled a little too smugly, she changed tacks. "Couldn't someone have smuggled the baby out under their clothing?"

"That would have been spotted immediately."

"Then how could you think the Hennings are involved? Even if they brought in the doll as a prop and Ethelda was in on it, someone would notice *something*."

"You'd think so."

"So you agree? Poof? The baby just vanished?" Randall asked.

"No. As I said before, we're pursuing every possibility. There *is* an explanation, and we're going to find it. Obviously, we're dealing with clever people."

"Is there a profile? Similar crimes?"

The room grew awkwardly quiet again with no reaction forthcoming. Finally, the detective took a deep breath and continued to stonewall, exasperation creeping into his voice. "Look. I do understand how frustrated you must feel. And your character references are appreciated."

"They're much more than friends. They're like family," Randall said, trying to keep concession out of his voice. He was losing the battle. "If there were only a way I could adequately convey what kind of people they are."

"You'd be surprised how little we know about people, even our nearest and dearest. Many are consummate actors." The detective handed each of them one of his cards. "If you think of anything useful, give me a call. Meanwhile, stick to moral support and let us do our job." As the detective rose and extended his hand, Barrie and Randall knee-jerked to their feet and departed on cue.

જીજી

"You wanted to fight and he wouldn't," Barrie muttered

to Randall as she dug through her kitchen drawer. "If the circumstances weren't so dire, it would have been funny—you having the luxury of being rude and him having to be professional. Did you notice? He said all the right things, as if he were reading from some script, but his body language didn't match his words. He's not on our side. He's our enemy."

"That bit about being actors was a dig at all of us."

"He's right, Randall. How many people stuck up for people who murdered their children? Speaking of digging, did you learn anything useful in his file?"

"Just that they decided not to request FBI intrusion into *their* case. Evidently, it's considered a local crime, and the fed needs an invitation. I'd wondered why the FBI wasn't all over this. I'm terrified that they're classifying the case as a murder rather than a kidnapping. That wouldn't trigger the fed's involvement, right? That means none of their agents is investigating the case. There's been no ransom demand and no indication of involvement across state lines. If only I'd had time to find the names of those anonymous tipsters. Maybe if we broke in—"

"Randall!"

"He said they've eliminated Ethelda Blake as a suspect, but I did read an upside down reference to a former employer. I couldn't make out the name. I'll see what Todd thinks about that. Maybe he can ask the bank's HR director to make an inquiry." He paused, aware of her actions. "What are you looking for?"

"My recipe folder."

"Your recipes fit in one folder?"

"Banking, flying, my pilot—I have to sleep sometime." She continued to riffle. "Ah, here it is. Kingsley's a chocoholic. Let's try this chocolate dump cake. All we have to do is dump the ingredients into a pan, stir it up, and bake. A monkey could do it. We can run it over later. I'd better go change. This could get messy." Barrie disappeared and reappeared in old cutoffs, bare feet, and a tee.

"Read me the ingredients, and I'll line them up." She crawled into the cave-like corner cupboard and retrieved a large mixing bowl and a Bundt pan. "Flour, sugar, oh dear, cocoa."

Randall searched a high cupboard. "Hot cocoa mix?"

"Good enough. Oops, I don't have any milk, much less sour milk and there's only one egg. Wait—there's eggnog left over from…"

"Christmas? That was four months ago!"

"Check it out." Randall probed the depths of the fridge and came up with an unopened quart that was stamped to expire January 1. It was frozen solid. "Nuke it on defrost, then smell it," she said. He grimaced but did as she asked, then raised his eyebrows. She smelled it too. "That'll do. Now—to make it sour. Let me think. Lemons! Look in the hydrator. I know I have one."

Randall sliced the lemon in half and squeezed it into a shot glass. "More?" She eyeballed it, shaking her head, and then rummaged for measuring cups, the sugar, and flour. "Now what?" he asked.

"Just dump it all in. Oh, and turn on the oven to three-fifty. Check it first. That's where I dry my undies when the microwave's not working."

"You need help."

"When I'm the chief financial officer of a major corporation I'll have a cook *and* a maid. Won't that be cool? We can spend all our free time flying around the world." She stirred the batter, then stuck her finger into the concoction and licked it. "Pretty good. Taste." She dipped it again, then dabbed it onto his lips. He licked his lower lip, and then she flicked her tongue on his upper.

"Very nice. And so is the batter." She dumped the concoction into the pan and, sliding it into the oven, set the timer for one hour.

"Leave the mess," he said, boosting her onto the only clean spot on the counter. She draped her arms over his shoulders then wiggled him closer and kissed him. "I feel guilty having this much fun."

"Don't, Barrie. If we can't keep our sense of humor and avoid a quagmire of depression ourselves, we'll be totally useless to them."

"Okay." She was thoughtful a moment then brightened. "Let's play a little game. I'll tell you something I love about you, then you tell me something you love about me."

"Okay. You go first.

"I love you because you wear silk boxer shorts."

He laughed. "I love you because you have short funny toes."

"And I love you because you're so tall."

"Five foot nine isn't tall, Barrie."

"From my height it is." Sliding herself to the edge of the counter, she encircled his torso with her bare legs. "I love you because you didn't put your best inches into your height." She smiled coyly and smoothed his thighs with her palms."

He groaned. "You're being saluted."

Barrie glanced over her shoulder and checked out the timer. "Got any plans for the next fifty minutes?"

"You bet I do."

Chapter 7

Kingsley awoke Saturday morning in Grammy's four-poster bed that faced her own front guestroom windows. Momentarily, she was perplexed, but then she remembered where she was and why. The petite-floral wallpaper closely resembled her room at Grammy's where she had slept many nights as a child. That's why she chose it. Streamers of light filtered through the giant oaks in the front yard, playing shadow games on her Amish double-wedding-ring quilt.

She glanced at the nightstand where a half glass of water sat beside an empty saucer on which had lain the other half of an Ambien tablet. Everyone had been right. Lack of sleep was hurting her more than an occasional sleeping pill. When had she taken the first half? Eight? Nine o'clock? She couldn't remember taking the second. Todd had taken the bottle downstairs to prevent her from being confused in the night and losing count.

She remembered fighting sleep until Todd became stern, finally propelling her into the guestroom. It would be quiet, he said, away from Billy's room and his own insomniac prowling and thrashing. Since the old house had been built in two stages, an eighteen-inch stone wall bisected the house, separating everything to the right of the foyer from the rest of the house. What now was their library, kitchen,

Billy's and their bedrooms had been added twenty years later.

What time was it anyway? She held the travel alarm close to her face and squinted. After nine! She hopped up. "Todd?" She called over and over and then, giving up, went into the large bathroom that yesteryear owners had added to the center front hall. Tablet paper was taped to the mirror.

Gone to work. Hope you slept well. See you for dinner. Love, T

She was alone. She located and used her breast pump, then dumped what she extracted into the sink. At first, she had saved and frozen the milk as she did for occasional bottles. Not doing so was her first unconscious concession to the inevitable. She stared as the last drops slid down the drain. Maybe being unprepared would hasten Billy's return. Opting for the shower instead of the oversized claw-foot tub, she turned the water to hot and stepped in. A flashback to February, the blizzard, that one last shower before Billy was born, still able to see her toes. She dabbed bath gel over her tummy, now flat as a board, and worked the lather down to her feet.

Billy! I've got to do something, anything constructive to pull myself back from the brink. When you come home, you'll need milk that isn't contaminated by pills. Somehow, some way, I've got to do better.

She thought of Todd and did not understand how he could be so matter-of-fact. From what reservoir did he draw such great strength? Was it just Todd, or did fathers, in general, feel less attachment than mothers?

Her stomach rumbled. Got to eat, she lectured herself. And inventory whatever food's left in the kitchen. Go to the grocery. Plan a real dinner. Maybe they'd grill—a petite fillet, shrimp, and scallops. The farmer's market would have out-of-season corn on the cob and great greens for a salad. When was the last time she did any laundry? She quickly shampooed her hair, toweled it, and threw on the jeans and sweater that she found on the floor.

ঙঌঌ

Kingsley pulled into the Giant Grocery Store's jammed parking lot and looked for a space. As she circled, she spotted a familiar car, then another and another. When somebody tapped a horn politely, she realized she had been blocking traffic.

Friends and grocery acquaintances were shopping. The meat, seafood, produce, and deli managers all knew her by name, as did the checkers. So many kind people had followed her pregnancy, congratulated her on the birth, and fussed over her baby. They'd all be staring or averting their eyes, or, not knowing, would blindside her with questions about Billy and how he was doing. Some, too, would blame her. She pulled out of the lot and, in minutes, was speeding north on the highway.

Just find a grocery out of the area. You don't have to like it. You just have to do it.

Forty-five minutes later she saw a billboard for a farmer's market. Exiting, she forced her mind onto the list on the passenger seat. At least she'd had the presence of mind to bring a small cooler and frozen ice packs for perishables.

Inside, the market was deliciously normal, the aroma of fresh strawberries, grapefruit, flavored coffees, and pastries blending with broasted chicken, sausage, and rioting flowers. Quickly she worked through her fresh list, paid, and hurried back to the car.

As she settled perishables into the cooler, she was struck by a thought. She had spent up to five minutes without thinking of Billy. How long had that taken when her first husband, Andy, had died? Weeks? Months? She couldn't remember. At least this time, *this time*, there was hope, and she clung fast to that thought. She knew, deep in her gut, that Billy was out there somewhere. But where? *Everyone has to be somewhere.*

Back on the highway, she checked for towns halfway to Allentown. Spotting an elevated sign for a grocery, she exited. Navigating strange aisles forced her to concentrate as she scanned the shelves for favorite labels and chanced strange store brands that might work. Having seen only strangers who looked through her as if lost in deep thoughts, Kingsley escaped into a glorious afternoon that pretended to know nothing of loss.

As she was wheeling her cart to the car, a familiar sight caught her eye. An infant, buckled into a newborn's carrier, wore a small hooded sweater with the same peculiar colors and homemade pattern as one of Billy's. She squinted into the brilliant sun's glare while wracking her brain. She had no recollection of the extra garments she'd left in the day-care's small chest of drawers and what had become of that sweater.

As the woman maneuvered the carrier into her old Ford, Kingsley perceived she was glancing furtively left and then right. When she stepped aside, Kingsley caught a glimpse of the baby. Billy! The baby was Billy! Shoving her cart aside, she started to run, shouting at them, but incessant honking forced her to turn. Her runaway cart was barreling toward a frail old couple frozen in its path. Giving chase, she overtook and shoved the cart out of their way, wasting precious seconds that enabled the woman with Billy to escape.

While jamming her keys into her lock and then the ignition, she darted glances at the old Ford, which had already exited the lot. An elderly man who had double-parked was helping his wife from their car. Somehow Kingsley squeaked by his Caddy and followed the Ford through the exit. Luck was with her as she quickly caught up with the car that was spiriting Billy away. As the strip malls gave way to Lehigh Valley farmland, she kept pace with the Ford. Soon it exited onto a lane that led to a dairy farm.

Kingsley followed while digging into her purse for her phone. She thumbed it on. How had she let the battery die?

She tossed it aside. By the time she pulled up to the farm-house, the woman had already gone inside and was emerging again.

"May I help you?" the woman asked as Kingsley hopped from her car. She had to be black-bumper Mennonite, Kingsley thought, noticing the pealing paint on the car's chrome. The woman's dress and hair were quite plain, and she didn't wear any makeup. Shortly a girl, who looked about ten, emerged from the house, carrying the baby. His face was turned into the girl's shoulder, away from Kingsley. Kingsley lunged toward the baby.

"Billy!"

"No, his name is Joshua," the young girl replied, turning the infant for Kingsley to see. It was not Billy.

"I'm, I'm sorry. I thought I knew him. I'm sorry." Blinking back tears she ducked into her car and left them staring after her dust.

∞∞∞

Kingsley sat on a bench in the Lehigh Valley Mall, looking for babies. So many! Then she prowled stores that sold baby things, looking instead for Billy and whoever might feel safe enough to venture into public with a stolen infant. Hours passed. Finally, she gave up, trudging to the parking lot and unlocking the car. The groceries! She lifted the cooler's lid and was relieved to find the interior still cold. But the rest of her food? She backtracked and, finding another grocery, auto piloted her way through the store.

By the time she got home, it was after eight, and Todd wasn't there. Quickly she lit the grill. While it heated she assembled a salad and then seared the steak. While it sizzled, she threaded the shrimp and scallops onto long metal skewers, then drizzled them with lemon juice followed by melted butter. In six minutes everything was grilled to tantalizing perfection.

Todd's car turned into the lane and circled to the back door. He wandered into the kitchen, looking bewildered. "You cooked?"

"One of your favorites. You must be starving after such a long day at the bank."

"Actually, I got home around five. I tried to call several times. If I'd only known, I wouldn't have eaten."

"You ate? Why didn't you wait?"

"It got to be seven, and I had no idea where you were, so I did fast food. Kingsley, why didn't you leave me a note? That's so unlike you."

"Everything's 'unlike,'" she said, dumping the salad into a large Zip Lock bag and tossing it into the fridge.

"Aren't you going to eat?"

"I'm not hungry." She looked at the platter. "I'll nuke this for lunch tomorrow. It should resurrect." Without further comment, she covered the platter with plastic wrap, jammed it into the fridge, and stalked from the room.

ↄ৹ↄ৹

Kingsley trudged up the stairs without flipping the light switch and stopped outside Billy's door. She stood, immobilized. Finally, she took a deep breath and, turning the knob, slipped into its gloom. She lit one small lamp, permitting her eyes to slide around the interior. Everything looked exactly the same as it did that long-ago Monday. What was it that Grammy would say?

You never know when you're going to do something for the last time.

She eased into her bentwood rocker and closed her eyes. Slowly she rocked. Was it possible for someone's aura to communicate with a distant loved one? She concentrated, sinking deep into her mind, trying to sense Billy.

The old wooden door creaked, and Todd's shadow spread over the floor. Backlit, she could see he was wearing his black warm-up suit and dark sneakers with reflecting silver stripes. "Where are you going?" she asked.

"Thought I'd go for a jog then work on my speech for the shareholders meeting on Tuesday." He started to leave. She jumped up and followed him into the hall.

"Hold on. Not so fast. Just tell me. How do you do it? I want to know. I watch you getting on with your life and, and—"

"What choice do I have?"

"Having feelings isn't about choice. Either you have them, or you don't."

"You don't think I have feelings? Because I don't cry or starve myself or quarrel with everybody who's trying to help?"

"I'm sorry this happened. It's all my fault. If I'd only stayed home." Todd did not answer, merely dropping his head. Her desperate need for reassurance had missed its mark. She tried again, being more blunt. "You don't blame me for returning to work, do you?"

"Being analytical won't help a bit. We can't rewrite the past."

"Then you do blame me!" She felt her face redden, her throat constricting as her heart rate took off, anger battering her gut.

"Logic means that if you and Billy had been somewhere else—"

"Logic? You said I was doing the right thing, going back to work. You said—"

"I said, 'If it's right for you, it will be all right for Billy.' That's not the same thing as telling you to go back to work." His voice boomed, words bitten yet exasperatingly measured as he drowned her out.

"But you spearheaded Keynote's daycare and the new security initiative. In fact, you were so proud of it."

"Of course! There are single parents and lower income families who can't pay their bills without jobs. Quality daycare is imperative. That's why I pushed it."

Kingsley's anger boiled and spilled. "Billy's kidnapping had nothing to do with my working. There's a monster out there who preyed on our family. You turned the scene into a circus. I bet you scared the kidnappers away. That's why we never got our ransom call."

"That's not fair! The whole damned building had to be searched, and that took manpower. Besides, the media monitors police calls."

"There was no Amber alert."

"How could there be? Billy could have been gone for hours before anyone missed him, and there were no witnesses, no vehicle descriptions, nothing to flag the public's attention. And you wouldn't let the media release pictures of him."

"You know very well why. If the kidnapper thought anyone would recognize him, they might have killed him. How hard would it be to bury such a small body where no one would find him?" Tears she missed with her sleeve burned a path past her chin on their way to the floor.

They glared at each other.

"Go. Just go. Go jog," she barely whispered before retreating into Billy's room and snapping the door shut.

Todd stretched in the driveway then angrily pitched his warm-up jacket aside. He loped the length of their lane, remembering the Valentine Day blizzard and how many times he had plowed the drifts to get Kingsley to the hospital in time. At the main road, he picked up his speed and headed west toward the neighboring farms.

The April night was soft and promising, a good night for camping. He approached their boundary where Billy would have watched from his stroller while his parents planted a snow fence of white pines. His mind began to shoot little pictures that fired faster and faster as he picked up his pace. Infant Billy safe with his dad. Billy in a backpack. In a sturdy red wagon. His first hiking boots. A little guy with a mop of dark hair asking endless questions. Climbing their trees. Hitting a T-ball. Throwing a football. Gangly Bill growing so fast that his knees ached. Sprawled on the grass to hear his dad talk about guy stuff—to respect girls and women, patriotism, God and his neighbor. The best fishing lures. The evil of drugs. Generations of family history and commitment that grown-up William Todd IV must remember and share.

Todd ran faster, heart pounding, lungs tearing as if he could catch up to Billy. He'd kill that bastard if only he knew who and where and for God's sake why he was taken. Faster. Go get him, but where? He ran to exhaustion and finally, lungs bursting, doubled over for great gulps of air. The night was so still beneath billions of stars, unspoiled by lights that did not defile the Amish countryside.

Overcome, he raged at the sky. "Billy! Where are you?" Nobody answered. "Where are you?" A small lick of breeze cooled his drenched head as he whispered into his soul, "What kind of man can't protect his own family?" Then he broke down and cried.

Chapter 8

Randall stormed into Barrie's condo without knocking. "You're not going to believe this!"

Startled, she jumped, sloshing her coffee onto the kitchen counter. "Why aren't you at the airport? You were supposed to be there an hour ago to fly those corporate clients to Chile."

"I phoned them to say I'd be late. Look at this." He tossed her the local section of the Sunday newspaper.

Barrie gasped. "Why, it's a picture of Kingsley. It looks like a cop is dragging her out of the bank." Together they huddled over the half-page spread, which included two detailed articles. Its headline screamed:

PARENTS QUESTIONED IN BABY'S DISAPPEARANCE
Police investigation shifts focus to family

Barrie scanned the body copy and then bolted into her living room. She yanked open her desk drawer and retrieved a magnifying glass. Quickly she swept it over the picture. "Look, Randall. This had to have been taken with a telephoto lens from the far side of the daycare parking lot the day Billy was kidnapped. On Kingsley's left is the cop who drove her car home. He's not taking her into custody, but they sure cropped this photo to look like he was. See?" She handed Randall the magnifying glass and tapped near the border with her nail. "You can make out Todd's hand supporting her upper arm. That's her keys in the officer's hand. I've told her a dozen times to get something more professional than that Kush ball key chain. Now I'm glad she didn't listen."

They reread the article that quoted "a source close to the investigation" whose identity the reporter was not divulging. "That is so bogus!" Barrie fumed. "They questioned *everybody* remotely connected to the Hennings—employees, customers, neighbors, shopkeepers, friends, felons. It's a travesty to even hint that they are responsible."

Randall stabbed a forefinger at a related article. "They went back to day one—Kingsley's family background, her first husband's death. They even drew a 'history of tragedy' to Todd's sister drowning. Is nothing sacred? No wonder they hate reporters so much."

Barrie scanned the pages. "There's good news—they didn't run a picture of Billy. That would be totally irresponsible. If the kidnappers saw it, they might—"

"Don't say it, hon. Don't even think it." He snapped a look at his watch. "I'm late. Gotta run. I'll be back Wednesday. If Todd and Kingsley want to blow this town for the weekend, tell them I'm good to go. I can file a flight plan on fifteen minutes' notice. Did you go ahead and arrange your vacation time from the bank?"

"Yeah, but Kiawah may be irrelevant now. I'll do whatever I can to help in the meantime. Speaking of help, where's my hug?"

ℰᴈℰᴈ

Cool civility shrouded the Hennings' home as they dissected the Sunday newspaper article. Numb, they retreated into their shells. Finally, she broke the silence. "I'm glad I went to early church," she said. "I knew if I didn't, I might never go back. It wasn't what I expected. There were no questions. No platitudes. No lectures about God's will. I couldn't have stood that."

"Had anyone seen the newspaper articles?" Todd asked.

"Judging from their supportive comments and anger, everyone did. They hugged me. Told me they'd keep us in their prayers. Asked how you were. Gave me open-ended offers for whatever we need. Stuff like that."

"And our priest?"

"He was livid about the article. Repeated what he's been saying all along—to call him if we need him, any time day or night, and that he'll stop by later today. All of our names have been put on the prayer list. The group that feels they have the power of intercessory prayer is focusing on us. I'm resolving, when this thing is over, to be more responsive to the needs of others."

Todd's demeanor softened. He smiled at his wife and mumbled, "As if you don't overextend already."

Kingsley's cell phone played muted music from its pouch on her purse. She dumped the paper and grabbed it. "Kingsley?" a familiar voice asked. "It's Callie Smith. I begged your cell phone number from Margaret, and I'm using mine. Please don't be mad at her. I was afraid your landline might be tapped—maybe mine, too."

Kingsley frowned. Why would anyone tap Callie's line? "I'm glad you called, Callie. I've been wondering how you and Sammy are getting along."

"We're good. I'm sorry to bother you at home, but ever since the police questioned me, I've felt so guilty. I can't stop thinking about it."

"Why? Do you know something? Or did you see something that you didn't tell them?"

"That's not it. It's my ex. I keep thinking there's no way he could have known where I was or about Sammy. Even if he did, he wouldn't come after him. I was—maybe—two weeks late when I realized I could be pregnant. I packed up and left, zigzagging the country using only the cash that I'd saved up. You know. Like Julia Roberts did in *Sleeping with the Enemy*. And before Sammy was born, legal aid helped me change my name. I told nobody. Have nobody. I even cut ties with the few friends I made in California. Please don't tell anyone."

"Of course not."

"The police asked me about any enemies who might have targeted Sammy. I had to give them my ex-boyfriend's name, but I lied about how long it had been since I'd seen him. They got back to me—told me that at the time of the kidnapping he was in jail for assaulting some girl who pressed charges. They eliminated him as a suspect without mentioning my name to him. And they didn't press me about Sammy's father. If anyone insists, I'm saying I had a one-night stand in Nebraska. I must protect Sammy."

"I don't understand why you feel guilty."

"Don't you see? The newspaper says there's no ransom demand, so why would anyone kidnap a baby whose family has money except by mistake? Nobody's that dumb. The day Billy was taken I wasn't there because of your kindness. You found a way for me to go to the dentist without burning a personal day. Sammy was safe from whoever did this."

"You feel guilty since my baby was kidnapped instead of yours? That's crazy! You mustn't! Both of them could have been taken. Now please, just love your baby and forget about guilt. Thank God Sammy's safe."

"There's something else—the main reason I called. The police zeroed in on why I was absent that day. Where had I been? Why that day and that time in particular? Whose idea was it? And so on. I stupidly volunteered that it was your idea to take a split shift. That you'd even arranged for my participation in the bank's dental plan. I wanted them to know what a good, caring person you are. That's when they branched into dozens of questions about you. I did my best to portray you as a loving, devoted mother, but they were, well, hostile. I thought you should know. I'm sorry.

"You didn't do anything wrong."

"Except that now they have the idea that you orchestrated the timeline for Billy's kidnapping. By the time I returned to the bank that day, it was all over. The place was swarming with cops, so I took Sammy back to my office. My supervisor was cool about that. She'd heard the daycare was closed. I am so sorry if I said anything that might hurt you and your family.

"You didn't, believe me. Now please, just enjoy Sammy. You don't need to exhaust your energy on something you can't do anything about. And hearing your voice really helps."

"Kingsley, you're such a good person. If there's anything I can do, anything at all."

"I'll let you know. And please, pray for all three of us?"

"Of course."

Kingsley punched *end* and wiped her eyes on her sleeve, feeling uplifted by Callie's compassion. She'd had enough dragons in her young life. Kingsley couldn't imagine not having her parents, aunts, uncles, dozens of cousins and friends to surround her with love and support. Callie had no one, no caring husband or family.

So many had called, sent notes, brought food, run errands, picked up the slack. Her poor staff members, who had covered for her maternity leave, were now doing double duty again. Long hours for salaried employees meant less time for their families without overtime pay. *I've got to go back to work. Please, God. Give me the strength. And bring my little one home. And if that's not possible, please let him be safe.*

"What was that all about?" Todd asked, removing his reading glasses and tossing the paper aside.

"That was Sammy's mother." Kingsley frowned, cradling her chin in her palm. "Callie Smith."

"What is it, K?"

She repeated what Callie had said about Sammy. "Why would anyone kidnap a baby if no ransom demands were to follow? Todd, is it possible that we've been thinking about this all wrong? Suppose Billy *wasn't* the target?"

"From what you've said about Callie's circumstances, the motive couldn't have been money. Where would she get it?"

"And that would explain why the kidnappers never called us. That might mean…"

"Some lunatic desperate for a baby or someone who steals babies for whatever reason."

"Since the police say this was expertly planned, I'm guessing the latter."

"Not necessarily. Maniacs can plan, K. Remember Ted Bundy was a genius."

⁂

Kingsley took a deep breath, stepped from her car, then straightened the seams of her flared pale -gray suit. After retrieving her briefcase and purse from the back seat, she scanned the bank property. Masses of azaleas were poised to burst into scrumptious colors. She remembered the first time she'd seen the magnificent building. It was late summer, two years ago, and one year after Andy's murder. Andrew Ward, MD, young ophthalmologist bent on saving the sight of the Third World. With the passage of time, she had realized the loss was much more to the world than to herself.

Then Todd had come out of nowhere. And Billy had made them a family. Strange how life unfolds. Had it not been for Andy's death, Billy would not exist. She would still live in Philadelphia with Andy, perhaps accompanying him on his annual trips to African free clinics. She remembered darkly how badly Andy disapproved of bringing children into this messed up world.

Get a grip. She clicked the doors locked. *You don't have to like this. You just have to do it.* With quick, resolute steps, she hurried into the building, past the atrium's towering five-story garden and fountain, and onto the elevator that whisked her to Four.

When she exited, a hush rippled through the outer office that formed the core of Commercial Lending. With professionalism she did not feel, she scurried toward the safety of her private office along the back wall. Her credenza under the window was stacked high with client files begging attention. She took a deep breath and exhaled slowly.

"So glad you're back," Kingsley's administrative assistant said briskly, handing her a client's file. "This simply can't wait. Could you put out the fire? Thanks." She started to leave.

"Marle?"

The stunning African American absently smoothed the poof where her cornrow braids met at her neck with a wispy silk scarf.

"Would you please ask the staff if we could gather in the conference room? I'd like to say a few words."

Marle nodded.

Kingsley waited ten minutes then picked up a file for something to do with her hands. Summoning her courage, she squared her shoulders. Once inside the conference room, she scanned the two dozen professionals from the Commercial Lending department. Good people. Kind people, all wanting information. The room grew quiet except for the hum of electronic equipment and the occasional swoosh of the elevator doors.

She took a deep breath. "First, thank you for your kindness to Todd and me. I want to apologize for the police prying into your lives, the inconvenience, uproar, and added demands to your workload. That's got to stop. I intend to make that a priority. And please extend my gratitude and apology to your families for whatever stress our crisis has caused them."

She paused and gathered her thoughts. *Focus. Do not cry. Be a professional and just get it said.* "I have a request that will help me immeasurably. Would everyone please try to act normal around me? I've missed the day-to-day chatter, whether it's your families' adventures, complaints about other departments, crises here in our world, even the gossip. And food. I've missed the recipe talk." That brought smiles.

"And don't try to shield me from departmental problems. I need that too. If anyone has any issues I need to address, please come see me. If I'm not here, Marle will know how to reach me. One more thing—I can't talk about the situation. So please. No questions, okay?" She nodded conclusion, and staff smiled agreement. "Thanks," she said and started to escape.

"Kingsley?" one of the administrative assistants called after her.

She halted and returned to face them.

"I think it's awful the way the press is treating you."

Kingsley scanned the assembly of nodding heads as people broke into murmured agreement. It didn't escape her attention, however, that several were glaring, deadpan. She made a mental note of which ones. "Thanks. I was almost afraid to come back for fear of what everyone might think."

"Ms. Henning. We were all interviewed by the police." She harrumphed. "We gave them an earful. Doubt they'll try that again."

Kingsley grinned, thanked them again, and returned to her office.

❦❦❦

Margaret Stiles let herself into Kingsley's office and closed the door behind her. Circling the desk, she moved into Kingsley's extended arms. "You did great, kiddo. I'm sure everyone is relieved. Nobody knew how to act."

Kingsley held her friend's hands at arms' length and absorbed her beauty that went far beyond her sapphire eyes, magnified as they were by oversized bifocals. They dropped hands, and Margaret settled into a guest chair opposite Kingsley's desk. She ran a hand over her smooth brown bob and adjusted her perfect linen pantsuit.

"What is it?" Kingsley asked.

"The shareholders meeting is tomorrow at five. If you're planning to attend, we can hang together. You can use me as a buffer."

"You *are* a dear friend. I've decided that going would be a mistake. I'd be expected to sit with the directors and their wives, which would be awkward, given the circumstances and the media splash. And, of course, the press would be there, which terrifies me. Besides, my presence would draw attention away from bank news. That wouldn't be fair. No, I'm staying home."

Margaret nodded agreement. "Figured that's what you'd say, but if you change your mind—"

"More to the point—I don't know how much more I can take. I can't risk making a scene. Strange, it's people's kindness that is the hardest. If I'm focused on something else and forget for a moment, it blindsides me. I could lose control and make everyone uncomfortable."

"Any news about the investigation?"

"Seems the police are considering Sammy as the possible target. And they're trying to match the abduction with the modus operandi of known kidnappers and perverts. They've questioned hundreds of people from felons to disgruntled customers, informants, known pedophiles, and even former employees."

"How did you find that out?"

"My father rattled his connections. And people who've been questioned keep calling. If they have any leads, they aren't sharing."

"How's Todd holding up?"

"He's withdrawn—never was much of a sleeper, but now he prowls most of the night."

"He must feel so helpless, like he has failed to protect his family."

"I hadn't thought of it that way. We used to be so close. 'Used to be.' One week can be an eternity." She glanced at the piles stacked on her credenza. "It's crazy. When I'm busy, time flies. I feel as if I should remain motionless—let time drag. Then, in the background, hundreds of people can use that time to look in every possible place of concealment."

"You're needed here, and being busy can't hurt. If there's any news about Billy, everyone knows where to find you. You're doing the right thing."

"Was it a mistake? My returning to work?"

"Of course not! Banish that thought from your mind."

"I needed to hear that. Maybe someday I can believe it." Margaret rose and, after a quick hug, was gone.

Chapter 9

Kingsley skimmed routine bank correspondence that she had brought home, finally realizing she hadn't the vaguest idea what she had just read. From the beginning, their library was her *sanctum sanctorum* and refuge from worldly intrusion. But now, even sunk in her favorite wingback chair with Pandora purring on her lap, the old house felt empty, its hollow silence exacerbating her fear and guilt.

Any attempt at distraction was useless. She closed her eyes in concentration. *Billy. Where are you?*

Dropping her papers onto the floor, she stared through the library windows at the gathering dusk that spread its pall of depression. Shivering, she wrapped her velour robe tighter and tucked her sock feet beneath her. She'd welcome a fire, but it wouldn't draw this late into spring, so she clicked on a lamp to frustrate her dragons. By the time Todd's headlights swung into their lane, it was dark.

Without calling his usual greeting, he walked slowly from the back door and dropped his overstuffed satchel in the foyer.

"How did it go?" she asked after they exchanged a perfunctory kiss that substituted for any semblance of intimacy.

"It went well, although the shareholders are always happy with increased profits and a free chicken dinner."

"I meant you. Was it difficult? Were you asked personal questions?"

"Dinner conversation was strictly business. One luxury of being president is that others let me initiate the topics. The directors invited me to join them afterward for drinks, but nobody pressed me when I declined."

"And Billy? Did anyone ask?"

"Not during the dinner that followed the meeting, but as I was leaving, a reporter cornered me. That caught me off guard. I walked away without comment."

"It's been ten days," Kingsley murmured. "Ten." He sighed wearily and started to turn from the room.

Suddenly three sharp raps of the pineapple knocker pierced the still air like so many red exclamation marks. From the library's double-hung window Todd saw the detectives' car and the pair at their doorstep. He motioned Kingsley toward the window.

"Why would they be here at this hour?" she whispered, unable to keep her voice from shaking.

"K, they must have found something." Todd threw open the front door to the same grim-faced detectives who had become their inquisitors.

"What do you want?"

"Mr. Henning. Mrs. Henning. We're here to notify you that an infant has been found. We want you to come with us to identify him."

Kingsley exploded with joy. "Really! Oh, Todd, that's wonderful—what we've been praying for." And to the detectives, "Do they think it's our baby? Where is he? Can we go get him? Right now?" Kingsley's excitement evaporated like mist in the wind as she digested the detectives' grim faces.

"Mr. and Mrs. Henning—we want you to make an identification."

"Identify? You mean like…"

The detective nodded. "We want you to come to the morgue."

Kingsley smothered a scream, whipping her head back and forth.

"It might or might not be your son," he repeated, but she had stopped listening. "We would like to escort you to the hospital."

Todd jumped in their faces. "We'll drive our own car. Just tell us where to go."

"It would be less complicated, easier for you, to just let us give you a ride."

"Are we under arrest? Because if we're not, we are not getting into that car."

"All right," he said. "We'll meet you inside the hospital's emergency entrance."

The pair piled back into their car.

Kingsley sprinted upstairs, two at a time, tearing at her robe as she went.

∽∾∽∾

The soft April evening with its light breeze and sweet smells of renewal seemed incongruous to Kingsley as she clutched Todd's arm and hurried toward the vast hospital's emergency entrance. The grim-faced detectives were waiting as the parents approached the reception area. They must have turned on the lights and sirens, as they had already completed the security procedures as evidenced by the big yellow visitor stickers affixed to their jackets.

After providing photo IDs, they, too, were given visitors' badges. While the four waited, the receptionist placed a call. "Someone will be here momentarily. Why don't you have a seat over there?" She motioned them toward oversized vinyl couches. Nobody sat.

Shortly a familiar-looking man strode toward them, a compassionate smile on his face. Todd recognized him immediately. "Kingsley, you remember Dr. Ruben from the fundraising banquet for the community center. Having a pathologist deliver an impassioned speech for our needing a safe after-school place for our kids drove home our community's need."

"It was my pleasure. I'm just sorry we have to meet again under such dire circumstances."

"Have you seen the baby? Do you think he could be ours?"

The doctor shook his head. "Knowing you, and having followed the story in the news, I thought it best to recuse myself." He cleared his throat. "I wouldn't have recognized him anyway, having missed his baptism. It was Easter, which coincided with Passover."

Kingsley tried to focus on what he was saying, but the clamor of patients with serious problems, the lights, and the smells, cluttered her senses.

"You have some choices," he was saying, obviously ignoring the detectives. "The assistant coroner can meet you in the pathology lab or in a viewing area near the chapel. The latter, he says, is more comfortable, but will take longer to set up. Or you could come back in the morning if that's more convenient."

"We'll go to the morgue now," the male detective interjected.

Ignoring him, Todd said. "Let's do it now. The quicker, the better."

Kingsley nodded.

To her he asked, "Are you okay with going to pathology?"

Again, she bobbed her head.

Dr. Ruben excused himself to relay their decision to the assistant coroner then returned quickly. "If you'll follow me, please."

Nobody spoke except for the occasional directions to turn this way, then that, ten shoes clattering in step like a parade. As they traversed what seemed to Kingsley like miles of corridors, she lost her sense of direction. In another life, she would have joked about leaving breadcrumbs.

Eventually, they emerged by a bank of elevators flanked by double doors with a red exit sign. Instead of pushing the button, their friend opened the stairwell door and motioned them downward. They descended into the bowels of the building, then continued traversing the maze. Finally, the pathologist stopped at a broad, unmarked wood-grain door. He rapped.

A flood of bright lights and cool air rushed past the assistant coroner who opened the door. His gentle face and sympathetic deportment had a calming effect that made Kingsley feel oddly safe.

As they shook hands, he echoed Dr. Ruben's sentiments. "I'm so sorry we have to meet under these circumstances. I'll make it as easy as possible." He opened the door wider, and they entered a large room that was bisected by an interior wall. A smell, similar to formaldehyde, shot her mind back to the frogs in her high school biology lab. Odd to remember that now.

Kingsley felt her temper roiling, barely under control, as the detectives glared at them. Even with her back turned, she could feel the woman stabbing her with mental accusations. The detectives weren't even trying to conceal that each was fixated on the same-gender suspect to catch the tiniest *tell* in their reactions. She wanted to explode, *Get the hell out of our private hell,* but tempered the urge. "Back off. We need to do this alone."

In a condescending tone, he said, "We've got to observe the identification. It's procedure."

The larger, immaculate room to the left with its stainless steel counters could have been a brand-new restaurant kitchen waiting for ovens to be installed had it not been for numerous specimen containers, labeled and arranged on shelves and a table. On the far wall of the cavernous space stood a two-tier bank of stainless steel doors with crank handles. Two chairs that she instinctively knew were out of place waited in the right front corner.

"Are you ready?" the assistant coroner asked, explaining what to expect.

"Let me go first," Todd said to Kingsley.

"No, I should."

"Take your time."

Kingsley studied his serious face and the concern in his eyes. She wondered how he could survive doing this kind of work. A wedding ring. Gold. He must be a father himself.

Todd, with his back to the detectives, angled himself directly in front of her, inches away from her face. "Just let me go first."

As he stepped farther into her personal space, she backed into one of the chairs and sat down. He turned toward the coroner and motioned for him to proceed.

He cranked open a door in the lower tier and pulled on a gurney that glided effortlessly onto the yellow tile floor. Todd's broad back completely obscured her view as she sat, braced for the worst. This wasn't real. The strange noises—unfastening, unwrapping, unzipping. Then quiet.

It could all end in a flash. Right here. Right now. All their hopes and dreams for that dear little person. *Oh please, God. Don't let it be Billy. But who then? Whose private hell? How could anyone ever hurt a small child?* Time stopped.

Finally, Todd spoke, his words reverberating crisply against the tile walls. "That isn't Billy. That's not our son. This child is too big, and his hair is blond. Our son has a mop of black hair."

Kingsley jumped from her chair but was unable to look for herself.

"May I see his feet?" Todd was asking. A few moments of silence followed. "The feet are all wrong."

"Oh my god, Todd. Are you sure? Let me look. Just the feet." She could not, dare not, trust him, just in case he was in denial. She tunneled her vision to one tiny foot. "Spread his toes," she said, and the coroner did as she asked. "He's right. That's not Billy."

Kingsley's jumbled emotions galloped aimlessly, flooding her with relief. She flopped back onto the chair. There was still hope, yet still, she trembled. As she scrambled for mental equilibrium and the ability to force her feeble body to a standing position, someone knocked on the exterior door.

As if reading their thoughts, the assistant coroner motioned them toward it. "Why don't you go home? If you have any questions, just call the switchboard tomorrow, and they'll locate me." As Todd opened the door, another pair of detectives was waiting outside with a man and a woman. The four cops communicated nonverbally, exchanging head-tips and eyebrow shrugs. Another couple, their faces anguished with apprehension, approached the pathology lab. For a brief moment, the four parents froze, grief passing among them. Nobody spoke. When the trance broke, the other couple passed into the brightly lit room.

"Where are you parked?" one detective asked. "I can take or direct you."

Kingsley turned to Todd. "I don't know about you, but I'd just as soon find our own way." To them, she added, "You're intruding. So—unless we're under arrest…"

"No. Not at this time."

"What happens next?"

"We'll continue our investigation and be in touch." They turned and disappeared around the first turn in the maze.

"Let's get out of here. Now!" Todd said as he tugged Kingsley's arm. Even through her jacket she could feel he was trembling. Glancing over his shoulder, he propelled her forward with unexpected urgency. As they approached the corridor's first turn, they heard a commotion behind them. Kingsley spun to locate the source.

The other mother.

She was screaming.

Todd grabbed his wife's arm and half dragged her toward the exit that ultimately led to the wrong side of the building. That didn't matter. The horror was somewhere behind the closed door.

Finally pausing and gulping fresh air, he said, "I need a drink."

"Me too."

☙❧

Todd reached into a high kitchen cupboard for bottles of twelve-year-old Bunnahabhain single malt scotch and Bacardi white rum. Clumsily, he dumped ice into two glasses, sending one cube skittering across the plank floor. To the rum, he glugged a thimbleful of tonic water but left the scotch undefiled.

He motioned her toward the living room where they sank into the couch. Both took a deep drink. She set her glass on the old trunk. At first, the rum, having been off limits for over a year, burned fire through her body.

Todd's voice was husky, merely a whisper, as he tipped his glass to study the ice. "I don't know how much more I can take. How much more waiting, not knowing, the calls like tonight's, and those that don't come. And the one that ultimately will."

He opened his mouth to say more, but instead shook his head slowly. He drained his glass and rose to leave the room, returning with a refill.

"Mine too," she handed him her sweaty glass, and again he returned.

"What's going to happen to us?" Kingsley asked. "There's three victims here, and we've come unglued."

He drained his second glass then set it beside hers on the trunk. He hugged her roughly against him. "Oh, K, I'm so sorry. About everything. About all of it."

"Me too. I've been so mean, so into myself. I should have understood that you were coping the best way you could."

"And I didn't grasp what it must be like for you as a mother."

She started to cry. "I've read that many marriages don't survive the—the death of a child. Promise me. Promise that there will still be an *us* if the next call or the next is the end."

"There will always be *us*." He wrapped her up with both arms and kissed her damp cheeks then pushed a stray curl from her forehead and kissed that too.

She took his hot face in her chilly hands, cooled by her fright and the icy glass. "Oh, Todd, promise me. Say it."

"I love you, K. I promise." He kissed her, tentatively at first, then again and again with increasing passion and urgency. The nightmare retreated as they shed their inhibitions along with their clothes, surrendering to primal lust and release that had waited entirely too long.

∽∾∽∾

Like exotic birds in courtship flight, Kingsley and Todd repeated a familiar ritual—he drawing the water, she lighting the candles and positioning the fluffy bath sheets near the old tub. From experience, he knew just how high the water should be to cover spent bodies without sloshing onto the floor. Sinking into its soothing heat, she pressed herself against his wet chest.

They languished, taking turns gently soaping each other. Finally, she tugged the plug's chain with her toe, letting the water take their jumbled emotions circling away. Refilling the tub with fresh water that splashed off their legs, Kingsley poured oil, gently distributing its silkiness throughout the ripples. She settled against him again. They relaxed until the fresh water cooled. "What are you thinking?" he finally asked.

"The police—we've got to face it. They've struck out. They're a whisper away from dropping Billy's file into their cold-case repository. All this time we've been pinning our hopes on the experts, but, Todd, they don't have a clue. And they don't know our world like we do. That building—it's our environment. Our turf. Our people. There's got to be something they've overlooked—something an insider might figure out. If they can't find Billy—Todd! We've got to find him ourselves."

"I'd tear that whole damned place apart with my bare hands if I thought there was one shred of evidence, anything that would point us in the right direction. I'd run from here to the coast to wrench Billy away from whoever did this to us. I'd do anything, give anything, promise anything."

"Have you struck deals with God?"

"Well, sure. Haven't you?"

"Every day. Todd, let's think. What about the staff? There's Alicia, its head, who strikes me as sterling."

"She came with incredible credentials and a long, uneventful history."

"And the grannies."

"I can't picture any of them masterminding a kidnapping," Todd said.

"And the Mennonite girl."

"They're deeply religious and not focused on worldly possessions. She'd have no motive."

"Two high school girls who spell the grannies at five o'clock came too late in the day. Todd, that leaves Ethelda Blake."

"What possible motive could she have? She's having a kid of her own."

"Money perhaps?"

Both were silent a moment, Todd absently rubbing her sides with the oil-soft water. "You've gotten so thin. And your muscles are as hard as this tub."

"Remember all that cream I lathered on my stomach before Billy was born, trying to make the stretched skin feel better?"

"Your belly was as hard as a bowling ball."

Kingsley turned so quickly that a small wave of water splashed from the tub. "Todd! That first day I met Ethelda Blake I crashed into her with my elbow. I was horrified that I might have hurt her. We both jumped back. But Todd, now that I think of it, her belly had *give*. Not soft, like a feather pillow. More like dense foam."

"What are you saying—that she wasn't pregnant?"

"What do we really know about her? And who can help us find out? Todd, could you ask Shirley Granger to chat up her former employer."

"I don't think a human resources professional can do that. Shirley's allowed to verify if and how long she held her last position and get her job description. Comments, even recommendations, positive or negative, are no longer legal."

"Ethelda told me her baby was due in two months. That would be June. If she left her last employer in December, she would have already been pregnant. Shirley could check on that, couldn't she?"

"Well, I suppose I could ask if…"

Kingsley clambered out of the tub. "She *must* be involved somehow. She's the only one in the entire scenario who could be."

"Where are you going?"

"To the bank. Come on. Get dressed."

"K, it's two in the morning." He followed her out of the tub and toweled himself quickly, knowing there would be no ritual drying of each other that night. He trailed her into their bedroom where she was grabbing at clothes.

"What are you planning to do?"

"Security's on duty twenty-four/seven. Let's get coffee at Wawa then look at every millimeter of that security footage. The answer is recorded somehow."

Chapter 10

Stars and a crescent moon broke through the canopy of racing clouds as Kingsley and Todd hurried into the bank. The guard behind the security desk snapped a look at his watch, then back at them in surprise.

"Charles Wasleski is expecting us," Todd said of the chief of security.

"He is? Oh, here comes Chas now."

"Great to see you again," Wasleski said, pumping their hands. "Working with you on that vault murder case was the most exciting thing I've done in years. And you figured it out."

"Couldn't have done it without your help," Todd said.

"Thank you for seeing us in the middle of the night," Kingsley said. "We're frantic, sleepless, and bent on exhausting even remote possibilities."

"No problem. I've been expecting your call. Just a matter of time, I told myself. You do know that everyone wants to help and doesn't know how. I'm at your disposal, any time, day or night."

"You're so kind," Kingsley said. Her mind flashed angry vignettes of their horrendous experience with the cops who, by comparison, were void of compassion. This guy was a blessed relief.

"I'm a parent too," he continued, leading them down a corridor to the right of the lobby. He swiped his ID that opened Security's inner sanctuary door and motioned them in. Numerous monitors displayed the live feed from strategically placed cameras throughout the building. The facility was dead at that hour.

"Have a seat," Chas said, pointing the Hennings to swivel captain's chairs positioned before several dark monitors. He fingers flew on his keyboard like a pianist playing Mozart's Concerto Number 21 in C major. "We transmitted digital copies of our files to the police's computers, going back to your son's first morning in daycare. What you'll see are the original, unaltered files. I'll set up the monitors to show you side-by-side, synchronized views recorded by the two daycare corridor's cameras."

The screens before them flickered to life.

Chas fast-forwarded to a strategic spot on both recordings. "There—see that lady in a plaid jacket? She's a good example. You can view her, front and back, if you glance quickly at both monitors. And, of course, I can pause them." He demonstrated several speeds as the woman seemed to fly or float down the corridor. "Before we begin, let me offer a suggestion," he continued. "I expect this could be quite disturbing. If you want me to stop at any time, just hold up a hand. We can take a break whenever and for as long as you wish."

"I think we're prepared," she said.

"Okay then. Let's go through it once, fast-forwarding through any dead spots."

"Look, Todd, there I am coming down the hall from the daycare's parking lot carrying Billy. Oh, his dear little face." She smiled at the image as tears filled her eyes.

"Here's my favorite part," Chas said. "You walk into the daycare, and in a few moments, come back into the hall and wave Billy's hand in our direction."

"I remember. Look what happened next. See? Miss Alicia came after me and pointed to the yellow line on the floor. I was supposed to sign him in *and* out before exiting the daycare, even though I'd just been there a few moments."

"Are they really that strict?" Chas asked.

"They are. It should have been the safest place in the world. Let's keep going."

Chas fast-forwarded through the footage of the empty corridor, stopping only to show people coming and going. It was getting old fast. Suddenly the hall filled with people.

"Now here's where the fire drill sequence begins," Chas said. All three focused intently. "There!" He froze the motion. "There's Ethelda Blake carrying Billy."

"Can you play that sequence again in slow motion?" Todd asked.

"Sure." They watched, transfixed, as Ethelda and Billy floated down the hall toward the door. Then he played the sequence one frame at a time. The feed from the camera facing the parking lot soon appeared to be flashing bright lights.

"What's causing that?" Kingsley asked.

"The camera's light meter reads what it sees. Whether it's a drill or the real thing, no doors may be propped open since oxygen would feed a real fire. Dozens of people streamed down that hall, pushed the door open, then let it shut. Sometimes it closed completely as gaps formed in the procession. When the door is wide open, the camera takes its light reading from outdoors, reading the corridor as dark. If the door is closed, it reads the hall light. With the constant opening and closing of the doors, what we can see is compromised."

"But we did see Billy," Kingsley said. "He lifted his head, yawned, and put it back down again."

"That's correct. So we know he was still in the building when the fire drill started. Shall I continue?"

"Please."

Chas proceeded at normal speed to the point where the last man exited the corridor. He turned right into the stairwell that led upstairs or to the rear exit on the back side of the building. Then the hall became quiet.

"Why didn't that man use the daycare door like the others?" Todd asked.

"It's procedure. Each department has its own assigned spot in the lot. We identified that man as an employee who was away from his office when the alarm sounded. His department assembles in the opposite side of the building. Given its geography, if he exited using the daycare corridor, he wouldn't have time to circle the building and make his roll call. Shall I go on?" The parents nodded.

Chas fast-forwarded through a long, dead space until the drill ended. The activity started again with the exterior door opening and closing, as the last group that exited re-entered first, passing the daycare's interior door and disappearing into the main part of the building. The daycare group brought up the rear. "There they come now!" Kingsley said, jumping up from her chair. She squinted. "Can you run it again in slow motion?"

"Sure." The images crawled, Ethelda with Billy, moving toward the interior camera, interspersed with flashes of daylight from outside the building. His fluff of dark hair peeked from his blanket, his little head supported by Ethelda's chin. As she turned to her right, into the daycare, she smiled sweetly at him and gave the top of his head a kiss. Then both disappeared.

"Can we see it again? Both sequences? And can you enlarge it?" she asked. Chas queued it up. They watched both monitors, then each individually in slow motion. When the staff re-entered the building, neither camera detailed Billy's face because he wasn't looking over Ethelda's shoulder. They could see his head with its tuft of hair and his little body wrapped in the monkey-print blanket.

"More?" Chas asked.

Kingsley sighed, disappointed. "There's no more to see. It's just as they said. The answer must be in the daycare itself."

"I'll queue that up." They watched a brief sequence as Ethelda passed the interior camera and disappeared into the baby's quiet room.

"Are there any more shots of Billy?"

Chas shook his head. "That's it. Of course, the police have everything we saved from the first day you arrived with your son."

Kingsley asked, "Could I see the sequence where Ethelda leaves the building that day?"

Chas glanced at a numbered list then fast-forwarded to the corresponding spot and pushed play. Shortly they saw the woman emerge. Coatless, she dangled keys in her right hand. A tiny purse with a long strap hung from her left shoulder. She wasn't carrying anything else. Finally, they watched the entire recording one more time without interruption.

Slowly they rose. "Thank you, Chas. We really appreciate it," Todd said.

"When you're ready to see it again, or any of our other recordings, just give me a call. I'll have it ready."

Kingsley and Todd exited the building into bright sunshine. Day eleven was underway. They walked upstream past employees reporting for work. "What are you thinking?" Todd asked.

"I'm disappointed. No, make that crushed. I was so sure that we'd see something the others had missed."

"Want to go home? Take a nap?"

"I just want to change clothes and get back to work. Todd, you'll talk to Shirley about Ethelda, won't you? Please?"

"I'll do it first thing."

₧₧₧

"You know I'll do whatever I can," Shirley Granger said as she faced Todd who sat in the guest chair opposite her desk. "It's the least I can do. Thanks to you, I'm no longer under the thumb of our crooked ex-president. And you encouraged me to get college credit for my life's work, to say nothing of my promotion. I'd never be part of the executive staff if you hadn't convinced me that I had potential."

"You don't owe me a thing. You did all the work."

She flipped a dismissing motion with her hand. "Whatever you need, I'll do it."

"I appreciate that, but let's have an understanding. It must be both legal *and* ethical. I won't have you compromise yourself, your job, or the bank."

She smiled. "What's our challenge?"

"Ethelda Blake. What do you really know about her?"

Shirley rolled her eyes and took a deep breath. "She quit. Never came back after the kidnapping."

"Really! What did she say?"

"*She* didn't. That redneck husband of hers came in with a handwritten note. Read me the riot act about not protecting employees from unwarranted harassment due to our lack of security. Said she'd already suffered one miscarriage and he wasn't risking another. That the police hounding her had made her quite ill, and he'll sue us if anything happened to her or their baby."

"Anything else?"

"Only that he was taking her to her parents in Michigan to recuperate."

"Shirley, do you know the HR director from her previous job?"

"Yes. We meet at professional functions. What do you want me to ask?"

"Kingsley said that Ethelda's baby was due in June. We suspect that she's not even pregnant. That she might have used that to help get this job, or to position herself to help with the kidnapping. If she lied so unnecessarily, the question is why? Can you find out?"

"Do you think Ethelda smuggled your baby out under her clothes?"

"That's impossible. Billy weighs twelve pounds and is tall for his age. And he's quite active when he's awake. I've seen the security footage. She'd be nailed the first time anyone looked at the video because Ethelda's too small to conceal him. But we shouldn't take anything as *fact*."

"If she didn't smuggle him out, what else could have happened?"

"I wish I knew. Just see what you can find out that doesn't fit. One more thing—could you supply me with the names of employees whose departments use the same parking lot as the daycare during a fire drill? Possibly include their home phone numbers?"

☙❧

"Leslie? It's Shirley Granger. I hope you can help me. One of our employees quit unexpectedly and wouldn't you know it? Hers was among the files that got shredded accidentally by that nice young man we hired to run our copy center. We believe in giving people with certain challenges an opportunity to work, but sometimes it blows up in our faces."

"Say no more, Shirley. What do you need to know?"

"The employee's name is Ethelda Blake. She worked for you prior to joining us. Can you give me her dates of employment and her job description? I need to reconstruct our records."

"I'll get her file."

While she was waiting Shirley jotted a few questions to pose then numbered them in their order of importance.

"Here it is—Ethelda Blake. She worked for us from June of last year through December, same year. Her title was Daycare Provider II. We were sorry to lose her. With over five hundred employees in our manufacturing facility, we have lots of families with young children. Our daycare space is always maxed out, and a really good Provider eases the crush."

"Sounds like you'd welcome her back in a heartbeat. Guess you're not allowed to say why she left, and I'm not asking."

"Just between you and me, we could use a dozen like her. You were lucky to get her. It's not often a registered nurse is willing to babysit. Frankly, I'm surprised that she'd take another daycare position after what she went through. Of course, I can't go into that."

Shirley crossed her fingers and prayed. "She told me all about her miscarriage and the trauma that brought it on."

"I've often wondered what became of Ethelda's friend. Imagine, being told your baby has died and being convinced that the deceased wasn't your baby. And no one believed her. According to the newspaper account, the mother swore that someone in the hospital switched her baby and altered the records. The investigation produced no evidence of foul play. The mother had a nervous breakdown, tried to kill herself, and ended up in a psych ward. I wonder if she's still committed.

"Ethelda told a coworker how she got involved. Guess it isn't a secret."

"Lived in the same neighborhood, right? They became friends. Ethelda said she suspected the woman used drugs, which could account for the infant's death. Ethelda exhausted herself trying to help, ignoring her own health and all the warnings."

"And Ethelda miscarried in September."

"No, December."

Shirley digested that quickly. "I meant December. Our staff says Ethelda is so softhearted and such a sweet person. From what she told me, I guess she got too emotionally involved with her friend. Did you know she's expecting again?"

"That's great," Leslie said. "Sometimes that's best. I just hope that she's up to it physically so soon after a miscarriage. My doctor told me to wait at least a year."

"One more thing. Her social security number, residence, and phone number."

"I can supply the SS, but mail sent to her home was returned, and the phone number's a disconnect. Do you want the address anyway?"

"Why not. And the name of her previous employer. I need to reconstruct her work history." Shirley crossed her fingers again. "I seem to recall it was a hospital?"

"Right. Here it is. Big one. Philadelphia. I'll give you the name of their HR director. Do you want the rest of her work history and education as well? Huh—that's interesting. She never stayed in one place for long. Oh, I see why. She was a student. Now that's odd—she undertook what had to be long commutes. Would you like the names of the schools she attended?"

"That would save me some phone calls." As excited as this information made her, Shirley knew she better not raise suspicion. Still, she pressed on.

"Her husband said he was taking her to her parents in Michigan to rest. I have some paperwork that needs her signature and her savings plan to process. Do you have the next of kin's information in your file?"

A long pause followed. "That's okay, Leslie, if you're unable to give out such information.

"Shirley, her parents are dead. A boating accident somewhere in the islands. I remember when she took compassionate leave to deal with their affairs."

"I, ah, must have misunderstood what he said. If you have a forwarding address, that would be helpful." The information Leslie ticked off was familiar to Shirley—a previous dead end. Time to punt. "Are you going to the human resources conference in San Diego?"

"Wouldn't miss it. Let's coordinate our flights—give us a chance to catch up. And good luck with those shredded files. Paperwork's a bitch."

☙❧

Kingsley closed her office door as soon as Todd began repeating what Shirley had learned. "That can't be right, Todd. Ethelda told me she was due in two months. You've seen the tapes. That looked about right, but if she miscarried in December, she couldn't have gotten pregnant until January or early February. That would make her due date no sooner than October. I knew it. I just knew it! She *is* the answer. But how did she do it? We should pass this information on to the police."

"No, K, we can't. Not without getting both Shirley and her counterpart in trouble. Ethelda's medical information should have been confidential. There's something more important we've got to consider. The police are hell bent on implicating us. If Ethelda is involved, what's to stop her from saying she did it for us? She could make up anything plausible in exchange for immunity. And even if Billy is never found, well, murder cases have been successfully prosecuted without a body."

Panic rose from her depth, its acid taste permeating her mouth. "Just when I thought this couldn't get any worse. If only there had been a camera in the parking lot or in his quiet room."

"There were lots of eyes in the lot. Maybe somebody saw something."

"I thought the police already questioned everybody. Nobody said they saw any strangers, vehicles, or anything remotely useful."

"Maybe they asked the wrong questions. Shirley gave me the personal phone numbers for employees assigned to that parking lot for the drill. She also included numbers for people who park there. That's a reach, but someone may have been reporting or leaving work at the same time as the fire drill. Let's call them from home."

Kingsley couldn't shrug off the creepy sensation of her office walls contracting, like a scene from Poe. She paced, not knowing quite what to do with herself. She jumped when the phone rang and was relieved when a prospect she'd courted wanted to see her ASAP. Quickly she resurrected the notes she had taken in what felt like a previous life.

Halfway to the prospect's office, the client called to reschedule—some kind of emergency that he must settle in person. Obviously frazzled, he apologized repeatedly. She looked at her watch—just ten a.m. Now what? She circled through MacDonald's, treating herself to coffee and a Danish, then parked to collect her thoughts while she munched. She decided not to return to the office, opting instead to follow a hunch.

Chapter 11

Navigating through older subdivisions, Kingsley located Ethelda Blake's house in a quiet neighborhood of 1950s ranchers dwarfed by overgrown maples. Halfway down the block, she found number 202. Weathered yellow paint peeled from the siding, revealing bare wood on numerous boards. One black shutter hung askew, and weeds choked what little remained of the lawn. She circled the block, parallel parking on the adjacent side street, and approached the house on foot.

No cars were parked in the driveway or on the sparsely stoned carport through which struggled more weeds. Kingsley rang the doorbell, and when nobody came, she rang it again. Apparently, no one was home. Finally, she squeezed behind the overgrown yews that were planted two feet from the foundation. She peered through the cracked drapery that covered the large picture window. Threadbare oversized furniture, fast-food bags, and debris littered what she could see of the badly worn carpet.

"They ain't there!"

Kingsley jumped and turned toward the voice, which came from the neighboring yard.

A dumpy woman, whom Kingsley judged to be in her late sixties, had been tapping a plant from its pot with a trowel. She wore muddy jeans, a work shirt, gardening gloves, and a floppy straw hat.

Kingsley approached her. "Do you know when they'll be back?"

The woman snorted. "Not ever, I hope. Just look at that place. No sense of pride." Kingsley glanced at the Blakes' house, a stark contrast to this woman's immaculate yard. Inside her white picket fence, a wide perennial border flourished, and rhododendrons rioted against her foundation.

"Oh dear," Kingsley said, unable to mask her disappointment. "I needed to see her."

"Well, you're too late. Moved out, lock, stock, and barrel."

"Are you sure? I saw furniture inside."

"It's a rental. Furnished. Oughta be a law. Just look at what happens when the landlord and tenants don't care."

"I lent her some books, one of which was quite valuable. Now I may never get it back." For a moment Kingsley retreated into her mind. *Another dead end.*

"Doubt if there's anything left, but if there is, I think I can help. Family before them had cats. I love cats, don't you? I used to critter sit when they went on vacation. They left a key under a rock. Maybe it's still there, but probably rusty by now. You a cat lover?"

"Why, yes. Her name is Pandora. A friend brought her to me as a kitten one stormy night. She came with her box."

The woman chuckled, eying Kingsley intently. "Say, aren't you that woman who's been in the papers?"

Kingsley sagged. The impulse to come here *was* a mistake. This woman had already revealed so much about two former tenants. She could not risk loose lips reaching the wrong ears. She should escape, the quicker, the better.

The woman broke into her thoughts. "I've been praying for youse and your baby." Kingsley looked up, startled. "That's why we were put on this earth—to take care of each other. It's God's will. Wait here." She went inside and returned shortly with a large ring of keys. She winked at Kingsley. "Here—take this." She handed over a small can of cat food and a can opener. "Anyone asks, you're doing it for me, seein' as how I'm digging some flowers for you. I thought I heard a poor little kitten crying. Probably got left behind. Be a shame if she went hungry, me with a key and all."

"Are you sure it's all right?"

"I ain't tellin' no one."

Kingsley followed her to the carport door. The woman unlocked it and stepped aside for Kingsley to enter. The smell of damp drywall, mold, and the ham-like scent of a working fireplace assaulted Kingsley's nose. "I'll leave you alone. Stop by the garden when you get finished. You know—for those flowers I promised?" Without waiting for a reply, the woman left Kingsley alone.

How do I do this? Where do I start? Kingsley took some deep breaths then explored the interior space systematically. She gave each room a cursory sweep—living room with its exterior door in the front corner. The kitchen, where she stood, was behind it. A hall that bisected the house led past a cellar door to several closed doors. Two opened into small bedrooms, one to a bathroom, and a fourth to access the attic.

Back in the kitchen, she opened cupboards and drawers, using a discarded sandwich bag as a glove. She found nothing but remnants of kitchen supplies. Then she looked hard in every conceivable place for evidence that Billy had been there or where he might have been taken, even under the cushions. Nothing again. The place really was empty, except for the abandoned living room furniture, dirt, and debris.

She opened the last door and peered down cellar steps into an unfinished basement. Bare light bulbs, one operated by a switch inside the doorframe, and three others with pull strings, lit the stark enclosure. Bare cinder block walls had never seen paint, and a few puddles betrayed water problems. The basement looked unused, its sole purpose being a foundation. She glanced at a gaping exit with rotting wood steps beneath Bilco doors that would lead to the back yard, but found no evidence of what—a tiny grave?

She returned to the living room fireplace, built against the carport wall. Someone had used it recently but neglected to shovel the ashes. The contents had burned inefficiently, leaving scraps of charred paper and shredded fabric. Quickly, she knelt for closer inspection. The paper scraps had numbers. Pulling the sandwich bag snugly around her hand, she started to reach for the papers.

Outside, slamming car doors grabbed her attention. She jumped, then crept to the living room window and peeked from behind the right side. Wrong angle, she realized, and scurried to the left and looked again, just in time to see two men and a woman in smart business attire striding toward the front door. They looked like bankers, attorneys, or real estate agents. Panicked, she tiptoed with giant steps through the living room and the kitchen, positioning herself at the carport door. Straining her ears while praying the trio would go no farther than the front door, she caught the sound of jingling keys and voices entering the living room.

Silently she grimaced as she turned the carport doorknob. It did not squeak. She eased the door open and slipped outside. She had two options—hide around back or make a beeline for the neighbor's yard.

"Let me show you the basement," she heard a male voice call to the others, followed by the clatter of multiple footsteps.

Without further hesitation, Kingsley strode toward the neighbor's back yard and circled around front. She caught her breath, and after her heart settled, knocked on the door.

"Find your books?" the woman asked, receiving the cat food and can opener.

"Afraid not. It was worth a try. Thanks for your help." She started to turn—took a chance. "By the way, did the couple who lived there have any children?"

"Nope, and the way he treated her, she'd be lucky to have the one she was carrying."

"Why? Did you see him abuse her?"

"The way he was letting her load up that U-Haul? She was pregnant, you know. Pig should have done it himself."

"Was she lifting heavy objects?"

"Nearly all of them boxes, close as I could see. Toted four to his one. Lazy son of a bitch."

"You've been quite helpful. I'd be grateful if you didn't repeat our conversation to anyone."

"Long as you don't let anyone know how you got in."

Kingsley smiled conspiratorially. "Why, the door opened when I knocked, and I swear I heard someone call for me to come in."

"If the family returns, should I…"

"No! I mean, I wouldn't want them to think I was snooping. I'll get in touch some other way." The woman nodded in what Kingsley interpreted as strategic agreement. She hurried back to her car, avoiding the front of the Blakes' house.

eↄeↄ

That evening Kingsley and Todd divvied up the 500 employees' names and numbers that Shirley had slipped him, noting the check marks beside employees' names whose fire drill assignments were located near the daycare's. They took turns calling, which yielded no new information. By the time each had made numerous calls, they were both proficient and disappointed.

Sighing, Kingsley dialed the phone one more time. "Brittney? This is Kingsley Henning. I'm sorry to bother you at home. I took a chance that yours was the number in the phone book." A forgivable lie under the circumstances, she thought, crossing her fingers. "I was wondering if you could help me. Todd and I are trying to envision the parking lot the day our baby was kidnapped."

The voice at the other end sounded flattered and somewhat awed. "Of course, Ms. Henning. What do you want to know?"

"The daycare and your department assemble next to each other in the lot. Did you see any strangers, even a child, in the parking lot near either group?"

"The police asked me that," Brittney said. "I'll tell you what I told them. There are twenty-three in our department. One person was absent. The drill took forever. First, we were annoyed, but then the fire engines came and stayed a long time. That was scary."

"Was your attention ever diverted?"

"Ms. Henning, there were no strangers walking around. Emergency personnel stayed on the front side of the building. We just hung out, not knowing what to think. Some of our staff got quite edgy. We were working tight deadlines before it all happened, and the lost time just made it that much worse, as did the potential for lost data from our system."

"So there was nothing unusual? Nothing at all? Not one little thing?"

Brittney chuckled. "Unless you're including that dog."

Kingsley jerked to attention. "What dog?"

"A black Lab wearing a red bandanna, carrying a Frisbee. He was so cute. Trotted into the parking lot from the grassy border in front of the woods. You know, that area beyond the asphalt? He must have been somebody's pet. It was adorable how he would drop the Frisbee at somebody's feet, then run toward the woods and turn expectantly. One of our guys threw it for him, and he brought it right back. He kept this up for five or ten minutes then didn't return."

"Was anyone with him? Back by the woods?"

"No. He was alone, as if he'd given his owner the slip and wanted to play. That sure broke up the monotony."

"Did you tell the police?"

"Well—no. They asked about people and cars. I didn't even think about the dog. Do you think it's important?"

"Not unless there was somebody with him. Did you hear anything back in the woods?

"Our location on the highway is fairly noisy. And our attention was directed toward the building. You know, to catch the *all clear*."

"Can you think of anything else?"

"I'm sorry. I can't."

"Thanks anyway, Brittney. I appreciate your time."

Kingsley kept her composure until the phone was securely cradled. "That's it, Todd! That's how it happened. Someone was out there in the woods with a dog to create a diversion. The dog kept playing until somebody signaled him. If everyone was watching the dog, that gave Ethelda time to swap the baby with the doll."

"But Kingsley, that doesn't fit. Remember the tape in close-up mode? The doll left in the crib had a smooth head with light brown painted hair. We saw Ethelda on tape with Billy's mop of dark hair. Besides, if she'd left him outside, he might have cried. The risk would have been phenomenal."

Kingsley threw the rest of the list aside on the desk. "This is so frustrating. Every time we think we've found one little clue, it gets shot down. Know what I'd like to do? Find Ethelda Blake and shake it out of her." Kingsley brightened. "That gives me an idea."

"You won't do Billy one bit of good if you're in jail."

"I promise I'll wear my nice person hat. Didn't Shirley tell you that Ethelda's husband said she was too upset to return to work? What would happen if I go to soothe her? Maybe she'll feel guilty enough or sufficiently off guard to let something slip."

"Shirley also said her husband was taking her home to her parents somewhere in the Midwest."

"But we know they're deceased. I've got to try talking to her."

"K, I don't know."

"Now don't try to stop me."

"God help the person who does."

Chapter 12

re you expecting someone?" Todd asked.
Kingsley turned a little too quickly from their living room's west-facing window where she'd been scrutinizing the sun's descent. Not realizing that Todd was paying attention, she had traveled between the library's front windows, through the foyer into the living room and back several times.

The woods that screened the front of their property from the access road to the highway gave way to the cleared farmland to the west and the north. The days were staying light longer as spring overtook winter, and Kingsley needed the cover of darkness.

"I'm just restless," she answered. "Think I'll go prowl the mall."

Todd set down his book. "I'll come along. I could use a few things—been putting it off."

"No. Actually, I also need to run by Barrie's. She's been having some difficulties. It's girl stuff. If she's not around, I should stop and see Margaret. I need to return some things that I borrowed."

"K, if you just need to be by yourself, it's okay. You don't have to make excuses for me."

"That's not what I'm doing. Now, if you really want to go to the mall…"

He smiled. "Actually, this book is quite good, and my

feet are too tired to tramp. Just be careful. Twilight driving can be tricky."

But not dangerous, she thought. Andy—the first real love of her life. That pitch black night with its interminable rain. Too dark to see faded lines on the road or the heating oil truck running the light. Or the killer closing in on him as he exited onto the ramp. How many more times would that memory blindside her when his death had receded into that recess where her mind hid her traumas?

"Don't worry. I'll be back in a couple of hours."

Kingsley had purposely parked the Lexus in the stone bank barn that served as their garage rather than leave the car behind the house. Built on a south-facing hill, its upper-level doors opened onto their lane. The ground had been backfilled against the barn by a former owner for second floor access. The lower level also was accessible to vehicles by a dirt driveway that sloped downhill beside the barn. In the old days, feed had been stored on top and lowered through traps to the animals below.

She circled on foot to the lower level where their garden tractor, tools, and supplies were kept. From a shelf, she grabbed several pairs of surgical latex gloves, which she often wore under her Wells LaMont leather gloves when pruning her roses. Then she retrieved a pair of eight-inch tweezers, a screwdriver, and pliers from a toolbox. A flashlight, she remembered, before returning topside to get into her car. She popped the trunk, and from a stash of office supplies, extracted two penlights. Sheltered by the trunk's lid, she checked the batteries and slid them into her jacket pocket.

Engine purring, she eased from the barn, straight up their lane and left onto the access road that led to the highway. Guilt gnawed its visceral intrusion as she rethought why she hadn't told Todd what she had planned. That was simple. He would have stopped her. His common sense and nega-tive fatalistic attitude were driving her nuts. And she was sick of playing by the rules. What good had that done Billy?

Or them, for that matter? Nevertheless, she checked her speed and slowed down.

The journey across town ate up enough time for complete darkness to blanket the Blakes' quiet neighborhood. That, she realized, had been built before underground utilities. The houses, while set back only twenty feet from the sidewalk, enjoyed deep back yards with twenty-foot rights-of-way to accommodate telephone poles, wires, and transformers. Homeowners, nevertheless, maintained the space. Tangled forsythia competed with lilacs and weedy vegetation.

She hadn't taken note of the streetlights' locations on her previous visit, but was relieved to find them at the end of each block. The blocks weren't long—five properties about eighty feet wide. Perpendicular side streets, without houses, connected more streets in a grid. Her fear that her car would scream intruder vanished as she circled, searching in vain for a parking place.

When the development was built in the '50s, homeowners parked their only car in their garages, leaving the street fairly empty. But now, with a vehicle for each licensed driver, even street parking was scarce. Kingsley's old Lexus, bought by Grammy the year that she died, did not look out of place in this working -class neighborhood.

By the time she had circled a third time, a vacated spot on a side street near the Blakes' yielded the perfect location. Enormous maples, growing between the sidewalk and the road, overhung the street, obscuring her from most windows. Stockade fences surrounded most properties, forming a tunnel through the right-of-way between the back yards. Resisting the urge to look around suspiciously, Kingsley walked directly from the side street into the right-of-way that led toward the Blakes' back yard.

Slowly her eyes adjusted to the darkness as she left the streetlights' glow behind. Down the block, a dog barked relentlessly, and an electrical buzz came from somewhere she couldn't discern. Otherwise, the neighborhood was quiet. Halting, she studied the ranchers surrounding the Blakes, which appeared identical in layout. Evening activities would take place in the street-facing living rooms or finished basements. If she were lucky, no one would be looking out the rear-facing bedroom windows. If they did, she hoped the distance, fences, overgrowth, and trees would obscure her from curious eyes as she cut behind the yards.

Finally, she reached the Blakes' rear foundation. She groped and squinted through the darkness, overturning any stone that might hide a key. As she reached for a promising sphere that was different from the others, a thorny bush raked her hand. She yanked it back, then groped more carefully, but raked her hand again. She sucked the salty ooze from the back of her hand, painstakingly removing the stickers. Determined, she snapped on her latex gloves and risking the penlight, examined the promising stone. It was hollow, its interior compartment yielding a key. Success!

Without any light, she entered the house by the carport door. From memory, she hurried through the kitchen and skirted the living room furniture. She knelt by the fireplace. Luck was with her as the ashes had not been disturbed. Deep from her pocket, she pulled several zipper bags and the tweezers. Glancing over her shoulder, she verified that the draperies were still drawn, cursing herself for not checking that first. Not wanting to waste any more time, she forced her attention to the task at hand, nerves be damned.

Crouching with the penlight clamped firmly in her teeth, she cautiously lifted the unburned paper scraps, none of which was more than a two-inch triangle. The papers had once been duplicates, printed in pairs—an original and a carbonless copy. Painstakingly, she separated each pair, taking care not to smudge them. Then she dropped the second page of each pair into a bag. Thank God she'd seen this done on TV, as she patiently worked her way through a dozen charred remains. Carefully she repositioned all the originals exactly as she had found them. Next, she tweezered through the ashes for any more scraps that hadn't been consumed. That yielded one more.

Her tweezers snagged what appeared to be lengths of unraveled thread. Lifting it carefully, she scrutinized the convoluted crimped strands. Ribbon? No, it appeared to be from a terrycloth towel—or yes! a baby's stretchy sleeper. Gently she blew the ash dust away. By the penlight's white stream, she saw what she swore looked *blue*.

Billy! If Billy had ever been in this house, could a dog detect his scent now? No way it could pick up a trail from a piece of charred thread. Still, Billy might have been placed on the couch. She wondered if this constituted probable cause. Kingsley replaced half the blue thread visibly on top of the ashes then dropped the other half in a plastic bag. Stiffly, she rose, putting the tweezers and bags into her pocket. Her mind raced, trying to formulate a plan that would bring the police and their dogs without throwing additional suspicion on her.

As she stealthily withdrew toward the kitchen to leave, brilliant lights stabbed through the ill-fitting draperies and the three small windows that topped the cheap front door. Simultaneously, doors slammed—three of them— accompanied by male voices. Kingsley froze, unable to choose the best route to escape. The three appeared to be separating, as if on different missions. She was trapped!

One crunched down the carport gravel toward the back yard. "It's not here!" he called in a rather high male voice. Another relayed the message from outside the carport door, inches from where she cowered. The key! She had dropped it into her pocket where it remained.

A dull thud, followed by splintering, came from the direction of the front door. From their crude language and vulgar attitude as they reassembled out front, Kingsley knew that none of these men were the professionals who had visited that afternoon. Frantically, she wracked her memory. Where could she hide?

If they were doing a walk-through of sorts, they would

check every closet and cupboard. In the seconds that preceded their boisterous entry, she hurried down the hall, past the cellar door toward the bedrooms, and circled to face the door that she prayed led to an attic. She yanked it open. Her penlight revealed two platform-like steps that led to a trapdoor. She crawled onto the lower platform and eased the door closed behind her. Crouched on the platform, she waited.

Within minutes the men had gathered in the living room. The one with the deep voice seemed to be in charge, shredding the others for their stupidity. "Blake took the key," he snarled, then unleashed an unabridged thesaurus of expletives when the fireplace caught his attention. "When I said destroy every trace, that meant ashes and all."

"See for yourself. There's nothing left," a third voice said in an unconcerned drawl. Clanking followed, which sounded like fireplace tools.

"There! You see? That paper didn't burn. What if the cops had gotten here first? Get that shit shoveled out, every last speck. You. Check the rest of the house."

As quickly and quietly as humanly possible, Kingsley mounted the second platform step and shifted the trap door just wide enough to haul herself into the darkness. Then she slid the door back into position, tearing several fingernails in her attempt to lower it gently to prevent it from thumping into its frame. Almost simultaneously, someone threw open the door beneath her and snapped on a light. A hair-width beam surrounded the trapdoor. He paused for what seemed like an interminable length of time.

"Hey! Footprints." More steps down the hall.

Deep voice snorted. "Checked the attic myself yesterday. Blake probably stored shit up there."

"But the footprints are small."

"Probably the woman's." The closet door closed.

Gingerly, without moving beyond the discarded plywood onto which she had crawled, Kingsley fingered her surroundings. Streetlights that seeped through the soffit re vealed just how close she had come to breaking through the living room ceiling. The beams, constructed eighteen inches off center, and pink rolled insulation were all that separated her from the living room below. One misstep and she would have crashed through the ceiling.

The air, dense with dust, grated her nose and throat. The more she gasped, the more she needed to cough. Carefully she slipped off her jacket, burying her face in its thickest folds and only permitted herself a bit of relief when the trio below started shouting. As she shifted her position, the sagging plywood creaked. How long could it hold her?

Kingsley sat motionless. A door opened, banged shut, then another. She could hear rustling paper. Somewhere near the kitchen a paper bag popped. "Who brought the beer?" No response. Another barrage of expletives, followed by the slamming front door.

It dawned on Kingsley that, besides being trapped for the moment, her clueless captors might squat here all night. She patted her pockets for her cell phone, and by its buttons' configuration, oriented it correctly. Holding it deep within the folds of her coat, she prayed as it powered up. Could they hear its machinations? When the electronic beeping finished, she peeked at the dial in time to witness the dying battery give up the ghost. She realized she'd have to get out of this mess by herself. Perhaps, since they'd already checked the house—she closed her eyes in concentration.

Knowing the men's vehicle was parked out front with nobody out back, everyone was accounted for. Repositioning herself to shield the penlight with her body, she examined her surroundings with peripheral light. The roof was quite shallow without standing room. The empty, floorless space was a sea of fresh insulation, the Pink Panther having arrived recently. The attic's failure to yield an escape route was obvious at a glance. There was no place to go except down.

She could wait until someone missed her. Would Todd suspect where she'd gone? With all that had happened to their family, would anyone think that she too had been abducted? Put out an APB on her car? If they found it in this neighborhood, would they know to search this particular house? She hadn't told Todd about her earlier visit. She was stuck and needed a bathroom.

Bathroom! Another problem. The trio was eating pizza and guzzling beer. They'd probably stay in that room since it was the only place with chairs. But sooner or later, with all that beer—if she intended to make a break, it had to be sooner. She walked her mind through the first floor layout. The front and side carport entrances—they were out. Basement Bilco doors, ditto. And she had no idea how noisy the old metal doors would be, and she'd have to pass through their line of vision to access the cellar stairs. Windows. The back corner bedroom had a side window, not visible from the carport or the bathroom window. If there were no complicated screens or storm windows, she could climb out.

Retrieving the screwdriver from her jacket pocket, she wedged open the trap door uneventfully. Carefully, she angled it aside. By now, the guys in the living room were getting louder. Maybe she should stay—see if she could learn anything useful about Billy. From the stories they were swapping, however, she had learned nothing remotely connected to his abduction. Cautiously, silently, she slid onto the top platform step, leaving the trap door cracked in case she needed to make a hasty retreat. Then she slid farther, skinning her back where her shirt had pulled away from her jeans. She clamped a hand over her mouth to stifle a cry.

When she was sure she could place all three voices in the living room, she cracked the door and slipped out, easing it shut. She crept to the far corner bedroom, and much to her overwhelming relief, found the door was still closed. If anyone approached the bathroom, nothing would look out of place. The knob turned silently. She entered the dark interior, pausing briefly while her eyes adjusted.

The room had two small double-hung windows, one side and one rear. The screens, which should be in the alumi-

num-frame tracks, were missing. Storm windows were anchored behind the upper sash, which meant the windows
themselves were single-pane glass. Choosing the side window, she felt for the lock, eased it open while praying the
sash wouldn't stick.

It would not budge.

She tried the rear window, which also appeared to be
painted shut. Removing her jacket, she wrapped the handle
of her screwdriver in it and tapped the frame's edges. Her
timid motion, while quiet, was unproductive. Pausing momentarily to listen, she tried again, digging and prodding
the corners with the screwdriver's blade. Heavy footsteps
hit the uncarpeted hall floor, approaching what she prayed
was the bathroom door. It was. He went.

The moment she heard the toilet flush, she braced both
palms under the sash's lower edge and pushed with every
shred of her strength. With a lurch it gave way, admitting a
rush of fresh air that rattled the bedroom door. Leaping, she
hoisted herself belly down over the narrow sill, somersault-
ing and crunching into the bushes below. To her dismay,
she realized there was no way to close the window through
which rushed a stiff breeze that continued to rattle the door.

Only after she had bolted through the fence and into the
right-of-way did she risk a glance over her shoulder. An
overhead light in the rear bedroom, which moments ago had
hidden her in darkness, splashed probing rays into the yard.
Its beam silhouetted a large man closing the open window.
As Kingsley tore through the right-of-way, she heard male
voices circling the house.

Chapter 13

After putting many streets between herself and the Blakes' neighborhood, Kingsley's white-knuckled hands relaxed their grip on the wheel. By the streetlights' ebbing and flowing, she noticed the dried blood on her left hand. It throbbed incessantly. She touched it gingerly with her right thumb while keeping an eye on the road. Fog crept over the lowlands, rolling intermittent volleys across the road, forcing increased concentration on the remote secondary roads. She was grateful to finally pull onto the highway where a tractor trailer's taillights lead her safely to her exit. She relaxed.

Just how long the car with one headlight had been following her she couldn't be sure. What was that called—a *piddle*? She recalled her parents' stories about how they had watched for them, the first one to shout *piddle* getting a prize. What that was her folks wouldn't divulge. She glanced in the rearview mirror again, concluding that she too was leading a driver through the fog. It would disburse, then reappear like a white wall into which they were forced to plunge blindly, saved only by those red truck lights.

Careful to put on her turn signals well ahead of her exit, Kingsley noticed the car pull closer, as if to realign it with the truck that she had been following. Instead, it followed her, sans signal, onto her exit. Even as she left the access road for their private lane, the car remained with her, just slowing momentarily as she left the blacktop. Then it took off at a speed which she thought was entirely too fast for conditions.

Abandoning her car by her back door, she hurried into her sanctuary. As the rear door snapped shut behind her, she sagged against it in relief. Deep breaths, she admonished herself as she hugged her jacket against her cold body. Pandora pattered downstairs and approached like the fog on little cat feet. Kingsley scooped her into her arms and buried her face in Pandora's warm, silky fur. She reset the security code and, taking a deep breath of relief, entered the kitchen to fire the teakettle and give Pandora a treat.

Todd had left the hurricane lamp lit on the table beside a scrawled note.

Gone to Randall's. Needs help with his books. Again! Randall afraid to ask Barrie, what with the shareholder's meeting and all of her deadlines. If experience holds, you shouldn't wait up. Love you. T

Chilled more by nerves than untamed drafts, Kingsley turned the shower to hot, enabling steam to envelop the room. Clothes shed, she stepped into its welcoming warmth, yelping in pain as the water stung the scrapes on her back, arms, and hand. Gingerly, she soaped her aching body with fragrant bath gel, shampooed her hair, and then wrapped herself in a thirsty bath sheet. Swiping the mirror with her towel, she turned to study her back, relieved to find the scrapes were superficial. Nevertheless, she gently patted antibiotic cream onto the rakings.

Kingsley couldn't pinpoint what caught her attention, but suddenly she prickled. Nonsense, she chided herself, but killed the bathroom light while groping into her terrycloth robe. On high alert, she imagined faint noises that appeared to be coming from beyond the front yard. The noise seemed familiar, but she couldn't place it. Feeling for switches, she killed both the overhead in the upper hall and the one suspended over the staircase's landing.

She crept into the guest room and eased the door shut. *Weird. Who could be out there?* She peered through the darkness and heard what sounded like a shovel's contact with the earth. She squinted beyond the front yard. What wasn't shrouded in fog was pitch black. In time, hearing nothing and seeing nothing, she tried to shake the creepy feeling, a probable by-product of her evening's adventure. She returned to the bathroom but left off the light.

Snug in fleece jammies and cozy plush socks, she retrieved her stash of sandwich bags from her jacket pockets. Looking around for a good hiding place, she hid the bag with the burnt fireplace scraps between Grammy's Bible and her first edition of *Gone with the Wind*. The bag containing what resembled blue thread she took to the kitchen. Retrieving liquid Tide from the basement laundry, she mixed a generous amount with water in a small mixing bowl. Then she let the thread soak while she blew her hair dry in the powder room. When finished, she gave the thread one final swish, rinsed it, and rolled it in a clean kitchen towel. With her blow dryer set on low she carefully dried the thread.

Under the glare of a hundred-watt bulb, and with the aid of a magnifying glass, she could see—positively—not only blue but the exact aquamarine of Billy's beaver suit. The crimped thread stretched into a length of nearly one foot. Lost in her imagination, she stretched and released it, stretched and released the thread in her hands, as she imagined how he felt the last time she dressed him. Finally, she forced herself back to the present and wrapped the thread tightly around two fingers to concentrate the color.

At the computer, she opened their photo document file and selected Billy. The quantity of shots taken in less than two months astounded her. Advancing from group to group, she quickly isolated the photo of Billy wearing the sleeper. She magnified the image as much as possible, verifying that it looked exactly as she remembered. Then she compared it to the thread in her hand. Of course, the computer's version wouldn't be faithful, but it was close enough to convince her that she had a match. Billy's garment, which had disappeared that fateful day, had ended up in Ethelda Blake's fireplace.

Todd broke her concentration as he entered the back hall. "Todd! In here. You've got to come see this!" He circled behind her to squint at the monitor, then at the thread she had wound around her fingers. "I didn't go see Barrie tonight," she confessed.

✌✍✌

"What did you think they would do?" Todd asked Kingsley as they watched from their car. Police, dogs, and volunteers swarmed the Blakes' property and the surrounding neighborhood. They worked systematically toward the community park that ended at the creek's bank. Something or someone splashed into the water.

"I thought that after I told them that I'd gone to chat with Ethelda and saw the blue thread in the fireplace that they would have their probable cause. Put out a APB on her and make her tell them where Billy was. Guess those men cleaned out the fireplace a little too well. But this? I don't understand this."

Todd smiled sardonically. "All this time you've been begging them to focus on Ethelda. Now that they're going full bore, you're upset?"

"This is not what I wanted. I wanted them to find *her*." They heard incessant barking that was growing dimmer.

"I overheard someone say he's a cadaver dog, K. After they finished with the house and the neighborhood, they turned their attention to the creek where the ground is soft from the rain."

She started to shiver. "What if he's out there in a shallow

grave? That all this publicity scared the Blakes off? That they killed and buried him? What if he's been dead all along? I'm not prepared—I'll never be prepared."

"Let's assume that they're taking you seriously and eliminating every possibility. At least now they'll look for the Blakes."

"If only they'd searched that house in the first place. Billy might still have been there. I know—don't say it. The crooks have all the rights." She sagged into the gloom of the passenger seat, watching flashlights stab points of light throughout the dark that was overtaking the woods.

Someone wrapped on the glass. "It's getting too dark. We'll pick it up in the morning."

The following day the group reassembled, systematically searching, probing, and eliminating suspicious places where the soft ground had been disturbed. "Over here!" a voice sounded off near the creek. "Found…"

"Looks like bones," someone else said. Kingsley threw open the car door and crashed through mud and tall weeds to the spot where the group was converging. Someone had unearthed remains.

"Small animal—fox or raccoon. Maybe a groundhog. Definitely not human," came the response.

Kingsley groaned in relief. "One of these times, Todd, we won't be as lucky. I'd rather be wrong about the Blakes than have it end some place like this." The group moved on, probing their grid until finally the area was covered. The dog, she learned, had not responded to the scent he'd been given.

☙❧

"What does this mean?" Kingsley asked the detectives who took what now appeared to be their assigned seat in their living room. "You're not giving up on the Blakes. You saw the thread…"

"Ms. Henning, who let you into their house?"

"Nobody. The door was slightly ajar. I knocked, it opened farther, and I thought I heard someone say to come in."

"We both know that's not true. The owner swears he locked it when he left earlier that day."

"He's wrong."

"And I suppose the man and woman who were with him and saw him do it were also mistaken?"

"What others?" she asked, trying to force her face back to an innocent demeanor. She'd trapped herself.

He measured his words. "Look. You, as a private citizen, may think you can get away with things that we can't because police are bound by laws, policies, and procedures. What you can do is disturb evidence, to say nothing of getting yourself sued or possibly arrested. You can't just ransack somebody's house."

"But I found the thread."

"Well, we didn't. And even if we had, you disturbed potential evidence. And you don't understand what's going on in that neighborhood. It's in decline—you can see that by driving around nearby blocks. Post WWII housing, sturdy but old, built for returning vets and their families. The Blakes' street has formed a little association devoted to keeping up property value. They paint, they landscape, they remodel, and upgrade. They saw that rental property as a threat, so they launched a campaign to vilify the owner as a slumlord and force him to sell. What they are is the 'pretty police.' The pair accompanying the owner had just inspected it for code violations. There were none. Everything that house needs is cosmetic. You're lucking out. The owner doesn't want any adverse publicity, which charging you with trespassing would cause. He has other properties and doesn't need the aggravation."

"But I didn't—"

"Enough. Please. Ms. Henning, you've got to quit playing detective. Let us do our job."

She glowered at him. "How many more times are we going to replay this conversation? Do I have to say it again? It's been thirteen days! Where is my baby? You may be an experienced detective, but you'll never be a mother or know how I feel."

"Fathers have feelings, too," he said. "Before I came here I was on a big city force. Lived in a working class neighborhood with my wife and my son. He was in the wrong place at the wrong time. Got caught in the crossfire of a drug deal gone bad. He was only eleven."

Kingsley opened her mouth to fire her next volley but stopped, stunned. "I'm sorry," she said. "It's just that I feel so helpless. That if I don't come up with something in time, we'll never find him. Each minute that passes he slips farther and farther away."

Todd, who had been listening in silence, rose from his chair. "I think we'd better call it a day. Thank you for the update."

The detective pulled his keys from his pocket and fingered them thoughtfully for a moment. "We'll have some more questions to ask you, perhaps at the station. But if you get any more inspirations, please. Don't take any action. Call us, okay?"

"And you'll take me seriously—yeah, right," she muttered.

Todd led the detectives out the front door, then returned and approached her. Silently they hugged. "What are you thinking?" he asked when he finally released her.

"That he's taking a different approach. I don't trust his kinder, friendlier veneer. I'm not buying that sad puppy look either. In fact, I bet he made up that story about his kid. And you'll notice he didn't tell us that we are no longer suspects. The police aren't our friends. We can't let down our guard for a minute. And if they think we're going to give up, they're insane."

⁂

The elegant lady in casual attire preceded her husband off the hotel elevator. She looked left and then right at the room numbering system. "Number six-zero-four should be that way," she said pointing left. Clutching his hand, she moved in its direction but stopped one room short.

"What's wrong?"

"Suddenly I'm scared. We've waited so long and been through so much. What if something goes wrong? What if—"

"Nothing will go wrong. I've made sure of that." Her husband propelled her forward by her elbow and stopped at room 604. He knocked. A matronly woman in a nurse's uniform admitted them wordlessly then disappeared into the connecting room.

Their attorney, a heavyset man in an impeccable gray suit, rose from a round table centered beneath the drawn draperies that shaded them from the midwestern sun. Beaming, he hurried toward them, his hand extended. She asked in a whisper, "Is he here? Can we see him?"

"I guess the paperwork can wait a few minutes. This way, please." The attorney approached the connecting room with a sweep of his hand as if to part the very air that separated the couple from their dream. She eased into the darkened room and approached the crib. A baby in yellow velour slept on his back, head turned ninety degrees, his tiny mouth making sucking motions.

"Matthew! May I?" Tentatively, she lifted the baby into her arms and looked in awe at her husband. "He is so sweet. And so small for five months."

The woman scowled. "Premature. Mother was probably malnourished too." To the husband's disapproving frown she quickly added, "Doctor says he's perfectly healthy. That he's catching up quickly."

The attorney touched the husband's elbow. "Why don't we wrap up the paperwork so you and your wife can take Matthew home?" He led the new parents back to the table on which he had laid several unmarked ten-by-twelve white envelopes. Abruptly his demeanor turned to business. As the attorney opened the envelopes, the woman nestled the baby in her arms. Awake now, he gazed in wonder at her.

"Make damned sure you keep your story straight. As I've emphasized to you from day one, the US does not have diplomatic relations with Matthew's birth country. One little slip could jeopardize your situation as well as the humanitarian efforts of those who are rescuing war orphans from squalid conditions. For your protection, as well as Matthew's, I cannot reveal which country."

"I understand. But you're positive that he has no family? You exhausted every possibility—"

The attorney lowered his head and shook it. "The civil war has been raging for years. Even if there were enough food and medicine for these orphans, in time, they'd become street waifs. Or they'd be dead. Part of your fee, besides paying off foreign bureaucrats, will provide for other less fortunate older youngsters who won't have Matthew's opportunities. That's part of their deal."

"You promised me an authentic birth certificate."

The attorney selected one envelope and withdrew several documents including the certificate. "Let me review, one more time, the story as you understand it, should anyone insist on knowing the details. You agreed that the identity of the baby's mother remains confidential. You don't know her name, where she's from, and agreed to research neither. All you know is that she's the adolescent daughter of a strict, religious family. In relinquishing parental rights, her identity will be protected as if the baby never existed."

"What can we tell him when he grows up? He's bound to ask difficult questions."

"When Matthew's an adult, you can share what little you know about his origins, even though he has no family or country to trace. I suggest you expand his records immediately. I've provided a social security number. Start his savings account, college fund, get him on a waiting list for your alma mater, and so on."

"Matthew's first appointment with the pediatrician we chose is on Thursday," the new mother said.

"Good." The attorney opened another white envelope and withdrew legal documents. "If you'll just sign at the Xs. Here, use my pen."

"And this states that…"

"Among other things, you'll make no attempt to locate the birth mother."

The couple signed and pushed the papers back to the attorney and, as if on cue, the husband took out his checkbook. He scribbled the date. "I believe the balance is two hundred thousand dollars?"

"On delivery."

New dad looked at new mom who was cuddling their baby now known as Matthew. Alert but quiet, the baby focused his deep blue eyes intently on her face. "'On delivery.' How appropriate." He finished writing the check.

The attorney smiled with deep satisfaction as he slipped the check into his folio. "There is no way that anyone, ever, can show up on your doorstep to disrupt your family. You have made a brilliant investment."

Chapter 14

Kingsley startled, grabbed the clock, and held it two inches from her nearsighted eyes. It was nearly eight-thirty. One more night had passed without any word, for better or worse. She moaned and dropped back onto her pillow, still clutching the clock.

"If we're going to make church, you'd better move it," Todd said.

She groped for her glasses and saw he was already dressed in a navy suit, sky blue and white striped shirt and a navy silk tie. She smiled at the man who had put up and shut up so many times during those awful days. Slipping out of bed, she encircled him in a hug.

"You are obscenely handsome, you know that?" she asked.

"Only if you say so. Now come on." He gave her butt a playful slap.

"Maybe this isn't the greatest idea."

"Last evening you thought that just being with our support system would give us a lift."

"To be honest, it's not about our church friends. I'm just so angry…"

"At God?"

"If God is all powerful, how could He let this awful thing happen?"

"He didn't. It's about free will, both good and evil. Let's

just put one foot in front of the other and wrestle with the theological questions some other time."

Following the service, they lingered over coffee in the large parish hall. Close friends ventured a few tactful questions, but soon everyone within earshot had gravitated toward them. Without planning to do so, they found themselves giving an impromptu update.

"You're really allowed to see the security video?" someone asked.

"We've seen them so many times that I see them in my sleep," Kingsley said. "It's so frustrating! I know there's a clue in there somewhere, but we can't find it." Heads nodded compassionately, and a long pause signaled the end of the briefing. The group drifted, collecting their families to go home to dinner.

One woman hung back. "You mentioned sleep. When I have a tough challenge, I make a list of all the details and my alternatives. I read it over one last time before bedtime, then I set it aside—let my subconscious chew on it while I'm asleep. You know what? Invariably in the morning, something clicks. Some detail that I've overlooked. It might work for you."

"I'll try it. Thank you," Kingsley said, returning her hug.

Todd gathered their umbrellas and helped Kingsley on with her raincoat. "Todd, could we run by the bank one more time? I need one more pass at the tapes."

"If we can eat first."

"I know just the place."

❧❧❧

"What do you expect to find that wasn't there yesterday?" he asked.

"Something on the blank footage we never watched frame by frame, thinking it was an empty corridor. Maybe it wasn't. Or someone who leaves for the fire drill and returns looking different. Or turns his face to blow his nose." Todd frowned, as if replaying what he had seen. "And behavior. Anything strange, no matter how trivial, especially avoiding the cameras."

Chas met them in the lobby, happily accepting their bag of Dunkin' Donuts' assorted croissant sandwiches and a tray of hot coffee. He settled them into the captain's chairs, brushing aside their apologies for disrupting his Sunday. They watched the entire recording as it glided in slow motion, including frames of the empty hall, while they sipped orange juice and coffee in between bites of their brunch.

"There," Kingsley said. "We never spoke to the man with the box. The one who brought up the rear but took the stairwell to the side exit. Who is he anyway?"

Todd looked through the folder of notes he'd collected from various sources. "His name is Nevin Green. He works in Purchasing on three. His group's assigned location is on the right side of the building."

"I'd like to call him. I know it's a stretch, but maybe he saw something he wouldn't know is important. Is his home number on Shirley's printout?" Todd rummaged through a folder and extracted the dog-eared sheets. He located the Gs. Kingsley poked his number into her phone.

Nevin Green answered immediately, his voice rich and jovial. "The wife and I were just saying how sorry we are about your little boy, and how we'd feel if it had been our baby years ago. If there's anything that we can do—the police asked all kinds of questions. I told them I saw nothing unusual, but my mind was focused on my own problems."

"Do you remember the events of that day?"

"Do I ever! It was the morning from hell. Our house has a one-car garage and single driveway. Rather than play musical cars every morning with the wife and our son, I park in the street. That morning my car wouldn't start. Dead as a doornail. Know what the mechanic found? Someone put sand—*sand!*—in my gas tank! By the time I'd had the thing towed, assessed the damage, called my insurance agent, got a ride home, and arranged for a rental, I didn't get to the bank until mid-afternoon."

"That's terrible. Do you remember where you were when the fire alarm sounded?"

"Sure do. I said, 'That's all I need.' I had just entered the lobby from the front entrance when the ruckus began. Since I had a rental, I'd parked in one of those choice visitor spots rather than hike to my assigned spot way up on the hill. I had an appointment with a vendor at three and already was late. So I called my fire drill captain and gave him my location. He said, 'Roger that,' and I jumped back in the rental and left for my meeting."

"Then you never went to your office?"

"Correct."

Kingsley sighed. "That's not what the tape shows. Are you sure you didn't exit across from the daycare"

"I made a U-turn around the fountain and left by the lobby entrance." Kingsley scrounged her memory for what she had seen on the video. "What were you wearing?"

"My favorite sports coat. It's a joke between the wife and me. She says I drink too much beer. That I'm getting fat. When that coat no longer fits, she's putting me on a diet. Damned thing got tight as sausage skin. Then about a month ago someone stole it from my car. Talk about luck! I found a ringer in the next size. Is that great or what?"

Kingsley covered the receiver and hissed to Todd that something didn't sound right. "Mr. Green, could you possibly come down to the bank and look at some security footage?"

Todd tapped her shoulder and whispered, "K, that's not a good idea. What if he's—"

She ignored him. "Just come as you are. We'll meet you at the security desk in the lobby."

❧❧❧

Nevin Green arrived in a Penn State sweatshirt and faded

jeans that drooped half-mast below his apple-shaped belly. Chas queued up the video. Nevin leaned forward, his beaky nose nearly touching the screen. His jaw dropped, face frozen in disbelief.

"Why, we could be twins! And look at that jacket!" Without being asked, Chas replayed the sequence in slow motion. "Stop there," Nevin directed. "Back up a bit and freeze it." Chas did. Everyone stared at the image.

"What do you see?" Todd asked.

"Sure as hell looks like me. Could be my double. But on closer inspection, not quite."

"In what way?"

"Hair's all wrong," He rubbed his hand through his coarse salt-and-pepper thatch. "This is all mine. That guy's got a rug."

"Are you sure?"

"How many fifty-year-olds do you know who got hair like mine? Comes from my mom's side of the family. That guy's wearing one ugly hairpiece."

"Do you recognize him?"

"Never seen him before. I'd remember 'cause it would sure give me a start. Run it by me again at regular speed." They all watched. "There. That's something. He toes straight ahead. I walk like a duck. And see how he's holding that box by the flap? I know shipping, and that box looks to be twelve by eight by four. His hand is quite small." Nevin held up a paw, which made everyone smile.

"Anything else?"

Nevin watched then hopped to his feet. "Hey! Now that's different. If I'm carrying anything, I fling the door wide—not hard enough to hit the wall, but enough so my elbow doesn't get whacked on the rebound. That's a good way to get bursitis. Now, this guy opened the door just wide enough to slip through and—looks to me like—I outweigh him by thirty pounds."

"Did you wear your hound's-tooth sports coat that day?"

"Sure did. When I see vendors, I make better deals if I look like one of them. Suit and tie doesn't cut it." They watched the video several more times until they exhausted the subject. At that point, Nevin left with their thanks.

Chas left briefly and returned with a small carton. "I've made copies for you to take home, although our system has options your home computer won't. The copies contain everything captured by our cameras from your son's first day with us."

The parents inspected the box that contained dozens of thumb drives. "That's quite a stash!"

"By *all*, I meant every camera throughout the complex. Knock yourselves out. Maybe you'll find something everyone missed, like Elvis coming or going. Come back any time. I mean it! In the meantime, I'll report our imposter to the police."

Kingsley asked, "Can you isolate and print the best picture you have of that man? Focus it as clearly as you can? I have an idea."

"You bet."

Kingsley patted his arm. "You'll never know how much it means to have someone like you on our side. We'll never forget it."

Back in their car, they rehashed what they'd learned. Todd rubbed his neck and closed his eyes as if looking into the back of his mind. "If somebody went to such extraordinary lengths to create an impostor, the question is *why*—and for what purpose? What did he hope to accomplish?"

"He never entered the daycare," Kingsley said. "If he's involved, why didn't he?"

"He was expert in moving his head with the changing light so we never got a clear view of his face. Maybe the police technicians can enhance the image."

❧

Kingsley directed Todd down the Blakes' street and

stopped by the next-door neighbor's white picket fence. Luck reigned as the woman was sitting out back in full view of the road. Kingsley opened the gate, calling a greeting as she circled the house. Todd brought up the rear.

"Have a seat," the woman said, motioning toward two Adirondack chairs. She eyed Todd approvingly, giving Kingsley a gap-toothed grin. "That's more excitement than this neighborhood has seen since the fire of eighty-nine. I'm glad they didn't find something awful."

"I'm sorry I made so much trouble."

"Trouble! In case you didn't notice, the slumlord's already painting that house. Rumor has it that he's going to sell. Now if we can just get a nice young family—you guys interested?"

Todd shook his head. "We already have a place of our own."

Kingsley opened the folder tucked under her arm. "Ma'am, would you please look at this photograph? It's only a partial profile, but does he look like Mr. Blake?"

The woman pushed her bifocals up on her nose and reacted immediately. "Blake's nothing like that. I'd say he's mid- to late-twenties, five-ten or eleven. Skinny—the sinewy type. Blond hair, a real brassy shade that must have been bleached. This guy's old enough to be his father."

"Have you ever seen him before?"

She shook her head. "Nope. And I'd remember. I'm in charge of the neighborhood watch, and we don't cotton to strangers. And that man looks like trouble! You like flowers? Have a garden? Come! I'll show you my perennials." She snipped a fragrant bouquet of lilacs for Kingsley. "Let's keep in touch," she said, handing over the bouquet that ranged from white to lavender to stormy purple. "If you turn your back on perennials for just a second, they take over. I love to share what I must divide. And these lilacs have sprouted lots of new plants."

"I'd love that," she said. "And thank you for all your help."

"You keep on looking, and we'll keep on praying. And, if they ever come back, I'll give you a call—that is, if you share your number."

As they climbed back into the car, Todd said, "They won't be back. So, any other ideas?"

"Only the manpower that this kidnapping took. And that terrifies me."

Chapter 15

Kingsley sat propped on their four-poster bed, having commandeered all the pillows. Copious notes escaped from her folders onto the sheets and comforter. She had watched the videos on their Mac until her eyes stung. Straining to leave nothing out, she organized her list and set it aside. It was only ten-thirty. Perhaps if she stayed up until midnight, she could sleep through the night.

She dreaded trying to sleep. She couldn't control old nightmares that sluiced from her depths and battered the gates of her mind. Sometimes they would retreat for months, but under stress, they would resurface. She would be drawn through a tunnel that only got darker in which there was no light, no sound, no feel, smell or temperature. Not a whisper of air and no guideposts. Nothingness. Everyone, everything, forever gone. She would awaken, gasping for air, exhausted and terrified that God didn't exist. Better to just stay awake a while longer.

She slid to the floor and set the list on the bedside table, then wandered to the front corner window. The coach lights between their lane and the front porch rippled a wave of light onto white bleeding hearts. She remembered her promise at Billy's baptism: *If anyone ever harms one hair on your head…*

If she could find the people responsible, would she be able to kill them? Could she, as they had promised on Billy's behalf, *respect the dignity of every human being*? Or would the people who perpetrated this horror even qualify as human?

Her eyes swept their bedroom, lovingly renovated. The glowing pine planks beneath Grammy's Persian rug, their own cherry dresser, armoire, rice-carved bed, and tall bedside tables. Todd's chair, ottoman, and floor lamp, angled in his corner. Her channel-back chair and needlepoint footstool in her front corner. And finally, against the original exterior stone wall that now separated their room from the bathroom and hall stood Grammy's vanity and bench replete with its original tapestry brocade.

She had sat on that bench while Todd straddled its end as she tried on her diamond earrings the evening he proposed. And she'd sat there drying her hair the day Billy was born, telling frantic Todd to relax. That first babies just don't fall out. She had waited so long that Billy was nearly born in the car during the Valentine blizzard. Billy. He occupied every corner of her mind, and would until the tunnel enclosed her for the last time.

She was tempted to sit in his room for a while but forced herself to a better alternative. She wanted to sleep. Was desperate to sleep. Perhaps a history book from the library downstairs.

Kingsley paused in the foyer outside the glass library doors. Soft lights illuminated the aging Appalachian cherry from which their ten-foot bookshelves were made. They had joked that they'd never fill three walls with books, but the addition of photos, keepsakes, antiques, and memorabilia made them look finished. As she entered, Todd tugged off his reading glasses and patted his lap. She snuggled against his broad chest.

"If that list is finished, it's bedtime," he said.

"It's too early. And I want to check one last sequence." She clicked the remote, fast forwarded, and stopped where the imposter entered the stairwell. She repeated it a second and then a third time, pausing every few frames."

"Anything?" Todd asked. She shook her head. "Enough, then. Tomorrow's another day."

ɔɔɛɔ

Kingsley awoke, or thought that she did, in the dead of night. Her body felt leaden, but her mind's eye was able to turn to her right. Todd was asleep, lying beside her. While knowing her eyelids were actually closed, she could still see. A great calm sustained her. The detachment of body and mind felt surreal yet almost normal.

Strange, she thought. She didn't need contacts or glasses to see. She gazed at the arched frame over her bed that supported a fishnet canopy. She should be worried that it shouldn't be there, but she wasn't. *Dreaming. I must be dreaming. I'm really asleep.* Her mind's eye studied the canopy then slid down the posters that held it up. The turns and twists were not her own but were dearly familiar. Grammy. She was dreaming of Grammy's own bedroom and the bed on which she had napped as a child. The same bed that now occupied her guest room across the hall.

Her mind turned toward Todd, but he hadn't moved. The wall in the corner behind his chair was painted white, and their wedding picture, snapped in her parents' garden, hung on the wall. She seemed to rise to a seated position, just high enough to see the opposite wall where Grammy's flowered wallpaper had somehow replaced the stone wall. She turned back toward the photo, but that wall was unchanged, and Todd hadn't moved.

Soon she was aware that Grammy's vanity and bench were no longer located on the opposite wall. They had moved to the interior wall facing the window. She remembered. That's where Grammy's had been. Far from alarmed and totally at peace, she was able to scan the whole room, while unable to move.

"Kingsley!" She looked toward motionless Todd then

around for the voice that was calling her name. "Kingsley!"

Grammy! She'd know that voice anywhere. She should be frightened, hearing it after so many years, but she wasn't. On Grammy's bench sat two figures. Her body strained to move toward them, but she couldn't lift as much as a finger.

She glanced back at Todd then at the bench. The two figures sharpened, and finally she saw them quite clearly. *Impossible*, she told herself. *This is a dream, but it feels so real*. Perhaps if she didn't move the dream would continue.

"Kingsley." The other one spoke. It was Andy, her young husband who had died in a fiery crash. His skin was now perfect and taut with an unworldly shine, unlike the blistered horror she'd seen in the morgue.

"He isn't with us," he said.

"*What*?" Kingsley thought, struggling to grasp what he meant.

He merely repeated, "Billy isn't with us."

Grammy spoke next. "Look for the shadow."

Her mind called soundlessly across the great chasm. "What shadow? What do you know? Tell me. Please tell me more. Do you know where he is?"

"He isn't with us," Andy repeated.

"The shadow. You must look for the shadow."

Kingsley wrenched her body from its moorings, finally succeeding in pulling herself into an upright position. Before she could reach the figures, the vision evaporated. She found herself standing alone in the middle of the room, barefooted on Grammy's rug. The wallpaper was gone, replaced with the stone wall, and the vanity was back in position.

"Kingsley?" Todd sat up in bed. "What's wrong? Are you all right?"

"I saw Grammy and Andy, over there. The vanity had moved." She crossed the room and touched its surface, then fingered the adjacent bare wall. "Grammy said, 'Look for the shadow,' and Andy said, 'He isn't with us.'" She shivered.

"Come here, K. You've been dreaming, and you're cold."

"It was so real. But I couldn't reach them." She crawled into bed and scrunched herself, fetal-like, against him. He held her tightly.

"I think Andy meant that Billy's alive. Grammy and Andy were such good people. They'd be in Heaven, and an innocent baby who died without knowing evil would be with them. What do you think Grammy meant about shadows?"

"Do you really think they could come back to give you a message?"

Kingsley sighed. "Of course not. But I believe love passes the vale—Grammy used to say, 'Nobody's ever completely gone as long as someone remembers and loves them.' My sleeping mind must have revealed something I saw and let them deliver the message. I'm convinced more than ever that Billy's alive. And we've got to find him ourselves."

The soft glow of dawn creased the side window and softened the room. "What time is it, hon?"

He tilted the clock on his bedside table. "Five-thirty."

"'*Look for the shadow.*' What could that mean? Surely not in this house. At the bank? In the daycare? On the video?"

Todd said, "Let's go look for some shadows."

৩৩৩

Kingsley concentrated on the bank's state-of-the-art video feed and, on the third slow-motion pass, she saw what she'd been missing. "That's it! Chas, is it okay if Todd walks down the hall on the live camera? I want to watch him."

"Sure. We can do that."

"Todd, go through the stairway door opposite the day-care, stand there a few moments, then turn around and walk back. Slowly."

"What are you looking for?"

"Just do it. I want to try a little experiment." He walked while she watched, then he returned to the studio. Both men looked baffled. "Chas, do you have a set of walkie-talkies we can use?"

"I'll get them." He returned shortly and handed her one.

"Watch me closely," she said into hers as she walked down the hall. "Can you see me all right?"

"Keep going."

"Okay then, follow me on the monitor and keep telling me where I am."

"You're approaching the daycare door—no, you're opening the stairwell door, passing through it, and I can no longer see you."

Several moments elapsed. "Now guess where I am."

"I assume that you're climbing the stairs or descending the short flight to the parking lot door at the bottom of the stairwell." A long pause followed with no communication.

"K? Where are you? What are you doing?" Todd asked into the walkie-talkie while studying the monitor for signs of his wife.

"If you were to bet where I am right now, where would that be?" she asked at last.

"In the stairwell."

"Are you watching closely?" As Todd and Chas studied the monitor, Kingsley stepped out of the daycare.

"How did you do that?"

"Watch the monitor again. I'm going to walk through the stairwell door and start toward the exit. Then I'll repeat it, heading upstairs. There's a light in the ceiling. Watch for my shadow on the far wall." She went through the motions.

"I see it," Todd said. "Or at least I could briefly when the door wasn't in the way."

She re-entered the hallway and waved to them. "Now watch again. Look for my shadow." She pushed the stairwell door open and passed through it. While the door was closing, they stared at the wall. There was no shadow.

Kingsley hurried back to the men. "That's how he did it. There's a blind spot. The camera shoots knee high and above. The man with the box went through the door, dropped to the ground behind the door, and then belly-crawled below camera range, across the hall, and into the nursery—its entry is right there. I'm betting the doll was in that box. Then he crawled back out the same way. He had plenty of time before the all-clear sounded, and if anyone saw him, he'd look like Nevin." Excitedly, Kingsley pointed to Chas's keyboard. "See if the video shows the stairwell door moving without anyone passing through it while everyone else was outside." They focused hard. "There! There it is, without a shadow. That's when he left after putting the doll in the nursery."

"I guess if anyone noticed at all, they'd assume that someone started to open the door from inside the stairwell, changed his mind, and went out the back door instead."

Todd darkened. "K, this is very revealing, but how does this help us find Billy? You've figured out how the kidnapper could put the doll in the crib, but nobody knows his identity."

"It gives us one more bad guy for the police to track down, and we've got his picture. Beyond that, we've just got to keep digging."

Chapter 16

Henry Alderson unlocked the front door of his family's secluded Georgian mansion in St. Davids and called to Sarah from the grand foyer. While straining to hear her response, he angled left through the living room then reversed right into the dining room. Fresh flowers spilled from a cut-glass pitcher, which meant Sarah had finished refreshing the vases.

He peered into the kitchen behind the dining room, then went back to the foyer and called her again. He tried his study behind the foyer then entered the sunroom in the left rear quadrant. A glance through the patio doors and the flagstones beyond told him his wife wasn't tending her gardens. He paused—remembering—nearly one year ago when Kingsley and Todd were married at the edge of the garden that bordered the woods.

"Sarah?" Her muffled response drew him toward her lower level studio. Sarah was perched on her long-legged chair, cordless phone in her hand. Artists' materials covered her workbench. Five antique blue mason jars filled with fresh flowers lined the far edge of its surface. Over her shoulder, he scrutinized her artwork. She had been sketching new scenes for her line of stationery that upscale boutiques carried throughout the Northeast.

"Pick up," Sarah said, covering the mouthpiece. "It's Kingsley. More trouble."

Henry crossed to a wicker grouping by the patio doors and sinking into a rocker, picked up the landline.

"Honey, Dad's on," Sarah said. "Start over. Bounce off him what you told me. He'll know what to do."

"Dad, those two detectives who questioned us last week—who suggested Billy was a hindrance to our careers? Today they 'invited' us to the police station to 'have a chat.' Showed us a picture of the kid who set off the fire alarm. She asked me questions like 'how long have you known this boy?' And 'Why did you put him up to it?' Seems the police had an anonymous tip linking us to the boy. It's creepy, Dad. She focuses cold, unblinking eyes on me while her partner goes after Todd."

"Tell Dad what you told her, honey."

"Todd started addressing both of them. It was like watching a tennis match. So I did likewise. Todd said he didn't recognize the boy. I told them everything I knew— that he's sort of a pet at the branch, according to Connie, the branch manager. He comes in with his mother. He loves the atrium garden. Sits on the wall to watch the fountain and feed the coy. He makes penny wishes. Connie gave up trying to get his mom to bank by direct deposit and the ATM. It's a biweekly outing for them on their way to Easter Seals, where he goes for physical therapy."

"The boy is disabled?"

"It's not obvious. He has mild cerebral palsy and a slight limp. Holds one arm a bit oddly. But it was enough for Connie to identify him, although a stranger might not have noticed."

"What else did you tell Detective Flynn?"

"That I'd never spoken to him. I had noticed him a couple times and heard people talk about him. Dad, he asked if we wanted to have an attorney present before they asked us any more questions."

"What did you say to that?"

"Before I could speak, Todd jumped in his face and told him that *he* would need an attorney if this persecution didn't cease immediately. That their 'inability to surface and investigate viable suspects underscores their incompetence, laziness, and lack of interest in finding our son.' That he'd 'better get the job done or Todd was going to hire professional help to clean up their mess and find our child.' I've never seen him that angry. He was livid. She backed down after Todd told them that the little Miranda ploy wouldn't work—that anyone who watches *Law and Order* knows that."

"Tell Dad how they responded to your FBI question."

"When I asked why the FBI wasn't all over this, he said that since there was no evidence of federal crime, like terrorism, or that 'the boy' was taken over state lines. It was a local crime—that the FBI would have to be 'invited' by local police." So Todd said, 'You're using our child's kidnapping to further a turf war with the feds? Take your pissing contest to a basketball court and get all the help you can muster. Maybe I'll call them myself.' Can we do that, Dad?"

Henry ignored that question, asking instead what happened next. "Todd said that if we weren't under arrest, we were leaving. And we did."

Henry was silent a moment. "Honey, your godfather is a damned fine attorney. He has called twice since he returned from Great Britain. He'd be appalled that you'd speak without representation. He wants to jump in, but you've got to invite him yourself."

"The detective insinuated that innocent people don't need attorneys."

"Bull! That's just a ploy to take unfair advantage of uninformed people."

"What if the so-called evidence is leaked to the press? Will everyone turn against us? Just when I think I can cope for five minutes—"

"I'm calling David. You three should talk."

"All right—if you don't think it will make us look guilty."

"*They* won't have to know."

"Honey, you can't worry about what other people think," Sarah said. "Remember what Grammy would say. 'Pray, then step back. Let God lead, and then follow.' I say, 'Focus.' You're making progress, even if it doesn't seem like you are. Tell Dad what else you thought about the boy."

"I'm convinced that the kidnapping couldn't have taken place without a diversion. We watched him hit the fire alarm on the security video. The boy told the police some kid at school bet him ten dollars he wouldn't do it. The boy said he needed the money to buy a Mother's Day present."

"But the detectives didn't believe him."

"They think he was put up to it, all right—by us. You know, there's something odd about that boy. Each time I watch the feed, I think something's wrong, but I can't put my finger on it."

"Describe the event and leave nothing out," Sarah said.

"It's a short sequence. The boy approaches the atrium fountain with his distinctive gait, half-circles the garden to the far side, enters the mouth of the corridor to his left, hits the alarm on the right-hand wall, then exits through the stairwell door that's just to the right of the alarm."

"Where are the security cameras?" Henry asked.

"There's one on the second floor balcony. It has a panoramic view of the front entrance, lobby, and the branch's glass wall. The other camera, on the opposite wall, catches the garden and radiating corridors."

"Did the cameras show the boy's expression?"

"His face looks, well, placid."

"He doesn't turn at all?" Henry asked.

"No."

"That's what's odd, Kingsley. Do you remember all the pranks you and your cousins used to play on each other? How did you figure out who did it?"

"That was easy—they looked guilty. Oh my gosh! That's it. Don't you think that a kid who'd been dared to pull a fire alarm at a five-story bank building would be nervous? That he'd look around to make sure no one was watching? He didn't. He hit the alarm as calmly as if he were pushing an elevator button. And he didn't sprint through the stairwell door, either. That had to be planned. He was coached."

"Honey, what are you going to do?" Sarah asked.

"Tell you what I'm not going to do. Share with the police. If I get myself into trouble, I'll call Uncle David. Meanwhile, Todd and I will try to talk to this kid and his mother."

"Honey, be careful," Sarah said, an edginess creeping into her tone.

"Talk to Uncle David anyway, you hear?" her father added.

"I *will* be careful, I promise. Love you both."

"We love you too."

৩৩৩

Incessant pounding brought Kingsley dashing to her front door. Through the peephole, she recognized the detective. Others, dressed in black jumpsuits, were disbursing throughout her front yard.

"Warrant to search the property," the detective said, thrusting a bundle of folded papers at her without making eye contact.

She scanned the yard, quickly comprehending the scene from TV and movies. A half dozen professionals began walking a grid, eyes sweeping the ground. "Why? What do you want? What are you looking for?"

"It's all in the warrant," he said, turning his attention to his mission. He called to several officers who carried shovels, "Start back by the woods."

Responding to the commotion, Todd strode through the foyer into the front yard. Kingsley gave him the papers. Quickly he scanned them. "What the hell—they're looking for evidence that Billy is buried on our property?"

He tipped the papers for her to follow where his finger jabbed. "Infant clothing, a blue garment in particular. Hey!" he screamed at the one barking the orders, charging toward him. "What's the meaning of this?"

"We have information that evidence pertinent to your son's kidnapping was buried in your yard. You'll have to stay back or go inside." His voice was cold. Cutting.

"What kind of evidence? Who told you that?"

"I'm not at liberty to say."

"Over here!" The entire group moved toward a spot where the lawn met the woods. "Looks freshly disturbed." Rather than attacking the spot with shovels, two of them probed the surface gently, enlarging it with trowels and gloved hands.

"Oh, dear God! Todd! Could anyone possibly have brought Billy here? Buried him in our woods? That would be the ultimate cruelty." Kingsley crept toward them, but immediately the police ordered her back.

"Found something." A voice at the edge of the woods signaled the others.

Kingsley wrenched herself free and dashed toward the man who held up a black plastic garbage bag. It appeared to be heavy. Setting it down, he slashed it open. Probing judiciously, he withdrew a smaller white bag that bore the logo of an upscale boutique. He set it down on the ground, eyeballed the contents. He reached inside. Grasped something.

Raising his hand above the bag's opening, he let dirt, tiny pebbles, and ashes trickle through his fingers back into the bag. What he withdrew appeared to be a small wad of cloth. Without letting the debris escape the bag's opening, he held up the cloth for inspection.

"Let me see that." The man in charge snapped on vinyl gloves and gingerly lifted the object by its edge. Gently he shook it, letting whatever clung to its surface fall back into the bag. The fabric was blue with a hint of red stitching.

"You recognize this? No, don't touch it." From somewhere in the woods that fronted the property, a series of light bulbs fired in rapid succession.

"Why, it's Billy's beaver suit. See the red embroidery that outlines the animal? How on earth did it get here?" She looked over the detective's shoulder at the search team, two of whom remained by the hole.

The others had returned to walking the grid. She heard one of them say *undisturbed*. They scanned the property, and then when something flagged their attention, headed toward the house's southern foundation.

"You were saying…"

Voice cracking, she struggled to speak. "The big bag—what's in it? Oh, dear God…"

"Appears to be nothing but dirt. Now—what about that garment?"

Kingsley gulped air, hyperventilating.

"Can't you see what a shock this is?" Todd snarled at him.

Kingsley held up her hand. "I'm okay." She looked at the fabric, still dangling from the detective's gloved hand. "After I fed Billy at noon on the day he was kidnapped, I left the beaver suit in his cubby in the babies' quiet room. It was too small to use as a spare, but I left it in his cubby, needing room in my bag for his laundry. I never saw it again."

"He didn't wear it that day?"

"No. He wore it once, weeks ago. It was a newborn size, and Billy weighed over ten pounds when he was born. I put it on him and took his picture to send to the friend who gave it to me. I hated to have her think that he couldn't use it. The sleeper was so cute. I intended to pack it away for another…" She choked, and couldn't continue.

"He didn't wear it that day?"

She took a deep breath. "Weren't you listening? It's too small. Look in the neck. If it's still there, the label should read *NB*—that's newborn. He weighs twelve pounds. If you check the security feed, you'll see that the outfit he wore had wide green and blue stripes."

Kingsley read the detective's expression as blatant disbelief. *Do not let him screw with your mind.*

Todd stepped a few inches closer. "Did I understand you to say that you had a tip? Tell me, Detective. Just how could anyone know about this unless *they* put it there? The trees are too dense for anyone stopping on the access road to see in. Amish farms border our property on the west and north. They have no reason to be near our property. And besides, they don't have phones or read our newspapers. To the east, beyond our land, is rental cropland. So how is it that someone could give you a tip?"

The detective smirked sardonically. "Our point. Exactly. Perhaps you or your confederate—"

"Todd! I heard something out here. The night you went to help Randall with his books. I was supposed to go to the mall. Remember? I couldn't make it out at the time, but the sound was familiar. Now I'm positive. It was digging. Lord knows I've dug enough holes in our gardens to recognize it." She couldn't stop staring at the remains of the blue beaver suit. "Are you going to arrest us for something?"

"We'll analyze everything."

Todd glared at the detective. "He couldn't anyway, K. There's no law against burying outgrown clothes on one's own property."

"Unless the contents contain evidence of a crime."

"You mean the dirt in the bag? Could anyone be ghoulish enough to..." Words failed her, but everyone grasped what he'd meant.

"We'll have it analyzed for remains."

Kingsley choked. "You mean like cremains? But why would they? And how?"

"K, someone's perpetrating a sadistic trick. Nothing more. And, if it's the last thing I do, whoever's responsible is going to pay."

A black Mercedes inched down the Hennings' driveway.

It stopped, door opening slowly. A shiny black wing tip touched the ground below a charcoal pinstriped leg. The man unfolded his tall slender frame, black-gloved hands adjusting a Scottish tam on his dense white hair.

"Uncle David!" Kingsley rushed toward his arms. With minimal steps, his long legs strode to the lead detective. He extended his business card to the police.

"In the future, direct all inquiries to me. You may not question the Hennings without my being present." He glared authoritatively, not needing to ask if that was understood. With one hand on each parent's shoulder, he piloted them into the house.

☙☙

Kingsley's godfather passed her his monogrammed handkerchief. "I am so sorry! I came as soon as I heard. We were touring Scotland and purposely did not stay in touch. Last evening I found your dad's messages and called him immediately. We had a long talk."

Todd left the two in the kitchen, returning to the foyer, drawn by the noise of renewed activity. En route, he snagged his Nikon field glasses and adjusted them to sweep the scene.

"I can't seem to get warm," Kingsley said, hugging her arms and rubbing them. "I deluded myself into thinking we could find Billy ourselves. But this! The pressure is enormous. We can't fight without help, and the cops think we're responsible." She gripped her mouth to try unsuccessfully to stop her teeth from chattering.

David draped his raincoat around her shoulders, the retained warmth of his body enveloping her. He settled her at the table. "Tea. Let me." He strode to the stove and snagged the kettle. "I hate this up-down-up-down spring weather— too warm for a fire, too chilly for comfort."

"What are we going to do?"

"Let's start by 'doing.' Tell me everything. From the beginning, one day at a time. Tell me every last detail you know, sense, or impression, even if it seems trivial. Anything you tell me, or a member of my firm, will be held in strictest confidence. So leave nothing out."

David lit the burner under the copper teakettle and pulled pottery mugs from the cupboard. He draped an Earl Gray teabag over each rim. She rose, leaving his coat on the chair, and absently performed good-hostess duties, assembling sugar, cream, lemon, and shortbread cookies. She described the drama, hour by hour, day by day. In between swallows, David inked pages with copious notes in his perfect square script. Occasionally, he jotted a question mark or an arrow in the margin but rarely interrupted unless clarification was essential.

Kingsley exhausted the timeline. Warmed by the tea and her godfather's devotion, she dredged up her fears. "If they're truly convinced that we staged the kidnapping, have they given up trying to find Billy? I flash morbid, hideous images of my baby, being abused, starved, ritualistically sacrificed, or dying even as we speak. That famous first twenty-four hours is a distant memory. What does it take to rattle them into action? Should we volunteer to take a polygraph test?"

"Absolutely not. No parent of a kidnapped, missing, or murdered child should ever do that, especially the mother. The reason is logical. Parents, at some level, always feel responsible—that if they had done something different, been more observant, diligent, protective, or informed, the event would not have happened. Think about the 'if only' that runs through the mind. 'If only I had researched the sitter more carefully, stayed home that evening, trusted my gut, not been late, driven more slowly' etcetera, etcetera. And I'll underscore that if anyone even suggests it."

David let that sink in, then continued. "You could take the polygraph, pass with flying colors, only to have them insist on their own, then lie about the results."

Kingsley jerked, miscalculating her mug's descent to the table, sloshing a small puddle. "Lie? That's awful! Why would they do that? Wouldn't they want to get at the truth?"

"At this point? They've got to cover their asses, having chosen the wrong direction and wasted precious time. Now, the trail is stone cold. In a high-profile case, results are expected from the district attorney down through the lowliest investigator. If they can't prove their case, they might fudge the evidence to ensure their jobs and protect their reputation. Or, convinced they are right, lie as a means to an end. If you were backed into a corner and felt you have no recourse, you might take a plea."

She jumped to her feet, knocking the ladder-back chair to the floor. "I would never, ever do that. Ever!"

"You, no. But the DA will try. They've got to clear ninety percent of the criminal cases without going to trial. Poor, young, innocent people with no family, friends, or money might feel it's their only option to avoid a long prison sentence. Criminal defense is not like a civil lawsuit where the attorney's fee is based on a percent of the award. A criminal lawyer, other than a public defender, requires cash up front, from which he draws anywhere from one hundred fifty to six hundred dollars plus, per hour, plus expenses. A private detective would cost more than the public defender's PI budget for the entire year. And he's got hundreds of cases."

He took another sip from his mug and grinned. "You, on the other hand, have the resources to fight like a tiger. And my fee is the enormous satisfaction I'll get by tearing them apart. I feel sorry for them already."

He circled the table and, righting the chair, guided her back to the table. "But, Kingsley, we've got to face facts. I apologize if saying this upsets you further. The case they're building against you could be…well, protracted. We need to be ahead of the police and DA's office every step of the way."

"The press—they keep calling. At first, they camped out, just beyond our property lines. Should we grant an interview? Tell them what happened? Ask for the public's help?"

"Absolutely not. The media are not your friends either. And at least they can't trespass. This house enjoys a considerable setback. Not one word to them. If any comment becomes necessary, our firm will draft *spin* to go on the offensive, but I'll do the talking."

"I feel so helpless, so incompetent, and yes, so guilty."

He shook his head. "Kingsley, I've known you all your life. Know the stuff that you're made of. Known your family since your dad and I were in college. You don't have an irresponsible bone in your body. And how anyone could make you feel *less* just makes me furious. What else do you need? How can I help?"

"Real police. Or an exceptional private detective. I understand a PI could lose his license by getting involved in an active police investigation. Surely that doesn't preclude research."

"That could hurt you since a PI must turn over pertinent evidence. Here's the deal. Our firm employs attorneys who serve in that capacity. Their title is *investigative counsel*. Privilege attaches to their research. Anything in particular that we should address first?"

"We tried to find Ethelda Blake and, when that failed, traced her life through her previous employers. We have her work history through two previous jobs, but nothing before that. Also, do you have access to a lab?"

"Do you have something you'd like to have analyzed?"

"Just a sec." Kingsley grabbed Billy's baby book into which she had scribed his earliest days. From the white leather volume, she extracted a tiny envelope that held a lock of his hair. Beside it on the table, she placed a plastic bag that held several strands of dark hair.

David bent over both, questioning her with a glance. She tapped the plastic bag. "The day Billy was kidnapped, I took this hair from Billy's blanket, thinking it was his. I desperately needed something to hang onto, and the police were keeping his possessions as evidence. The more I looked at it, the less I thought it resembled his."

"I assume that's his newborn hair."

"Yes, but there's a problem with that. The amniotic fluid probably damaged the mop he was born with. By now, it could be falling out or coming in lighter. I need a lab to compare the strands. If they're both human hair, are both specimens his? If not, could the strand in the bag belong to the kidnapper? I know it's a stretch..."

"But one worth pursuing. It couldn't be either of yours. Todd's is curly, and your hair is auburn." They packaged a few strands of each and sealed them in separate bags. David secured them in his briefcase. "Now—about security for you and this property..."

"We subscribe to the company that installed the system. They'll come if we call or they'll contact us if there's any service disruption."

"That's not good enough. I want on site security at all times. No one sets foot on this property without permission. If and when you need a bodyguard, they'll supply that as well."

"Isn't that extreme?"

"Absolutely not. I want to send professionals we know personally from Philadelphia. It's too difficult to run background checks on out-of-town subcontractors. I'll take care of that personally—it's the least I can do. But keep your present security company for the moment. It may take a couple days to coordinate overlapping coverage."

"What's that going to cost?"

"Let's see." He smoothed his thick white hair thoughtfully. "Dinner for four—make that six, including your folks—that great filet and scallop thing Todd grills so well. Those wonderful Delmonico potatoes your grandmother made. I'll leave the rest up to you. Oh—and we'll have this celebration *with* Billy being passed from lap to lap."

"I'll never be able to thank you enough."

"Why don't I smuggle the two of you out for a really fine lunch? I spotted an historic inn along the highway. And Kingsley? Remember. Whatever you need, personal or professional, you needn't ask twice. I'll do it, find it, or surface who can."

Todd's yell, followed by expletives, echoed down the hall from the foyer. Kingsley bolted toward the outburst, followed by David. "What is it? What's happened?"

Before Todd could explain, she grasped the situation. The cops were destroying the flowerbeds that she had lovingly restored and coaxed to life during their renovation, Todd having joked that they had gardens before electricity. Now, on the grass by the western foundation lay uprooted antique tea and floribunda rose bushes. Clumps of bulbs were being piled haphazardly onto the lawn. Blooming daffodils, crocuses, and Lenten roses poked sadly from clods of wet earth. Several men were headed out back to her perennial bed that spanned their entire back lawn.

"You can't just dig up my gardens. Some of those roses are a hundred years old. And my perennials, Grammy's peonies, my…"

"Ms. Henning, go back in the house, or we'll be forced to remove you. The warrant specifies 'disturbed earth' and this is—"

"My garden! You idiot! My beautiful flowers! Botanical wonders nurtured by generations! Survivors, progeny lovingly tended. This destruction is barbaric! Sadistic! Hedonistic! Reprehensible!"

David grabbed her by the shoulder and pivoted her, still spluttering oaths, back toward the house. Todd trailed helplessly. Overwhelmed by the magnitude of the escalating nightmare, she sobbed hysterically. "Who could do this to us? Hate us so much? And those animals—they're the criminals."

David propelled Kingsley into the kitchen, pulling the pocket doors shut as he went until the destruction outside could not be heard. After resettling her by the fire and pouring her a stiff drink, he powered his cell phone to call reinforcements. "Peter? Dave Wentworth here. I need your best landscape professionals at the following address, STAT. We have some historic specimens to save from a brutal assault. Have your foreman call me ASAP. I'll give him the details. And thanks." He hung up and turned to them. "Kingsley, Todd, we're getting out of here. Now."

Kingsley buried her face in her hands, plugging her ears with her index fingers as David's Mercedes propelled them away from the destruction.

Chapter 17

T here it is—last house on the left with a bike in the driveway." Todd parallel parked on the street. Kingsley, who sat numbly beside him, could barely focus on the mission at hand. Todd sagged, dropping his chin to his chest. "We cannot interview these people unless you're all right. Perhaps we should do this some other time."

Desensitized, she shook her head. Raging against the assault on her honesty, to say nothing of her gardens, had left her exhausted. At David's insistence, they had dawdled over lunch. By the time they parted company, the wine, warm food, and his soothing reassurance helped her get a grip on her ragged emotions.

Todd continued. "Hopefully, the police will be gone by the time we get home. We'll put on our boots and direct the landscapers as they work their magic. With any luck, your prized specimens won't know they've been moved."

Kingsley looked up. "Before we ever moved in, before the plumbing and electrical updates, and while you were sanding all those pine floors, I dug every shovel of dirt. Those roses, all tangled among the weeds, revealed themselves to my eternal joy. And that first summer they bloomed. The old couple who lived here forever took photos of the original garden. And now—"

"K. Don't. Stop. Come on. Task at hand. We've got to do something constructive."

She nodded consent. Side by side they climbed the narrow concrete strips that formed a driveway, tire-width apart. Dandelions carpeted the dirt in between and dotted the narrow front yard. Todd knocked on the weathered front door. A young boy, whom Kingsley instantly recognized, opened the door of the modest white saltbox.

He stood, motionless, for a few moments, until his mother appeared behind him. "Yes?"

"Mrs. Edgerton? I'm Todd Henning from Keynote National Bank, and this is my wife, Kingsley. May we speak with you for a moment? It's very important."

Recognition dawned in the mother's eyes. "You're his parents—the baby I read about in the newspaper."

"I'm afraid so. I was hoping your son would be willing to help us. I heard that he's friendly with the folks at the branch and might have seen something." Todd's smile thawed the boy a bit. He shyly smiled back.

"Please. Come in." Mrs. Edgerton opened the storm door and motioned them into the small living room. It was shabby but clean, and the picture window sparkled. "May I get you something to drink? Coffee? Soda? Ice tea?"

"No thank you. We just had lunch. We're fine," Kingsley said. She settled beside Todd on slipcovered chairs that faced a matching sofa. She focused her attention on the boy. "I understand you were in the bank when the fire alarm sounded."

Before she could transition to her questions, Mrs. Edgerton cut her off. "Dwight's not that popular at the bank anymore, not after pulling that fool stunt. Brought all those fire engines and police running. I'm terrified they're going to bill us for that." The boy dropped his head and studied the toe of the sneaker that he was rubbing with the opposite foot. "He has been punished, and I assure you that he will never do anything like that again. Tell them you're sorry."

"I'm sorry. I'll never do it again."

Todd nodded acceptance. "When I was about your age, I wanted to buy my mother a beautiful pin that she had admired in a jewelry store window. I mowed lawns, ran errands, even tried to borrow money from my sister. But it wasn't nearly enough. The Saturday before her birthday, I bought her a pendant in a department store instead. It was all I could afford."

"Did she like it?" the boy asked.

"She said it was just what she'd always wanted."

"Did you ever buy her the pin?"

"Years later, after I was grown I found something similar and told her the story. Know what she said?"

"No, what?"

"That the pendant had always been her favorite. And she still wears it. Son, I understand how you feel. You must love your mother very much."

Dwight nodded as he wiped his nose on the back of his sleeve.

"Would you like to make up for what happened?"

The boy looked up, bewildered, then brightened and nodded.

"Do you know what a coincidence is?" Todd asked.

"I think so," Dwight said.

"After the fire alarm sounded that day, somebody stole our baby from the bank's daycare. Everyone said that was a coincidence—the confusion created by the fire alarm and the kidnapping. We don't think so. We were hoping that you might have seen something. Would you mind, please, telling us what happened that day? I heard that a kid at school dared you to do it?"

The boy squirmed, repeating exactly what they had seen on the tape.

"Dwight," Kingsley said. "Why didn't you look around to make sure nobody was watching?"

"I was told not to." Busted, the boy's eyes widened, and he gulped air.

"Who?" Kingsley asked. "Who told you? It's all right.

You can tell us. You're not in any trouble. But we need to know. Who told you not to look around?"

Tears formed in his eyes. "I was told not to tell anyone."

"Dwight, whenever anyone tells you not to tell, that's exactly what you should tell your mother," Todd said.

He looked at his mother who nodded agreement. "Go ahead, son," his mother said sternly. "Tell Mr. Henning the truth."

"Who told you not to tell?"

"The scurry man."

"Scurry?"

"You know. The guy who makes sure nobody ever, ever gets burned up in a fire."

"Do you mean *security*?" Todd asked.

"Yeah, that's it." Fright overtook the boy's face.

"What is it?" Kingsley asked.

"What if the building burns to the ground because I told about the test? And lots of people get hurt or die?"

"That's not going to happen, I promise," Todd said. "Now please. Tell us what really happened. Why did you pull the fire alarm?"

"Well, it was like this. I wanted to buy my mom a really nice present. Then this man asked if he could hire me to help with an important test. I said yes. He said all I had to do was pull the alarm then leave the building by that stairway, circle the building, then meet my mom at her car. He told me what day to do it. He said nobody who worked at the bank could do the test 'cause everyone would know it wasn't a real fire. I'd be a real hero."

"What did he promise you?"

"A hundred bucks."

Kingsley's eyes widened. "One hundred dollars? That's a lot of money. Did he give you the money?"

"Yeah. He slipped me an envelope."

"When? Where?" his mother demanded, alarmed.

"Outside. He told me he'd be in the visitors' lot in a black car near my mom's."

"Did you notice what kind of car it was?"

The boy shook his head. "I was told not to look at the car—just walk by as if I didn't see it. Pass close enough to take the envelope then hide it so no one would see."

"The story you told the police about the kid at school?"

"It wasn't exactly a lie. It was part of the test."

"And the torn ten dollar bill you gave the police?"

"The scurry man gave it to me, only he gave me both halves. If I got caught, I was to say the kid gave me one half before and the other half after I got it done. That if I got into trouble he would tell all about the test and make it okay."

"If you got into trouble, how would you get in touch with the man?"

Anguish overspread Dwight's face. He darted looks back and forth from his mother to Todd and Kingsley, then started to sob. "I don't know! I—I didn't think about that."

Mrs. Edgerton stroked his arm gently. "Dwight—tell me. Is that why you refused to give the police the other boy's name?"

"I did something terrible, didn't I?" Tears streaked the boy's freckled face.

"Son, you did not," Todd said. "You were tricked by a very bad grownup. You thought you were helping save lives. Where is the money?" The boy eyed his mother who nodded emphatically. "Dwight?" Todd called after him as he left the room. The boy stopped and turned. "Let me help you. We must not finger the envelope."

Todd held the envelope by the corner with a tissue, lifted the flap with his pen, then blew on the bills, separating them sufficiently to count them. "Here's what I'd like you to do," Todd said to Mrs. Edgerton. "Give this envelope to the police. Dwight, tell them exactly what you told us. And please, don't handle the envelope or money in case there are fingerprints." He crossed the room and set it down on an end table.

The others stared as if it might come alive.

Todd focused on Dwight. "How would you like to help solve a real crime?"

The boy nodded enthusiastically.

"Do you think you could help the police by describing the security man? Maybe look at some pictures?"

"Yes, sir!"

Todd pulled a photo from an envelope. "Is this the man?"

The boy scrunched his face. "A little. Except he was bald."

"One more thing," Todd said, extracting his wallet. "Here." He counted out five twenty-dollar bills.

His mother jumped from the couch. "He can't accept that."

"He completed a job with the best of intentions, for which he deserves to be paid."

As they were leaving, Todd beckoned for the boy's mother to follow him outside. "I don't mean to alarm you, but Dwight could be in danger. We're dealing with sophisticated criminals here. Please urge the police to protect Dwight's identity and the information he shares."

❧❧❧

"I don't think that even occurred to her," Todd said, looking glum as the Edgertons' house grew smaller in the rearview mirror. "I hated doing that. Such a death of innocence, as if she didn't have enough worries, what with the boy's disability."

A death of innocence. How naïve, Kingsley realized, she had been. How protected from evil that now seemed everywhere. Throughout her life, until Andy died, she'd been sequestered in Mainline Philadelphia society. Her Ivy League education barely covered the basics of dealing with the real world. And the honesty of her well-known family would not have been doubted. She sighed, as if to expel evil vapors. "Now what?" she asked.

"Let's ask Chas to scan the security tapes for any shots of the boy talking with that man—go back to the date when Dwight said he was approached."

"I have a terrible feeling that he knew exactly how to avoid the cameras. But it's worth a shot. We've got nothing to lose."

"Which raises an interesting point. Someone had to be intimately familiar with Keynote's layout and procedures. Let's ask Chas to include all men, not just strangers. This could be an inside job."

"But who? And why?"

Hours later, Chas called back. "You were right, Todd. I can see Dwight on several occasions, obviously talking with someone. But that person never comes into view. Either he was one lucky bastard, or he knew exactly where to stand."

"Was anybody else nearby when the man and the boy were talking?"

"A witness would have been nice. But no."

Chapter 18

Barrie?"

The assistant controller looked up from her stack of spreadsheets, the margins of which were covered with tiny jottings and question marks. "Kingsley, hey! Who let you in?"

"You busy? I have an idea."

"Hang onto it—it's in a strange place. Hey! That's a joke—what's on your mind?"

Kingsley turned somber eyes to her friend. "Todd and I spent hours with the gardeners, trying to replant my torn up flowerbeds. If I don't do something, I'm going to lose it."

"Got something in mind?"

"An employee who was out in the parking lot when we evacuated the building noticed a black Lab. Apparently, for no reason, it chose that time and place to play Frisbee. She described him as a magnificent animal. Suppose the dog *did* slip away from a local or a hiker at the time the kidnapper escaped through the woods? That owner might, in my wildest dreams, be a key witness without realizing the significance of what had been seen. Perhaps that person doesn't watch TV, read the papers, and so on."

"What's your plan?"

"Find that Lab. Question the owner. It's worth a try."

"Has it crossed your mind that whoever you find just

might be involved? You could be in danger. Even harm Bil-ly—force them to cut their losses and run."

"I'll make up an innocent, plausible reason for asking. Canvas neighborhoods within walking distance. Talk to vets. Breeders. Lab clubs, if there is such a thing. Whatever it takes to find a certain dog that would have a reason to be near our bank." She shook her head to Barrie's offer of her visitor's chair. "I'll go nuts if I sit. I've got to keep mov-ing."

"There must be something Randall and I can do."

"You could help piece together the fragments of infor-mation. My mind is mush."

"I know—let's have an old fashioned brainstorming ses-sion. Works in business when we're stuck for ideas." A big grin warmed Barrie's face with the light of inspiration. "I'll call Randall, and we'll plan a session. Just leave it to me."

As soon as Kingsley left, Barrie dialed Randall, who was about to fly home from Maryland. She could picture him thinking, eyes on the ground as he paced the tarmac, run-ning his hand through his shock of red hair.

"Since tomorrow's the day we were supposed to fly to Kiawah, you guys are scheduled for vacation anyway. I'll pick up fresh crabs. Preparing a feast takes lots of work, which will free up our peripheral minds. Over a long dinner, we'll consider those fragments. We'll sleep on it, then to-morrow sort it out."

"Randall, I've gotta run to a meeting. Pick up some ex-cellent wine. No, wait. Pick me up at my condo at six. Then we'll get wine. Oh, call Todd first. Warn him we're coming. Decide what to tell him."

Randall laughed. "I sure hope you've got your meeting planned better than this conversation."

❧❦❧

Kingsley circled through several strip malls until she

found the one she remembered. Sandwiched between a pet supply shop and a nail boutique stood a store that sold every magazine imaginable as well as newspapers and writing supplies. She approached a girl behind the counter who was in between customers.

"Do you sell county maps? I need one that shows all the local streets and subdivisions."

The girl shook her head. "Sorry. We have maps of the entire USA, the northeast, and some state maps, but county? Nope."

"I really, *really* need one. Do you know anybody who does?"

"Just a sec. I think I have something that might work." She disappeared through a door marked *Employees Only* and returned shortly with a folded glossy brochure.

"This what you want?" She unfolded a huge sheet bordered with two-inch advertisements for myriad local businesses and services. She tapped a map in the lower right corner with her index finger. "That's our county, divided by boroughs, with all major roads."

"I'm afraid I need more detail."

With the flourish of a magician who snatched rabbits from hats, the girl flipped the sheet, revealing the entire layout of roads. "Da da!" she sing-songed, delighting in Kingsley's reaction.

"That's it! That's just what I need. How much is it?"

"Well, we don't sell them. Got a couple dozen from the Visitor's Bureau to promote local businesses." She wiggled her left fingers for Kingsley to admire an exquisite diamond. "I'm getting married in a few weeks. Needed maps for out-of-town family." She folded the brochure. "Here. This one's for you."

"It must have cost something. Please let me pay you for it." Even though the girl shook her head, Kingsley pressed a twenty into her hand. "Thanks. I can't tell you how helpful this is. And congratulations."

Back in her car Kingsley unfolded and propped the map against the steering wheel, studying the area closest to the bank. Her eye swept the quadrants, looking for roads and subdivisions within dog-walking distance. She quickly eliminated the entire stretch on the far side of the highway, which, in addition to suggesting a dangerous crossing, was undeveloped and bordered by the landfill.

The bank was the last significant structure after a series of industrial parks. Beyond it to the south the land was sparsely populated, the map showing a handful of rural roads. A large subdivision with convoluted loops and cul-de-sacs lay beyond the bank's south parking lot where Billy had been taken. To the east was the view Kingsley saw from her office window—undeveloped land, still thick with native white pine, maple, oak, and rhododendron and bordered by a rushing stream.

Kingsley scrutinized the highway's off ramp south of the bank and plotted her route toward the subdivision. She dug a small tablet and pen from her armrest, writing down the turns in large letters before hitting the road. After exiting the four-lane, she reached the subdivision, then cruised the entire neighborhood, getting a feel for the challenge—how to find one friendly black Lab who liked to play Frisbee. The streets were laid out in an undulating grid with lots that couldn't be more than one-quarter acre. Amazing, she thought, that with all that land, 3,000-plus square foot houses would end up bunched together.

Better for me, she thought, as she hit on a plan. Big dogs leave big poop. Halfway down the first block, she spotted a lawn with circles of lush green near yellow circles. She parked and knocked on the door. Shortly an older woman opened it. Behind her, an elderly collie mix ambled gingerly as if in pain.

"Hi. I'm trying to find the family that owns a black Lab—wears a red bandana—likes to play Frisbee. Would you know if he lives on this block?"

The woman looked startled. "Why? Did you hit it or something?"

"No, nothing like that. I saw the dog at a distance, and he was magnificent. I'm looking for a breeder. You know the problems with puppy farms. We want a strong, healthy dog for our little boy."

"Problem is," the woman snorted, "people are too snooty. For my money, I'll take a mixed breed anytime. Morty here's fifteen years old and still has his marbles." She looked behind her at the old dog, who smiled at his mistress, tail swishing lazily.

"Would you know if a dog like that lives in this neighborhood?"

The woman shook her head as she scanned the block over Kingsley's shoulder. "Not on this block, the two beyond it, or the side streets. Where did you say you saw the dog?"

"It came into Keynote National Bank's parking lot from the woods. I figured it must live around here."

"Try that way." She pointed to the streets that paralleled hers.

"Thanks for your help."

Kingsley eased down the road. The woman was still watching from behind her glass storm door. As she passed the second side street, she could see a cul-de-sac and turned in the direction the woman had suggested. She isolated a promising yard among the next series of blocks.

Her knock brought a skinny young woman to the door with a toy Pomeranian tucked under one arm and a toddler affixed to her opposite leg. From the looks of the lawn, Kingsley suspected they rarely cleaned up after the dog. Kingsley explained a more polished version of her fabrication.

"Nope. And I wouldn't go any farther down this street. There's a pair of Dobermans in the next block that the owner insists stay in their yard and wouldn't hurt a fly. Ha! Beasts only listen to the man. The teenagers let them out after school. Bitches laughed fiendishly when the dogs backed us down the street. My husband swears if they ever come near our daughter, he'll put a bullet between their eyes. He can, and he will."

"Thanks. I'll be careful."

After Kingsley struck out on the third and last series of streets, she studied the map again. An isolated road beyond the subdivisions snaked into the area nearest the bank. Returning to the access road from which the subdivision had sprouted, she turned right and traveled the half mile that paralleled the highway.

A narrow asphalt road with a battered street sign looked rutted but passable. She turned right and slowly eased around potholes. The road weaved past occasional houses on huge wooded lots. Disreputable bungalows with peeling paint bordered others that resembled hunting lodges. Stone, cedar, brick, and vinyl—no similarity of materials or architecture existed. Clearly, this was a place where people came to express themselves—privately, please.

As the road threaded westward, the houses dwindled, ultimately disappearing, as did the asphalt. Kingsley braked and oriented herself by the sun's position. Then she studied the map. If her sense was correct, the dirt road extended a quarter mile in the direction of Keynote's parking lot. She coaxed her car forward until the potholes became tank traps. She parked and got out of the car, wishing she could swap her pantsuit for jeans. She managed to find some old sneakers in the trunk and proceeded a quarter mile on foot.

The road, she realized, had once been rough coated, but now was pockmarked with weeds and bristling pine seedlings. The woods seemed determined to reclaim itself.

"Hey there!" Startled, she scanned a steep hill onto which was nestled a log house with a deck. It looked one with the woods. She shaded her eyes and located a man with a full white beard, wearing a red flannel shirt.

Summoning her courage, she shouted. "Could I talk with you for a minute?"

"Come around this way." He pointed down the hill to his right.

At the base, Kingsley found timbers recessed into the hill, forming square-yard mini terraces that ascended the hill. Gingerly she picked her way toward the man. He sounded friendly enough, but she stopped before reaching the deck.

"You lost or something? You're hardly dressed to go hiking."

She glanced in dismay at her fawn-colored pantsuit, now covered with burrs and twigs. Lamely, she began her story again, this time adding that her map had deluded her into thinking the road led to a housing development.

"You aren't far wrong," he said. "Developer who did a subdivision over yonder was going to continue around here. People who owned large tracts of land threw a fit—held him up so long he went broke, or so goes the story. Most folks just wanted to be left alone."

Kingsley pointed. "Am I right that Keynote National Bank is farther that way?"

"Yep. You'll run into the back. No, I guess it's the side."

Briefly, she told the improved, polished version of her quest for a dog. "Is he yours? He was spotted in the bank parking lot where I work. I was trying to locate the owner."

The man squinted into the distance, as if replaying a scene. "My dog's a boxer, but now that you mention it, I did see such a dog. Must have been, oh, two or three weeks ago. I remember it started out sunny, then one of those damp spells moved in. I'd been sitting on my deck with my wife." He motioned to the screened structure anchored into the hillside by six-by-six supports.

"This beautiful dog came trotting from the direction of the bank, shiny black coat, red handkerchief around its neck. Something orange in its mouth. Assumed he lived down yonder," he said, pointing in the direction from which Kingsley had come. "But I'd never seen him before. Haven't since. You might want to knock on a few doors."

"That's a good idea. I'll try that next." She turned to dismount the steps.

He called after her. "If I come across that dog, how can I reach you?"

She rummaged in her jacket pocket and found a slightly bent business card and added her personal phone numbers. Mounting the steps, she handed it to him. He studied the printing. "If I see the owners, should I pass this along?"

"No! Please don't. I mean, I'd rather approach them myself."

He shrugged. "Okay. Can I offer you something before you go? The wife's inside. She can't get around and misses having company."

"Perhaps some other time. I really must get back. Thanks for your help."

By the time she got home, Kingsley was truly exhausted after tramping unsuccessfully to isolated doors. A number of unfriendly dogs and people underscored that they truly did not appreciate strangers. After dropping her filthy pantsuit onto the dry-cleaning pile, she changed into jeans and a soft cotton sweater. She sank into the living room couch and hugged into her chenille throw.

A dull buzz rose in her ears as she drifted away. In a dream she was out back by her garden, throwing a Frisbee to the beautiful Lab, a golden-haired toddler in hot pursuit. Her mind searched the little girl's face, but she was a stranger. A distant ringing that only got louder drowned out the little one's laughter. She groped for the phone. "Ms. Henning? My husband gave me your card. I think I saw your black Lab."

☙❧

Kingsley came awake instantly. "Do you live in the log house overlooking the dirt road?"

"That would be me. You're trying to locate a breeder?"

"Not exactly. I'm hoping to find the dog's owner. He or she may be a witness to something that happened." Kingsley was tired of lying and undone from learning nothing. "It's important."

"My husband thought you might be that woman in the newspaper. The one whose baby was snatched from the daycare? Was it that bank? At the end of the road?"

Kingsley flashed on a dozen good reasons not to go any further, but felt she had no choice but to trust her. "Somebody has to have seen something."

"I'm dreadfully sorry for you and your family. Sounds like the cops are worthless, as usual. A hit-and-run driver mowed me down, and they did nothing to locate the bastard who put me in this wheelchair. In fact, they blamed me. I didn't plan to have car trouble. Cars die where they die."

"Oh, my. I'm terribly sorry." Kingsley's carefully worded story no longer fit. But the woman continued anyway.

"I'm an avid birder, helping to count migrating flocks. A friend got me interested after the accident. My husband got me some excellent field glasses, and I spend a lot of time scanning the woods. That's why I'm calling. I did see something that might interest you. You're not really trying to locate a breeder, are you?"

Kingsley couldn't help herself, as she blurted the truth. "It's been awful. The police suspect we're involved, and even if I locate the kidnapper himself, he could say we put him up to it in exchange for a deal. All we want is to rescue our baby."

"I understand. Well, here's what I saw—a slender young man dressed in black pants. He looked Amish. He wore suspenders rather than a belt. A collarless jacket and a blue dress shirt buttoned high at the neck. No tie. A sun-bleached straw hat shaded his face, which was florid— sunburned like he wasn't used to being outside. Vigilant blue eyes. Alert, as if being careful not to be noticed. From behind my black screens, he couldn't see me. He was just standing there, all alone."

"You're quite observant."

She chuckled. "I'm hooked on mysteries. Writing is one thing I can do from my chair, so I've read everything I can get my hands on about craft. Anyway, I watched the man, imagining what he might be doing. You know—to trigger a plot idea. Another thing—I need to describe the birds that I see. Intricate detail separates one from another. It's good training for a writer, wouldn't you think? Anyway, this man was cocking his head like he was straining to hear. Suddenly he blew several short puffs on what looked like a whistle, but there was no sound. Moments later, a dog like the one you described appeared and dropped an orange Frisbee at the man's feet."

"Which way did he come from?"

"The dog? From my deck, it would be to the right, as if from that bank. I could hear the man say, 'Good boy! Now park it.' The dog flopped on his butt. Did I mention the bike? The young man had a faded green Deluxe Schwinn Breeze. Had one myself as a kid, so that's how I knew what it was. He'd stashed the bike in the bushes on the far side of the road. 'Stay,' he said. I thought that was odd. If the man were Amish, wouldn't he have spoken to the dog in Pennsylvania Dutch? Anyway, the dog watched his master as the man pedaled down the road toward the bank. That dog just waited all by himself. Shortly, the young man reappeared, a cardboard box braced on his hip. Before securing the carton into the bike's newspaper basket—that was bolted to the rear rack—he reached into the box. He didn't take anything out of the box, just opened what appeared to be white wrappings. Like thin Styrofoam sheeting. He nodded, smiling, like he was satisfied and secured the box to the bike with black bungee cords.

"Then he did the strangest thing. He took what appeared to be a plastic pump bottle from the bicycle's basket, like the kind you use to spray for insects, then jogged back toward the bank. He returned the same way, arching a mist from the spray bottle as he swept the dirt with a hemlock branch. Like he was covering his tracks."

Kingsley was stunned. "You saw all that? Your powers of observation are incredible. Could you see what was in the box?"

"Wish I could, love. My glasses have super magnification, but X-ray vision? Afraid not. The lid's flaps were too high."

"What happened next?"

"He said, 'Let's go, Champ.' The dog trotted beside the bike, warily watching his master's feet as the guy pedaled or hit the coaster brakes. Tires were big—sixteen-inch street treads, I believe, and the terrain's so uneven." She paused for a breath. "Here's where it gets really strange. The fellow had attached that branch to the rear of the bike and dragged it as if he were trying to obliterate the wheels' tracks. They proceeded toward the paved road. The last thing I could see was a Chevy pickup truck that had stopped. The driver jumped out. His shoes were covered with cloth booties. The men didn't appear to speak. The driver freed the box and slid it onto the passenger seat while the young man stowed his bike and the dog in the back of the truck. They were all but out of my line of vision, but I did see the young man changing his clothes—exchanging that Amish getup for jeans and a sweatshirt."

"And the box was…"

"Must have been between them on the front seat. Last I saw was their dust."

"You said it was a Chevy truck? I don't suppose you caught the license plate."

"If I'd had any idea it was important, I would have tried harder. I did note it was Pennsylvania and started with a Y, but it was muddy. I assumed they were part of a crew spraying for pests, like mosquitoes."

"Was there a logo on the truck? A construction vehicle perhaps?"

"Nope. Just two-tone brown and filthy."

"Can you think of anything else?"

The woman paused momentarily. "No. But I'll call you if anything triggers."

Kingsley paid for her information by listening to the homebound woman expound about her accident, her politics, and her view of the world. Kingsley did, however, secure the woman's agreement to keep what she'd seen to herself.

After Kingsley hung up, she just sat, absently twisting the corner of the chenille throw. So that's how they could have done it! Billy was carried into the parking lot where the dog created a distraction, during which time Billy was swapped for a doll. The all clear sounded. Dog owner whistled. The dog retreated. Bank personnel vacated the lot. The kidnapper collected the box. Put it into the bicycle basket. Rendezvoused with the getaway vehicle. And vanished.

She hung her head. So many unanswered questions. If the scenario was true, how could Ethelda have been seen carrying Billy back into the daycare? And where was he now? And how had the bloodhound missed his scent? None of that seemed to matter. Billy could be anywhere in the world by now, and the trail was stone cold.

✌✌

"We're doing beach night," Randall announced, as he and Barrie lugged coolers into the Hennings' kitchen and thunked them onto the floor. "Da da!"

"Live crabs!" Kingsley gaped at the struggling crustaceans that crawled all over each other.

"These guys were luxuriating in Maryland waters only this morning," Randall said. "Boy, are they legal! Brought corn—it needs husking—and cabbage for coleslaw. If we all pitch in, we might eat before midnight. Let's put newspapers on the kitchen table. This is going to get messy."

"I'll get the pots," Todd said. "Do we have any Old Bay?"

"Top shelf. Lemons are in the right-hand hydrator."

Barrie snagged one of the larger crabs and turned it loose. "Crab on the floor!" she shrieked in mock fear as she directed the hapless creature in Randall's direction. Randall, in turn, selected another and aimed it toward her. Todd dipped into the chest and turned two more loose as the group succumbed to hysterical laughter. Finally, they rounded them up and dropped them back into the cooler.

At first, Kingsley waved off the chilled Chardonnay but finally accepted just a half glass. Someone refilled it in increments whenever she wasn't looking. They nibbled Havarti, whole-wheat crackers, grapes, and cashews while cooking and cracking the crab. A soft May breeze mingled its silkiness with their candlelight and camaraderie. In spite of herself, Kingsley's cares slipped away.

Pandora feigned boredom as she slinked near the forbidden table to nab her share of the crab. Her white bib splashed radiantly onto her long, shiny black fur that framed her emerald green eyes. Finally, she gave up the pretense and jumped onto the table.

Barrie snagged her and asked, "Do you remember that stormy evening when I brought you Pandora under my raincoat? I begged you to take her. Her owner's child was allergic."

"I remember you bribed me with excellent wine and hinted she'd be destroyed if I didn't take her. She was so tiny."

Todd said, "How about the time she fell into the toilet? And landed in the clumping kitty litter? That was the first time you entertained me for dinner."

"But you didn't get fed until you helped clean up the mess." He began rolling the newspapers on which was piled crab debris. He stuffed the mess into a heavy-duty garbage bag. "You must admit I was pretty good at policing the area."

"There's a perfect evening outside," Randall said right on cue.

"Why don't you guys stay over?" Todd asked. "We can drag out the hammock—rush the season a bit. I've got a powerful new lens for my telescope. We can let this business rest until morning when we're rested."

The three turned to Kingsley who had withdrawn into dark thoughts. "K, tomorrow we'll lay everything out. Refocus our efforts. Brainstorm and pinpoint ideas to research."

"And," Randall injected, "take nothing for granted, even if we know it as gospel truth. Lay every shred bare."

Kingsley smiled. "Thanks, guys. I appreciate everything you're doing. Every time I feel like I'm falling through hell, you pull me back. If we ever survive this, I'm going to fulfill all those rash promises I made to God. And I want to be the kind of friend that you've been to me." She looked at the clock. "I can't believe I'm so sleepy. If you don't mind…"

"I'll come up with you," Barrie said. "I'll need to borrow some stuff." The girls walked arm in arm down the hall, giggling as they feigned bouncing off one wall and then the other. "Back in a minute," Barrie enunciated carefully to Randall over the banister.

Todd took Randall into the dining room and opened the doors below the dry sink, which was angled in the back interior corner. "Here's the good stuff," he said. "Help yourself. Take it outside. You don't need us to party. There's the swing out front. And we can locate the lawn chairs. If it gets chilly, grab coats from the pegs in the back hall."

"Perfect," Randall said, inspecting the bottles. "Ah, here's something Barrie will love. Get her into the mood. Make her putty in my hands. Be my submissive slave. That back guest room is pretty soundproof, didn't you say?"

"Stone walls tend to do that." Todd turned serious. "Do you really expect her to wait around forever? The guys at the bank are forming a line that wends around the corner."

"Todd. She said no."

"When?"

"Any number of times."

"I'm sorry. I just assumed—"

"That it's incomprehensible that a woman should ever refuse an offer of marriage?"

"Did she give you a reason?"

"She says, 'We're fine, just as we are, so why mess it up?' Barrie's a contradiction. She can tell you, down to the minute, where her career is going through the next decade, but I can't pin her down to where our relationship should be this time next month or next year."

"What is it she wants?"

"By job description, to be the chief financial officer of a major corporation. Personally, to be independent enough to take care of herself—to never again depend on a man."

"But you're not just any man, and you respect her. You're certainly not like that guy who used her to get through med school then dumped her. Surely, she knows how loyal you are. And that you don't require *dependence*."

"It's a circle. Whenever I bring that up, she reverts to her professional goal, how long it will take, her freedom to relocate, work late, have no responsibilities for a family, etc. ad nauseum."

"Know what I think? You need better bait. She wants to climb the corporate ladder? You've incorporated, and your business is growing so fast that it's horrible. I helped with your books before Barrie showed up, knowing how badly you need expertise. She wants to climb? Take her to Home Depot. Buy her a ladder."

"If only it were that easy."

"How many years have I been telling you that you need a partner to handle the business?"

"Yeah, yeah, yeah."

"Speaking of Barrie, I almost forgot. I've got something for you that slipped my mind with everything that's happened. Kingsley and Barrie were shopping in Philly some time ago. Kingsley came home all excited and gave me a jeweler's card." He led Randall into the library and rummaged through a holder of business cards. "Here. The salesman slipped Kingsley the information about a ring that Barrie went nuts over. It's an heirloom setting, heck of a rock."

Randall took the card, a smile overtaking his face. "I'm no good at this kind of thing. I thought if I could get her to say yes I'd have her pick something out."

Todd shook his head. "Even *I* know that's not romantic. There is a downside to this ring, Buddy. Kingsley said the price is over six thousand bucks."

"I'd sell my soul if that's what it took."

"Randall! Just what kind of ring do you think you could buy for twenty-four dollars and fifty cents?"

Chapter 19

Randall scanned the pristine heavens then stepped back into the Hennings' kitchen. Friday, May third, and the nineteenth day of their endless ordeal, would have been perfect had the situation been different. The five would have been flying to South Carolina to start their vacation. "We should fly somewhere—anywhere," he said, gazing longingly at the heavens. Kingsley passed raspberry rugelachs and refilled their mugs with Green Mountain Coffee, a gift from a friend and proprietor of a fine coffee boutique.

When everyone was stuffed with pastries and fruit ka-bobs, the four began poring over timelines, people, and facts, squeezing their brains for inspiration and fresh angles.

"Thanks for viewing the videos again," Todd said. "I know it wasn't easy fitting it into your schedule the other times either. And now, getting up early—"

"That's okay," Randall said, faking a yawn. "Couldn't sleep anyway. The vixen here talks in her sleep." As Barrie elbowed his ribs, he feigned excruciating pain, clutching his sides, doubled over.

Barrie said, "If we're going to brainstorm, let's do it right. Randall, please fetch the marketing stuff from the trunk." Shortly he reappeared with two easels onto which he propped a large whiteboard. She fanned an array of colored felt-tipped markers onto the table. Going to the board, she drew four black vertical lines to create five columns. Atop each, she printed titles in different colors: *Who? Why? When? Where? How?*

"Ground rules for brainstorming," she instructed. "I'll be the facilitator. Randall, you scribe, neatly, please. Todd, start a new Word table on your laptop and save our thoughts. Everyone think! As we enter ideas, absolutely no critiquing and no getting chatty until we've wrung every thought from our brains. Every idea goes on the board. Nothing's too stupid or irrelevant. Any questions?"

The others were quiet. "Let's do *Where* first. That's easiest. Where did the kidnapping take place?"

"That's obvious. In Keynote's daycare."

"Tut!" Barrie interrupted. "No critiquing. Randall, print *In the daycare* under *Where*. Where else, guys?"

"Parking lot. The hallway."

"Come on—be specific!"

"The nursery, the woods, the stairwell…" The group got silent momentarily. "The quiet room, the bathroom." They stalled.

"Okay. Let's do *When*." Barrie said.

Todd said. "During the fire drill."

"Wait!" Kingsley said. "Write down between twelve-twenty and three p.m. I personally saw him at twelve-twenty, and the granny discovered the doll at three p.m. We have no first-hand knowledge that narrows it further."

"Excellent. Too definitive, but okay for now. Randall, write it down. Now let's do *Who*? Who would have a reason to kidnap Billy? I'll get us started. Randall, write down *Aliens*." Everyone laughed, but Randall wrote it anyway. "Now fire off as many as you can think of, without critiquing."

"Jealous person, insane person, opportunist, delivery person, repair person, someone posing as security or police, an employee, an outsider, a customer…" Randall scribed as quickly as possible while keeping it legible. "Anyone in any kind of a uniform."

"Specifics, please?"

"UPS, USPS, FedEx, carpet cleaner, water delivery guy, nurse, EMT..." Kingsley watched the list grow, wishing she could supply a real name. Like the woman in Lending who had wanted her job but was passed over. And that other gal who thought Todd would be hers. Finally, she named them; they were included.

"Okay. Let's do *Why?*"

A cumulative sigh escaped from the foursome. "Ransom, research, organ procurement, commodity procurement, hate, profit, jealousy, mental dysfunction, psychopath, needy mother, needy father, child hater..." A long pause preceded a fresh rash of ideas, stripped from the headlines.

"Now, the big question: *How?*"

"During a diversion, dressed like a girl, under someone's clothes, in a large bag, wrapped like a parcel, through a hidden door in the nursery or corridor, through the ceiling, bundled with linens, placed in the dumpster, handed off outside, beamed aboard..."

The kitchen grew quiet, save Todd's keying, as everyone studied the expanding chart.

"Miss Scarlet in the library with the candlestick!"

"Randall!" Barrie snapped. "That's in terrible taste!"

Todd sat transfixed by the chart. "Can we critique now? I think the *when* and the *where* aren't as important as the other three categories, unless they trip someone up. *Motive* is everything. If we only knew *Why*, then we could narrow down *Who*."

Kingsley said, "Wait a minute. Thread, Ziploc bags, paper scraps..."

"What on earth are you talking about?" Randall asked.

She gave the others an abbreviated rundown of ransacking the Blakes' house, including what she had stolen. She was met with stunned silence. She shrugged. "It didn't lead anywhere. I found nothing useful. Heard nothing and made the cops furious. They searched the Blakes' house, yard, and neighborhood to no avail. That also exhausted many good volunteers. I'm sorry about that. But I'm convinced the search failed because they waited too long. All I netted was a strand of blue thread and some burned paper scraps that are too consumed to read."

"I want to see them—the scraps," Randall said.

"Let's finish here first." Kingsley frowned at her notes. "We all saw Billy with Ethelda when she exited with him and brought him back in. Everyone agree?"

They nodded.

"The most obvious answer is that someone, somehow, swapped Billy for the doll. But how, when, and where? Since the place was torn apart by professionals, let's assume for the moment that there's no alternate entrance into and out of the daycare. That means the swap had to take place outside." Kingsley quickly related her conversation with Brittany, about the black Lab, and the homebound woman with the field glasses. "The Lab playing Frisbee was the perfect distraction."

"But the doll in his crib didn't look one bit like Billy," Barrie said. "We saw him when Ethelda brought him in— all that dark hair."

"I just wish we could have seen more than his head," Kingsley said.

"What did we see? Exactly? Did he move? Were his eyes open? Was he asleep?"

"Ethelda, Billy, his blanket..." Todd jumped to his feet. "That's it! That's how she did it!"

Kingsley jerked to attention. "But we've seen her on the video with him dozens of times."

Todd stabbed his finger toward the whiteboard. "To be literal, as in limiting our thinking to just what we *personally* know, we saw Ethelda, Billy's head, and his blanket. His head! That's all we saw of Billy. *His head*." The others looked puzzled.

"So?"

"Suppose that's all there was? That we couldn't see more than his head because there *was only* a head."

"Todd, that's impossible…"

"Suppose, as we suspect from our 'looking-for-the-shadow,' that the doll was put in the crib while everyone else was outside. And suppose Billy was switched outside, not for a doll, but for a doll's *head* that was wadded in his blanket. That could have taken place during the Frisbee distraction. If the head was supposed to look like Sammy, it would have looked like Billy as well. Remember Sammy also had dark hair, and although two months older, was small for his age."

"But Sammy was absent."

"Callie Smith, Sammy's mother, may have nailed it—Billy wasn't the target. But having gone through all that prep work, they needed a baby. Billy was the only infant in the room. Perhaps the kidnapper didn't know the difference."

"Someone could have left a container behind the dumpster to put Sammy in. But how would they keep him from crying?" Randall asked.

"Now that I think of it," Kingsley said, "Callie said Sammy had his first cold. There are cold and allergy remedies that make children drowsy. She mentioned that she had Dimetapp for Sammy and joked she was getting a little more sleep. A generous squirt and Billy would have zonked out without any real harm."

"You're forgetting one important detail," Randall said. "The bloodhound. Didn't the handler say he went as far as the edge of the parking lot, circled as if confused, then sniffed his way back to the building?" The four sat in silence a minute.

Kingsley got to her feet and paced. "So Ethelda brings up the rear with a doll's head and uses his blanket to shield its face, keeping a little distance between herself and the others. She slips back the blanket just far enough for the camera to catch the top of its head. And as she passes the camera entering the daycare, she bends to kiss him. Her face not only blocks his but keeps the head from falling out of the blanket."

"So where's the doll's head?" Randall asked.

"Had to have been in that little purse, which she took home. And she was long gone, without being searched, before anyone knew Billy was missing and started to check employees' purses and packages."

"I doubt they would have looked in such a little purse anyway," Barrie said.

Kingsley took a deep breath and expelled it. "If that's really what happened, she took a huge chance. Wait a sec. I may have something to prove this." She hurried into the study, returning momentarily with a tiny white envelope and a small plastic bag. She spread the contents onto pieces of white paper while the others nearly bumped heads to look.

"Both, supposedly, are strands of his hair. At least I thought that they were. I gave the police a few hairs for his DNA. The other lock was stuck to his blanket. I gave samples of each to Uncle David to have analyzed. I thought it might identify the kidnapper—that if I could discover a likely accomplice I could swipe a discarded coffee cup for DNA, like they do on TV." She shrugged. "I know—that sounds ridiculous even to me."

Barrie eyeballed the strands through the magnifying glass that Kingsley had brought from her library desk. She scrunched her face in disbelief. "They don't look identical to me." With a delicate touch, she stroked one, then the other. "The strand you found on his blanket looks heavier. Rougher."

Kingsley sighed. "I assumed any difference was baby oil, shampoo, or something he'd come in contact with since I'd last bathed him. What if, suppose, it was Ethelda's? She had short dark hair and probably used lots of product on it."

"This is all well and good," Todd said, "but it just leads us back to what we already know—that Ethelda Blake has vanished off the face of the earth and taken the knowledge of Billy's whereabouts with her. If we just had one little clue that could tell us where she might have gone."

"Didn't you say the Blakes' neighbor said they used a U-Haul? Did anyone try to trace it?" Randall asked.

"Dead end," Todd said. "It was abandoned in a subdivision of new houses that are still under construction. Nobody noticed there weren't any new neighbors until a couple days passed. The truck was empty and spotless. These people are good."

"Could they be traced through their credit card use?" Barrie asked.

"I tried that through our banking connections. They didn't use any—at least not in their own names. Kingsley, could you have missed anything at their house? Like papers lining the silverware drawers or cabinets? Did you see garbage bags? Or scraps of paper that could have blown into the window wells?"

"The only scraps I found, besides old fast-food bags, were in the fireplace, and those thugs cleaned it out before the police searched the place."

Barrie looked up, perplexed. "What are you talking about? What burned paper?"

"The scraps I found in the fireplace turned out to be useless except that it prompted the search of the woods, which yielded nothing. I couldn't make sense of them."

"Do you still have them?"

"Well—sure. Hang on a sec." She left the kitchen and returned with the Ziploc bags. "See for yourself. I was hoping for names, addresses, bank statements, records of any kind." She dumped the scorched scraps onto white printer paper and separated the pieces with tweezers.

"Pass me the magnifying glass," Todd said. The four bent, their heads nearly touching, to examine what now looked to Kingsley like their last straw, and a burned one at that.

"That one has a nine-digit number," Barrie said. "And something before it that's nearly obliterated."

"Can't be a credit or debit card number—they're much longer than that," Kingsley said. They brainstormed ideas that ranged from map coordinates to bank account numbers.

"Looks like part of a sideways X," Todd said, pointing to a faint mark that preceded the others. "Could it be a four?"

"If so, that makes ten digits," Randall said. "Bet it's a phone number. And if that X is a four, and you add the next two numbers, that makes four-one-two, which is the area code for downtown Pittsburgh."

"Who do we know at the phone company?" Kingsley asked, but Randall was already reaching for his cell phone.

"It's past eight o'clock. Let's see who's home. Barrie, grab a tablet and something to write with." He fired the phone. Barrie turned to a fresh sheet and readied her pen as Randall motioned for her to move closer. "Get your boss on the line—now!" Randall bellowed at whoever picked up the phone.

Barrie jumped, then recovering, moved back toward the phone, smiling in amusement at his creativity. Randall angled the phone away from his ear so the huddled group could hear.

A woman's professional voice quavered after a pause. "Excuse me?"

"Your boss knows darned well I have to file a flight plan to be there by eleven for our appointment. Where *is* your boss anyway? Someone was supposed to get back to me."

"I'm sorry, sir. He's taking a deposition this morning."

Barrie nodded and jotted, *Pittsburgh lawyer, male, with at least one staffer.* They overheard what sounded like the woman riffling through papers.

"I apologize, sir," she said again. "My predecessor, whom I never met, departed suddenly without entering appointments for any time today. Would you please give me your name?"

Randall eyed the ceiling then grinned. "Jones. Mac-Corkle Jones." Barrie turned away, gripping her mouth to smother an explosive laugh. She sidled back.

"Sir, since Mr. Shure told me he would be in later this morning, I'm putting you on his calendar immediately. Would you please spell your name?" Randall obliged.

"I apologize for being so abrupt. I'm slightly rattled. Would you please give me directions to your office? And how your firm's name reads on the directory?"

"Certainly, Mr. Jones. The directory reads 'L. Gerard Shure, Esq. and Associates, PC.'" Randall gave Barrie a thumbs-up after she scribbled it perfectly. He thanked the lady for the detailed directions then disconnected the phone.

"Internet!" he said, triumphantly striding into the library. Quickly he accessed the Allegheny County Bar Association, the Membership Directory, then clicked on the S block and scrolled the subdirectory. "Here it is! Name, address, phone, fax, no other particulars."

"See if his firm has a website," Todd said. Randall Googled and found it quickly. The other three hunched over his shoulder to read the sales pitch. "Damn! He's an adoption attorney, but wait a minute—it says he specializes in foreign adoptions?" They exchanged puzzled looks.

Kingsley straightened and searched their faces. "Do you think it's possible that he *steals* babies?"

"Now we should call the detective—find out what they know about this phone number."

"Wait a minute," Kingsley said. "I'd have to tell them how we came by this information. I left the fireplace looking untouched, except for the threads, but all that was gone by the time they searched."

"Were they in plain sight? In the fireplace?" Randall asked.

"I repositioned them as best I could—yes."

"Then say you noticed burned scraps with what looked like phone numbers, so you wrote them down. You knew they'd be ticked if you touched them, but you forgot to mention them at the time. You were too focused on the blue threads."

Todd nodded his head in agreement. "Sounds reasonable to me."

"Uncle David would not approve."

"Sometimes," Randall said, "it's easier to get forgiveness than permission. Besides, if we're sitting on evidence—"

"Just do it."

༄༅

Kingsley and Todd sat at their library desks that abutted each other in the center of the room. Barrie and Randall listened attentively as Todd dialed the detective's number. When the phone began ringing, Kingsley hit the conference call button. As usual, the detective sounded prickly with forced civility. Todd's patience dissolved quickly, as the conversation went south.

"Look, Detective, you told us to call you if we thought of anything, and my wife observed something that could be important. We're sick of your innuendoes and insults. Level with us, or I'll unleash every weapon in our legal arsenal and make your life as unbearable as you're making ours."

"Calm down. What is it you want to know?"

"Information. Not to be kept in the dark. A modicum of respect would be appreciated. And we need to know about that phone number."

"You must appreciate that we have procedures. We can't jeopardize our investigation by sharing the details with you."

"You've got that backward, Detective. My wife noticed something important and had the presence of mind to memorize it then write it down. You had a possible lead to track down."

"I'm sorry, but—"

"Then I'm going to go to the office of one L. Gerard Shure of Pittsburgh Pennsylvania, and—" He didn't need to go further.

"All right," the detective said. "Since you seem to know about him, I'll tell you it's a dead end."

Todd jumped to his feet. "What do you mean 'a dead end'?"

"We pulled the Blakes' LUDs—that is, the Local Uses Detail—and found three calls had been placed to Mr. Shure's office. One lasted fifteen minutes, the others less than three. Mr. Shure was more than cooperative. According to Pittsburgh Police Detective Greer, Mr. Shure said that he had indeed received calls from Mr. Blake. Blake wanted to refer pregnant teenagers whom he found at a homeless shelter to his practice. Of course, he wanted a finder's fee."

Todd took notes in rapid succession, including *which shelter?* The detective continued. "Mr. Shure said he told Mr. Blake that he wasn't interested. He also said he had trouble getting the guy off the phone. Imagine that, coming from a lawyer. Anyway, when Blake got offensive, Shure cut him off.

"And the other two calls?"

"He said he didn't take them. He told his secretary not to put any more through, so she fielded them."

"What did his secretary say?"

"Unfortunately, the police weren't able to question her. She died three weeks ago."

"Aren't you going to search Shure's office? His home? You're not going to just let this drop."

"We don't have probable cause for a search warrant. As I said, he was cooperative. And everything he told us, right down to the dates and duration of the calls, matched what we knew. Naturally, we didn't tell him everything—just that we understand he'd received 'a call' from Mr. Blake. He volunteered additional details that included the two other calls."

Neither spoke for a moment. "Mr. Henning—a word of warning—you could get yourself into more legal trouble if you pursue Mr. Shure. We can't protect you from yourself."

"To date, you have not protected my family from any-thing."

From across the room Randall mouthed for Todd to let it go. "Okay. I appreciate your talking to us. My wife and I won't approach Mr. Shure."

"Of course there's an APB out on the Blakes. I know you're finding this hard to believe, but the police are doing everything they can. We've been inundated with tips, which consume endless man hours to investigate."

"Yeah, right. Like coming after us." He slammed down the handset.

"And we," Randall said, "are going to do everything that *we* can. 'Mrs. Jones,'" he said to Barrie, who looked up in surprise at the strange-sounding name. "I think it's high time we adopted a baby. Jackets, everyone, and, ladies, grab your purses. We're flying to Pittsburgh for an eleven a.m. meeting."

Chapter 20

The Cessna Citation glistened in the clean morning air as the four friends approached the air steps. Once inside, Randall and Barrie disappeared into the cockpit while Todd and Kingsley stowed their carry-ons and sank into the soft velour seats. Shortly, Barrie returned, bright-eyed with anticipation, and apparently unfazed by the impromptu departure with minimal sleep.

"Do you realize that if Randall keels over mid-flight, as the newly qualified copilot, I have your life in my hands?" She grinned and punched "yes!" into the air. Then she sobered. "You guys keep the faith and relax. Nothing's happening until eleven o'clock. We're not coming back without satisfaction." She punctuated that thought by stabbing an exclamation mark with her index finger. "I'm going to assist Randall with takeoff preparations. Estimated flight time, thirty-five to forty-five minutes." She shot them a reassuring smile, then disappeared.

Todd laughed, in spite of himself. "That Barrie! I can't imagine life without them as a couple. She is exactly what he has needed for such a long time. How much longer do you think they can keep up this dance?"

"She isn't fluff, Todd. For all her zany behavior, she was a Phi Beta Kappa and the most focused woman I've ever known. But she loves big—too big, and she knows it.

"Can she trust any man?"

"It's not about men. It's about trusting herself—to control her own heart and her own destiny. She had a history of spending more emotionally than she could afford to lose. Those scars haven't healed. She's learned to hold back. The more she loves, the more she fears, and the more she resists. So she dances and focuses just on the moment."

Kingsley took Todd's hand and fingered his ring, her mood darkening as she remembered their mission. "Look at them out there on the tarmac—all that bustling activity. Corporate executives, vacationers, pilots, and ground crews preparing for an ordinary day. I wonder what their lives are like. What deals they're chasing. What's plaguing their lives. What if we're on the wrong track? Or that we're not smart enough to recognize what we're seeing? The answer precedes the question? What if—"

"I have a question for you. Do you have any idea how much I love you? What I would do for you if I could? The extent I would go to fix this? I never, ever meant to imply that this was your fault. I do understand that women need to use their brains just as much as their male counterparts. Returning to work was never an issue. Billy should have been safe."

"I don't deserve you. I am so sorry that I have neglected you. Made you be the parent for both of us. Been a child when you needed a grownup."

"Don't you see, K? That's my salvation. To be strong, to provide, to shield and protect, to make things right for my family. Some things never change."

She settled into her seat, holding his hand across the narrow aisle as the engine's roar signaled imminent departure. The Cessna taxied into position, waiting its turn to take off. Minutes later they enjoyed a bird's eye view of southeast Pennsylvania transformed into an undulating quilt of green, brown, blue, and gold squares, splashed with the shadows of cumulus clouds. Banking, the jet headed west.

"What happens when we reach Pittsburgh?" she asked.

"Randall says we'll land at Allegheny County Airport where he has reserved a fleet van. We'll drive to the Golden Triangle and park in a garage a few blocks from Shure's office. You and I will kill time while they keep the meeting. He doesn't want us seen together, and I agree. If this man Shure is smart enough to perpetrate a sophisticated kidnapping, and if Randall's story set off any alarms, they could be under surveillance from the time they approach his building. And we would be recognized.

"He wants us to duck when he approaches the garage then wait while he scopes out the deck. Five minutes after he leaves the garage, we're to find lunch, get take-out for them, then come back to the van and wait."

"I wish I could be a spider on the wall when they go into Shure's office and pitch an adoption. Those two are crazy, and together, there's a synergistic effect."

"I wonder if they know what a funny tag team they are— if it's planned or if it comes naturally. If Shure's involved, they won't be fooled."

"Todd, could they be in any real danger?"

"Randall can handle himself. I just hope it's not another dead end."

"What if it is? We'd be out of leads."

"There is one more avenue we can pursue, although it's a long shot. The dog. The bloodhound that is. That breed is famous for tracking a scent through air, water, and deceptive tricks, even days later. The bloodhound appeared to lose the trail by the dumpster. That doesn't make sense. Or should I say 'scents.' Had Billy been carted away in a receptacle, a trained dog would have followed his trail easily. If we come back from Pittsburgh empty handed, let's interview the handler. She couldn't be that hard to find. Let's ask her how her dog behaved."

"You don't suppose the handler's involved."

"That could explain a lot. A murmured command to call the dog off could mean nothing to those within earshot."

"I still think if Pittsburgh doesn't yield anything, we're out of luck."

"K, try to be patient. We've got to keep a positive attitude and stay focused." As the Cessna knifed through crystal space, the couple withdrew into private thoughts. Before they stopped talking altogether, though, they agreed that at least they were doing *something*. And that provided a measure of comfort.

☙❧

As Randall's fleet van emerged from the Fort Pitt Tunnel, Pittsburgh's Golden Triangle burst upon their senses in panoramic splendor. Navigating the eclectic mix of historical structures and dazzling skyscrapers, he maneuvered the van into the parking garage at 6th and Penn Streets. Luckily, the garage was devoid of people at that time of day. After taking the stairs to street level, Randall and Barrie continued alone, hustling past Heinz Hall toward the office of L. Gerard Shure.

Meanwhile, having seen neither suspicious vehicles nor foot traffic, Kingsley and Todd ventured onto Sixth and walked the short distance to Market Square. Business people, tourists, and shoppers alike relaxed at small sidewalk tables, dawdling over an early lunch. A band played in the square. Gratefully, they blended anonymously into the mix of friendly strangers and briefly enjoyed being tourists.

A few blocks away, Randall and Barrie elevated to the tenth floor office of L. Gerard Shure and entered his opulent suite. A woman whose nameplate said "Ruth" rose to greet them. She extended her hand. Barrie was surprised by how cold and bony it felt. Still, Ruth seemed the proficient executive complement.

"Please have a seat for a minute," Ruth said. "May I offer you a beverage?"

"We're fine, thanks," Randall answered for them both

while Barrie studied the woman. She was skinny and at least sixty-five. Barrie tried not to stare at her hair, which was dyed the starkest of blacks, except for a two-inch strip of pure white that was cut short and waved to one side of her forehead. The rest of her hair was pulled severely into a French twist. Barrie pushed *skunk* out of her mind and forbade herself to catch Randall's eye, lest she explode in uncontrollable laughter.

At precisely eleven, Ruth showed Mr. and Mrs. MacCorkle Jones into L. Gerard Shure's sumptuous office. Towering windows back-dropped the rotund lawyer's chair, showcasing a panoramic view of Pittsburgh, alive with gleaming buildings that had risen from the ashes of the once defeated steel-making capital.

Barrie inventoried the scene peripherally, noting the packing cartons stowed behind his desk. Through a closet door that stood slightly ajar, she noticed transparent bags filled with cross-shredded paper.

Framed composites groaned with family photos on both side walls—babies alone, babies with sibs, babies with parents, and many older children in similar combinations with family. What was most striking was the ethnic diversity. Many of the children were Asian girls and black children with every manner of parent. The photo array was overwhelming.

Shure seemed relaxed in his element and obviously proud of his accomplishments. "I specialize in foreign adoptions," he said after offering coffee, which they declined. "Take China, for instance. Years ago, the Chinese government realized their country was being crushed by its own population. So they encouraged couples, through various means, to limit themselves to one child.

"You see, in their culture the eldest son is responsible for his aging parents. When a daughter marries, she becomes part of her husband's family and devotes herself to his obligations. If a young couple has a son first, that's great. They're done. But if they have a daughter, they are allowed to try again. If they have a second daughter..." L. Gerard shrugged. "That's where it gets sticky. Many are aborted; some are kept at great penalty to the parents, but the less fortunate end up in orphanages or worse. This is especially tragic if a second daughter has medical problems since a second girl receives no governmental health care. I help American couples adopt one or more of these sweet little girls."

"Do all your babies come from foreign countries?" Randall asked.

"Just about. I had a vision that one day each little child in our global community would be matched with loving parents who want and need them. Here's an idea I've nurtured that I hope takes off." He pointed to pictures of several black families. "African American couples, with or without children, are tracing their roots and adopting orphans from their own ancestral regions. Ditto war-torn countries like Bosnia. The Middle East. How's that for an idea begging its hour?"

Barrie glanced at Randall and shifted uncomfortably in her chair. "I'm sorry I'm not better prepared for this interview," the attorney continued. "My former secretary didn't inform me of our appointment. Please. Fill me in. What brought you here?"

"We understood that we would be seeing photographs of babies you hope to place. We hadn't considered anything, well, exotic," Randall said, gesturing toward the photo array.

L. Gerard chuckled. "You were hoping to find a baby that looks like yourselves." Barrie nodded. "Would that it were that easy! Thanks to birth control, legal abortions, and the vanquished stigma of being a single parent, babies who look like you have disappeared into a ten-year waiting game, unless you're willing to accept a child with certain challenges."

"Ten years!" Barrie shot Randall a look of despair. "My mother's been nagging since we got engaged. There's a family fortune dependent upon heirs, with lots of strings attached. Surely there's some way…"

Randall pulled himself high in his chair. "Fortune has smiled on my business, enabling me to invest in whatever makes my lovely wife happy. And she wants a child. So surely you can think of a way to fast-forward the process? There must be, ah, situations that require more capital for whatever reason? Perhaps lots of it?"

Shure laughed. "To put it bluntly, you who 'got bucks' get bumped to the top of the list."

Randall smiled benignly and patted Barrie's thigh. "Something like that. Or perhaps something, ah, creative?"

If Shure noticed the bait, he ignored it. "The reality is that I've had terrible luck with those teenage moms who get knocked up, bail out, then want to reclaim their kids several years later. And with the courts siding with birth mothers— whew! Even the strictest legal documents can be over- turned." He tipped back in his chair and rolled his eyes across the ceiling.

He sat up quickly and thumped his palms on his desk. "I could tell you horror stories of devastated adoptive parents, howling tykes dragged from the only family they've ever known, heartbroken grandparents." He angled the last part at Barrie. "Nope, I won't go there again. Not anymore."

"But I thought it was difficult for birth parents to reclaim a child once he'd been adopted."

Shure shrugged. "Sure. If both birth parents sign off ini- tially and no problems arise during specified time frames. But suppose Mom says she doesn't know who the father is. Or the boyfriend at the time didn't know about the baby. Or she lied. And Dad shows up, not having signed off, and de- mands his rights to the child."

Randall smiled innocently but riveted Shure with mogul eyes. "I'm thinking about extreme incentive. Perhaps a situ- ation that requires, ah, confidentiality?"

L. Gerard studied Randall's face, then focused on Barrie. "The law is specific. You cannot buy a baby. Now, Mrs.

Jones—you look quite young. Are you sure that you have exhausted all your options? How many times have you failed at in vitro?"

"Well, I, ah…"

"At least been working with a fertility expert?" They exchanged glances. An answer to that sort of question had not been rehearsed. "Signed a five-year lease where they don't allow kids?" Tension broken, everyone laughed as Shure reached over his belly and rummaged in his top drawer. "Here. These doctors work miracles. Since you have resources, you can afford the best specialists and the finest facilities. That's your best option."

"And you," he said to Randall. "How about putting that successful business on hold for a while? Take your lovely wife on a world cruise. You know. Boozin' and cruising'. Chewin' and screwin'." He winked at Randall and laughed. Then he turned serious. "You might consider a less stressful job, looser underwear, and more time relaxing." He smiled with fatherly gratification as he swept his hand toward the pictures surrounding them. "On the other hand, if you'd consider a foreign sweetheart or a dear little American orphan with medical challenges, you'd never have a contrite birth mother invading your dream."

Barrie frowned. "My parents—they would *not* understand."

"I see." L. Gerard rose from his desk and extended his hand. "I'm sorry I'm not able to offer you any encouragement. And again, I apologize about our little mix-up." He swept them into the outer office. "If you'll excuse me, I have a luncheon engagement. Good luck to you both." As quickly as it began, Randall and Barrie were again alone with Ruth in Shure's outer office.

Chapter 21

"How did you make out?" Ruth asked the Joneses. "Was Mr. Shure able to help you?"

"I'm so disappointed," Barrie said, allowing her eyes to well with tears. "The other lady, your coworker, was so encouraging. I actually thought we were going to see baby pictures today."

"Where is she?" Randall asked.

"Who?"

"The other woman we spoke to."

Ruth angled her hand beside her mouth and lowered her voice, even though the outer office was empty except for the three. "She's dead. Happened right here in this building, just three weeks ago."

"Did she have a heart attack or something?" Barrie asked.

Ruth fleetingly glanced at Randall. "I mustn't gossip. It's unprofessional."

Barrie made a small circular hand motion for Randall that was out of Ruth's line of vision. "I need a restroom," he said, catching on. "And, honey, will you give me a few minutes? I must return a few client calls." He turned back to Ruth. "Can she wait here?"

Barrie looked helplessly around the reception area then back at the secretary. Ruth responded as if on cue. "Sure. You can hang out with me if you wish." Randall left while

Barrie worked up more tears and made a big production of not finding a tissue.

"Here, dear," Ruth said, offering a decorator box from her desk.

"I'm sorry," Barrie said, sniffling. "It's just that the other lady—what was her name? I have it here somewhere." She rummaged some more. "Something lyrical."

"Libby."

"Yes, that's it. She was positive, so encouraging that Mr. Shure could help us. Said something about a perfect baby boy. An infant, two or three months old? He sounded precious—lots of dark hair and eyes the color of the Blue Grotto. Didn't she leave some sort of file about us? Say something to you about what she had in mind? Maybe it's in the baby's file. Perhaps you could look—"

Ruth shook her head. "I did look after your husband called this morning. I found nothing. As I told him, I've only been here three weeks."

"You—never spoke with her?"

"We never met."

Barrie mopped her eyes and blew her nose, buying time to think. She'd gone too far with Billy's description, and for what? She'd learned nothing, and Ruth might repeat her comments to Shure. She needed damage control and to ask better questions.

"Mr. Shure mentioned foreign adoptions. I, we, hadn't considered anything like that. Perhaps if I could talk with some of those adoptive parents? Find out how it's working for them. Could you give me a couple of references? Maybe—"

"I'm sorry, Mrs. Jones. That information is confidential."

Barrie sighed deeply and ran down her mental list. Geography. If she could just nail that down. "Is Mr. Shure's practice local?"

"I know you must think I'm being unhelpful, but really—I *am* new, and between you and me, I'm clueless. I inherited a mess." She gestured helplessly around her space. "It's worse than coming in after somebody's quit or was fired. At least there's a chance of calling them up if you're desperate. But her death—"

"You said she died right here in this office?"

"Not 'here,' as in this suite." When Ruth lowered her voice to gossip level, Barrie prickled with anticipation. Underneath her professional demeanor, this woman needed to talk.

"What happened?" That was too blunt; she kicked herself mentally, but for some reason it worked. Ruth relented.

"She committed suicide. Threw herself off the roof."

"No! That's horrible! Why did she do it? Did she leave a note?"

"No, there was no note, but the girls told me what Mr. Shure told the police. It was awful for him. She actually told him what was bothering her. He didn't take her seriously and really beat himself up about it afterward." Ruth lowered her voice even further, and Barrie leaned in.

"Libby was, as my mother would have said, an old maid. Had actually entered a convent once, but left before taking her final vows. You know what they say about women that age being more likely to be struck by lightning or killed by a terrorist than finding a husband? Anyway, at this late date—she was forty-eight, I think—she met *the* man. First time in her life. She threw herself into it. The romance went hot and heavy for over six months, but with no mention of marriage. Wouldn't you just know it? According to Mr. Shure, he *was* too good to be true. Mr. Right was married."

"Did she tell Mr. Shure she intended to kill herself?"

"Not in so many words, although in retrospect he said he should have paid more attention. He said he wasn't comfortable with touchy-feely female conversations. He told police she said she couldn't live with such sin on her conscience."

Barrie started to protest that first, Libby was duped, and second, that suicide was unthinkable for a Catholic. She caught herself just in time and shut her mouth. She was playing a role, must stay in character, and steer dear Ruth in a useful direction.

"Did Mr. Shure meet the man? I mean, maybe he felt guilty about not reading the situation."

"He said he had no idea she was even seeing someone— that there's a strict policy about personal calls. And he didn't recall a gentleman picking her up after work. The relationship was very hush-hush."

"What a shame to get such a nice job at someone else's expense." Barrie made a great show of ogling the grandeur of the sumptuous office. "Bet the pay's really great."

Ruth snorted. "I'm just a temp. Barely more than minimum wage. You'd think these lawyers would pay a bundle, charging like they do. Oh! Please don't repeat that. I don't want to get fired. I need the money."

Bingo. Now Barrie had leverage. "Of course not. Did you say a temp agency sent you? If Mr. Shure really likes you, maybe he'll hire you directly and pay you accordingly. My husband insists on paying his people well. Says if he takes care of them, they'll go the distance for him."

"That won't happen."

"I noticed some boxes," Barrie whispered, hoping to pry Shure's destination out of the woman. "Maybe he'll do some local consulting. If he lives nearby and needs secretarial help, you may be in luck."

Ruth took the bait. "Not him, lucky stiff. He's out of here. Imagine, just forty-five. I overheard him negotiating to buy his own island. Now how much do you think he has to charge to do that by age forty-five?"

"An Island? Oh, I'd just love to live in the Caribbean."

Ruth looked left and right, as if witnesses had pressed their ears to the walls. Without making a sound, she mouthed, "Fiji," then put her finger to her lips. Barrie nodded, conspiratorially.

"What's it called?" Barrie mouthed back without a sound.

Ruth took out a pen and wrote, *Egomaniac is naming it after himself—Gere Island. It's a nickname for Gerard.* She crumpled the paper and buried it in her handbag. The women exchanged sinful grins.

Barrie dug in her purse for a pen. "My husband was saying—just the other day—that one of his Pittsburgh clients is desperate for a good administrative assistant. Why don't you give me your full name and number?"

Ruth's face lit up, but then her smile faded. "I'm afraid I'm deficient when it comes to computers."

"That's okay. Someone can train you or send you to classes if your professional skills are solid."

"I was a Katie Gibbs girl. Was a great secretary years ago, but then I quit, as women did in my day, to raise a family. I never thought I'd have to work. We'd planned for every contingency, or thought that we had. Then my husband—he was a lot older than me—he had a stroke and needed a nursing home for many years. That cleaned out our nest egg."

"Do you have any children who could help?"

"I will never, ever depend on my children. My parents didn't do that to me. No, ma'am! That's a marriage wrecker. I'd rather starve or live in a shelter than do that to them. Besides, I like to work."

"I admire your spirit," Barrie said. "You shouldn't have any trouble finding a job. You have something to offer, and someone will always pay you for that. Besides, you're so youthful and professional."

Ruth sat a little straighter and smoothed her suit sleeves into perfect position over the cuffs of her blouse. "Do you think so? Truth is I'm sixty-seven."

"I would have guessed mid-forties. That client of my husband's says he needs a seasoned professional—one of those ladies who can still take dictation, give old-fashioned service, and never, ever gossip. He abhors email and won't hire chicks for his staff. Says they make his wife 'uncomfortable.' I think he means jealous or threatened."

"I did work for IBM years ago. Do you have your husband's card? Perhaps I could mention your name when I apply."

Barrie felt her face redden. "Ah, not with me. Why don't you jot down where *he* could reach *you*?" Ruth carefully wrote her particulars in perfect cursive.

"It might be a good idea if you didn't mention our conversation about Libby. If your boss gets the idea that you've been gossiping, well, a negative comment like that might make it harder for my husband to help you."

Ruth looked startled. "You won't repeat anything that I told you—"

"Of course not." Barrie rose and extended her hand. "I'd better catch up with him. Thank you for trying to help us. I can tell that you're a real professional." Ruth nodded self-consciously, a smile of relief overtaking her face. Barrie escaped.

As soon as they reached the elevator's privacy, Barrie began to fill Randall in. "We've got to work fast. He's clearing out. Soon. Some island in Fiji."

"He sure looked legit on the surface and did not snap at such blatant bait. But what original lines! My ass! That bastard is smooth."

"Yeah, from practice."

"And something else. I flew a group of adoptive parents to China some time ago. According to them, the countries from which Americans can adopt children are limited. And Bosnia wasn't mentioned."

"Any idea where to start?"

"Ruth, the temp, said something that didn't fit. Evidently, Libby, the secretary she replaced, was despondent about being deceived by a married lover. That she committed suicide. But she also revealed that the woman was a devout Catholic. She would *not* kill herself. If she felt she'd sinned, she'd go to confession."

"Did she leave a note?"

"Not according to Ruth. But supposedly she confided her anguish to Shure the afternoon of the evening she died. Or something like that."

"After we meet up with Todd and Kingsley let's check out that suicide."

"By the way, Randall—we need to find a job for our new friend Ruth, or at least go through the motions to ingratiate her."

He gave her a withering look then grinned and nodded. "Babe, whatever it takes."

As the cylindrical glass elevator slid silently to ground, Barrie glimpsed a figure on the balcony, all but concealed by a pillar that rose from the lobby into the stratosphere. An elbow, a flash of gray flannel, a cell phone clamped to an ear, the man gesturing adamantly as he spoke. Before Barrie could get Randall's attention, they arrived in the lobby. The man, who she was positive was Shure, was nowhere in sight.

As Randall started toward the revolving doors, Barrie grabbed him by the elbow. "We didn't come all this way to leave empty handed. I swear I saw Shure on the balcony, spying on us. Come on! If Ruth is also out of the office, let's toss it."

"But how?"

"Brought my lock picks."

∽∾

"Let's check around back for a freight elevator." Before Randall could argue, Barrie had propelled him through the lobby toward double utility doors marked *authorized personnel only*. That led to an ancient elevator door painted with Rustoleum. "If we get caught we'll say we forgot something. Your pen. My sunglasses. Maybe Ruth left the door open."

Pressing a black button brought the conveyance groaning

to life. With a flourish, she motioned Randall into its depth. Glancing both ways, she hit 10, grinning at him conspiratorially.

"You must have been one hellion of a kid," he said shaking his head. "Sweet little thing, all ribbons and bows, robbing banks or something. If it weren't for the gravity of the situation, this would be hysterical." When they arrived at ten, it shuddered to a stop, doors creaking open to disgorge them.

Barrie pulled Randall along by his sleeve, stopping just long enough to stand on tiptoe to peer through the metal door's tiny safety-glass window. The elegant hallway beyond the utility corridor where they hid appeared empty. Barrie could see that their approach was sheltered from office and elevator doors. A quick right brought them back to Shure's entrance, which was directly across from both men's and ladies' rooms. "Check 'em out," Randall hissed. Both bathrooms were empty.

Barrie, noticing Shure's outer office was dark, tried the doorknob with a gloved hand. Finding it locked, she put her ear to the frame, and hearing nothing, pulled the lock pick from her purse. With a series of jiggles, it clicked. "Aa ha! We're in," she whispered.

"What if…"

Barrie whipped a finger to her lips. "She must have forgotten to lock it."

Silently, they edged toward Shure's private office, protected by the layout's dogleg design. Though the outer office was quiet as a tomb, Shure's light was still on. Suddenly he shouted so loudly that both of them jumped. In seconds, however, they realized that he was on the phone. Judging from the trajectory of his voice, he must be standing behind his desk. His voice rose and fell, as if he were pacing. Like statues, the pair poised to listen or flee.

Shure said, "Well, circle the block. They should have been out by now. He's five-eight or nine, stocky, red hair, wearing a tan bomber jacket and black slacks. She's a knockout—tiny blonde, looks like a model, only way too short. Black pantsuit. Turquoise jewelry. See where they go and who they meet."

They heard a beep, which probably signaled the end of a cell phone conversation. Silence followed. As they started to beat a hasty retreat, faint beeps that sounded like dialing emanated from the room.

"How was the sound from Ruth's office?" A long pause. "Did she feed them the right details? She's too dumb to do anything else. She mentioned the convent! Oh, shit. Any reaction? Good. Okay. If they aren't legitimate, they'll be chasing their tails for a long time."

A long pause. "I'd still like to know what brought them here. Only thing I can figure is that the sister hired them to investigate Kathleen's death. Did you come up with any-thing on the name MacCorkle Jones? You'd think they'd invent something more suitable if they were PIs. Name's amateurish—make that ridiculous."

Barrie elbowed Randall, who shrugged, looking heav-enward. They refocused on the task at hand.

"And there's no record of any such people? Keep dig-ging. The visitors' chairs in my office—dust them for prints. Kathleen? I personally scrubbed over her calendar before I destroyed it. Checked every drawer, every pocket, her purse, everything. There was no mention of anyone named Jones. I'd made a big hairy deal about not accepting new clients. You did say you found nothing in her apart-ment…That's right. The disk—the one I saw her trying to hide? No disks." A short pause. "And you took the comput-er." From their place of concealment, Barrie and Randall exchanged puzzled looks.

Shure sighed. "Maybe it's moot. If Kathleen had wanted to copy my files, she needed to duplicate my keys and ac-cess my office. There was no opportunity. I guard my shrine. Besides, I didn't find any duplicate keys. I searched everywhere systematically. She couldn't have seen that screen for more than a moment. She always returned from lunch promptly at one. I found her in my office at five after. She seemed flustered, but that's not unusual, given her personality. She's jittery by nature—like I'd think she swiped paper clips. She said she was looking for our holiday mailing list—which she'd deleted on hers by mistake and was looking for it on mine. She hadn't found it, she said, and asked for my help. I emailed it to her computer, and she seemed satisfied. Subject of that document never came up again, but she tipped her hand when I told her I was retiring. Immediately she asked too many probing questions. She was testing, all right, but her religious background betrayed her. She was one lousy liar. I have no doubt that she would have called the police. We had no choice."

A long silence.

"No way. She was no mole. Wrong type. Besides—I would have been questioned by now." More pausing. "You're getting paranoid. Speaking of loose ends, I've got a tail on the Joneses, or whoever the hell they are. We may need to deal with them too. We're too close to completion to get sloppy and blow it. Time frame—Ruth will unknowingly keep up the pretense of business for several more weeks, but in three days, we're done."

Shure took a noisy, deep breath. "I think we can safely forget the disk. If anyone finds it, they won't know what it means. And there is no way that Kathleen had time to copy my files. In the meantime, check my website for hits. See if there's anything that remotely connects the Joneses with our recent activities. Gotta run."

Barrie and Randall jolted from their nearly hypnotic state, having been captivated by Shure's conversation. "Go! Go! Go!" Randall mouthed to Barrie, propelling her out through the outer office into the hall. He invested several precious seconds to ease the outer office door closed. He bolted after her toward the utility corridor, the dense carpet concealing their footsteps. The freight elevator, unused since their ascent, was waiting, its door ajar. Only after they were safely inside did they compare notes in whispers.

Chapter 22

Barrie and Randall swept through the revolving door and stepped from Shure's building into the sunlight. Squinting, Randall located his aviator sunglasses, then glanced at his watch. "That didn't take as much time as we planned. We have an hour to kill. Any ideas?"

"Kaufmann's Department Store. I hear it's a great place to disappear for a while." She put on her shades.

"Do you know where it is?" She pointed to the right.

❦

From an office window above the lofty atrium, an operative speed dialed Shure's office. "They're heading up Sixth, but some guy is following them."

"One of ours?"

"Negative.

"What's he look like?"

"Moves like an undercover cop. Or a fed. Or PI. A little too smooth to be coincidental. Should I follow them?"

"Let it go. Expedite wrapping things up."

They disconnected.

❦

Barrie glanced at the nearest street sign and gestured. "If

we cut over to Fifth, then find Smithfield Street, it should be at that intersection. A friend said we'd know it by the clock on the corner. It's a landmark and place where people meet." They started. "You're awfully quiet. Does the prospect of shopping depress you that much?"

"Don't make any sudden moves and do *not* turn around. We're being followed."

"Are you sure?"

"Easy. Easy. Maintain the speed. Up ahead. Stop at the far side of that big window and pretend something has caught your eye. Let me get on your left. I can scope out the sidewalk in the reflection."

Barrie approached the window that displayed women's accessories. She stopped and pointed for Randall to look. "That's good—point at something else, then look at my face."

With her back to the stalker she whispered, "Chunky? Black slacks, gray jacket, and sunglasses?"

"That's him."

"What makes you think—"

"Let's keep moving. Next block, same drill." They repeated the motions.

"What did he do?"

"Stopped when we did, started following again. Quick! The light's changing. Dash to the other side, then let's walk slowly again. See what he does." From the corner of his eye, Randall could see the stranger jaywalk through traffic against the red light.

"What's the plan? We don't want him to follow us, and we don't want him to know he's been made."

"Just keep moving then stop halfway up the next block while I rummage for something. Let's see what he does." Barrie did as he asked, using the reflection from a passing limo's tinted glass for a peek. The man appeared to be asking directions from a pedestrian who was pointing toward one of the buildings.

She nudged Randall. "Let's go. See if he cuts his conversation short." The two began walking, Randall pretending to take in the height of the buildings while stealing a look. The man had picked up his speed and closed the distance to a half block.

"There's Kaufmann's!" Barrie gestured toward the department store where a cluster of people obstructed the entry "What shall we do?"

"Cut through it and lose him." Taking Barrie's elbow, he hustled her toward the entry. "It's closed! Boarded up! What the hell! Duck behind that clump of people." Randall rummaged in his bag, pulling out two black wigs. Both yanked off their jackets and shrugged into oversized navy windbreakers, balling and zipping their own jackets against their chests and pulling on the wigs. "You go right; I'll go uphill. Meet me on the opposite corner of the building. First one there, hail a cab."

Converging on Forbes, they zigzagged to Grant Street. Luck was with them as a cab approached and stopped for Randall's frantic flag. They scrambled inside.

"Where to?"

"Oakland. The Cathedral of Learning. And hurry. We're late for a meeting."

Randall put the folder he'd carried to Shure's office between his face and the window and motioned for Barrie to duck. She pretended to take a stone from her shoe, complaining noisily about women's styles. Luck was with them again as the cabby ran a red light and sped toward the parkway.

As they approached Oakland, Randall fired his cell phone and pretended to dial. "This is Dr. Gray. I'm running five minutes late. They did what? Where? What time? Why didn't somebody contact me? All right. We'll be there as soon as possible, but this is most inconvenient." He closed the phone and turned to Barrie. "Dr. Morgan. They've moved the meeting to the Gateway Center." He got the cabby's attention. "Take us back to the Hilton, will you? By the fastest route possible. We're already late."

❦❦❦

They scrunched into an alcove just inside the entrance of the parking garage, both scanning the view from their place of concealment. "If we weren't positive before that Shure was involved, we are now," Barrie said. They kept watch for a while. "Can we assume that we've lost our tail?"

"To be safe, let's take the stairs then check out the van from a distance. If the coast is clear, we'll wait in the back seat." On the third deck, they peered through the fire door's reinforced safety glass for several minutes then slipped the few spaces that separated them from the van. No activity broke the midday lull among the rows of vehicles ensconced until rush hour.

Barrie eyed Randall's fiery hair. "If we're going to keep doing this sort of thing, we've got to dye that mop a drab color."

Randall grinned. "Maybe I'll shave it."

"Don't you dare!" As they unlocked the van, they spotted Todd and Kingsley exiting the elevator. Randall made a thumbs-up motion, and the Hennings approached without acknowledging them. Quickly they converged on the van and piled in.

"Drive!" Randall said, tossing Todd the keys. Exiting, he turned right onto Sixth, right onto Liberty, and then crossed the Fort Pitt Bridge. The Fort Pitt Tunnel swallowed them into its safety under Mount Washington.

❦❦❦

As they sped across Route 279 toward the airport, Kingsley began unwrapping their lunch, filling the van with the aroma of Primante Brothers' Pitts-burger cheese steaks. "You get an A-plus in hunting and gathering," Randall said, as he began to demolish the sandwich, which bulged with fries, coleslaw, tomatoes, and onions. "Todd, head for the airport while I eat and make a few calls. We picked up a lead."

He attacked the rest of his sandwich, licking his fingers. Barrie ate part of hers, then like a well-practiced dance, handed the remaining two-thirds to him, which he inhaled. Then he scanned her box. Wordlessly, she passed it over for him to finish the stray scraps of tomatoes and most of the fries.

Satiated, he wiped his mouth and hands on a pile of fresh napkins, took a deep breath, and patted his belly. "This adoption business is hungry work." He smiled at Barrie and leaned over to kiss her. She opened a bottle of raspberry Snapple, took a swallow, then handed it to him while he hit the speed dial on his cell phone.

"Randall here," he said to the employee who picked up the phone at his base of operations. "Got a minute, Greg?"

"Sure do. Got as long as you want. What's up?"

"Go on the internet to the *Pittsburgh Post-Gazette's* Website. I need you to research an obituary for me." Via the speaker, they could hear Greg keying in rapid fire.

"Got it. I need a date."

"Start around April eighth of this year and work forward in the classified obits for a woman whose first name is Libby. Read me whatever it says." While Greg keyed, Randall clicked a Cross pen and opened a small spiral notebook while Barrie held his bottle of tea.

"Nope. Nobody here by that name."

"There has to be. She died in this city. Look for someone with a middle initial, L. Oh, and it would be a suicide, so look for something that does not indicate natural causes." Time seemed to drag.

"Sorry to keep you waiting," Greg said. "I'm still coming up empty. Any idea how old she would be?"

"Late forties, or thereabouts."

"Hello! Here's something promising. 'O'Connor, Kathleen E. on Friday, April twelfth. Beloved sister of Mary

Margaret O'Connor of Seattle, Washington." He paused a minute too long.

"What?"

"I was just scrolling to read the obits before and after this one. Some have photos and long lists of relatives. Kathleen's is skimpy by comparison with no other relatives listed except for the sister. That's odd."

"What else does it say? I'd like the name and address of the sister."

"All it says is 'Mary Margaret O'Connor.' No further address is mentioned."

"Is a funeral home noted? If so, give me the name and the town." Greg did so then said, "Here's something interesting. Most list where friends could pay their respects or send donations or flowers. Nothing here."

"Maybe she's buried here in Pittsburgh. There could have been a memorial service in Seattle without her body."

"No," Greg said. "It says 'A funeral prayer was offered at nine a.m. and a Mass of Christian Burial was held at ten.' Interment is noted at a cemetery, all of which are in Seattle."

"Thanks, Greg. You've been a big help."

"Anything else?"

"Locate a Seattle phone directory on line. See if you can get a number for Mary Margaret O'Connor and the funeral home." Again, more clicking.

"There are lots of O'Connors, including a Mark O'Connor and an M., but no Mary Margaret. The phone might be listed under a husband, or possibly unlisted."

"Give me the address and phone number for M." He jotted as Greg recited, then took down the particulars about the funeral home. "Got it. I'll call the funeral home if 'M' doesn't work out. They should know which O'Connor."

"Next?"

"That's everything, thanks."

Randall handed Kingsley the number Greg had retrieved from the Seattle directory. She eyed it warily. "If I find out she *is* the sister, what should I say? I can't just lay out our suspicions."

"What *are* our suspicions?" Todd asked.

Randall and Barrie exchanged knowing glances. "From what we overheard, Kathleen O'Connor was an innocent bystander who got too close to something illegal and either tried to learn too much or even blackmailed the felons."

"Ruth certainly told us a different scenario," Barrie said, repeating the corporately correct version per Ruth.

"Do you realize Ruth may have given us the secretary's wrong name on purpose?" Barrie said. "She may be up to her neck in this, too."

Todd did mental math, frowning, as he counted bodies onto a second hand. "Ethelda Blake and her husband, the man in the bank's stairwell with the box, Shure, Ruth— there's got to be more."

Kingsley held up a finger. "Don't forget what Ethelda's former HR director said. Ethelda resigned, supposedly upset over a friend's baby who was born dead. The mother was sure her baby had been switched. If she was involved in that too, we're talking substantial manpower."

"And the guy who tailed us from Shure's office," Randall said.

Kingsley gasped. "What guy? What have we stumbled into? We better hope that Shure can't figure out who the 'Joneses' really are."

Randall repeated Shure's end of the overheard conversation. "My fingerprints are on file in Washington since I was in the military. How about you, Barrie?"

"Yep. For a security clearance. If those bastards have access, they'll make us fast."

Todd scowled ahead at the highway, teeth grinding, a small muscle rippling in his cheek. "Everything we've learned could delude us into thinking we're making progress, but goddamn it, they're so sophisticated we might never find Billy. I am so angry, not just for Billy but for every victim of this kind of treachery. And for what! Money?"

"'More money does not make more happy.' That's what Grammy used to say." Todd glanced at her, twisting her ring, lips taut, blinking quickly. He knew that look—the one that said that she would not cry, no matter what. He took her left hand in his right, kissed it, then pressed it to his cheek while continuing to steer.

The tar-filled expansion joints ticked rhythmically under the van's Michelins. Finally, Kingsley broke the silence, turning to Randall. "I can do this. I'll call Seattle and see what I can learn." She took Randall's notes. "I'll try this M first. Perhaps I'll get lucky. If not, I'll call the funeral home."

A young-sounding male answered the phone. "I'm calling from Pittsburgh," Kingsley began. "I'm trying to reach the family of Kathleen O'Connor. Do I have the right number?" A long pause followed.

"Well, yeah, sort of. She's my—was —my aunt, but she passed away three weeks ago."

Kingsley shot the group a thumbs-up. "I just heard, and I am so sorry for your loss. I'd been looking forward to meeting her, then missed her by such a short time. Is there someone else I can talk to?"

"There's my aunt. Just a minute." Kingsley waited. "Aunt Mare! It's some lady from Pittsburgh who knew Aunt Lib." Another pause followed in which Kingsley could hear footsteps approaching the phone.

"Hello?"

"Ms. O'Connor?"

"I'm Mary Margaret O'Connor. Can I help you?"

Kingsley struggled, knowing that if she misspoke, it might kill their chances. "I'm so sorry to bother you. It's just that I, we, are so frustrated. We just missed Kathleen by a few weeks, and I, my husband and I, were hoping she had information we need. We heard she was such a good person, so strong, such a devoted family person and Christian, and we'd counted on her helping us."

"Kathleen was my sister. More than my sister. My other half. We were identical twins. And yes, she was a wonderful soul, not at all like the terrible person folks in Pittsburgh described." Kingsley heard the woman's voice crack as she struggled to finish her sentence.

Kingsley sensed that she had connected with a benevolent person and took a chance. "We had been hoping to meet her at her place of employment. There was some confusion—the secretary told us her name was Libby."

"Her middle name was Elizabeth. Libby's a nickname, although I don't understand why they would use it. She detested the nickname and never used it—said it sounded like canned fruit."

"We just met Mr. Shure a short time ago."

"Shure! As if her death weren't bad enough. He had the nerve to defame her, making up lies about suicide. Suicide! Kathleen was a devout Catholic. Suicide is a mortal sin. She never, ever, *ever*, would have jumped off that roof!" The woman started to cry. "Somebody pushed her. I just know it. That's the only way it could have happened, and nobody believes me."

"Surely, they considered it."

"Seems the police had anonymous phone calls. You know, from cowards who won't get involved? After the news broke, the informants confirmed the lies that man Shure told the police and the press. Who's going to believe me? A sister who lives twenty-five hundred miles away? They were condescending and patronizing. Practically patted me on the head like a child in denial."

"I believe you. And there's a chance we can prove it. What do you think really happened?"

"Kathleen said Shure and some others were involved in something illegal, but that she was safe because she had insurance. My read on it was white-collar crime, like tax evasion or hiring illegals to do menial work. Since she wasn't a bookkeeper or accountant, she didn't have access to his financial records that would make her a threat. I tried to get her to tell me more, but she said not to worry. That she had the situation in hand. That she was positioning herself to retire. It had something to do with a pension or a reward or insurance."

"Did she say what kind of insurance?"

"She sent me the policy, but it's on a disk, and I don't know how to use a computer. I've been too busy, too upset, to look into it, and afraid to show it to anyone else. Her death has been a terrible ordeal, trying to arrange burial in consecrated ground. I had to agree she was mentally ill." Kingsley could hear her blowing her nose.

"About Mr. Shure—"

"I'm sorry. I don't feel comfortable discussing this on the phone."

"Could you hold for a minute?" Kingsley covered the mouthpiece and turned to Randall. "Could we go to Seattle?"

"Sure. We'll need to fly home and get the Gulfstream. How about first thing in the morning? I'll need to file a flight plan." As he reached for his phone, Kingsley motioned for him to hold on.

"Ms. O'Connor, would you be willing to meet with my husband and me tomorrow morning? I'm sorry to be so insistent, but our concerns are quite urgent. And I think we can help each other."

"Who did you say you were?"

"My name's Kingsley Ward Henning. Please. We must talk to you. Our baby was kidnapped, and I fear that your sister's death may be somehow related—that she stumbled onto something that Shure was doing."

"Well, all right." She sounded so hesitant that Kingsley feared she'd change her mind and hang up any second.

"Could you give me directions to your home?"

"No! You can't come here. That might not be safe. I'll meet you, and we'll go somewhere private."

"I'm going to put our baby's godfather and our best friend on the phone. He's our pilot and knows Seattle. His name is Randall. Here he is." She passed the phone to the back seat.

"Hi. Yes, I've used Boeing Field. Okay. We'll meet you at the parking lot outside the fixed base operation's terminal. Eight tomorrow morning is fine. How will we know you? A green Aerostar—Okay. We're coming in on a Gulfstream IV. You'll recognize me by my awful red hair. See you then." Before Randall could pass the phone back to Kingsley, the woman hung up.

"What now?" Kingsley asked.

"We'll fly home, grab some sleep, and meet at the airport in the morning." He held up his left hand and ticked off the time with his right index finger. "The Gulfstream can make it nonstop in five and a half hours. We gain three hours flying west, and our appointment's at eight. We must take off by five."

"Let's do it."

Chapter 23

Silent as the fog that concealed them, the black-clad pair crept from the wood's dense protection and circled toward the Hennings' rear entry. The lead kept his hand close to his weapon, moving swiftly with expert stealth. Convinced they were alone and no one was home, he motioned her forward with a jerk of his head.

Within seconds, she had the knob and deadbolt unlocked and swiftly disarmed the security system, unaware of the luminous green eyes that watched every move. Suddenly alert, the woman strained toward the thumping that receded as quickly as it had began. They waited, unmoving, for several moments. At length, the man shrugged. The two tiptoed down the center hall's Persian runner, past the kitchen on their left, verifying their location as they proceeded. Both stopped in mid-step as they came to the library entrance, its glass doors open. He pointed and both took a giant step from carpet to carpet, careful not to clatter on the old pine floors.

Efficiently she studied the neatly stacked papers assembled on the wife's desk and speed-read the contents. "It's all here. Lots of notes," she whispered, focusing her tiny camera to capture the details that suited her purpose. Then she ran expert fingers through Kingsley's Pendaflex folders, dismissing the mundane minutia, then searched her belly drawer.

He searched the man's desk, careful not to displace even the chair, then passed latex-gloved fingers over the computer's keyboard. On the open desktop, he searched the most recent activity by clicking Microsoft Internet Explorer History/Today and clicking on acba/GetMember and then there it was—Shure's membership listing. He beckoned for her to come have a look. Back-arrowing to ACBA he mouthed, "Allegheny County Bar Association."

Taking her turn, she followed the history's progression, verifying that someone had indeed identified Shure and visited his Website. Before he could stop her, she had clicked one too many back arrows and had shut the PC down.

He stared at the dark screen then snapped in a whisper, "The damn thing was on!" Futilely he tried to reboot the computer without success.

"Forget it. They probably won't notice. Think they quit it themselves, or that the electricity blinked. We got what we came for. Let's book."

Retracing their steps they approached the security keypad and, using a micro-sensing device, she rearmed the system. Sliver by sliver, he cracked the back door. Finding the expanse of back acreage deserted, he motioned for her to follow. Within moments they were swallowed back into the wood's dark protection.

ⲉⲟⲉⲟ

By the time the foursome reached the Hennings' back door, crimson clouds that had streaked the western horizon had faded from brilliant fuchsia to slate and then inky black. Todd, keys and penlight in hand, suddenly snapped to attention and waved off the others.

"What's wrong?" Kingsley asked, instinctively lowering her voice to a whisper.

Tentatively he touched the doorframe, which yielded a trace of brown smudges. As if zapped by a surge of electricity, he jerked his hand back. He retreated, pulling his cell phone from his jacket to speed dial the security company's number.

"Mr. Henning! We've been trying to reach you. We had an alert from your home. The alarm must have frightened away the intruder. We checked all the doors and windows and found no evidence of a break-in. We'd like to inspect the interior before you go in."

"I'd appreciate that."

"Wait outside and don't touch anything until we arrive."

Within fifteen minutes, a pair of uniformed men jumped from a white panel truck that bore the security company's distinct blue and green logo. After cursory introductions, they began their investigation, beaming flashlights around the exterior glass, then aiming their lights inside. "Your keys, please," the man in charge said. Gingerly he unlocked the back door, opened it, and circled the beam through the center hall.

"Wait here."

Kingsley, Barrie, and Randall hung back while Todd circled the house at a safe distance. In a few minutes, he reappeared, shrugging. "Looks normal to me."

Shortly the man called to them. "You can come in now. Tell us if anything's missing or looks out of place." The Hennings followed him throughout the house while Randall and Barrie hung in the kitchen. Todd stopped dead at his desk.

"The computer's turned off. I left it on." He circled the desk, looking hard at its surface. "My papers—the difference is subtle, but I don't stack things that way."

"We'd better call the police—have the desk dusted," the man said.

Todd hesitated. "No, that won't be necessary. I'm probably not remembering it right. We were in such a hurry this morning."

"Todd, are you sure?" Kingsley asked. "You're so methodical that—" Todd turned his back to the security man and warned Kingsley off with a dart of his eyes. "I guess you're right," she said. "Nothing appears to be missing. And we did leave in a rush."

The second security man joined them in the library. "If you're satisfied that nothing is disturbed, we'll finish checking the interior. Don't forget to lock up, arm the system, and call us if you're concerned." Silently, he held up a card for Todd to read, simultaneously putting a finger to his lips. It read, *We're going to sweep the house for bugs.* Todd nodded agreement. The pair disappeared down the back hall and returned with electronic wands. Stealthily they moved throughout the house systematically.

"Where did the girls go?" Todd asked Randall as they watched the men work.

"They went to the kitchen to fix us a snack. Everyone's famished."

Randall stalled, killing time with inane chatter about a particular jet engine that he thought would overtake the market and how it could change how he scheduled his work. Todd rolled his eyes and tried not to laugh. The lead security man finally returned and held up two fingers, one on each hand.

"Where?" Todd mouthed.

He pointed upstairs toward the bedroom and mouthed, "Lamp. Right side. And the lamp on her desk." He produced a second index card that read, *What do you want us to do?* Without hesitation, Todd jerked his thumb over his shoulder. The man removed the bug and dropped it into an insulated black pouch. "We're finished here," he said in a normal voice.

Todd followed the pair to their truck that was parked in the lane. "If I were you, I'd notify the police, keep your security system armed at all times, and have the house swept regularly, at least until your situation is resolved."

"We'll do that. And thanks." Todd watched the van disappear up the lane, staring long after its taillights vanished. Then he trudged back to their library.

"This doesn't make any sense," Todd said in hushed tones. "If someone got in, they didn't have time to access the computer, search the desks, and retreat before the alarm went off."

"Don't you think you should call the police?"

Todd gave Randall a weary look. "We're not one hundred percent sure that the devices weren't left by the cops."

"Wouldn't they need a warrant to do that?"

"Of course, to search, but to plant a listening device? They wouldn't tell us about that. What would be the point?"

Todd opened a desk drawer and inspected the contents. "I left our notes right here, including the ones about Shure. They're disarranged. I just don't understand how they got in and why the alarm tripped *after* the fact."

"Obviously, they knew how to bypass the system but screwed it up when they left. Were the motion detectors operational?"

"We never turn them on. Small matter of the cat."

Before he could explain further, Pandora abandoned her hiding place under the couch. Feigning boredom, the luxurious feline stretched and yawned innocently, then headed toward the activity in the kitchen.

"Whoever reset the alarm must have turned on the motion detectors, never reckoning on Pandora. She would have run upstairs the minute she heard strange voices and hid until they left."

"You better have that security company re-evaluate your system or hire a pet sitter."

"Our attorney promised onsite security, but they won't get here until tomorrow. They would have been here today had background checks not been so complicated. David Wentworth is being painstakingly thorough about anyone who gets close to Kingsley. His scrutiny borders on paranoia."

Randall poked at the papers piled on the desk. "What brought them here, and what did they want? You say nothing appears to be missing."

Todd frowned, pacing, then froze. He snapped his fingers. "Shure's website! Damn! We should have known better. They could have traced our activity. That means they know who we are. We've lost our advantage. And if we've gotten close enough to spook them, we might never find Billy."

"In case you haven't noticed, we're not safe ourselves, smart guy," Randall said. "But we still have the advantage if they don't know we found Kathleen's sister. Hopefully, we'll learn a lot more tomorrow."

"I won't be able to sleep," Todd said.

"I better round up the vixen. Let's meet at the airfield at five in the morning." He gave Todd's arm a compassionate punch. "Get some sleep, buddy."

୧୬୧୬

Kingsley peeled off her clothes and stepped into a hot, steamy shower. She lathered herself with silky body wash and shampooed her hair. She imagined the circling bubbles were drawing her troubles down the drain. Hair dried and dressed in lemon-yellow satin pajamas, she had just pulled on socks when she heard the phone ring. She hesitated, almost afraid to pick the thing up.

"Are you ready for some interesting news?" David Wentworth's voice sounded downright jovial. "Our investigative counsel did some excellent sleuthing."

Kingsley came to life instantly. "Let me get Todd on the extension." She hollered downstairs and heard him pick up. "Tell me!"

"First—the hair. The strand you picked up in the crib isn't human. It's mohair."

"Like a sweater? Somebody's garment?"

"Not a sweater. A wig."

"You mean—"

"Let me finish. This mohair is particularly fine and soft.

According to an expert, it's used in dolls' wigs, specifically infant baby dolls. We checked with a supplier of infant wigs and learned there's a specialty market for people who make, repair, or restore baby dolls. Their line includes complete dolls that look for all the world like real children, as well as parts, such as eyes, arms, legs, and, yes, wigs. They are particularly proud of how realistic their infant line is. The wigs are soft, with or without curls, and perfectly styled and colored to resemble every ethnic diversity."

"Can we get a list of who bought wigs that corresponds with the strand that I found?"

"We'd have to know which company to approach, get a warrant if they wouldn't cooperate, and still be faced with bogus names and post office boxes. Infant wigs aren't big-ticket items and could be purchased with a money order, cash, or a stolen credit card. On the plus side, that explains *how* the kidnapper made the doll's head look like Billy and Sammy."

"What if she'd been caught with it in her possession?"

"She didn't risk it—the doll in the crib had a painted head. If she'd put the wig on that doll, Ethelda would have been suspected immediately. They'd know to search Ethelda's house. They would have held her for questioning before she had a chance to escape. As it was, everyone was clueless as to how Billy returned safely to the nursery but disappeared from his crib."

"You are trying to find her—"

"Even as we speak. Which brings me to item two. Who is the Blake woman? We did an extensive background check on Ethelda, finding one more previous employer, then nothing. It was as if she never existed. But we caught a break. An employee from a previous job, who suspected she was stealing from coworkers, decided to snoop. Among her personal stuff, she found a reference to a rural town in Georgia. Ethelda said she was from Detroit, born and raised. The employee dismissed that tidbit, having no interest in why she would lie."

"How does that help us?"

"We acquired her social security number, then had an operative check vital statistics in rural Georgia. Bingo—it was the name of a real person. However, many jurisdictions do not or cannot cross-reference birth and death certificates."

"Let me guess. The real Ethelda Blake died in infancy, or something like that."

"Actually she was a young teen, which is why she had a SS number. She worked part time at a fast-food joint when she was fourteen. And get this—she had a twin named Emelda."

"You've got to be kidding. Ethelda and Emelda. Huh!"

"Emelda Blake, who is now married and goes by her husband's name, *Black*."

"Uncle David, can we sit on this for a while? We need time to track down a lead of our own." She and Todd took turns filling him in on their day's expedition and what they had learned, including their upcoming meeting the following morning.

David groaned. "First, we'll have your house secured by tomorrow. And you should take a bodyguard. And, I wonder if we should confide in the authorities."

"I've thought about that, but I'm not willing to share until they concede that we're not involved. I want a public statement to that effect."

"That would be worthless. They could go back on their word in a heartbeat."

"Can't you demand that they give you any evidence they're collecting against us?"

"If they charge you with a crime, I can file for discovery. But since they haven't—"

"I get it. Okay, here's the deal. As long as the possibility exists that the kidnapper could claim they were working for us, we are simply not sharing. I'm not obligated, am I?"

"You need not tell anyone what you suspect. Nor must you turn over anything that could incriminate you. But,

Kingsley—you too, Todd—be careful. You could be in danger."

"Nobody knows where we're going—it's just an overnight trip to Seattle. But if this escalates, then, yes—we'll take you up on that bodyguard."

ოოო

The woman tapped her French-manicured nails impatiently on the Corian counter as she stared unseeing across the lush landscape that embellished her elegant townhome in north Jersey. Cell phone clamped to her ear, she paced as she staccatoed her report. "I got a call. They've made the connection! Or at least they will shortly. That hit to your website came from the Hennings' home computer."

"Damn!"

"What are we going to do? This is a runaway train."

"Get hold of yourself," he said. "Indulging in hysteria will only muddle your thinking. No one will ever find traces of you in my records that aren't totally legitimate. You're listed as an outsource professional who does research for prestigious law firms. Every cent you've been paid has been declared to the IRS. That's where lesser minds screw up."

"If you're sure—"

"Shortly I'll know who the Joneses really are. If they're close to the Hennings, that shouldn't be difficult. I'll put a tail on all four then decide how best to proceed. Look— your exposure is negligible, but nevertheless, double-check your precautions. Make damned sure you've cross-shredded and burned your instructions, IDs, and pertinent documents."

"What about you? What if—"

"I'm wrapping up my business in Pittsburgh and will be out of the country in forty-eight hours."

"And these four people?"

"Just loose ends. Such details needn't concern you. They

will be addressed like all the others, and the less you know about that, the better. Now—I believe we're up to date on your remuneration? Let's review our concluding protocol."

"I finished my checklist, burned it, and am good to go. Directly, I might add."

"It's been a pleasure. If you're ever near my island—"

"I doubt that, but thanks anyway."

The new Ms. Vanessa Smyth-Wyatt opened her bag and checked her virgin driver's license, passport, and array of credit, debit, and medical ID cards. She looked at her platinum Rolex—almost time for her ride. Her copious luggage, grouped near the door, would cost a bundle in overage fees, but that was okay. She needed her stuff. Ticket to Paris— that was tucked in the pouch of her Coach carry-on. One last walkthrough, she thought, as she opened every closet, door, and compartment throughout her luxury rental digs. Six hours from now, she'd be in the air. A free, obscenely rich woman.

She checked the powder room mirror for a final adjustment to her long, auburn wig, and inserted brown contacts. In response to a toot, she opened her door and summoned the driver to help with her luggage. As the sleek limo eased away from the condo, she bade a silent goodbye to Ethelda Blake, who no longer existed. The only thing left was her *remuneration*, which she intended to enjoy.

⌘

The Hennings' old stone farmhouse was finally silent. Sock footed, Kingsley prowled its interior, its sense of protection like an old friend. She had always felt safe in the Amish countryside, surrounded by gentle people and obscured by the woods. And, from day one, she had felt its ethereal warmth and connection to those long-ago families who had built, loved, and lived out their lives within its shelter. Her and Todd's painstaking restoration, the act of touching every square inch with paper and paint, had made it their own.

The security men had been thorough, efficient, professional, and polite. They had dispelled any feeling of possible danger. Nevertheless, Pandora and her box, food, water, and treats, would be closed in their bedroom, the security system fully armed.

"Kingsley, come to bed. We have to leave in just a few hours."

Kingsley took one last look, switching off the lamps that were lit in each room, and ascended the staircase. She paused in the upper hall and glanced into her little son's room. How many frivolous things had she prayed for in her lifetime? Was there such a thing as a quota? *Dear God in Heaven,* she prayed silently. *Give us strength. Give us courage. Give us the insight to understand what we find.* She thought of her Grammy. *"Watch...He will lead ...follow."*

⌘

Daybreak outlined the distant Appalachians in a pencil-thin tangerine line that pushed aside the last remnants of night. As the Gulfstream soared westward, the first rays of sunshine bounced gleaming light off its silvery body. Todd fell asleep immediately, but Kingsley, edgy and anxious, was unable to nap more than twenty minutes. Tired of thinking and praying and reviewing all that she knew, she prowled the short aisle. She watched the sun's progression that seemed to be chasing the jet, eventually overtaking them. After what seemed like an eternity, the jet landed at Boeing Field near Seattle and taxied to the fixed base operation.

Mary Margaret O'Connor was hardly what Kingsley expected. Although they arrived thirty minutes early, Kathleen's sister was already waiting in her hunter green Aerostar. She was short and plump, her steel gray hair side-parted in a short bob that just covered her ears. She wore a long-sleeved white jersey over a gathered denim skirt and canvas flats. Mary Margaret's flawless complexion needed no makeup, and her features were soft and motherly. She smiled with her eyes that showed no trace of the fear that Kingsley had heard on the phone.

"I know a private place where we can talk," she said after they exchanged introductions. The five piled into her van, and Mary Margaret sped to the highway. She maneuvered side roads that ultimately wound to a secluded Puget Sound inlet. As they stepped out of the van, she directed them toward the shore where several picnic tables sat beside a barbecue pit. No one was around.

Mary Margaret seated herself across from Kingsley and Todd while Barrie and Randall wandered toward the water to give the others privacy. Dragonflies, born on gossamer wings, skimmed among cattails that swayed gently as the water rippled against the silt shore. The Pacific Northwest, known for its months of soggy weather, gave up its secret that morning. Following months of heavy weather when even the gulls were reduced to walking, a spectacular season unfolded that sometimes started as early as April and persisted into the fall.

A soft morning breeze lifted Mary Margaret's hair. She exuded a peace that belied the grievous nature of her information, beginning her story as soon as they settled. "I begged my sister to give up her job and come home. Kathleen was a smart lady and scrupulously honest. No one could have persuaded her to look the other way." She paused a minute, looking beyond her folded hands to the inlet's opposite shore, then back at them.

"She never felt prayer was enough. Her favorite Bible passage was from Matthew when Jesus says, 'I was hungry, and you fed me; thirsty and you gave me something to drink…' He continues to say that whatever you do for the least of my brothers, you do for me. That was Kathleen's inspiration. To address need in Jesus's name. She felt privileged to sail into battle on behalf of less fortunate people, especially those who had tried to help themselves, only to fail. Evidently, she stumbled across something at Shure's firm that dealt with victimizing families."

"What exactly did she say?"

"Let me back up. At first, she thought Shure was involved in some kind of 'victimless crime,' like tax evasion. High-level accounting was over her head. Then she alluded that he was cheating people, perhaps by billing for inflated hours. There were people being paid for projects and services about which there was no documentation.

"Shortly before she died, she made a huge discovery. She was terribly upset—said she suspected her boss was victimizing families, but she needed time to find proof. She offered no details. Said she had everything under control. But in spite of her reassurances, my intuition went crazy. There was this—something—in her voice that didn't feel right. She was scared. And unaccustomed to lying, she mixed up the details. In any event, I bought a plane ticket east. We needed to talk face to face."

"What did you learn?"

"I was too late."

"Then there was no man in her life?"

"I'm positive. In the first place, she would have told me. More important, she wasn't impulsive. We were alike in that way. It takes both of us time to warm up to strangers. I know what people think—that I'm in denial. But she was my twin. Once, when she broke her arm, I felt the pain from a hundred miles away. Sometimes I'd become sad, for no reason at all, and she'd call with a problem that she was facing. Twins have a mystical bond. It defies logic, but it's there all the same."

She lowered her gaze, breaking eye contact with Kingsley, holding her hands as if in prayer. She bobbed them rhythmically against the edge of the table. "This is difficult to talk about. We both were squeamish about being touched. We had problems as children, being premature. We had numerous surgeries and treatments. All of that probing left us, well, raw. And we were schooled by strict nuns. We don't relate well to men. Not socially anyway. No, if there had been a man in her life, I would have known. But a married man? She'd have gone straight to her priest."

A cleansing breeze that rippled the water carried the scent of warmed Douglas fir. Sunlight dazzled the water, and gulls that approached them departed haughtily when no food was offered.

It was absurd, Kingsley thought, to feel overwhelmed by evil on such a spectacular morning.

"You said your baby was kidnapped?" Mary Margaret asked.

Kingsley condensed their anguishing weeks as briefly as possible, ending with how they obtained Shure's phone number and braved an appointment for Barrie and Randall.

"What name did you say they called my sister?"

"Libby."

Concern overtook Mary Margaret's serene face. "The only way they could know that was through reading her private papers. Those she kept under lock and key in her apartment. You're in danger, just like she was. You must go to the police."

Todd huffed. "They're convinced we staged our son's kidnapping, which is ludicrous."

"You mentioned a disk," Kingsley said. "That it contained an insurance policy."

"After we spoke on the phone, I realized that she never used the word 'policy.' She said 'insurance.' She had me go to my priest to whom she had spoken and entrusted with a package. He gave it to me, and I did as she asked."

"And you have no idea what's on the disk? Aren't you curious, given all that has happened?"

"Yes, but she told me not to read it unless I received instructions to do so."

"What did she ask you to do if something happened to her? Give the disk to the authorities? Or back to your priest?"

"She said she would send me a contact's name under separate cover, but that never came. I think she died before she had time to finalize her plan."

"I am so sorry. Please forgive us for bringing more trouble to your doorstep. We wouldn't do so if we weren't desperate."

"It doesn't matter." She gazed across the water as if reflecting on a lifetime of precious memories. Shortly she came back to the present. She dug into her purse and produced an unlabeled CD in a clear plastic sleeve. "Here. I'm giving you Kathleen's insurance with the understanding that, if it yields anything relevant, you'll help me clear Kathleen's good name. She did not kill herself. She was not mentally ill. I'm not as generous as my sister. I want whoever did this to her to be punished in this lifetime too."

"Of course. I'm just sorry we didn't have the honor of knowing your sister. Thank you for trusting us and for confirming what we suspected."

The lady smiled, a peace spreading over her countenance as if a great burden had been lifted. "How can we safely stay in touch?" Kingsley asked. "Your phone might be tapped."

"My priest says to call him any time. I'll give you his number."

"Are there other copies of this disk?" Todd asked.

"That's the only one. I entrust it to you."

"We will safeguard it and use it properly."

They sat for a while, talking of families and faith, no one wishing to leave. Finally, Todd rose, breathing the fir-scented air. "I know a banker, here in Seattle, who has offered to help us. Ms. O'Connor, could you drop us downtown?"

"Of course. And call me Mare. Everyone does."

Chapter 24

Kingsley was surprised by how desolate she felt as Mary Margaret's taillights disappeared, leaving them alone on a Seattle street corner. Mare's serenity and the peaceful lakeside setting had calmed her anxieties and made her feel stronger—somehow detached from the horrific reality. Now reality dropped its pall on her spirit. She took a ragged breath.

"This way." Todd directed them through the historic bank's brass-trimmed door. The four passed into the main branch's lobby.

"How much do we have to tell Lloyd Peterson?" she asked.

"Lloyd already knows about the kidnapping. He called me as soon as it happened to offer condolences and whatever help we might need. He sounded delighted that we'd be in town."

The bank's mammoth interior with its marble floors, brass teller cages and vaulted ceiling supported by pillars, oozed century-old integrity and stability.

Footsteps echoed, as bankers and customers hustled to transact their business. Half-round windows that topped the two-story casements wore gathered sheers drawn to a knot. Beneath them hung mauve jabots, swags, and floor-length draperies.

Along the floor's perimeter walls, officers whose nameplates bespoke their importance worked behind low wooden dividers with matching gates.

"There he is now," Todd said, pointing to a thin man who stood before a huge open vault. The man smiled broadly as he strode toward them, quickly closing the gap. Kingsley warmed immediately to Lloyd Peterson, whose soft-spoken greeting and genuine warmth reminded her of British nobility. While his face was quite ordinary—brown eyes that were small, a nose rather large, and thinning brown hair that was slicked back with no part—he was nevertheless elegant in a muted, starched way. Beneath his gray trousers his black wingtips shined. Casual Friday, to say nothing of Saturday, had not reached this man.

"Let's take the elevator to my floor," Lloyd said, steering Todd gently by the shoulder. They might have been prep school roommates or fraternity brothers, Kingsley thought, judging by Lloyd's genuine pleasure at seeing his friend.

Lloyd showed them into his corner office, which was surprisingly modest compared to the elegant lobby. A time-line of family photos marched across the credenza behind him. On the side walls, which were papered with grass cloth, hung plaques of appreciation from numerous professional and nonprofit organizations. A tall carafe, coffee cups, creamer and sugar sat on a small table beside his desk. He began pouring and passing the cups, then pushed the condiment tray within reach.

"I'm at your disposal," Lloyd said, bringing focus to the assembly. "Todd, let me start by saying you don't need to elaborate on details, especially since you indicated on the phone that time is of the essence. Just tell me what you need, and we'll hop to it."

Kingsley pulled the disk from her purse. "We're hoping this contains information about what happened to our son. Regardless, there's evidence of a crime."

Todd said, "I must warn you that the information it contains could put you in danger. Our goal is not cracking a kidnapping ring. Our goal is to locate our son, if it's not already too late, and to safeguard our family and friends."

"What's on the disk?" Lloyd asked.

"That's what we're here to find out. We need a computer with a disk drive. What comes next depends upon what we learn."

"Nobody's working on this floor today. You'll have complete privacy. I'll put you in that vacant office across the way, which still has an older PC with a disk drive."

୧ର୧ର

Settled before a Hewlett Packard computer and monitor, Todd pushed the disk into the slot, double-clicked the icon that appeared on the screen, and then opened the first of many folders. The computer dutifully opened Microsoft Word.

"That appears to be a personnel list," Barrie said. "Look. There's Ruth's name." She rummaged in her purse for the paper Ruth had provided. "The address and phone number aren't on this list. What are the numbers that follow it?"

"Looks like account numbers, but no institution is listed," Todd said.

"Try another document," Randall said. Todd double clicked an Excel icon, and a spreadsheet sprang onto the screen.

"That looks like expenses," Todd said, squinting at the columns of tiny numbers. He positioned the down arrow, then asked the Excel genie to sort the document's columns by name rather than date. He picked one at random. "There. It's a list of expenditures by the person's name, with two different date columns and some type of code explanation."

"Bet the first date is the target and the second, completion," Randall said.

Kingsley was getting impatient. "Never mind the details—keep opening documents. There's got to be something more useful."

Todd opened document *Three*, its title being *Families*. The name of a city followed each couple's names. Todd slowly scrolled to the bottom of the list while the others read it in silence.

He tapped Page Up, and the two-page document zapped to the beginning. "A mailing list? But there aren't any addresses. Just cities," Kingsley said. "That's disappointing. I was expecting, well, I don't know what I was expecting."

"How about detailed directions to Billy? That would have been nice," Barrie said with a note of sarcasm. "That's what I hoped."

"Why is the list so short?" Kingsley asked. "You said his bulletin boards were groaning with pictures. If he stashed enough money to retire to his own private island, he must have had more than a few dozen clients."

"It's more like thirty," Todd said, scrolling the document again. "Make that thirty-three."

"You're forgetting something important," Kingsley said. "Kathleen's sister said that this disk contained Kathleen's insurance. Wouldn't that mean something other than routine data? Above and beyond legitimate business? And," she said, brightening at a new idea, "she thought she could retire with the *rewards*? She did say rewards, right?"

"Kathleen didn't sound like the blackmailing type," Todd said. "Maybe her reward was the joy of recovering kidnapped children and protecting future families from his crimes."

Todd was rapidly opening and closing more documents. "Let's go out on a limb here," Randall said, interrupting the tour of the disk. "Suppose these *Families* are the names of people who hide kidnapped children. Or maybe they're the ones who are adopting them. Having secured that information, Kathleen could have researched each one, then passed the information to the authorities. Exposed the whole operation."

"But something went wrong," Kingsley said. "Or something spooked her and forced her to act too quickly. Or perhaps she thought what she knew kept her safe, especially if nobody knew where she hid the disk. Mary Margaret did say her Seattle house was broken into during the funeral and thoroughly tossed. The police suspected it was part of a series of robberies where the thieves get their victims' names from the newspapers and rob houses during the services. No one was house-sitting during Kathleen's mass."

The group fell silent for a moment. "So," Randall broke into their thoughts. "Where are we going with this information?"

"Let's make some assumptions," Todd said. "First, let's say it's a list of people who acquired their children through less than legitimate means. And they may or may not have been in on the crime."

Kingsley frowned. "If they're wealthy and would stoop to that, they could flee until it's safe to return or leave the country forever. Then we would never find Billy."

"On the other hand," Todd said, "suppose the families are perfectly innocent? Then Billy would be safe as long as we find him before the kidnappers learn that we're close and remove him—maybe harm him this time."

"You heard what Shure insinuated," Randall said. "There's a ten-year waiting list. If an individual 'got bucks' and was willing to pay 'huge' to be bumped to the top of the list, wouldn't that be a hell of a payday to feather his tropical nest? Times thirty-three? And don't forget, there wouldn't be any taxes to pay. All that, on top of his legitimate earnings."

"But Randall and I couldn't bait him into offering us a child for big bucks."

"If he's that smart, you didn't fool him," Kingsley said. "Remember, someone traced our little adventure back to our PC the same day."

"Focus, guys," Todd said. "Let's assume he steals American kids and passes them off as foreign orphans. His legitimate foreign adoption practice would be a perfect cover." The four looked back at the computer screen as Todd selected *Families*, queuing up the print dialog box and typing the command for four copies. He took his copy and returned to Lloyd's office. When he rapped on the doorframe, Lloyd looked up and motioned him in. "Did you find what you needed?" he asked.

"Possibly. May I ask one more favor?"

"Sure. Shoot."

"Do you have a conference room with several phones, or could we use several individual offices?"

"Of course." He led Todd through the labyrinth of cubicles to the opposite corner of the executive suite to the boardroom. "Here you go," he said, pointing to the large table with several phones strategically placed. "Help yourself. Dial seven-one to access the wide-area usage line."

"I owe you."

"No, you don't. Just find that baby."

•••

"This is not going to be easy," Barrie said, scanning her list one more time. "Some of these names are so common, but at least we have the husbands' first names and their home towns." Randall snapped a look at his watch. "It's nearly eleven. Let's divvy up the list, call information, and nail down as many as we can." Kingsley drew pencil lines to bracket her share, then started to dial. The others did likewise. A competitive atmosphere overtook the conference room as they dialed and scarfed information rapid-fire from directory assistance, seeing who could finish their list first. Many names were unusual, and all included middle initials, which facilitated the task. Todd triumphantly held his hand high after just fifteen minutes.

"We can't just call and say, 'do you have my baby who was kidnapped three weeks ago?' How can we do this?" Kingsley asked.

"I've got an idea," Barrie said. "Let's pose as representatives of a company that deals in baby products and ask their opinion. Chat them up a bit."

"That could take a lot of chatting, *if* they'll talk to us and *if* we can somehow work *adoption* into the conversation," Randall said. "You've got to ask something compelling—then cut to the chase."

"What subject would keep them on the phone?" Barrie asked the parents.

"Health issues would do it for me," Kingsley said. "If I'd just adopted a baby from a foreign country or a native teenager, I'd listen long enough to make sure my baby was healthy."

Todd, who had risen from his chair, began pacing, eyes on the carpet, stroking his chin. Finally, he spoke. "Don't forget Shure. We can't say anything that would trigger a call to him, such as asking about diseases or immunization. Shure would know immediately that something was wrong. That could impact what might happen to Billy. We've been assuming that one of the couples on this list has him. He might still be en route or on hold somewhere else."

The four exchanged furtive glances, nobody daring to say the D word.

"I've got it!" Barrie said, jumping from her chair with a cheerleader's grin. "Oh, this is so perfect. And we can quickly eliminate girls from the list if we do it."

"What?"

"Let's pose as pharmaceutical representatives from some big name company like Pfizer or Merck. Now, what do baby boys have done that baby girls don't?" She didn't wait for the obvious answer. "We'll say we're doing a follow-up check on little patients who were circumcised within the last three months using our new local anesthetic. Did the baby seem comfortable immediately afterward? Any rash near the site? Let's make up an off-the-wall sounding rash so there's no way it could be confused with diaper rash."

"Great idea, Barrie, since that question would be a non-issue for these parents," Todd said. "If each child on this list was kidnapped and passed off as a foreign orphan, he would have already been circumcised or not, or would have been by the adoptive parents' physician. The parent *should* respond that they don't know since the baby was adopted."

"And if the baby is a girl, we're off the phone fast and on to the next," Barrie said.

"I don't know about you, but I need a script," Kingsley said. "I'm terrified that I might trigger an alarm, and it's just too important." Barrie was already attacking a legal tablet and scribbling ideas.

"You girls better do it," Randall said. "I'm no good at this chatting-up business."

Todd nodded. "They'll be more willing to talk to a woman, especially if you say you're a mother yourself."

Barrie slipped into her role along with an ingratiating smile to get her mood right. She dialed the first number at the top of her list.

"Hi, Mrs. Szyler? I'm Suzy Little, a new mom and a representative of Merck Pharmaceutical. I'm calling other moms whose infant boys may have used one of our miracle products during their recent circumcisions." A long pause followed. "Oh, that's so sweet. I'm so happy for you. How old is your daughter now? Wow, she must be in preschool by now." Barrie held up four fingers. "Well, congratulations, and thanks anyway for your time."

"Well?"

"She was thrilled to brag about her baby. We've got to fine-tune this script a bit to force them to mention adoption." She scribbled some phrases and passed it to Kingsley.

"Ready?" Barrie asked Kingsley.

"I better listen one more time." Barrie dialed the second number, and Kingsley listened intently while being careful not to distract her with eye contact. In less than two minutes Barrie hung up.

"That was a boy, but he's three and a half. And guess what! She volunteered that he was adopted and that she had no idea what was used for his operation."

Todd frowned at the list. "If there's a chance that these names are in order, with the oldest ones first, let's work from the bottom. Here—go to the third from the end."

Barrie pointed to Kingsley who picked up the phone. Kingsley willed her hands to stop shaking as she dialed the phone and demanded her mind to snap into the role. "Hi, Mrs. DeLong? I'm Suzy Little…"

"What did she say?"

"We're getting closer," Kingsley said, trying to quell her excitement. "The DeLong baby was adopted too, but it's a six-month-old girl. I'll do another." She dialed again, chatted much longer, and then reported back. "A six-month-old boy, but get this—she says his eye color doesn't match— one blue and one brown—and she wonders how soon small children can wear colored contacts. She's concerned about his being teased."

Randall, who had been watching the scene quietly, spoke up. "Todd, all three mothers said their babies were adopted? Is there any way to ask how these babies became available for adoption?"

"That *would* trigger a phone call to Shure. We don't know what these parents were told. If they're innocent and grateful to him, they might call to ask if they said anything wrong. Let's stick to the script."

"My turn," Barrie said, and dialed number twenty-eight that belonged to a family named Manatawney. She started her spiel, then listened intently. Immediately Kingsley noticed the change in her tone. "I wouldn't worry too much. What is he, almost five months? I bet he'll have a growth spurt soon. Are you and your husband short people? Oh, well then, maybe the birth parents were short. Perhaps he'll grow up to be a fine surgeon. Doctors don't have to be tall." She shot Kingsley a look, making wild circular motions with her free hand to grab her a pencil.

"He sounds beautiful," Barrie was saying. "Is he sleeping well for you? My little guy is up every three hours." She listened for what seemed to the others like forever. Randall went for the conference call button. Barrie shot him a look, covered the mouthpiece, and mouthed "No!"

"Do I detect a midwestern accent?" Barrie asked sweetly. "Oh, what part of Ohio? Really? What a coincidence! My husband is being transferred to Columbus. Do you have a nice neighborhood to recommend?" Barrie scribbled a notation, then finally moved the conversation to a conclusion. She hung up.

Kingsley leaped from her chair. "Do you think that you found him? What did she say?" Her insides were jumping and she could feel the familiar tingle of milk letting down. Automatically she clamped her forearm across her breasts to stop it.

"She described him as thin, and yes, adopted. He has a lot of dark hair and gorgeous blue eyes. He's really cute, but all our mothers said that."

"Why was she concerned about his size? Billy is big for his age."

"Not if she thinks he's five months old. That's Sammy's age. She said she was told that he spent his first four months in an overseas orphanage—then stopped abruptly and corrected herself saying, 'I meant to say Appalachia, not overseas.' She said he's perfectly healthy and was told by the agency that he'll catch up quickly. She said her pediatrician agrees—even speculated that he might have been premature and his mother, malnourished."

Kingsley jumped to collect her things, but Todd stopped her. "Not so fast. We've got to work our way upstream on that list. This may not be Billy."

Kingsley sighed and dropped her stuff back on the table. "Okay, but we can't rule out the possibility that one of them could call Shure, and if several of them do—"

Barrie interrupted. "Isn't that a good reason not to make too many calls?"

"Let's just do enough from the bottom of the list to verify that we're out of the age range." Barrie and Kingsley began calling simultaneously from opposite ends of the conference table, backs to each other. That got old fast as they mapped a progression of children who passed from eight to twenty months, proving that the list was chronological.

"You say the family lives near Columbus?" Randall asked Barrie.

"A small city called Upper Arlington."

"You are good! Now, while you guys call a cab or hit our friend Lloyd for a ride to Boeing Field, I'll phone for a flight plan. Next stop—Columbus, Ohio."

Chapter 25

L Gerard Shure pounced on his cell phone the second it vibrated. Sequestered in his luxurious penthouse, his eyes glazed in rapt concentration. His operative began his report.

"The blonde was fingerprinted for a security clearance, and the guy who called himself Jones was in the military. His name's Randall Shannon. Graduate of the Air Force Academy. Flew with them for twelve years, then resigned his commission. Spent a couple years traveling around before starting his charter company. That is flourishing. He flies rich people and corporate types around the world for business or pleasure."

"He's not a PI? Then what the hell was he doing on my doorstep? Especially using that stupid name? And who's the woman?"

"His corporate headquarters is located in southeast Pennsylvania. And get this—according to school records, he graduated from high school with William Todd Henning."

Shure lowered his voice through clenched teeth, lips touching the phone. "I could strangle the Blake woman with my bare hands. It was bad enough kidnapping a high-profile baby by mistake, but from a family with that kind of resources? What else did you find?"

"The blonde's name is Barrie Brown. She's assistant controller at the bank where the Hennings both work. That's the connection."

"Terrific!"

"It gets worse. According to Shannon's flight plan, he's in Seattle right now and—hold it a minute—he just filed another for Columbus, Ohio. What do you want us to do?"

"Any idea why he was in Seattle?"

"Could be nothing—company business or pleasure, but according to the ground crew, four of them left together. However, the descriptions match the Hennings and the Brown woman. Of course, she's his co-pilot so that would explain her."

Shure strained into the back of his mind. "There's something curiously reassuring about all of this. If they've picked up our trail, why aren't the cops all over it too?"

"We planted enough misinformation and sightings, supposedly from reliable sources, as well as a flood of anonymous tips, to make the Hennings look guilty. They look at family first, and they've taken the bait. The cops are trying their damnedest to prove the Hennings disposed of the kid. So, whatever the Hennings think they have learned, they must be keeping it to themselves."

"Excellent. Have you learned anything else about Kathleen's disk?"

"It hasn't turned up. We searched her apartment, took her PC. Nothing. Ditto the sister's place in Seattle. You searched the office. She had no safe deposit box, rental space, didn't make any friends. Kept to herself. I think it's safe to put a check mark beside that."

"No. That's got to be why they're in Seattle. Kathleen must have sent the disk to her sister. Here's what I want you to do. Track Shannon's flight and their credit card use and get back to me. When you find them, eliminate the problem. It shouldn't be hard to intercept them in Columbus. Just make sure it looks like an accident. Planes crash all the time. And deal with the adoptive parents as well."

"What about the kid?"

"Separate him from that couple then dump him out of state. Some place like the Ozarks or Appalachia. One more thing—make damned sure that everything's shredded and burned. Your account will be paid in the usual way, half now, half when completed."

"For this type of risk, I want it up front."

"You know I need proof. Keeps everyone honest."

"Seventy-thirty."

"Oh, hell. Just do it right."

"And the disk?"

"We can assume the sister doesn't know what she's got, or we would have heard about it by now. If we eliminate the four, knowledge of the disk ends with them.

The operative disconnected, scowling at the man behind the wheel. "That bastard's losin' it big time. 'Make it look like an accident,'" he singsonged contemptuously. "Yeah, right. Like spur of the moment, all four of them. And Appalachia? Drag the kid over state lines?" He emptied his unabridged cache of expletives.

His companion drummed on the wheel. "I say the minute the cash hits the account, we disappear. Forego the balance."

"With his connections, he'd find us."

"Then how do you suggest we handle this?"

"Let's stake out the adoptive parents' place first, then hit them when the neighborhood's quiet. Like Sunday morning. Slit a baggie where he falls, stash another in a cereal box or in the fridge. Cops will think it's a drug deal gone south. He's got to be up to no good to live like he does."

"This deal's been wrong from day one."

"No shit. Man's got a god complex. And this job's got to be costing him more than he's making. Should have eliminated the problem as soon as he knew the wrong kid was snatched."

"Speaking of the kid…"

"Collateral damage. As for the Shannon foursome, they'll need a rental in Columbus. We can rig it or the plane."

❧❧

Lloyd Peterson approached the conference room, clearing his throat to announce his intrusion. "How's everyone doing? Did you find what you're looking for?"

"I think so," Todd said as he finished gathering his notes and research materials. "I just wish we had time to study each document we found on this disk."

"Do you have a laptop?"

"Well, yes. But it doesn't have a disk drive. Just USB ports."

"Why don't you save each document on our desktop computer, then drag each to a flash drive? I'll get you a supply.

"That would be great." Lloyd disappeared and returned shortly with several thumb drives. Todd wasted no time copying the files, then Lloyd agreed to safeguard Mare's CD in their vault.

"What's next?" Lloyd asked as he shut down the computer.

"We'll return to Boeing Field, then fly to Columbus, Ohio, which is where the trail leads."

"Then you were successful?"

"Thanks to an unselfish lady who values justice more than her safety." Todd weighed the thumb drives in his hand. "Mary Margaret trusted us with the only evidence that could clear her sister's name. If it leads to our son, we'll never be able to thank her enough."

"Call from Columbus and let me know what you find. I'll give you my unlisted number."

❧❧

Randall led the way up the Gulfstream IV's airstairs. Barrie headed straight for the cockpit while Randall followed the Hennings into the cabin. He was unusually somber and professional, focused on task. "Fixed-base operation personnel ordered some food from one of their caterers." He pointed to the galley in the rear of the jet. "Please. Help yourself. You've got to eat, whether you feel like it or not. If you can manage, you're on your own." He snapped a look at his watch. "It's one o'clock now. With the time change flying east, we should land at Port Columbus International about eight-thirty their time."

"I wish we knew someone in Columbus," Kingsley said.

"We do," Randall said. "Dan Griffith, the industrial designer whose firm did extensive renovation at your bank. I flew him to Columbus after one of your meetings when he'd missed his return flight. I hit him with one of my better sales pitches. Not only did he become a regular customer, but also sent first-rate business my way. Columbus is a city of opportunity where business, government, and education intersect. It's been a cash cow for me. I should open a branch office there."

"He did say if I was ever in Columbus to give him a call," Todd said.

"I'll get him on the sky phone. We'll need suggestions for dinner and lodging as well." He started to leave and turned back to Kingsley. "Take care of your guy. I can't play mother hen forever." He flapped his arms and clucked, enjoying his joke, then hustled to prepare for departure.

❦

"He sleeps!" Fran, Beth Manatawney's next-door neighbor in Upper Arlington, gently touched Matthew, who was sacked out on Beth's shoulder. The two resumed wandering their perennial gardens, checking on spring's progression. "You look exhausted. Is he sleeping much yet?"

"Three hours, tops, but rarely at night." Beth caught herself peering between their two houses and tried to shake a creepy sensation.

"Beth, are you expecting someone?"

"No, but—Fran, have you noticed any strange cars on our street?"

"Strange? Not really. People have been stopping across the street to check out the house that's on the market. Why?"

"There's this black car. I've seen it a couple times now. It wouldn't have caught my attention had it not parked and just sat up the street. Why would anyone do that?"

"Could you tell who was in it?"

"They weren't neighbors—I know their cars. From behind my bedroom sheers, I could make out two men. They didn't do anything except wait, but it bothers me."

Fran chuckled. "Maybe they're private investigators. Maybe someone's suspected of having an affair."

"That couldn't be it. Everyone at that end of the street has lived here forever. They have grown grandchildren."

"If you're concerned and see them again, call the police. I don't suppose you could make out the license."

"Just that it is Ohio's."

"Well, keep your alarm on, just in case."

"We never installed one. Nicodemus would bark at anything that moved, and he sounded ferocious. We were waiting for the next litter of pups when we got the call about Matthew."

"All the more reason to get an alarm. I'll give you the number of our provider." The pair continued their garden inspection, both now glancing warily at each passing car.

৶৩৶৩

"You hardly ate anything," Todd said of the excellent spread that the caterer had stowed in the galley. "And it's been such a long time since breakfast. Come on. Eat something."

"You sound like my mother."

"I'm being practical. Besides, didn't you say something about being an adult?" She elbowed him, splashing his soda onto his shirt.

"Serves you right." She dabbed at the damage before turning serious attention to her neglected tray. "You're right. Butterflies be damned. By the way, what time is it now?"

"Thirty minutes later than the last time you asked. Here." He unbuckled his watch and handed it to her. "Your turn. You keep track." She pulled the strap to its tightest hole, laughing when it flopped ridiculously on her narrow wrist. When it righted itself, she observed: three more hours. Then what?

Todd stowed his tray then, settling into a captain's chair, opened his leather carry-on tote. One by one, he extracted the manila folders into which he had organized pertinent documents. Slowly he dealt the pages onto the table like so many cards. "I hope I've brought enough proof. It won't be enough to just say that he's ours or that we recognize him."

He opened several bulging envelopes, one at a time, and let the contents slide onto the smooth surface. "So many newspaper articles. I just wish I'd asked the clipping service to do a national search so that I'd know what else has been said. And why didn't I ask them to research Shure? Perhaps he's been sued."

He continued to scan, then reinserted the clippings into their envelopes. He got up and prowled, then examined the documents a second and third time, interspersed with more pacing. Finally, he flopped heavily, closing his eyes and rubbing his temples.

Kingsley approached the back of his seat and gently massaged his neck and shoulders. "Give it a rest, hon. Those papers haven't changed in the last twenty-four hours."

He held up the glossy hospital print on which were inked two tiny footprints and one of her thumb. Then he stared at Billy's hospital picture and one with their family and priest by the Baptismal font. He gazed at a photo of Billy, cheek to cheek with his mother, then stroked a few strands of their baby's dark hair, secured with a golden thread, between his thumb and finger. "How could anyone hurt such a tiny little person?"

Kingsley collected the papers, sorting and stuffing them into their folders and envelopes, then tugged at his arm to coax him onto the divan beside her. "We need to talk. There's stuff that's got to be said."

He glanced at the bundle of envelopes and then at her, almost unseeing.

"If Columbus is another disappointment, we don't have a plan B. We have to consider that we might never know what happened to him."

Todd leaned forward, hands folded, arms supported by his thighs, and stared at the carpet. He nodded. "Tell me the truth," she said. "Are you beginning to accept, even in the abstract, that he might be dead?"

"Someone would have to prove that to me."

"But do you think it?"

"Of course. I keep telling myself I must be prepared. Maybe it's survival to keep me from losing my mind. But I feel, in my gut, that he's out there somewhere. We wouldn't be allowed to come this far without a reason. Would we?"

"Nobody answered the prayers of six million Holocaust victims. I'm sorry. That wasn't helpful. In fact, it was cruel. I go back and forth. Back and forth. There's no magic prayer."

Todd rubbed his eyes and studied her blearily, somewhere beyond comprehension.

"Did you sleep at all last night?" she asked.

"Not really."

"There's room to stretch out on this divan." He glanced at it sideways. "Come on—lie down with me awhile." She looked at his watch that swung from her wrist. "It's been, oh, I can't compute the hours, what with changing time zones. I could use a speed nap myself if you could make me lie still."

She kicked off her shoes and wedged herself against the back of the soft tweed divan, then fluffed, grouped, repositioned, and angled the oversized pillows, wiggling and readjusting herself. Todd watched indulgently then started to smile. "You must have been a very good dog in a previous life. Are you quite finished?"

She beckoned and snuggled deeper, holding up her arms to encircle him. "Park it, mister." He relented and pulled off his shoes. Without opening her eyes, she said, "If I have to stop obsessing, then so do you. Deal?" She buried her face in the curve of his shoulder.

"That's a deal."

Another thought demanded its due, and she sat abruptly. "Wouldn't it be a kicker if Shure was legitimate? That every last thing we have learned could be explained in some other way? He has partners, doesn't he? And subordinates with the run of his office. Maybe—"

Todd lifted his head to focus on her. "There's too much of it, K. Way too much. Here's a plan B. If we fail tomorrow, we'll backtrack and find the wrong turn. Like working a maze. Put everything under the microscope and try again. Hold onto that thought."

She sat up again, this time clipping his jaw with her head. "Look around you. We're better off than ninety-nine percent of the world, but I'd trade everything we have or ever will have to get Billy back."

"Except that there's no one willing to bargain. Now, weren't you the lady who needed a nap? We could beat this to death from here to Columbus. Picture something pleasant. Something that makes you happy."

"Hummm. It's been a long time since I had one pleasant thought. Our gardens at home—they should be ready to burst, if they survived the butchering by those insensitive boors. And we have the white-pine fence row to plant for a windbreak."

"That's your idea of a pleasant thought? Me digging dozens of holes through clay, rock, and roots? You can do better than that."

"Billy is watching us from his Pack 'n Play." She peered at Todd's face. His eyes were closed, but he was smiling. Better, she thought, feeling less like screaming herself. They had survived one more trip through the depths. How much longer could they go through this? What if...

She closed her eyes and forced concentration on their wonderful old house, nestled in Pennsylvania Amish farmland. She pictured her back yard and the two ancient maples that defined the left corner under which they had enjoyed their first picnic. She imagined the old roses' fragrance mingled with other perennials in the garden that anchored the center back yard, back-dropped by acres of sprouting corn that the Amish farmer had planted. The corn shoots would be knee high by the Fourth of July and would crackle audibly as they grew in the heat.

That open place in the back right corner—what should it be? A swing set sprang to mind—a wooden one with a playhouse on top. Playmates! Little people with sippy cups and peanut butter sandwiches cut in quarters, laughing at their own silliness. She imagined the hum of the jet engines was the drone of the bees and summer insects. She saw butterflies on flowers, nesting robins, and bluebirds in boxes at the edge of the field. A ballet of barn swallows swooping in patterns.

The Gulfstream knifed through a periwinkle sky, as if drawn by an invisible cord, retracting the distance between parents and child. Somewhere above Middle America they fell asleep.

From the cockpit Randall placed a call to the head of security at Port Columbus, arranging private-duty security to guard the Gulfstream from the time it landed until its departure. Randall said he was transporting corporate executives whose jitters vacillated from nervous to paranoid over airline security. Not exactly a lie. Besides, nobody needed an in-depth explanation after nine-eleven.

Signing off, he patted Barrie's hand and grinned at her radiant face. "We've done all we can for the moment," he said to the love of his life.

"Thank you for that."

Chapter 26

I t's still broad daylight!" Kingsley said as she stepped from the Gulfstream at Port Columbus International. She squinted, shielding her eyes from the glare.

"Columbus sits west in the time zone," Randall said. He led their party into Million Air Terminal, his favorite fixed-base operation. "There's Dan now," he said of the man loping toward them.

Turning, Kingsley saw a young professional in khakis, a short-sleeved white polo shirt with an Ohio State emblem, black socks, and Dockers. He was six feet and brown eyed with closely cropped curly brown hair and a trim moustache and goatee. As he strode, his arms swung from his muscular body. He was an athlete, of that she was certain—one of those guys who hadn't let flab overtake him when school sports had ended.

"You better repaint that jet if you're going to do business here," Dan joked, pumping Randall's hand and giving him a friendly slap on the back. "Replace those gold and blue stripes with scarlet and gray. And add a few buckeyes."

"You haven't met the ladies yet." Randall introduced Kingsley and Barrie.

Dan shook hands with everyone, then rubbed his hands together in anticipation. He looked ready for action. "Okay, what's first? Food?"

"Food is good."

"And you mentioned lodging."

"Any suggestions?"

"If you like upscale, I recommend the Crown Plaza, the Westin or the Hyatt Regency. They're in downtown Columbus in the heart of the business district." He jerked his head toward the Gulfstream. "That's where many jetsetters, celebrities, and athletes like to stay."

"We need something a bit more low key with easy access to Upper Arlington."

"Then I suggest the Homewood Suites on Lane Avenue, which borders the north end of the Ohio State campus. You should call them from here, as it's a popular location for sporting events and its proximity to the OSU Medical Center."

"I was unable to secure a fleet car," Randall said. "Know where I can get a rental at this time of night?"

"I can do better than that. I'll take you wherever you want to go for dinner. Afterward, I'll pick up my wife's car, then leave mine with you. It's that red SUV in the lot. No extra charge for the dog and cat hair. Just kidding about the charge, not the pet hair." Kingsley laughed, taking an instant liking to their affable host. "Tell you what," Dan continued. "Ask the hotel to hold your reservations for late arrival. Then we can have a leisurely dinner."

Todd reached for his wallet and selected the Visa he used for travel expenses. "I'll secure it right away."

"I'm taking you to BD's Mongolian Grill. If you've never been there, you're in for unique, interactive dining—the world's number one create-your-own stir-fry experience.

"You're making this too easy," Todd said. "We hadn't expected to be in Columbus, much less stay overnight. Just give us a few minutes to round up our gear."

Reservations made, the five crammed into Dan's OSU red Ford Explorer and headed downtown.

လာ

How on earth? The woman must have slipped past security onto the tarmac, but when? By the time Randall's security guard noticed her, she was approaching his Gulfstream. He called after her, assuming a menacing stance, his crisp uniform and visible sidearm underscoring that he meant business.

She turned, beaming a hundred-watt smile. "Oh dear," she cooed. "Am I on your runway?"

"Miss, this tarmac is a secure area. I'm going to have to ask you to move away from the plane. Go inside the terminal, or you'll be instructed to leave."

She tossed her shimmering black hair as she looked at the jet in frustration, pointing toward it with a black-gloved hand. "My friends—I was supposed to meet their flight, but I got tied up in traffic. They don't have a car. We're going to have dinner together. They said, 'Come to the plane.' Or something like that. But they're nowhere! Maybe they left me a note in the plane. Can't I just take a peek?" She couldn't have looked more dismayed than if she'd landed in Boise by mistake.

The guard was no stranger to the dumb ploy. Having provided security for touring rock stars in downtown Columbus's entertainment venues, he was accustomed to fending off groupies. This woman, elegantly turned out in designer clothing and major jewelry, was no groupie. But she struck him as *off*. "If you don't comply, I'll have to arrest you."

"You can't do that—can you?" she murmured with a bit of Marilyn Monroe that nevertheless demonstrated she understood his limited authority.

Bad acting aside, he knew she was right, although he still could sound the alarm. As he was weighing his options, his partner slipped up beside him, sat on his haunches, and fixated on her purse. The guard placed his hand on the dog's shoulder and felt his muscles tense. When the dog had retired from police K-9 duty after being shot in the line of duty, his partner was allowed to keep Otto. The dog, trained to detect explosives rather than narcotics, alerted with a rolling rumble deep in his throat that intensified into a growl.

"Okay!" she said. "Call off your mutt. I'm leaving. But my friends are going to be very upset. They're very important people, you know. Just look at that plane."

He jerked his head toward the terminal. As she stomped from his view, the guard noticed her oversized purse. He switched on his phone. Without leaving his post, he alerted airport security and the bomb squad, who surrounded, apprehended, and whisked her away.

☙☙☙

Dan parked in the Arena Grand parking garage and directed the others toward BD's Mongolian Grill on Marconi. The five were ushered past an angled bar into a cavernous room with lofty exposed steel and wood beams. Hardwood gleamed under their feet. Upbeat rock music mingled with laughter and the occasional sound of a gong.

Kingsley, impatient to storm Upper Arlington to wrench Billy from the arms of his captors, tried to push the do-or-die urgency out of her mind. Usually, the distraction of the unique, the unfamiliar, helped her ignore her problems temporarily, but now the pall of anxiety and excess adrenaline overwhelmed her. A server named Matt snapped her into the scene as he ran down their choices of drinks.

"What do you recommend?" Todd asked.

Dan said, "Cold beer is great for a burning tongue if you like spicy food, which I do. CBC—Columbus Brewing Company's IPA—that's India Pale Ale, their flagship beer, is good. And you can support the local economy."

"Make that five," Randall said.

"I'm driving, but you guys knock yourselves out."

Kingsley watched the mixture of diners—midget cheerleaders with their coach, a bachelorette party, Ohio State fans wearing scarlet and gray, a group of girlfriends, an emaciated, sick-looking father with a young son. As a family with a baby was seated nearby, she felt her resolve slipping away. "I can't shake off the feeling of impending doom," she whispered to Todd. "What if..." Her voice cracked, and she blinked quickly, pretending to retrieve a dropped napkin to buy a few moments grace. It was no use.

Hot tears spilled onto her cheeks. Quickly she dabbed them, but with their route established, fresh ones took their place. Her heart began pounding as she panicked about making a scene. She wanted to run, but where? She was trapped with no way to escape.

Todd patted her thigh and smiled understandingly, which only escalated her emotional upheaval. Since she was little, she had felt humiliated by her sensitive nature, how easily she cried, and how uncomfortable that made others feel. She ransacked her mind for her old tricks, like counting by an unlikely number. She tried seventeen. Thirty-four. Up twenty, down three. That would make fifty-one. Their server reappeared with the beer before she reached the four hundreds.

"Hey, this is fantastic," Barrie said, taking a swig, then a gulp.

"Better tap a keg for the vixen," Randall said to their server. She elbowed him smartly, but not before he saw it coming and put down his glass.

"Go ahead, K," Todd said. "She's right. You'll love it."

"I shouldn't."

He edged the glass toward her hand, letting the din hide his words. "Go for it. For luck. It's like washing the car or leaving the windows open during a drought. When, not if, we find Billy tomorrow, then you can worry about your blood alcohol level."

"I suppose one glass wouldn't hurt." She took a sip, and another, followed by a gulp. "It's incredibly good." She chugged half the glass, and soon the warmth spread down her arms, her legs, and on toward her feet. Her springs relaxed.

"Here's the deal," Dan was saying. "We get in the buffet line, heap a bowl with beef, chicken or seafood and veggies. Then add a ladle of oil and a couple of sauce. Spices—watch out for the ones labeled C, unless you like it hot. The cooks will dump your bowl onto that huge round grill—it's called a yurk—and stir-fry it using long metal tools—"

A rolling gong that only grew louder before it abated interrupted him. "What was that?" Kingsley asked.

"Anyone who puts a tip in the jar for the cooks gets to whack the gong that's hung over the counter."

Kingsley watched the customers work their way down both sides of the buffet, filling their bowls, then placing them on the high counter for the cooks to pick up.

"There. Watch." Dan pointed to a girl in tight black slacks and a bare-midriff knit top who wound up and belted the gong. She jumped back, giggling at her boyfriend who swung his tanned, tattooed arm and outdid her. The girl laughed delightedly into her manicured hands, bracelets dropping to her elbow. Shortly a cook plunked both their plates onto the high counter, and they left for their table.

"Looks like fun," Todd said.

"Wait till you taste it. And you can go back for seconds. Let's go."

"Shrimp! Scallops! Calamari? I'm in love!" Randall said, heaping his bowl.

"Food's the first thing he loved that loved him back," Barrie said, pinching his spare tire.

Randall groped for his cell phone, studied the number, and excused himself. From the sidewalk's privacy, he returned the guard's call. "Shannon here. You called?"

"I thought you should know," the guard explained. "The woman who was supposed to meet your party is in custody."

"What woman? We weren't expecting anyone."

"Five-six, slender, straight black hair. Dressed to kill. Sounded dumb, although that felt like an act. She wanted to wait for you in the plane."

"You didn't let her!"

"Hell no. Otto warned me. I hadn't given him the order to search, but he was edgy nevertheless. And the woman was carrying a leather purse—large enough to hold explosives."

"She lied. I have no idea who she was. Stay vigilant. And if you need additional people, get them. If anyone else approaches the plane, don't put yourself or your dog at risk. Call security. Turn them in. And check out anyone new, including the ground crew. Anything else?"

"A minor observation. She wore leather gloves. That caught my attention because it's too warm."

Randall made a note to ask David Wentworth's investigative counsel to check out the woman if her image had been captured on airport security. He re-entered the restaurant.

Back at their table Kingsley and Barrie munched while the men scarfed and ordered more beer. Barrie and Randall exchanged knowing glances as Todd switched his glass for Kingsley's one more time.

As the dinner wound down, Kingsley looked at Todd's watch, but her eyes wouldn't focus. "What time is it?" she asked Barrie.

"Nearly eleven."

Todd reached for his wallet, but Dan held up his hand. "My turf, my treat. You're money's no good in Columbus."

As Todd slid from the table, Kingsley tried to stand up. Wobbling, she grabbed for Todd's arm, giggling in embarrassment. "How much did I drink?"

"A gallon or two," he said, supporting her as they wended their way through the restaurant. Dan tossed Todd a spare set of keys. "Take these now, and when I get home, a neighbor and I will drop the SUV in your hotel's parking garage. You've got my number—give me a call on Sunday and we'll figure out how to undo it."

"Are you sure that your wife doesn't mind?"

"She's out of town doing surgery at a free spay and neuter clinic in Kentucky. She won't return until Sunday night. You guys saved me from an evening of reruns and leftovers."

"I can't thank you enough for all your help," Todd said, lagging behind the others. "My wife can't take much more pressure. I had no idea how we'd manage these last few hours." He motioned toward the other three who, arm in arm, had started to sing "God Bless America" as they weaved toward the garage. "Don't think she'll have much trouble sleeping tonight."

"Glad I could help."

Back at the hotel, Dan braked under the carport and discharged his passengers. "Hey," he called back through the open passenger window. "If you need a nightcap, I recommend Limoncello." That brought groans and withering looks.

❧❧❧

"Can you manage?" Todd asked Kingsley as she tried to walk the straight line to the elevator, knees buckling every few steps.

"Of course." She enunciated carefully, but clung to his arm nevertheless. He unlocked their door and let her precede him into the room where she dropped her purse and flopped face down onto the bed in one fluid motion. First one, then the other shoe slipped from her feet. He smiled, shaking his head.

A quick inspection of the room's earth-tone tranquility pleased him. Fresh, clean, and newly appointed, a taupe duvet draped the king-size bed. He crossed the room to draw the heavy blackout draperies but paused to check the street scene six stories below. Nothing seemed suspicious, but would he know the difference?

Saturday night was still jumping on Lane. Partying students crammed into a Jeep waved to a couple in a vintage Corvette. His mind flashed back to his student days at Harvard. He'd been so serious most of the time—a typical oldest child, driven to excel, idealistic, and bent on family tradition. His mindset had been cleanly bisected—the time before and the time after his little sister had drowned in Lake Erie. His eyes followed the Corvette until it disappeared. He wondered, fleetingly, whether he should have allowed himself some frivolity. No, he'd been happy being himself. He remained a few minutes, scanning the parking lot and the neighboring streets. Deciding that no menace had followed them, he closed the draperies.

Kingsley stirred and propped herself up on one elbow, rubbing her hand through her disheveled hair. "I'm a mess," she said, struggling to her feet and heading for the bathroom. Shortly she returned. Rummaging through her purse she unearthed a toothbrush and paste. She grinned at him. "I'll share if you're really, really nice to me. We've shared spit before." Shortly he heard water running.

She re-emerged and sat on the edge of the bed where he joined her. "How about a shower?" he asked. "I feel pretty grubby myself, and we've been up since four."

"I'll wash your back, if you'll wash mine," she said in silky tones. Pulling off her sweater and shell and lobbing them onto the floor, she gave him an innocent smile. He overdid a lascivious look, licking his lips.

"Get the water adjusted and I'll be right in." He listened until he heard the toilet flush, then the rush of the shower. Then it shut off. The bathroom was quiet.

He knocked on the door. "Are you okay?" When she didn't answer, he cracked it and peered in. "Hon?"

Kingsley's underwear lay in a heap. She was standing in front of the mirror running her right index finger between her collarbone and her left breast. "My pump. I never thought."

"Are you all right?"

"The engorgement—it's so painful. And for what? All these weeks! And I may never see him again."

"I'll get a cab. Find a drug store that's still open and get whatever you need."

She turned from the mirror, dropping her eyes without making contact with him, but he could see she was crying. "I am so sorry," she said, coming to him and taking his face in her hands. "You are so strong and so good. You'd do just about anything for me, wouldn't you? Have I let you think that Billy is the only important thing in my life? Without you, nothing's worth doing. You're trying so hard, and I want so badly to be like you. I'm just not. I'm sorry. I just can't."

"K, you've got to stop apologizing. There's nothing to forgive. We will get past this—tomorrow, and the next day and the next. One foot in front of the other. Remember, we agreed that as long as there's 'us,' we'll be okay.'"

"But I can't stop crying."

"That's supposed to be cathartic."

"And you have to keep buoying me up. Why can't it ever be the other way around?"

"You sustain me in so many ways that I can't explain. Now come on—I believe I owe you a back wash." He wrapped strong arms around her and hugged."

"Ouch!" She jerked back, crossing her arms over both breasts. He started to speak, but she held up her hand. She thought a moment and then asked in a whisper. "You can help me out here, if you don't think it's disgusting."

☙❧

Warm, steamy water enveloped their bodies, as they tore the paper from small bars of soap. Synchronized, they massaged each other's temples, cheeks, chins, and necks, succumbing to laughter when soap got in their mouths.

"Turn," she said, and worked lathered hands down his torso. "Magnificent butt." Slowly she traveled down to his feet. "Your muscles are tight as banjo strings."

He helped her up, then turned her gently, lingering soapy hands to massage her shoulders, down to her waist and the small of her back. As he rubbed, she groaned ecstatically. He said, "We didn't have any dessert, and I have an appetite. Do you?" She lowered her gaze, then tipping her face, looked through dripping lashes, and ran her tongue over her lips. Todd killed the water and groped for a towel, then carried her into the bedroom.

Chapter 27

An hour later, Todd slipped from her embrace and eased himself to the edge of the bed, trying his best not to rock it and wake her. He needn't have worried, he thought with a grin. Kingsley was out cold. Ever so quietly he circled the bed and bent to his wife. As he kissed her damp tousled hair, he breathed the mingled fragrance of herbal shampoo and vanilla soap. He untangled the sheet, covering her loveliness with a light blanket, and prayed. *Please, God. Don't disappoint her.*

He crossed to the bathroom. Pulling the door nearly shut, he groped around the jam for the switch. By the light's slender beam he located his laptop and carry-on tote that contained the documents he'd brought from the plane. When he crossed the room without looking, he tripped on a chair leg and smothered a curse. Shrouded in darkness, he rummaged for a legal tablet, a pen, and the thumb drives that Lloyd had provided in Seattle. Thank God Lloyd had the presence of mind to check whether his laptop had the right drive. It did.

Quietly he slipped into the bathroom, closed the door and plugged in the laptop. He angled it on the edge of the vanity facing the toilet, then sat down on the lid. While the laptop completed its startup, Todd fanned the thumb drives like so many cards. He groaned at his stupidity. How many more seconds would it have taken to label them? And why didn't he print the directory from the screen? Maybe the backups were in order. Perhaps he'd get lucky.

He inserted the first thumb drive and double clicked its icon. He waited then double-clicked the icon that led to the document folders. *Families*—that contained the list they had hoped were the parents. He copied it to his hard drive, closed it, ejected the thumb drive, and inserted the next. The document that opened was the Excel spreadsheet titled *Expenses*, which they'd seen at Lloyd's bank. With the luxury of time, he scanned the first column, which looked like initials. "EB." Could that stand for Ethelda Blake? How many others were on the list? A dozen?

Quickly, he copied and closed that file and inserted a third thumb drive. That one contained individuals' expense reports. The codes beside the initials meant nothing to him, and there was no key. But he scrutinized another and yet another report. Finally, one titled "EB" sprang to life. Ethelda Blake! But why was only her name in quotations? Was it an alias? The first entry, which was listed chronologically by date, was posted in February. Two years ago! He studied the categories above each column of numbers, but still could not guess what they meant. *Think of something you know.* Scrolling, he looked for 04/15, the day that Billy was kidnapped.

And there it was! An entry for $5,000 dated 04/16. Who in their right mind would risk a lifetime in prison for five thousand bucks? Of course, if Billy wasn't her only assignment—he scrolled backward to January and found an identical entry in the same column. January! Billy hadn't even been born, but the diabolical plot was already in motion. If these initials identified the members of the kidnapping ring, they would be meaningless unless they could be matched with real names or social security numbers. Maybe that list was in here somewhere?

Kathleen's disk held a wealth of information. No wonder it put her in peril. Had she honestly thought that hiding this evidence could buy her protection? Or that she could unravel the plot without help? His pulse raced as he organized a plan—open every last file, then read them in order of their importance. His fingers flew as he opened, made a notation on his legal pad, then closed and moved on. Some documents made no sense at all, and he clicked through them with growing urgency. Just like Barrie, he'd become greedy for a quick route to Billy.

Suddenly a different format sprang to life on the screen. *My God*, he thought. I*t's a letter from Kathleen to Mary Margaret*. It was dated Thursday, April eleventh. From everything Mare had told them that morning, he realized that she'd never seen it. His mind shot through what Randall's employee, Greg, had read from Kathleen's obituary in the *Pittsburgh Post Gazette*. She had died the following evening, Friday, April twelfth. Greedily, he read what Kathleen had written:

My Dearest Mare,

If you are reading this, you will know that I failed. I am so sorry for any grief that my passing will cause you and our family. Especially you. You've been my soul mate from our conception, and you never failed to be strong when I wasn't. You must not grieve. It isn't your fault. Please remember that I did what I thought was right. Nothing that you or anyone else could have said or done would have dissuaded me.

My faith in God, His presence, and His work through others' hands has never flagged. For most of my life, however, I did not believe in the devil. Now I do. I have seen evil personified in the persona of Gerard Shure.

I have tried to collect all the information necessary to reunite parents with the children he and his soulless colleagues have stolen. On the surface, that sounds like a joyous end, but my heart grieves for the innocent adoptive parents who believed there was no way that their babies could be reclaimed. From what I've overheard, these poor people were told that their infants were war orphans—Bosnia, Croatia, and other war-torn countries.

If I am to receive any rewards, please donate them in our parents' names to the American Red Cross's Disaster Relief Fund, to Catholic Charities and to the Salvation Army. Worldwide, they serve need and spend precious little on overhead. In a separate note, I am sending you the name of the person to whom you should entrust the data on this disk.

My dear Mare, do not dishonor me by wanting revenge. I view this as an opportunity—poor Lazarus found on my doorstep. Not seizing the opportunity gratefully would be a travesty.

Give my love to every one of our family and friends. But most especially, take care of "my other half." I love you and will pray for you always.

Kathleen

Stunned, Todd sat frozen, forgetting momentarily just where he was. Returning to the present, he wiped a tear on the nearest towel as reality struck him. Shure! Of course, they were right! He snapped off the laptop, tucked it under his arm, and hurried into the bedroom in search of his clothes. He pulled on slacks without his jockeys, turned his shirt right side out, and thrust his bare feet into his loafers. Grabbing his room key, his cell phone, and notes, he hurried into the hall.

The lobby was deserted at two-thirty a.m. Todd had no trouble finding a private table near an electrical outlet in a lounge. Quickly he rooted for Mary Margaret's phone number while practicing what he might say. Already eleven-thirty in Seattle, they might not answer the phone. He rebooted the laptop as his cell phone began ringing Mare's number. Was this a mistake? Two rings. Could murderous ears be pressed to the line? Another ring, then the young-sounding male.

"Hello?"

"I'm sorry to bother you this late in the evening, but it's

important that I speak to Mary Margaret. Would you mind waking her for me if she isn't still up?" A long pause followed. "Hello? Are you there?"

Todd heard a snuffle, followed by the young man clearing his throat. "You can't."

"It's *very* important. She'll understand."

"No, *you* don't understand. Aunt Mare has been in a terrible accident."

"What kind of accident?"

"Hit and run—the police said there weren't any skid marks. They're investigating, but nobody saw anything."

"Is she—"

"She's in a coma. They don't expect her to live."

Todd didn't remember what he said next or when they hung up. Time hung suspended in an opaque, surreal miasma. His head started to clear. The priest! He'd call the priest. Frantically he groped for the number, which only yesterday Mary Margaret had given to him. He found it and dialed. There was no answer.

Suddenly Todd thought of Lloyd Peterson. Had Mary Margaret's nemesis followed Todd and the others to Lloyd's bank? Perhaps followed him to the airport? He must have! Todd located Lloyd's business card and punched his unlisted number. A sleepy man answered the phone.

"Lloyd! This is Todd. You may be in danger." Even to him, that sounded paranoid. He was making no sense.

"Todd. Back up. What's happened?"

"That lady who gave me the disk just this morning? She was in a wreck shortly after she dropped us off at your bank. It wasn't an accident. Please, please, get some protection for yourself and your family. This evil thing has followed us from one coast to the other."

"I'll do it."

"You're not going to tell me I'm overreacting?"

"No way. I'll phone the police and bring the Seattle police up to date. But what about you?"

Todd was silent a moment. "Our only safety is getting to the bottom of this fast. We will be careful."

"Todd, call the local police."

"Tomorrow, when we know more. In the meantime, see what you can find out about the accident and let me know what the newspapers say. And be careful which phone you use. I have no idea how these people circumvent electronic devices, but they're extraordinarily proficient."

☙❧

Todd rapped softly on Randall's door, then knocked louder when no one responded.

"*What?*"

"It's me. Open the door."

Momentarily Randall unbolted and pulled it open, adjusting the elastic of his inside-out silk boxers. He rubbed his eyes groggily.

"What's up?"

"One of those drives contained a letter from Kathleen to her sister implicating Shure. There's a wealth of information on Kathleen's disk, and someone tried to kill Mary Margaret. She may not live." Todd fleshed out the details as he understood them while Randall frowned in silence.

"What do you think we should do?"

Todd looked for his watch, which wasn't there. "If you want to bail, get the hell out of Dodge, and take Barrie home, that's fine. I don't want you guys to get hurt. I know Kingsley will insist that she and I stick with the plan. We're just that close. But even if they're right behind us, maybe our luck will keep holding."

"And the police?"

Todd scrounged through his thoughts. "I'll call them if our Upper Arlington lead is productive, but for now, we still have no proof that Billy is there. If we dump everything we know on the locals, they'll want to call Pennsylvania and check out our story. At best their procedures could cost precious time, and at worst, they could stop us or warn the family that's got him."

Randall nodded. "That sounds about right."

"What do you want to do?"

"We're sticking."

"But Barrie…"

He cracked a smile. "That woman is fearless. I wouldn't mess with her, would you? As for me, I'm with you so I can get paid. You owe me dinner and a fifth of single malt Scotch. Oh, and my books. They could sure use your help."

Todd laughed. "You got it." Randall flipped him a sleepy wave, turned slowly, and ambled into the room's inky interior. Todd watched him briefly and pulled the door shut. "Hey! Lock it!" Momentarily, he heard the click. If only he had Randall's military nerves.

Chapter 28

Over breakfast in the hotel's spacious dining room, the four scrutinized their plan. Barrie tapped her finger on the map of Columbus and its environs. "Here it is—the street in Upper Arlington where the Manatawneys live."

"Thank God, they had an unusual name," Kingsley said, pushing aside her half-eaten waffles. She looked where Barrie was pointing. "How far is it?"

Barrie put the tip of one nail on their hotel's location, then traced a route with her left index finger. "Twenty minutes tops. And since it's Sunday, there won't be much traffic."

Randall ambled to the beverage station to refill his coffee mug. Without comment, Barrie picked up her unfinished breakfast and swapped it with his polished plate. "What's the plan?" Todd asked.

Randall swallowed more bacon and eggs and washed them down with a gulp of coffee, then cleared his throat. "I suggest we scope out the neighborhood first. Find the house, and then decide what seems reasonable."

"Don't forget I spoke to the woman. She sounded friendly. Approachable." Barrie said. "I could knock on her door and re-introduce myself. Remind her that she'd recommended her neighborhood's school district and championship golf course.

"That won't work," Todd said. "Sufficient time hasn't elapsed. You placed that call less than twenty-four hours ago."

"We could stay over—let me ring her doorbell tomorrow."

Randall tossed his napkin onto the table. "Guys, let's buzz the place, then decide. Barrie, you done with that juice?" She passed him the glass, and he drained it. Kingsley, who couldn't conceal her amusement, hid a giggle with her napkin.

Exiting the dining room, Todd headed to the front desk. "Are there any messages for Henning or Shannon?" The Guest Services Representative checked under the counter and produced an envelope bearing his name. Todd extracted a diagram and rotated it several times, scowling.

"It's from a friend who's lending us his car. He's an industrial designer who made an intricate drawing that resembles a blueprint of where we'd find it, but I don't remember seeing anything like this."

"May I?" Todd passed the drawing to the woman. "Oh, yes, of course. He used our parking garage. Go to your right, around the desk, and down the corridor past the elevator and through the glass doors. Looks like your car's in the far corner."

"Thanks." Todd said and, refolding the paper, beckoned for the others to huddle. "You guys collect your stuff, and I'll bring Dan's car around front. Meet me by the front door."

They disbursed. As Todd turned from the desk, the GSR called after him. "Sir? There was a call, a man asking if you were registered here."

"Who was it? What did he say? What did you tell him?"

"Well, nothing, sir. It's against policy. We're not allowed to give out information about our guests."

"Thanks. If anyone asks, please—we value our privacy and are *not* expecting anyone." She smiled and nodded.

Todd quickly strode into the garage where he spotted the red Ford Explorer.

No sooner had the glass doors to the parking garage closed behind him than a skinny man wearing black jeans and a black crew-neck cotton sweater with sleeves pushed to the elbow approached the front desk. "I'm supposed to meet friends who are staying here. Names are Henning and Shannon. What are their room numbers?"

The GSR startled. Eying the man, the tingle that crept down her spine warned her that *friend* didn't fit. She forced her best professional face. "I'm sorry, sir. We cannot confirm names or give out room numbers. I can call the room and pass you the receiver. Or you can leave your friends a message, but I can't…"

"What do you mean, 'can't'?" He lowered his slash of black eyebrows and narrowing his eyes, snarled. "Get your manager out here. *Now!*" The woman jumped when he smacked the counter with his fist.

"Sir. He'll say the same thing. The rules are—"

Bang! The man, who had only become more agitated, pummeled the counter with his fist and shot expletives in a menacing voice.

"I'll see if I can find him." She stole a few precious seconds to scan her computer and flip off the monitor to make sure nothing useful was showing. Then she hurried toward the back office.

Out in the parking garage, Todd found and unlocked the SUV. He couldn't help smile when he saw the back seat, draped with an old army blanket. Dan hadn't been kidding about the pet hair. He took a minute to roll and stow the holey blanket then hopped in and looked for an exit. None faced the front of the building.

Exiting to the rear, he turned left into an alley and paused. How much time would it take them to grab their stuff? Ten? Fifteen more minutes? He waited five then circled to the front entrance. As if on cue, the others emerged from the lobby.

"You drive, Todd," Randall said, maneuvering Barrie into the back seat. Kingsley took the copilot's seat. "Take a right onto Lane. We need to go west."

"Can't. It's blocked—some kind of bridge work."

"Then make three lefts."

Todd pulled onto the street and turned east onto Lane.

Inside the lobby the GSR reappeared with the hunk of a manager and a grim-faced security guard. The man in black shot daggers from one to another before turning to check the lobby's front entrance.

Freezing, he straightened and scrutinized something beyond the front windows. Three passengers were piling into a red Explorer. There was no mistaking the red-headed man. He lunged for the door as the SUV disappeared. Sprinting toward an idling Crown Vic, he jumped into the passenger seat, rattling off orders to the wheelman.

Randall wasn't sure just what caught his attention, but whatever it was lurked in Todd's side-view mirror. "We're being followed. Go!" Todd hung a left onto Neil Avenue and shot down the street.

"Where?"

"Just go. Fast! Several blocks to Dodridge, up ahead at the traffic light. Then make a left."

"Is he still following us?"

Randall swiveled, squinting through the glare. He watched intently. The light at Dodridge was stale yellow as Todd approached the intersection—red by the time he got there. "Run that light, but don't gun it. Just drive like you don't respect traffic signals." Todd looked left, praying as much for their borrowed SUV as their personal safety. He sighed in relief as he got away with it.

Randall repositioned himself to have a clear view of the side-view mirror without making himself visible. "Girls, get down."

"What's he doing now?"

"Damn! He slowed a little then gunned it straight through the red. We're being followed, all right."

"What are we going to do?" Kingsley begged in a small, frightened voice.

"My cell phone's in my bag. Get it out," Todd said.

"Should I call nine-one-one? What do we tell them?"

Randall barked orders from the back seat. "Left again onto the Olentangy River Road. Go a short distance like we haven't made them, then as soon as we're out of his sight, floor it back up to Lane." Todd obeyed. "Now right onto Lane, beyond the barricade, then floor it again."

"Oh, god, don't roll it," Barrie said, grabbing for the seat belt that she had neglected to fasten.

Todd shot onto Lane. "Where is he now?" he asked, concentrating hard on the road and his steering.

Randall looked out the back window. "We lost them in the dip in the road. There! Make a left and then take that off-ramp."

"It's the wrong way! We'll crash into oncoming traffic!"

"Just do it! Nobody's coming."

Todd yanked hard on the wheel. When he lined up for the ramp, the Explorer rocked as it grazed the curb that bordered a small, grassy island. He continued to protest. "I can't go up there—that's a super highway."

"Just go! Stay far right on the berm. Stop fast at the top, then quick! Make a hard right onto the highway. Cross to the far inside lane, then stop above the overpass."

Todd sped up the off-ramp, eyeing the sliver of berm to his right, their only margin of safety from oncoming cars. Two startled motorists, exiting north off Route 315, passed them, mouths gaping, but having no time to honk. At Route 315's juncture, the sole vehicle going northbound was in the center lane. Todd cut the wheel hard, and without stopping, squirted toward the overpass and skidded to a stop above Lane. Nobody breathed.

"Get your four-ways on, Todd," Randall barked without taking his eyes off the back window. Tick. Tick. Tick. No one dared speak. Todd, with a death grip on the wheel, fixated on the rearview mirror. Randall jerked his head back and forth, watching the traffic on Lane Avenue as it passed underneath them. The black car shot past in a westward trajectory.

"There he goes! He didn't see us. He stayed on Lane. Quick! Floor it into the far right lane in case one of them looks up and spots us."

Todd pulled quickly over three lanes and resumed normal speed. "What if he'd seen us and simply taken the southbound exit?" Kingsley asked Randall.

"Then we'd have made a U-ie, taken the exit we just came up and gone east on Lane. There's no way he can make a three-point turn on this limited access highway, and the grass median is a gully."

Todd drove conservatively on Route 315 North and exited east onto North Broadway. A quarter mile farther he pulled off the road. Kingsley stared at her thumb, which she had unconsciously rubbed until it was raw. "We can't give up, not after getting this close. We can't proceed, and we can't call the police. What are we going to do?"

"Would someone please remind me why we can't call the police *now*? Isn't our predicament rather obvious?" Barrie asked.

Kingsley quieted. "We can't be positive the Manatawneys aren't involved, and seeing the cops, they might panic and hurt Billy. Or they might just haul ass, leaving those bastards time to vanish."

"Oh, Kingsley, I really don't think—"

"Guys! Let's stick with the plan, but first, we need a different car," Randall interrupted, annoyance creeping into his voice. "It's safe to assume one person in a strange car won't be easily spotted. The others can stay low."

"Then we need to find a car rental that's open this morning," Todd said. "We can swap a fresh ride back for Dan's car later." They circled through sleepy suburbs and finding a convenience store that was open, asked for a phone book. Todd thumbed through the list. "There's an Avis on Lane and a Budget on the Olentangy River Road. Both are open on Sundays. Let's do it."

Todd eased toward the highway and took the onramp to 315 South. The other three rode in silence, eyes scanning the roads for black cars. "They could have the Manatawney's house staked out," Todd finally said. "If that car shows up again, we'll be forced to call nine-one-one. We could say some idiot, probably drunk, tried to run us off the road. Give a description and a location. That should buy us some time."

The back-seat passengers kept the vigil, but there was no trace of their tail. Kingsley loosened her grip on Todd's cell phone as he blended into the church-going traffic. At least for the moment, they were passing for ordinary people.

Todd approached Upper Arlington, turned left onto Tremont, and crawled through its beautiful neighborhoods in a rented beige Impala. Substantial custom-built homes shaded by mature trees evoked the aura of class and conservative old money. They slid past stone Tudors with hundred-foot facades, anchored by carriage houses and surrounded with immaculate landscaping.

As Todd looped serpentine streets, the only signs of life were an occasional jogger and a distinguished-looking man in a bathrobe fetching his Sunday newspaper. Eventually, he happened upon the Manatawney's street. Braking, he gazed down its tree-canopied depth. "This is it."

"See anything?" Randall asked, risking discovery from the back seat.

"No cars parallel parked and none in the driveways. No one's about. Thank God, it's Sunday."

"Just drive down the block and check the house numbers," Kingsley said. She rubbed her neck and stretched out the kinks from being crunched out of sight for so long. "It's in the two hundred block, and I see number five on that house to our right."

Todd edged down the first block, then stopped midway to consider. "Everyone must have partied last night."

"I think it's safe to scope out the house," Randall said. "Go. Careful—I spotted a fifteen MPH speed limit sign." The others gave him a withering look as the speedometer hovered near five.

Barrie looked left and then right, gaping at the parade of elegant homes as they eased into the third block. "There! That's it. Up ahead on the left! Hello! Talk about luck! A realtor's sign. Right across the street. There's our excuse to knock on their door."

Todd pulled to the curb in front of the Tudor with a realtor's sign. Opposite, on the Manatawney's side of the street, the spacious lots had been staggered to prevent windows from facing each other. The Manatawney's two-story home was stone, as deep as it was wide, and enjoyed a seventy-five foot setback. A two-car garage abutted its right, and the lawn was deep green and blade perfect. They could make out a fence in the back yard, and through its pickets, a large swimming pool.

Kingsley, nerves jumping, started to fidget. "We can't just sit here."

Suddenly both of the Manatawney's garage doors started to rise, one slightly ahead of the other. Two cars came into view as the doors climbed. The car nearest the house was a BMW convertible with its top down, the one by the outside wall, a Mercedes. "Pretty shabby," Barrie said, breaking the tension. Fascinated, they continued to watch.

Momentarily a middle-aged man in tan slacks, a yellow golf shirt and white golf shoes with tan saddles emerged from the garage's depth and circled to the back of the BMW.

"Must have come out through a laundry or the kitchen," Kingsley whispered as if he could hear her. The man crossed to the back of the Mercedes then set down the golf bag that was slung on his shoulder. He extended his hand, and the trunk glided open. He busied himself fitting the clubs into the trunk, then returned from the direction he had come. Soon he reappeared with a tan duffel bag, adjusting a golf cap that matched his slacks.

As they watched, a woman joined him. He tossed the duffel into the trunk and, when he extended his arm once again, the lid glided shut. Briefly, they kissed. As she retreated, he got into the Mercedes and backed down the driveway. Returning her wave, he headed down the street, away from the Impala. The woman disappeared into the garage but did not put down the doors.

"Duck!" All four hit the seats. Nobody moved until Randall, who had pulled on a gray baseball cap, peeked out and observed for a moment. "Wait. Just a few minutes." Time crawled, and he peeked out again. "They're gone."

"What? Who?"

"That damn car."

"The same black one?" Kingsley asked, eyes darting up and down the now quiet neighborhood.

"Same damn Crown Vic. It's gone now. Barrie—write this down."

When a quick rummage through her purse yielded no pen and paper, she uncapped a lipstick and pulled up her sleeve. He dictated from memory while she wrote the license number in two-inch letters and numerals. Minutes crawled as they practiced patience nobody had, but the black car did not return.

As they were debating what their next move should be, the woman emerged from the garage pushing a stroller. It was elegant, obviously expensive, and had a lowered sunbonnet.

"That's got to be Beth Manatawney," Barrie said. "Come on, Randall. Showtime. Let's go chat up the woman about real estate and take a peek at the baby."

"We can't let you do that," Kingsley said. "What if that black car comes back? Or the woman is dangerous?"

"Look, kiddo, we have the luxury of a little more distance. There's less chance that we'll freak. Randall, you
ready?" She tugged at his arm. "Let's get into the role." She
reached over the back seat and squeezed Kingsley's shoulder. "We won't blow it. I promise." Without waiting for a
response, she opened her door. "Watch our backs."

Kingsley reached for the cell phone and held it up like a
weapon. As Barrie and Randall ambled toward the Tudor
with the realtor's sign, Kingsley realized she was holding
her breath. Riveted, she watched them make discrete ges-
tures in the house's direction, first toward the roof and then
the back yard. They made sweeping motions with their
hands, finally facing each other as if discussing its relative
merits. Barrie made a show of surprise at seeing Beth Manatawney, who was now pushing the stroller down the opposite sidewalk in their direction. She poked Randall's arm,
gesturing toward Beth, but he appeared fixated on the Tudor.

Barrie half crossed the street, stopped and turned, then
called something to Randall, motioning impatiently for him
to follow. Kingsley stared, willing her friend to go faster,
run, and grab her baby. But Barrie sauntered, feigning interest in the houses that flanked the Manatawney's. When she
stopped to say something to the mother, she didn't even
glance at the baby.

Barrie said something and smiled when the mother replied, no doubt to answer a question. Then she motioned
toward the house with the realtor's sign and toward Randall,
who was taking his time catching up. He kept turning back
toward the house. Barrie put her hands on her hips and
glared impatiently at him.

Finally, after what seemed like all eternity, she pretended to notice the baby. She made a hand motion toward the
stroller and then looked up laughing along with the mother.
She must have said something that delighted the mother.
With that, the mother lifted the stroller's bonnet. Barrie
bent, smiling, and made silly faces. She reached toward the

baby, as if to tickle his tummy, then stood, smiling, and spoke to the mother, who was beaming.

Ever so slowly, Barrie turned her attention back to the Tudor. This time, however, she turned her face squarely toward the Impala. She lifted her chin, as if to study the sky, then lowered her chin to her chest. Slowly she repeated the motion. Up and then down. Up and then down.

"It's him! It's Billy!" Kingsley grabbed the door handle.

Todd caught her arm and yanked her back. "Wait! We can't do this alone. Now we need help."

Cell phone in hand, Todd dialed 9-1-1. "This is an emergency. We need the police. My name is Todd Henning. Our baby was kidnapped in Pennsylvania, and we've spotted him at an Upper Arlington home. I'll give you the address. No, I'll tell you whatever you need just as soon as you get someone rolling. Our child could be in danger. Wait! A black car that's been stalking us just turned onto this street. It's two blocks away and closing. Send help! Fast!"

Barrie noticed it first and grabbed Randall's arm, then swung, wild-eyed toward the woman. "Quick! We're all in danger. Into the house!"

The woman froze, mouth open, as the car entered the block. Obviously not comprehending, she appeared nailed to the sidewalk.

Chapter 29

ow! Into the house!" Barrie grabbed at the stroller's handle and started to turn it, but the mother, coming to life, wrenched it from her and dashed toward the garage. Barrie and Randall bolted beside her, keeping an eye on the approaching menace.

"The doors! Hit the down-buttons!" Randall commanded. "Get in the house! Lock the doors!" Barrie palmed the garage door openers, and both surged to life.

Todd and Kingsley watched the black car approach with illogical fascination. She threw herself at the passenger door and wrenching it open, dumped herself onto the grassy strip that separated the curb from the sidewalk. Scrambling on hands and knees, she crawled to the front of the car and peered around the front tire. Todd flattened himself across the front seats.

The driver stopped, blocking the Manatawney's driveway. As the occupants slowly opened their doors, the Manatawney's left-hand garage door began to rebound, having struck an object dropped on the floor. The men exchanged nods. The skinny one made motions to the wheelman, who withdrew a shiny metallic object that had been stuffed in his belt. Each man was exiting the car, one foot on the ground, when Kingsley first saw flashing lights blocks away. Two police cruisers were steaming their way.

Both men jerked to attention and lunged into the car, slamming the doors simultaneously. With a burst of speed, the driver plunged the car into a U-turn. Todd dived for the passenger seat as the charging black vehicle lurched toward the Impala, missing it by a mini scintilla. In seconds, the car reached the intersection and vanished around the quiet, curved street.

"The house! We've got to get in there!" Kingsley scrambled to her feet and bolted toward the open garage door, which, as if possessed, had reversed direction again. She tried to slither underneath, bumping her back, which caused it to rebound one more time. The police, who had spilled from the cruisers, halted her progress with a sharp bark.

As the scene unfolded in what seemed like slow motion, Kingsley was struck by the contradictions. One cruiser's radio crackled with messages against the incongruous cacophony of twittering birds, oblivious to the drama unfolding below.

The pair of female officers listened attentively to Todd's explanation, which he staccatoed with names, dates, and places. Todd clutched Kingsley's arm to keep her from bolting. Each time she moved, he tightened his grip, only relaxing it slightly when she stopped struggling.

Kingsley could stand it no longer. "Please! Can't details wait? Get in there and rescue our baby before it's too late. What if she hurts him? What if—"

"Wait here!" one of the officers ordered Kingsley. A young male officer, newly arrived, motioned for one of the other officers to approached the homeowner, who by now had opened the front door wide enough for Kingsley to see she was holding the baby. Beth Manatawney, neatly dressed and immaculately made up, was beckoning frantically to the police. She looked both angry and scared; Kingsley could see that Billy was crying.

Kingsley tried unsuccessfully to run for the door. "Don't let her hurt him!"

Beth urged the officers to approach, opening the glass

storm door just wide enough for them to enter. They did, uneventfully. She slammed the front door.

"Please wait outside!" the policewomen, who had been on the radio, directed Kingsley in a professional, authoritative voice. Awash in maternal instincts, Kingsley disobeyed, dashing beneath the malfunctioning garage door and into the house, through a laundry room hallway, and into the kitchen. She froze at an archway to the grand foyer so quickly that Todd nearly trampled her. The police officer in pursuit collided with both, and they teetered like dominos.

"This is Matthew," Beth Manatawney was saying to the officers she had admitted. "He's ours, and we have the papers to prove it. He was a foreign war orphan, and we adopted him. It's all legal and final. I don't know who these people are or why they think they can barge in here. Please make them leave."

For a woman facing three police officers, four deranged strangers and one sinister black car with occupants of questionable character, Kingsley thought Beth Manatawney was entirely too calm, to say nothing of confident. A wee flicker of doubt pulsed through her mind. What if the infant wasn't Billy? Just a baby who looked like him? She'd made that mistake once before. She had to get closer.

The Upper Arlington's Police sergeant arrived in a Ford Explorer. "Don't move!" one officer told the Hennings as one of the officers exited via the front door to greet her sergeant. Out in the driveway, Kingsley could see the officers speaking, hands pointing in animation. She prayed the sergeant would at least try to verify the details that Todd had unleashed.

Their attention was drawn back to the foyer. "I'm sure we can straighten this out," one officer said, trying to placate Beth. She was quite young and professional, yet soft-spoken, which appeared to have a calming effect. "Let's move somewhere more comfortable."

Beth hesitated momentarily, glancing behind her and frowning. Randall, who had been hanging back in the grand foyer with Barrie, pounced on the sergeant the minute she entered. He pointed emphatically toward the infant. "That baby is William Todd Henning IV, and I ought to know. I'm his godfather. He was kidnapped on April fifteenth and hasn't changed that much in three weeks. The kidnappers are one step behind us. They're driving a black Crown Vic—"

Barrie cut him off, addressing the officer attached to her side. She pulled up her sleeve to reveal the license numbers and letters smudged on her skin.

"Please," the officer said. "My sergeant will take your information." Randall studied the officer's name badge. Smith. Right.

"I'm calling my husband." Beth started to leave the foyer with the baby.

"Why don't I come with you?" Officer Smith asked in the same tone with which she might offer to carry her groceries. She not only did not object but looked somewhat relieved for the officer's protection. Randall and Barrie started to follow. "Wait here, please." They turned to face the sergeant, whose attitude commanded respect. They acquiesced.

"Please have a seat in the living room." It was hardly a request they could ignore.

"Perfect place for a baby," Barrie said under her breath as she surveyed the white brocade sofa and matching chairs positioned on miles of the palest taupe carpet. They chose two needlepoint medallion-back chairs that afforded the best overall view.

The spacious living room flowed into a vast dining room where a Queen Ann cherry table, surrounded by twelve matching chairs, sat on a peach Persian rug. Beyond that was a large family room filled with all manner of baby contraptions.

Back in the foyer, the sergeant spoke with her officers. "First, we must separate these people. One of you take Mrs. Manatawney back to the family room. The other, collect the

Hennings and their companions and sequester them in the living room."

"Both are saying they have documentation, and the Manatawneys are well-known community leaders. How do we decide who gets the baby?" one asked.

"I'll notify the FBI and request that an agent meet us at the station. They'll interface with Pennsylvania authorities. Family Services is sending their representative."

"She'll take the baby?"

"I prefer to have an impartial buffer who understands children's rights. And I'll put out an APB on that black car. It's probably rented or stolen, but the Highway Patrol may be able to find it before it gets ditched."

Duties assigned, they disbursed. One of the female officers, who collected Kingsley and Todd in the hallway, directed them into the living room. Kingsley's eyes darted everywhere. "Where is my baby? I demand that you bring me my child."

"Mrs. Henning—"

Kingsley's rage rose, fueled by what felt like the condescension in the officer's voice. Ignoring her direction to sit and be patient, she broke from the room. Todd followed as she tore through the dining room, into the family room, and then back through the dining room into the kitchen behind the grand foyer. Beth Manatawney, who was standing in front of the sink, looked up in fright.

"Billy! Oh my God! It's really you. Oh, thank God!" She ran toward the baby, reaching for him. Billy turned his beautiful face toward his mother and smiled. "Give me my child!"

Beth Manatawney clutched the baby and pivoted away, colliding with Officer Smith. "Mrs. Henning! I'll have to ask you to return to the living room, or I swear, I'll be forced to arrest you."

"But that's my baby. She has my Billy. They stole our child!"

"His name is Matthew, and he's mine!"

The officer grabbed a deep breath. Positioning herself between the two women, she gripped Kingsley's elbow with surprising strength and propelled her out of the kitchen.

"Beth!" A bull of a man erupted through the front door with a stranger in tow. "What the hell's going on here? Beth! Are you all right? Is Matthew?"

Beth hurried toward her husband's protection, clutching the baby who had started to cry. He was straining his head in Kingsley's direction. Any semblance of order disappeared in the pristine living room, everyone shouting at once. The woman from Family Services arrived, which only added to the confusion.

"Quiet!" the sergeant demanded. "All of you." The racket stopped immediately, save for the baby's crying. She faced the big man. "Who are you?"

"I'm Burton Manatawney. This is my home, and this is our lawyer. I demand to know what's going on here."

The sergeant faced the big man. At least six-two, tan and athletically built, Burton's genes had favored him with a shock of hair that sported no gray.

"These folks are the Hennings from Pennsylvania," the sergeant said evenly, pointing to Todd and Kingsley. "They claim to have tracked their kidnapped son to this location."

"That's a lie! Our son was adopted through proper legal channels, which I don't mind telling you, was expensive. I've got the paperwork to prove it." He stalked toward an antique desk in his office that was sequestered off the foyer.

One officer got between him and the desk. "Sir. If you don't mind—"

"You think I got a gun in there? Go ahead! Open it yourself. Look anywhere you want. There are no weapons in this house. We have nothing to hide."

The officer slid the drawer open. "This?" He extracted several white envelopes when Burton grunted in the affirmative. He gave the contents a cursory inspection then handed the envelopes to Burton.

"You want proof?" Burton exploded triumphantly. "It's all right here, right down to his footprints. The originals are in our safe deposit box, which I can produce first thing Monday."

Todd, who had been pacing the floor at the juncture of the living and dining rooms, jabbed a finger into the air. "Footprints? I have newborn footprints in my possession on the same page as my wife's thumbprint. I have his birth certificate and photographs from his birth February fourteenth up to the day before he was kidnapped."

"February fourteenth?" Beth looked up with surprise, relief flooding her face. "Then this can't be your baby. Our Matthew is five months old."

Barrie weighed in. "I suppose you were told he was small for his age? That he had some kind of developmental delays due to the circumstances of his birth? Or that he was premature? Look at him! He's big for his age."

Beth studied the baby, a flicker of comprehension gripping her briefly. Just as quickly she shook it off, denial regained. She clung tighter to her Matthew.

"So!" Todd shouted at Manatawney. "Were you in on the kidnapping? Did you have any part in stealing our son? Or did you pay someone to do it for you?"

Manatawney started to charge the twenty feet that separated the men, but the officers intervened.

"Sit!" the sergeant barked, at last losing her professional patience. Everybody obeyed. "This will not be settled here. The FBI will review the records, coordinate with the authorities in Pennsylvania, and make a determination."

The baby, who had started to fuss, digressed from whimpers into real tears. "He's hungry," Beth said. "And it's time for his nap. Can I go get him his bottle?"

"Go ahead. The lady from Family Services will hold him while you get it ready."

Beth nodded toward Kingsley. "You won't give him to her—"

"I repeat—the nice lady will hold him."

"Your sarcasm is not appreciated," Beth retorted and stalked from the room. In a few minutes, she returned with the bottle.

"You didn't microwave that, did you?" Kingsley demanded. "It could have hot spots and burn his little mouth."

"Why don't I test it?" the woman holding Billy said over the baby's screams.

But when she tried to settle and feed him, he only wailed louder. Pulling his face away from the nipple, he craned his head, turning it nearly upside down until he was looking at Kingsley. He bawled.

Kingsley jumped to her feet. "He won't take a bottle if I'm in the room. Nursing babies won't do that."

Todd shouted over the din. "If I can prove, right here and now, that he is my son, will you at least let my wife feed him?" Todd didn't wait for a reply. "Take off his socks."

More from surprise than anything else, the woman holding Billy complied.

"Look between his three smallest toes." Those closest huddled over the baby, as the woman placed her index finger under them. "Spread them gently," Todd said.

"Why, he has little webs!"

"Now look at my feet." He had kicked off one loafer and jerked off a sock with one motion.

The group moved their attention to him then looked up at each other.

"Why, he's got them too."

"I'm going to let Mrs. Henning feed the baby," the woman said.

Kingsley met them halfway, over Beth's protests, and scooped Billy into her arms, oblivious to anything else in the room. Turning her back on the group, she settled in the far corner with Todd at her side. Silence. The baby gulped, and Kingsley cried with joy and relief.

"We're not caving in," Manatawney said, angrily clenching and unclenching his fists.

Todd addressed the police collectively. "We have evidence in our possession that will prove that our son's kidnapping was part of a much larger conspiracy. A woman in Pittsburgh, who was subsequently murdered, collected that evidence. I'm not handing it over to anyone who can't guarantee that it will be pursued properly. It's urgent. By now the kidnappers know they've been identified and could be leaving the country."

"That would be a matter for the FBI. Under the circumstances, we're moving all of you to our facility."

The Manatawneys huddled with their attorney, shock and realization taking over. "You can't think we had anything to do with this."

"That's not for me to decide."

Kingsley observed the couple, as if seeing them for the first time. Their look of despair moved her deeply. If she hadn't known the adoptive parents were victims also, she knew it now. She went to the woman. "If I tell you the name of the person who we believe is responsible for all this misery, will you promise not to call him? We must give the police time to apprehend him. He has the resources to disappear and never be punished for what he has done."

Beth nodded agreement. Her husband glowered. Kingsley turned to Todd and touched his arm gently. He stiffened but grudgingly agreed. "Was his name 'Shure' spelled with an 'h'?"

The shock on their faces answered her question. Manatawney responded, as if in a trance. "He assured us. And we paid. Over a half million dollars."

✺

As the strange assembly of peace officers and civilians grouped and regrouped for transport to the Upper Arlington Police Department, Kingsley felt overwhelmed by a deep peace. With Billy safe in her arms and the warmth of Todd's hand on her shoulder, she didn't care how long they stood on the lawn while those in charge decided who rode with whom. And she didn't care that the woman from the Office of Families and Children stayed attached to her side.

She glanced at the Manatawneys, who by now were listening intently to their family attorney. Had *he* checked out Shure? Or had Burton Manatawney, with his business savvy and wealth, suspected that something was wrong and chosen to ignore it? Did he really think he could buy whatever he wanted? Their family attorney spoke rapidly in hushed tones. Could they interfere with Billy's leaving this place? Beth looked as if she might fall down and, for whatever reason, could not look at the Hennings. Kingsley felt the knot in her stomach return.

Todd whispered to Kingsley. "It doesn't look like the police are assuming they're innocent victims. I wouldn't want to be in their shoes. At best, they'll look like fools. And they're out all that money."

"How many times did both of us say we'd give everything we had to get Billy back, and we meant it? Nothing can compensate for the loss of a child."

"Another thing I love about you, K. You don't have a mean bone in your body."

Chapter 30

Randall completed his discussion with the officers and strode over to them. "They don't need Barrie and me. Why don't I take the rental car back, pick up and deliver Dan's, and meet you wherever?"

Todd handed Randall the keys. "I have no idea how long this will take. It could be a long time." He looked at his watch. "I'll keep you posted, but let's assume it will run into evening. Take Barrie shopping, to dinner, whatever you want, and we'll play it by ear."

"Shopping. Yes. I'll take her to a hardware store."

"You can do better than that."

"Not for what I have in mind."

☙❧

Randall parked in the Easton Town Center's lot. They strolled the mall and the adjoining brick sidewalks that crosshatched the village of upscale shops. Small children squealed as they ran through water jets that rose from a courtyard surrounded by benches and gardens. Their parents laughingly lamented not bringing dry clothes but didn't interfere with their fun.

"Dan recommended Brio's Tuscan Grille. It's over there, across the plaza." They wandered closer and studied the menu posted outside. "Food! Hummm—would the lady enjoy calamari fritto mistro, lobster bisque, filet mignon, shrimp risotto and broiler lobster tail, a fine Italian wine, half the dessert menu?"

Barrie looked down at herself in disgust. "I can't do 'fine dining' in the same clothes I've worn for two days. I'm a rumpled, spilled-upon mess. I wouldn't turn down some fast food, though. Oh! Let's get some of those roasted pistachios."

They wandered and munched, then bought Cokes from a vendor. "I have a little errand to run, which would bore you to tears. Why don't you browse through these stores and choose an outfit that makes you feel as gorgeous as you are? I'll meet you back here."

"I could run your errand with you."

"It's about hardware, and I don't mean computer."

"In that case, shopping is good."

Randall smiled with satisfaction and reached into his pocket for the silver money clip that Barrie had put in his Christmas stocking. He stripped off three one-hundred-dollar bills. Instinctively she pulled her hand behind her back, but he caught it. "Get something you'll love wearing to dinner. Take your time."

"I can buy my own clothes."

"I know you *can*."

"I'll bring back lots of change."

"You better not." He tilted her chin and gave her a respectful in-public kiss, then let her go. "Take as long as you want. I'll be right here, playing with the other kids in the fountain."

"You would!"

Two hours later, they met at Brio's, which was alive with festive diners. Servers sailed back and forth from the exposed half-walled kitchen. The manager called orders, and staff quickly assembled gourmet dishes and placed them on a high counter that separated staff from the main dining room. Barrie gazed at the unique ceiling, draped like a maypole from a high central point with wide swaths of silky peach fabric that radiated and were secured halfway down the interior walls. "It's like an elegant parachute," she said as they were led to a table in the center of the room.

He touched her leg briefly under the table. "That outfit's fantastic. A silk flower garden." She tucked a stray curl behind her ear, revealing a cluster of periwinkle flowers that looked as if they had escaped from her dress. "You are so beautiful."

"I'm okay for a Sunday evening."

"You're fantastic for the whole twenty-second century!" He continued to grin as he studied the menu. "I don't know about you, but I'm starving. Do you realize we haven't eaten for over twelve hours?"

She chuckled. "That's a life record for you." They ordered then turned their attention to dinner. Ravenously, Randall bolted his filet.

"Slow down! You're supposed to savor your dinner."

His fork stopped mid-lift, and he laughed. "I savor quickly." He popped the forkful into his mouth then reloaded while he concentrated on whatever would be the next bite. She watched him, smiling, and wondered at what point his idiosyncrasies became so endearing.

She smothered a grin with her linen napkin then nibbled her shrimp. He had finished and was watching her, swirling his second Chianti. "That was outstanding. You take such good care of me. Thank you," she said. She squeezed his hand; he trapped hers between his.

He eyeballed her plate. "That's the first time I've ever seen you finish a meal. Shall we look at the dessert menu?"

"I don't think I could eat one more bite."

"Good. Then I can eat both." He studied the selections entirely too long without really moving his eyes.

Barrie watched until he looked up. "You're awfully quiet for someone who should be in a celebratory mood. You look downright serious. What are you thinking?"

"I was just trying to remember what we were doing before Billy was kidnapped. I was flying from one place to another in between trying to run my burgeoning business. Weeks, months, even years ran together, but to where? And for what?" He shrugged. "That's what I was thinking about."

"It's been a wake-up call for me too," she said. "Just look at the Manatawneys. They have their wealth and possessions, but that Monet on their living room wall isn't worth one little child. It makes me wonder what I'm chasing too."

"You have your goals, and I admire that. And I do understand why you live day to day, at least in your personal life."

She studied him over the rim of her wineglass, elbows propped on the table. "Have I ever told you how much I appreciate a man who doesn't believe women should only make dinner and babies? If I couldn't use my mind, I would lose it, but you've never made me feel like less of a woman because—"

"You're perfect partner material, you know that?" He squeezed her hand again then abruptly pushed back his chair. "I'll be right back."

Barrie sipped and let her mind drift to where she had been before and after they'd met at Kingsley and Todd's wedding. The contrasts! She thought he was crazy—outspoken, brash, smart, and yet funny, but loyal to that sentimental core, which he tried hard to hide. From day one, he had treated her like a treasure. He restored her sense of self-worth. She smiled and looked at the menu. If their server returned before him, she would order for both.

Randall reappeared with a jubilant air and a hardware store bag tucked under his arm. He set the sack on the floor and dropped onto his chair. "Barrie, I've made a decision. Todd's right. My business has grown out of control like a kudzu vine. It's so good that it's awful. I *do* need a partner, but not just anyone, however qualified. I need *you*. So, here's my job offer. You could fly as much as you want or manage the business. Hire whomever you need while I fly and court customers. Or any combination of both."

Barrie opened her mouth, but before she could speak, Randall stopped her, palm out. He erupted out of his seat. Reaching, he retrieved the hardware store bag from the floor and whipped out a bundle of wood strips and rope.

A hush rippled throughout the restaurant as Randall hopped onto the chair facing hers. She gasped as he held his hands high, unfurling a rope-and-rung ladder. "You want to climb a corporate ladder?" he asked in a ringing voice. "I have a corporation, and here is a ladder." He leapt from the chair and bundled the ropes and rungs into a ball. Then he circled around to her side and placed the jumble onto her lap.

Before she had any time to react, he pulled a small box from his pocket and dropped to one knee. "I'm asking you to be my partner in every sense of the word." He opened the velvet box and placed it in her hands. "Will you marry me, Barrie?"

She broke into a smile and gasped in wonder and delight at the azure-cut diamond flanked with baguettes. "Why, it's the ring Kingsley, and I saw in Philadelphia. How did you know? Where did you find it? I don't deserve—"

"I deserve *you*!" Randall jumped to his feet and shouted to the entranced captive audience around them. "I think she should marry me, don't you?" Applause and hoots filled Brio's, as Barrie got to her feet to hug and then kiss him.

"What?"

"Yes! I said yes!"

೮ン೮ン

Twilight hushed the city of Upper Arlington. The police station, which had bustled with activity all day, now had grown quiet, its carpeted hallways and soft lights in the public area cocooning those in its confines. As Billy slept on his mother's lap, Todd emerged from the council committee room, where the parents had spent hours with the Upper Arlington Police and the FBI agents. Todd dropped onto the leather couch beside her in the comfortable visitors' lobby.

"Are they convinced?" she asked.

"They are. I'm awed by how quickly and professionally they interfaced to verify Billy's identity. They're satisfied that he's ours. And the Manatawneys aren't interfering."

Kingsley grinned, first at him and then at the baby, who was exhausted after his long day's ordeal. He slept on her lap, head by her knees, little legs bunched against her stomach. Rhythmically, she smoothed his tummy and gazed at his sweet little face, turned to one side, thumb in his mouth.

"What about Kathleen's disk?" she asked. "Those files that led us to Billy cost Kathleen her life. Can the information be used against Shure?"

"I explained what I knew or suspected of each document, along with the people through whom it has passed and where to find the originals. I phoned a heads-up to Lloyd in Seattle. The FBI will interface with the local authorities. They aren't divulging their plan, but I imagine they'll coordinate nationwide wherever the trail leads. I've got Kathleen's files saved to my hard drive and gave them the thumb drives. If Lloyd hadn't suggested that, I never would have seen Kathleen's letter to Mary Margaret."

"Are Shure's accomplices identified on the disk?"

"He must have been paranoid about tax evasion. One of those documents contained a list of employees' social security numbers. They correspond with the payroll records."

"You mean—"

"For every task, the operative was paid as an employee with all the appropriate withholdings for what looked like legitimate work."

"Then how can the police separate the good guys from the bad ones? He must have had some honest employees."

"That may be tough since every assignment is identified by a code. Those codes also appear on each individual's expense reports. How they'll decipher the codes is beyond me because there's no key."

"Why would he keep such detailed records when they're so damning?"

"Oh, K—he had to. Just think of the complexity of running so many schemes concurrently along with legitimate work. That would require extensive bookkeeping just to keep it all straight. And then there's his arrogance. He must have thought he would never get caught. It's possible that the files on Kathleen's disk are the only ones left in existence—that every incriminating document has been shredded or erased. He was scrupulous about every detail except one, which led to his downfall. His operatives should have been instructed to abort any plan that required improvisation. Ethelda knew Billy wasn't Sammy, but she went ahead with the kidnapping anyway."

"Where do you think she is now?"

"One of those documents contains addresses. Perhaps they're safe houses."

Kingsley's eyes widened. "Or locations where they hid children until they would be placed?"

"There's one big disappointment. Shure kept a calendar, and by now he's supposed to be out of the country. The police and the FBI may be able to round up his accomplices, but if the dates are correct, he's already slipped through the net."

Kingsley scowled. "That's not fair! But even if they can catch him—can he be convicted with the material on the disk?"

"It's passed through so many hands a defense attorney could argue that it's been altered, fabricated, or tainted. Or that anybody could have made it up to defame him. There could be chain-of-custody issues as well. But now that the police know where to look, they can follow it backward."

"What about the other thirty-two families?"

"If the authorities can cross-reference each child included in the *Families* list against a database of missing children, at least they can reunite families. And the adoptive families will undoubtedly rage against Shure. As we speak, search warrants are being obtained for his home and office, and an APB has been put out on him. And K, the press will be all over this story. Every unsolved kidnapping for the last several years will be re-examined. And Shure's accomplices, if arrested, will be anxious to make deals with the district attorney. Had the police followed the same trail that we did, they would have inevitably discovered the disk."

"Should we have waited? Told the police everything as we found it?"

Todd shook his head. "They didn't trust us, and we didn't trust them. And I still believe that every moment was precious. The clock in my head never stopped ticking."

"Did the police say what will happen to the Manatawneys?"

"They haven't been charged with anything yet, as far as I know."

"They must have been questioned for hours. I haven't seen them or their attorney leave."

Billy stirred and slowly opened his eyes. His parents bent toward him, their cheeks brushing each other's. The baby brightened, returning their coos with a smile.

"Todd, do you realize what date this is?"

"I do. It's the fifth of May."

"I can't imagine a better anniversary present." Oblivious to the desk sergeant, they kissed while Billy continued to smile.

"Can we go now?" Kingsley finally asked.

Todd splayed his hands on his thighs and pushed to leverage his stiff legs into action. He rose. "I'll call a cab."

"But where are we going?"

Todd looked at his watch. "Randall says he'll meet us at the hotel. Then we'll fly home, which just takes fifty minutes."

"Home! Billy, did you hear what your daddy just said?" As she lifted him high, Billy grinned until his eyes squinted shut.

"Do you think we can stand being normal again?"

"That would be simply magnificent."

At that moment Burton and Beth Manatawney emerged from the depths of the building. He was still wearing his golf attire, and she, the Capri pants and knit top from that morning. Everyone froze. Kingsley forced a weak, conflicted smile, not wanting to convey anger or victory either. Beth approached her hesitantly.

"We had no idea. I hope you can believe that."

"I do."

She glanced at Billy who only had eyes for his mother. "He's such a dear baby. This is—so hard." Fresh tears wet her red, swollen eyes. For a split second Kingsley was tempted to offer to let her hold him again, but the little voice in her head cautioned to just wrap it up.

"We bought him so many clothes, and there was a shower last week. If you want to come by the house—"

"I appreciate that, but there won't be time." Kingsley compelled her voice to sound convincing, even though she knew she was lying. "We're being flown home within the hour and must meet our pilot. The woman from Family Services gave us the few things we need."

Burton stood rigid, stoic, not even glancing at Todd. "Beth, we'd better go. Our attorney is waiting to take us home." She nodded. He squared his arm around her shoulder and pivoted her toward the front door.

Kingsley turned to Todd. "Do you realize we didn't bring any baby things with us? My diaper bag, his clothes, blankets—I never believed we'd find him so quickly."

"Burton?" Todd called after the man. He turned. "I'm sorry about your being victimized, too. I know how you must feel."

"You have no idea." And with that, they were gone.

Chapter 31

San Diego! L. Gerard Shure drank in its beauty, excitement mounting as his cab arched across the Coronado Bay Bridge. The perfect end to the perfect plan—well almost perfect, assuming everyone executed their final assignments with customary perfection. And hadn't they always? The scheme, which had spanned so many years, had now reached fruition. And the success rate! One hundred percent!

"Where to, sir?"

"To the Del."

"Wonderful place. Business or pleasure?"

"Pleasure. Pure pleasure."

"Staying long?"

"Just long enough to enjoy their Sunday buffet. Then back to the airport." Shortly the cab arrived at the Hotel Del Coronado, the historic treasure that was the nation's oldest wooden hotel. Shure left a huge tip then hurried into the Del's splendid Victorian lobby. Thanks to the time change, he wouldn't miss the world-famous buffet. This wasn't the plan. He should get out of extradition range fast. Oh, well. A later flight to Hawaii shouldn't make any difference.

"How's this, sir?" The friendly server motioned him toward a table near the buffet.

"View's perfect!" He winked, refusing the menu she offered. "That's what I'll have."

Fruit, he thought. I'll sample it all then decide what comes next. He ambled toward the groaning table, draped in linens and splashed with magnificent flowers. He made the first of many selections.

Once seated with his first course, his juice and coffee, he allowed himself the luxury of looking around and engaging in one of his favorite pastimes—reading people. Most looked like tourists. Those two, who slipped in under the wire, holding hands and murmuring to each other, must be a honeymoon couple. That smiling middle-aged couple just out of focus would be celebrating a milestone. The husband reminded him of someone he couldn't quite place from that distance. And them, the ones ignoring each other, would be wrapping it up.

Shure's mind flashed through his disastrous first marriage that ended before it began, way back before law school. Her wealthy, blue-blooded parents never thought he was good enough for their princess. He was not one of them. He had no potential. They poisoned that marriage.

After that and a brief second marriage not worth remembering, he was too busy for committed relationships. As his fortunes skyrocketed, eager women, tired of supporting themselves and finding the good men all taken, were only too happy to spend time with him in hopes of spending his money as well. Food—now there was something that never denied him. Once he was settled on his own island, he'd have his gardeners grow all varieties of tropical fruit.

From the breast pocket of his silk-blend sports coat, he withdrew a small leather notebook with onionskin pages. The book opened automatically to the black satin ribbon. He took a sip of fresh pineapple juice as he looked at the entries in his own special code. Shure smiled with satisfaction at all the check marks, right down to each list's lower margin.

He scrutinized another page of new bank account numbers, opened to accept the fruits of his labor. He touched his breast pocket, reassuring himself that the envelope holding his cashiers' checks was still there. And the code. Nobody would ever untangle the code identifying his operatives' work without this one page, even if Kathleen's disk had survived. This book, too, would be destroyed in a few days after he square-knotted every loose end. Champagne! This sumptuous brunch required champagne. He motioned, and his server appeared.

Shure left his fruit plate on the table and returned to the buffet to select the next round of mouth-watering delicacies. Would there be quail eggs? He glanced at his watch. The later flight left plenty of time to saunter the Del's walkways and drink in the sounds and the scent of the sea. He felt exhilarated and relaxed simultaneously.

Maybe he'd break with the plan—stay a few days on the big island of Hawaii. Pick up one of those elegant girls with long hair and long legs and short flowered skirts with leis over a teensy bikini. Just the thought of it made him excited. He returned to his table and, before tasting his eggs, toasted himself. Whoever said that was bad luck? He savored his second flute.

At a remote table, the Greers finished their coffee then accepted a refill from the attentive server. "What a wonderful week. Have I thanked you enough?" she said, smiling at her husband of twenty-five years.

"Once or twice. Have I thanked you for tolerating my crazy life all these years? The erratic hours, the time spent away, the fear and the toll that marriage to a cop must have taken? I like to think that I'm pretty tough, but clearly, you are the strong one."

"So you'd marry me all over again?"

"I'd steal you from the sandbox to give us more time."

"Guess living on the edge keeps things in perspective. Like the time you were shot." She traced the scar that ran up his arm and disappeared beneath his golf shirt.

"I promised you when we were engaged that I'd bring you here. At the time I was in the navy, stationed in San Diego. When I saw the Del I said to myself, 'What a wonderful place to bring my bride!' I'm only sorry it took so long."

She smiled. "It's not exactly around the corner from Pittsburgh. This trip cost a fortune, and I love you for making it special."

Lieutenant Greer tipped back in his seat and lazily scanned the gracious Victorian dining room. His trained eye, however, was not on vacation. It stopped on one guest in particular.

"Honey, I want you to do something for me. First, keep that exact expression, no matter what I might say."

Her face jolted nevertheless. "Are you all right?" she asked.

"I'm fine. Now, smile. That's good. Hold that expression and keep looking at me. I've spotted someone across the room whom I recognize from a new APB. Let's finish our coffee then casually walk toward the lobby. Just do not look around."

Mrs. Greer took one last swallow, retrieved her purse, then stood, and accompanied him into the lobby, their backs turned toward the guests. He flashed his badge at the desk. "I need to speak with your manager and head of security immediately."

Within ten minutes, two plain-clothed detectives entered the Hotel Del Coronado accompanied by two uniformed officers, who had arrived without lights and sirens. The four huddled with the vacationing lieutenant, the manager, and the chief of security. The contingency then crossed the vast lobby and approached the open doors to the dining room.

"Over there," Greer said to the others.

"That's him, all right."

L. Gerard Shure was enjoying his last drops of champagne, oblivious to his surroundings. Even without looking in his pocket, he could picture his new passport and driver's license. Davis. So easy. So innocuous. So downright blendy. He'd have to practice it until it was flawless—second nature.

"Mr. Shure?"

"Yes?" he answered reflexively.

"FBI." They flashed their IDs. "Would you come with us, please?"

The big man, blinking in disbelief, came to his senses. "There must be some mistake. The name's D—Davis," he stammered, starting to reach in his pocket.

A uniformed officer stopped him, insisting he keep his hands within sight. "Mr. Shure, you are under arrest for the kidnapping of William Henning. You have the right to remain silent—"

A hush blanketed the vast dining room as the man was handcuffed and led away.

Lieutenant Greer returned to the lobby, rejoining his wife.

"Was that who you thought it was?"

"It was."

"But how did you know?"

"Do you remember reading about the baby who was kidnapped from a bank's daycare facility in southeast Pennsylvania? I subsequently interviewed an adoption attorney in Pittsburgh as a potential witness. Even though the suspect had phoned him on three separate occasions, it appeared to be a coincidence. It wasn't pursued any further. The attorney, a man named Shure, wasn't considered a person of interest. This morning I learned that an APB had been put out on him. He's wanted, not only in connection with the Henning kidnapping, but also for questioning in a string of others. And there he was, right across the room, enjoying his meal. I could scarcely believe it. Since kidnapping under these circumstances is a federal offense, I contacted the FBI."

"And he didn't recognize you?"

"Apparently not."

She sucked in a breath. "What were the odds of that happening?"

"Slim to none. Since he's this far from home and probably traveling with false identification, he could have been long gone before his brunch was digested."

She squeezed his arm. "You're good, do you know that?"

"That's what they pay me the big bucks for, baby."

೮౩౬౩

The phone would not stop ringing. Caller ID winnowed some, but most were from intimates. While Todd manned the phones, Kingsley folded Billy's beach togs into his bag. Before snapping the latches, she removed a tiny beach hat that would shield his face from prying eyes. That she set on his dressing table beside the onesie and little bib overalls he'd wear for the flight to Charleston.

Satisfied, she dropped his suitcase by the hall banister alongside her own.

Todd mounted the staircase and paused on the landing to peer through the ripple-glass windows. Satisfied that the back yard was devoid of intrusion, he climbed the remaining six steps. Billy was draped over his shoulder, his sleeping face pressed against a small blanket, oblivious to the commotion his return had created.

"That news helicopter just won't give up," Todd said, "but security's doing a great job of keeping reporters off our property. Oh! I almost forgot. The woman who owns the bloodhound that couldn't track Billy? She'd like you to call her."

Mystified, Kingsley dialed the number. After identifying herself, she asked the burning question. "Why did your dog stop tracking our baby?"

"He followed the scent to the edge of the lot where he encountered a scent pool. He sniffed all around the pavement from the daycare group's location to the dumpster. But when he stepped into the grass, he sneezed, recoiled, and wouldn't go any farther."

"You mean as if he'd smelled pepper, like in the movie, *Cool Hand Luke*?"

"No, that wouldn't trick a bloodhound. Might make him sneeze, but he would keep tracking. He appeared to have lost the scent, so we returned to the building. In retrospect, that wasn't normal. I'd come on short notice and had urgent business, so we left the bank directly. That evening, my dog was terribly sick—gagging, drooling, eyes watering and nose running, sneezing and rubbing his face with his feet. I rushed him straight to the vet who suspected toxicity. My dog acted lethargic and embarrassed over losing his faculties. He was one sick puppy for days but slowly recovered. Nothing remotely similar had happened before, and we don't keep anything poisonous where he could reach it. Then we read how the kidnapping was staged."

"Then he's all right?"

"Health wise, apparently. But when I took him out on his next search, he seemed timid. If you ask me, anyone who would poison a dog should be shot."

A commotion outside drew Kingsley to the window. She angled to see through the rippled glass. Armed guards were ejecting a jeep that had cut through the Amish farmer's cornfield.

"You don't suppose they'll follow us to South Carolina," she asked Todd after finishing her conversation with the bloodhound's owner.

"Security arranged for a decoy, using our Explorer to draw them off. Should be easy since we use the bank barn as a garage. The decoy will proceed to Harrisburg International while we meet Randall at his private airstrip. The worst that can happen is that the photographers will get some good shots of the Explorer. Once we're on Kiawah Island, we'll have privacy. Your dad called—they'll join us tomorrow." He handed Billy to Kingsley and picked up their bags.

The library's landline jangled for their attention. "Would you mind repeating that for my wife?" Todd said to the caller as he punched the speaker button. A familiar young man's voice began speaking. Instantly, Kingsley recognized Mare and Kathleen O'Connor's nephew.

"Can you hang on a minute? There's someone who wants to talk to you," he said. A long pause followed, blended with rumpled noises and the young man speaking to someone nearby.

"Thank you," a small voice whispered. "Thank you."

The young man came back on the line. "Could you hear that?"

"Oh, my God—was that your Aunt Mare?"

"Yes! She regained consciousness. She's too weak to talk, but she saw the newscast and insisted on thanking you herself."

"You tell her we'll bring Billy to Seattle to thank her in person as soon as she's well."

Todd's cell phone rang. Shirley Granger, Keynote's EVP and HR director, bubbled through the line. "Thought you'd be interested in a missing puzzle piece. Remember the cleaning woman who was murdered, necessitating a substitute the day Billy was kidnapped? Now that some of the details have become public, the deceased woman's husband called me, hoping to get your home number. I didn't give it up, of course, so he settled for telling me his story. Strange—people don't attach meaning to odd events at the time they occur. It seems the man's wife once worked at the same hospital where Ethelda Blake was a nurse. The wife kept to herself, but naturally was privy to personal business. Ethelda was missing part of two fingers. As fate would have it, the cleaning woman recognized Ethelda at our daycare and reminded her of where they had met. Ethelda denied it—said she must resemble somebody else. The foolish woman, however, pointed out the problem with her hand. Ethelda still insisted she was mistaken."

"Do you see the irony in this?" Kingsley asked. "If Ethelda hadn't ordered the killing, the regular cleaning woman would have done her job in the morning and been long gone by noon. And the substitute, who worked in the daycare later that day, would not have shuffled the baby's cribs at the same time the kidnapping unfolded. She would have been required to go outside with the daycare group. Not knowing anyone personally, she would have been a quiet observer, thwarting the opportunity to take Billy."

"Do you think Ethelda would have aborted the mission?"

"If she had half a brain, she would. Ironic, isn't it? How close it came to not happening?"

"The husband is beating himself up," Shirley said. "Wishes he'd paid more attention, but he had no interest in office gossip. He'd tuned her out."

Another commotion out by the highway drew his attention. Todd thanked Shirley and wrapped up the call.

"Have you heard if the police have make any progress locating Ethelda Blake and her husband?" Kingsley asked Todd.

"Huh! They're not telling me squat, especially since we did their job for them. All they'll say is that 'the investigation is on-gong.' Translation—no."

"Todd—there's the van." As they watched through the library window, the security guards parted to let a vehicle with dark-tinted glass glide down their lane. Slowly it circled to the back of the barn toward the massive equipment doors. A man and a woman, sized like the Hennings and carrying a small bundle, walked from the house and disappeared into the barn. They emerged thirty minutes later in Todd's SUV, turning onto the access road that led to the highway. An assortment of vehicles followed, while others appeared to give up. The news chopper cleared the trees, its thumping racket diminishing.

Inside the house, Kingsley slipped Billy's sweater over his head and tied a hat under his chubby chin. She smiled at Todd. "We're ready. Let's get on with the rest of our lives."

ACKNOWLEDGMENTS

There is no way I can adequately thank all the people who patiently provided details, colorful descriptors, and answered my technical questions. From *Vanished: A Trust Mystery*'s first keystroke to its final hash mark, ten years elapsed, my three other novels intervening. I am grateful to everyone who provided, then checked, details—twice—to ensure my work's accuracy.

I'm particularly indebted to the following professionals for sharing their time, expertise, and for saving me from making egregious errors: Forensic Pathologist Neil A. Hoffman, MD; Angel Cabrera, Criminal Investigator, retired, Reading, PA Police Department; Officers Kurt Bowman and Karena Wilka, City of Upper Arlington Police Department; Stephen A. Hoare, Sr., Captain USAF, and Civilian Airline Transport Pilot; Daniel W. Hughes, NCIDQ, Senior Technical Design Coordinator; Elaine D. Hughes, DVM; Lora J. H. Bean, PhD, FACMG, Assoc. Professor, Emory University, and Senior Molecular Director EGL Genetics, Eurofins Clinical Diagnostics.

The following organizations provided me with resources, programs, friendship, and guidance to grow in the field of crime writing through the dedication and effort of many volunteers: The Mystery Writers of America, New York Chapter; International Thrill Writers; Sisters in Crime; and Penn Writers. And my readers, book club buddies, friends and fellow writers who encourage and inspire me. Thank you!

My publisher, Black Opal Books, deserves my enduring gratitude for having confidence in me and my work. I am indebted to BOB's editor, Lauri Wellington, and to my editor, Faith C, for her skill, dedication to detail, and putting up with my idiosyncrasies. Jack Jackson's beautiful fourth cover, once again, captured the essence of this novel and is worth more than a thousand words. Behind the scenes, Black Opal's staff handles myriad details and challenges with speed, grace, and humor. Bless you all; you are the best!

And as always, my love and my rock, my husband, Bill Hughes. Thank you for having my back every step of the way.

About the Author

Nancy Hughes's family says of her work: "She murders people." On paper, that is. She made the leap from journalist, media, community relations and PR specialist to follow her heart and write mystery novels. She credits her love of writing to her parents, who were voracious readers. When Hughes was small, they spent hours reading to her, which fueled her lively imagination. Transplanted from Key West at age two, she never adjusted to the cold. While walking to grade school, then Penn State classes, she invented mystery stories to distract herself from the snow and ice. Now, nothing stirs the creative juices like a hot shower.

The view from her rural Pennsylvania home-office window is just as distracting as big city chaos when the deer munch her beloved azaleas. A three-hour commute to Manhattan connects Hughes to the Mystery Writers of America's New York Chapter meetings. Their devoted leaders provide timely updates, inspiration, mentor programs, workshops, seminars, tours, legal tips, and boundless moral support. And friends! With whom she exchanges war stories and encouragement.